The Mystery of the Sea

The Mystery of the Sea

Bram Stoker

MINT EDITIONS

The Mystery of the Sea was first published in 1902.

This edition published by Mint Editions 2021.

ISBN 9781513271514 | E-ISBN 9781513276519

Published by Mint Editions®

 **MINT
EDITIONS**

minteditionbooks.com

Publishing Director: Jennifer Newens
Design & Production: Rachel Lopez Metzger
Project Manager: Micaela Clark
Typesetting: Westchester Publishing Services

Contents

Appendices

I

Second Sight

I had just arrived at Cruden Bay on my annual visit, and after a late breakfast was sitting on the low wall which was a continuation of the escarpment of the bridge over the Water of Cruden. Opposite to me, across the road and standing under the only little clump of trees in the place was a tall, gaunt old woman, who kept looking at me intently. As I sat, a little group, consisting of a man and two women, went by. I found my eyes follow them, for it seemed to me after they had passed me that the two women walked together and the man alone in front carrying on his shoulder a little black box—a coffin. I shuddered as I thought, but a moment later I saw all three abreast just as they had been. The old woman was now looking at me with eyes that blazed. She came across the road and said to me without preface:

"What saw ye then, that yer e'en looked so awed?" I did not like to tell her so I did not answer. Her great eyes were fixed keenly upon me, seeming to look me through and through. I felt that I grew quite red, whereupon she said, apparently to herself: "I thocht so! Even I did not see that which he saw."

"How do you mean?" I queried. She answered ambiguously: "Wait! Ye shall perhaps know before this hour to-morrow!"

Her answer interested me and I tried to get her to say more; but she would not. She moved away with a grand stately movement that seemed to become her great gaunt form.

After dinner whilst I was sitting in front of the hotel, there was a great commotion in the village; much running to and fro of men and women with sad mien. On questioning them I found that a child had been drowned in the little harbour below. Just then a woman and a man, the same that had passed the bridge earlier in the day, ran by with wild looks. One of the bystanders looked after them pityingly as he said:

"Puir souls. It's a sad home-comin' for them the nicht."

"Who are they?" I asked. The man took off his cap reverently as he answered:

"The father and mother of the child that was drowned!" As he spoke I looked round as though some one had called me.

There stood the gaunt woman with a look of triumph on her face.

THE CURVED SHORE OF CRUDEN Bay, Aberdeenshire, is backed by a waste of sandhills in whose hollows seagrass and moss and wild violets, together with the pretty "grass of Parnassus" form a green carpet. The surface of the hills is held together by bent-grass and is eternally shifting as the wind takes the fine sand and drifts it to and fro. All behind is green, from the meadows that mark the southern edge of the bay to the swelling uplands that stretch away and away far in the distance, till the blue mist of the mountains at Braemar sets a kind of barrier. In the centre of the bay the highest point of the land that runs downward to the sea looks like a miniature hill known as the Hawklaw; from this point onward to the extreme south, the land runs high with a gentle trend downwards.

Cruden sands are wide and firm and the sea runs out a considerable distance. When there is a storm with the wind on shore the whole bay is a mass of leaping waves and broken water that threatens every instant to annihilate the stake-nets which stretch out here and there along the shore. More than a few vessels have been lost on these wide stretching sands, and it was perhaps the roaring of the shallow seas and the terror which they inspired which sent the crews to the spirit room and the bodies of those of them which came to shore later on, to the churchyard on the hill.

If Cruden Bay is to be taken figuratively as a mouth, with the sand hills for soft palate, and the green Hawklaw as the tongue, the rocks which work the extremities are its teeth. To the north the rocks of red granite rise jagged and broken. To the south, a mile and a half away as the crow flies, Nature seems to have manifested its wildest forces. It is here, where the little promontory called Whinnyfold juts out, that the two great geological features of the Aberdeen coast meet. The red sienite of the north joins the black gneiss of the south. That union must have been originally a wild one; there are evidences of an upheaval which must have shaken the earth to its centre. Here and there are great masses of either species of rock hurled upwards in every conceivable variety of form, sometimes fused or pressed together so that it is impossible to say exactly where gneiss ends or sienite begins; but broadly speaking here is an irregular line of separation. This line runs seawards to the east and its strength is shown in its outcrop. For half a mile or more the rocks rise through the sea singly or in broken masses ending in a dangerous cluster known as "The Skares" and which has had for centuries its full toll of wreck and disaster. Did the sea hold its dead where they fell, its floor around the Skares would be whitened with their bones, and new islands could build themselves with the piling wreckage. At times one may see here the ocean in her fiercest mood; for it is when the tempest drives from the south-east that the sea is fretted amongst the rugged rocks and sends its spume landwards. The rocks that at calmer times rise dark from the briny deep are lost to sight for moments in the grand onrush of the waves. The seagulls which usually whiten them, now flutter around screaming, and the sound of their shrieks comes in on the gale almost in a continuous note, for the single cries are merged in the multitudinous roar of sea and air.

The village, squatted beside the emboucher of the Water of Cruden at the northern side of the bay is simple enough; a few rows of fishermen's cottages, two or three great red-tiled drying-sheds nestled in the sand-heap behind the fishers' houses. For the rest of the place as it was when first I saw it, a little lookout beside a tall flagstaff on the northern cliff, a few scattered farms over the inland prospect, one little hotel down on the western bank of the Water of Cruden with a fringe of willows protecting its sunk garden which was always full of fruits and flowers.

From the most southern part of the beach of Cruden Bay to Whinnyfold village the distance is but a few hundred yards; first a steep pull up the face of the rock; and then an even way, beside part of which runs a tiny stream. To the left of this path, going towards Whinnyfold, the ground rises in a bold slope and then falls again all round, forming a sort of wide miniature hill of some eighteen or twenty acres. Of this the southern side is sheer, the black rock dipping into the waters of the little bay of Whinnyfold, in the centre of which is a picturesque island of rock shelving steeply from the water on the northern side, as is the tendency of all the gneiss and granite in this part. But to east and north there are irregular bays or openings, so that the furthest points of the promontory stretch out like fingers. At the tips of these are reefs of sunken rock falling down to deep water and whose existence can only be suspected in bad weather when the rush of the current beneath sends up swirling eddies or curling masses of foam. These little bays are mostly curved and are green where falling earth or drifting sand have hidden the outmost side of the rocks and given a foothold to the seagrass and clover. Here have been at some time or other great caves, now either fallen in or silted up with sand, or obliterated with the earth brought down in the rush of surface-water in times of long rain. In one of these bays, Broad Haven, facing right out to the Skares, stands an isolated pillar of rock called locally the "Puir mon" through whose base, time and weather have worn a hole through which one may walk dryshod.

Through the masses of rocks that run down to the sea from the sides and shores of all these bays are here and there natural channels with straight edges as though cut on purpose for the taking in of the cobbles belonging to the fisher folk of Whinnyfold.

When first I saw the place I fell in love with it. Had it been possible I should have spent my summer there, in a house of my own, but the want of any place in which to live forbade such an opportunity. So I stayed in the little hotel, the Kilmarnock Arms.

The next year I came again, and the next, and the next. And then I arranged to take a feu at Whinnyfold and to build a house overlooking the Skares for myself. The details of this kept me constantly going to Whinnyfold, and my house to be was always in my thoughts.

Hitherto my life had been an uneventful one. At school I was, though secretly ambitious, dull as to results. At College I was better off, for my big body and athletic powers gave me a certain position in which I had to overcome my natural shyness. When I was about eight and twenty I found myself nominally a barrister, with no knowledge whatever of the practice of law and but little less of the theory, and with a commission in the Devil's Own—the irreverent name given to the Inns of Court Volunteers. I had few relatives, but a comfortable, though not great, fortune; and I had been round the world, dilettante fashion.

II

GORMALA

All that night I thought of the dead child and of the peculiar vision which had come to me. Sleeping or waking it was all the same; my mind could not leave the parents in procession as seen in imagination, or their distracted mien in reality. Mingled with them was the great-eyed, aquiline-featured, gaunt old woman who had taken such an interest in the affair, and in my part of it. I asked the landlord if he knew her, since, from his position as postmaster he knew almost everyone for miles around. He told me that she was a stranger to the place. Then he added:

"I can't imagine what brings her here. She has come over from Peterhead two or three times lately; but she doesn't seem to have anything at all to do. She has nothing to sell and she buys nothing. She's not a tripper, and she's not a beggar, and she's not a thief, and she's not a worker of any sort. She's a queer-looking lot anyhow. I fancy from her speech that she's from the west; probably from some of the far-out islands. I can tell that she has the Gaelic from the way she speaks."

Later on in the day, when I was walking on the shore near the Hawklaw, she came up to speak to me. The shore was quite lonely, for in those days it was rare to see anyone on the beach except when the salmon fishers drew their nets at the ebbing tide. I was walking towards Whinnyfold when she came upon me silently from behind. She must have been hidden among the bent-grass of the sandhills for had she been anywhere in view I must have seen her on that desolate shore. She was evidently a most imperious person; she at once addressed me in a tone and manner which made me feel as though I were in some way an inferior, and in somehow to blame:

"What for did ye no tell me what ye saw yesterday?" Instinctively I answered:

"I don't know why. Perhaps because it seemed so ridiculous." Her stern features hardened into scorn as she replied:

"Are Death and the Doom then so redeekulous that they pleasure ye intil silence?" I somehow felt that this was a little too much and was about to make a sharp answer, when suddenly it struck me as a remarkable thing that she knew already. Filled with surprise I straightway asked her:

"Why, how on earth do you know? I told no one." I stopped for I felt all at sea; there was some mystery here which I could not fathom. She seemed to read my mind like an open book, for she went on looking at me as she spoke, searchingly and with an odd smile.

"Eh! laddie, do ye no ken that ye hae een that can see? Do ye no understand that ye hae een that can speak? Is it that one with the Gift o' Second Sight has no an understandin' o' it. Why, yer face when ye saw the mark o' the Doom, was like a printed book to een like mine."

"Do you mean to tell me" I asked "that you could tell what I saw, simply by looking at my face?"

"Na! na! laddie. Not all that, though a Seer am I; but I knew that you had seen the Doom! It's no that varied that there need be any mistake. After all Death is only one, in whatever way we may speak!" After a pause of thought I asked her:

"If you have the power of Second Sight why did you not see the vision, or whatever it was, yourself?"

"Eh! laddie" she answered, shaking her head "'Tis little ye ken o' the wark o' the Fates! Learn ye then that the Voice speaks only as it listeth into chosen ears, and the Vision comes only to chosen een. None can will to hear or to see, to pleasure themselves."

"Then" I said, and I felt that there was a measure of triumph in my tone "if to none but the chosen is given to know, how comes it that you, who seem not to have been chosen on this occasion at all events, know all the same?" She answered with a touch of impatience:

"Do ye ken, young sir, that even mortal een have power to see much, if there be behind them the thocht, an' the knowledge and the experience to guide them aright. How, think ye, is it that some can see much, and learn much as they gang; while others go blind as the mowdiwart, at the end o' the journey as before it?"

"Then perhaps you will tell me how much you saw, and how you saw it?"

"Ah! to them that have seen the Doom there needs but sma' guidance to their thochts. Too lang, an' too often hae I mysen seen the death-sark an' the watch-candle an' the dead-hole, not to know when they are seen tae ither een. Na, na! laddie, what I kent o' yer seein' was no by the Gift but only by the use o' my proper een. I kent not the muckle o' what ye saw. Not whether it was ane or ither o' the garnishins o' the dead; but weel I kent that it was o' death."

"Then," I said interrogatively "Second Sight is altogether a matter of chance?"

"Chance! chance!" she repeated with scorn. "Na! young sir; when the Voice has spoken there is no more chance than that the nicht will follow the day."

"You mistake me," I said, feeling somewhat superior now that I had caught her in an error, "I did not for a moment mean that the Doom—whatever it is—is not a true forerunner. What I meant was that it seems to be a matter of chance in whose ear the Voice—whatever it is—speaks; when once it has been ordained that it is to sound in the ear of some one." Again she answered with scorn:

"Na, na! there is no chance o' ocht aboot the Doom. Them that send forth the Voice and the Seein' know well to whom it is sent and why. Can ye no comprehend that it is for no bairn-play that such goes forth. When the Voice speaks, it is mainly followed by tears an' woe an' lamentation! Nae! nor is it only one bit manifestation that stands by its lanes, remote and isolate from all ither. Truly 'tis but a pairt o' the great scheme o' things; an' be sure that whoso is chosen to see or to hear is chosen weel, an' must hae their pairt in what is to be, on to the verra end."

"Am I to take it" I asked, "that Second Sight is but a little bit of some great purpose which has to be wrought out by means of many kinds; and that whoso sees the Vision or hears the Voice is but the blind unconscious instrument of Fate?"

"Aye! laddie. Weel eneuch the Fates know their wishes an' their wark, no to need the help or the thocht of any human—blind or seein', sane or silly, conscious or unconscious."

All through her speaking I had been struck by the old woman's use of the word 'Fate,' and more especially when she used it in the plural. It was evident that, Christian though she might be—and in the West they are generally devout observants of the duties of their creed—her belief in this respect came from some of the old pagan mythologies. I should have liked to question her on this point; but I feared to shut her lips against me. Instead I asked her:

"Tell me, will you, if you don't mind, of some case you have known yourself of Second Sight?"

"'Tis no for them to brag or boast to whom has been given to see the wark o' the hand o' Fate. But sine ye are yerself a Seer an' would learn, then I may speak. I hae seen the sea ruffle wi'oot cause in the verra spot where later a boat was to gang doon, I hae heard on a lone moor the hammerin' o' the coffin-wright when one passed me who was soon to dee. I hae seen the death-sark fold round the speerit o' a drowned one, in baith ma sleepin' an' ma wakin' dreams. I hae heard the settin' doom o' the Spaiks, an' I hae seen the Weepers on a' the crood that walked. Aye, an' in mony anither way hae I seen an' heard the Coming o' the Doom."

"But did all the seeings and hearings come true?" I asked. "Did it ever happen that you heard queer sounds or saw strange sights and that yet nothing came of them? I gather that you do not always know to whom something is going to happen; but only that death is coming to some one!" She was not displeased at my questioning but replied at once:

"Na doot! but there are times when what is seen or heard has no manifest following. But think ye, young sir, how mony a corp, still waited for, lies in the depths o' the sea; how mony lie oot on the hillsides, or are fallen in deep places where their bones whiten unkent. Nay! more, to how many has Death come in a way that men think the wark o' nature when his hastening has come frae the hand of man, untold." This was a difficult matter to answer so I changed or rather varied the subject.

"How long must elapse before the warning comes true?"

"Ye know yersel', for but yestreen ye hae seen, how the Death can follow hard upon the Doom; but there be times, nay mostly are they so, when days or weeks pass away ere the Doom is fulfilled."

"Is this so?" I asked "when you know the person regarding whom the Doom is spoken." She answered with an air of certainty which somehow carried conviction, secretly, with it.

"Even so! I know one who walks the airth now in all the pride o' his strength. But the Doom has been spoken of him. I saw him with these verra een lie prone on rocks, wi' the water rinnin' down from his hair. An' again I heard the minute bells as he went by me on a road where is no bell for a score o' miles. Aye, an' yet again I saw him in the kirk itsel' wi' corbies flyin' round him, an' mair gatherin' from afar!"

Here was indeed a case where Second Sight might be tested; so I asked her at once, though to do so I had to overcome a strange sort of repugnance:

"Could this be proved? Would it not be a splendid case to make known; so that if the death happened it would prove beyond all doubt the existence of such a thing as Second Sight." My suggestion was not well received. She answered with slow scorn:

"Beyon' all doot! Doot! Wha is there that doots the bein' o' the Doom? Learn ye too, young sir, that the Doom an' all thereby is no for traffickin' wi' them that only cares for curiosity and publeecity. The Voice and the Vision o' the Seer is no for fine madams and idle gentles to while away their time in play-toy make-believe!" I climbed down at once.

"Pardon me!" I said "I spoke without thinking. I should not have said so—to you at any rate." She accepted my apology with a sort of regal inclination; but the moment after she showed by her words she was after all but a woman!

"I will tell ye; that so in the full time ye may hae no doot yersel'. For ye are a Seer and as Them that has the power hae gien ye the Gift it is no for the like o' me to cumber the road o' their doin'. Know ye then, and remember weel, how it was told ye by Gormala MacNiel that Lauchlane Macleod o' the Outer Isles hae been Called; tho' as yet the Voice has no sounded in his ears but only in mine. But ye will see the time—"

She stopped suddenly as though some thought had struck her, and then went on impressively:

"When I saw him lie prone on the rocks there was ane that bent ower him that I kent not in the nicht wha it was, though the licht o' the moon was around him. We shall see! We shall see!"

Without a word more she turned and left me. She would not listen to my calling after her; but with long strides passed up the beach and was lost among the sandhills.

III

An Ancient Rune

On the next day I rode on my bicycle to Peterhead, and walked on the pier. It was a bright clear day, and a fresh northern breeze was blowing. The fishing boats were ready to start at the turn of the tide; and as I came up the first of them began to pass out through the harbour mouth. Their movement was beautiful to see; at first slowly, and then getting faster as the sails were hoisted, till at last they swept through the narrow entrance, scuppers under, righting themselves as they swung before the wind in the open sea. Now and again a belated smacksman came hurrying along to catch his boat before she should leave the pier.

The eastern pier of Peterhead is guarded by a massive wall of granite, built in several steps or tiers, which breaks the fury of the gale. When a northern storm is on, it is a wild spot; the waves dash over it in walls of solid green topped with mountainous masses of foam and spray. But at present, with the July sun beating down, it was a vantage post from which to see the whole harbour and the sea without. I climbed up and sat on the top, looking on admiringly, and lazily smoked in quiet enjoyment. Presently I noticed some one very like Gormala come hurrying along the pier, and now and again crouching behind one of the mooring posts. I said nothing but kept an eye on her, for I supposed that she was at her usual game of watching some one.

Soon a tall man strode leisurely along, and from every movement of the woman I could see that he was the subject of her watching. He came near where I sat, and stood there with that calm unconcerned patience which is a characteristic of the fisherman.

He was a fine-looking fellow, well over six feet high, with a tangled mass of thick red-yellow hair and curly, bushy beard. He had lustrous, far-seeing golden-brown eyes, and massive, finely-cut features. His pilot-cloth trousers spangled all over with silver herring scales, were tucked into great, bucket-boots. He wore a heavy blue jersey and a cap of weazel skin. I had been thinking of the decline of the herring from the action of the trawlers in certain waters, and fancied this would be a good opportunity to get a local opinion. Before long I strolled over and joined this son of the Vikings. He gave it, and it was a decided one, uncompromisingly against the trawlers and the laws which allowed them to do their nefarious work. He spoke in a sort of old-fashioned, biblical language which was moderate and devoid of epithets, but full of apposite illustration. When he had pointed out that certain fishing grounds, formerly most prolific of result to the fishers, were now absolutely worthless he ended his argument:

"And, sure, good master, it stands to rayson. Suppose you be a farmer, and when you have prepared your land and manured it, you sow your seed and plough the ridges and make it all safe from wind and devastatin' storm. If, when the green corn be shootin' frae the airth, you take your harrow and drag it ath'art the springin' seed, where be then the promise of your golden grain?"

For a moment or two the beauty of his voice, the deep, resonant, earnestness of his tone and the magnificent, simple purity of the man took me away from the scene. He seemed as though I had looked him through and through, and had found him to be throughout of golden worth. Possibly it was the imagery of his own speech and the colour which his eyes and hair and cap suggested, but he seemed to me for an instant as a small figure projected against a background of rolling upland clothed in ripe grain. Round his feet were massed the folds of a great white sheet whose edges faded into air. In a moment the image passed, and he stood before me in his full stature.

I almost gasped, for just behind him, where she had silently come, stood Gormala, gazing not at the fisherman but at me, with eyes that positively blazed with a sort of baleful eagerness. She was looking straight into my eyes; I knew it when I caught the look of hers.

The fisherman went on talking. I did not, however, hear what he was saying, for again some mysterious change had come over our surroundings. The blue sea had over it the mystery of the darkness of the night; the high noon sun had lost its fiery vigour and shone with the pale yellow splendour of a full moon. All around me, before and on either hand, was a waste of waters; the very air and earth seemed filmed with moving water, and the sound of falling waters was in my ears. Again, the golden fisherman was before me for an instant, not as a moving speck but in full size now he lay prone; limp and lifeless, with waxen cold cheeks, in the eloquent inaction of death. The white sheet—I could see now that it was a shroud—was around him up to his heart. I seemed to feel Gormala's eyes burning into my brain as I looked. All at once everything seemed to resume its proper proportion, and I was listening calmly to the holding forth of the Viking.

I turned instinctively and looked at Gormala. For an instant her eyes seemed to blaze triumphantly; then she pulled the little shawl which she wore closer round her shoulders and, with a gesture full of modesty and deference turned away. She climbed up the ridges of the harbour wall and sat looking across as at the sea beyond, now studded with a myriad of brown sails.

A little later the stolid indifference as to time slipped all at once from the fisherman. He was instinct with life and action, and with a touch of his cap and a "Farewell good Master!" stood poised on the very edge of the pier ready to spring on a trim, weather-beaten smack which came rushing along almost grazing the rough stone work. It made our hearts jump as he sprang on board and taking the tiller from the hand of the steersman turned the boat's head to the open sea. As she rushed out through the harbour mouth we heard behind us the voice of an old fisherman who had hobbled up to us:

"He'll do that once too often! Lauchlane Macleod is like all these men from Uist and the rest of the Out Islanders. They don't care 'naught about naught.'"

Lauchlane Macleod! The very man of whom Gormala had prophesied! The very mention of his name seemed to turn me cold.

After lunch at the hotel I played golf on the links till evening drew near. Then I got on my bicycle to return home. I had laboured slowly up the long hill to the Stirling quarry when I saw Gormala sitting on the roadside on a great boulder of red granite. She was evidently looking out for me, for when I came near she rose up and deliberately stood in the roadway in my path. I jumped off my wheel and asked her point blank what she wanted with me so much that she stopped me on the road.

Gormala was naturally an impressive figure, but at present she looked weird and almost unearthly. Her tall, gaunt form lit by the afterglow in a soft mysterious light was projected against the grey of the darkening sea, whose sombreness was emphasised by the brilliant emerald green of the sward which fell from where we stood to the jagged cliff-line.

The loneliness of the spot was profound. From where we stood not a house was to be seen, and the darkening sea was desert of sails. It seemed as if we two were the only living things in nature's vast expanse. To me it was a little awesome. Gormala's first mysterious greeting when I had seen the mourning for the child, and her persistent following of me ever since, had begun to get on my nerves. She had become a sort of enforced condition to me, and whether she was present in the flesh or not, the expectation or the apprehension of her coming—I hardly knew which it was—kept my thoughts perpetually interested in her. Now, her weird, statuesque attitude and the scene around us finished my intellectual subjugation. The weather had changed to an almost inconceivable degree. The bright clear sky of the morning had become darkly mysterious, and the wind had died away to an ominous calm. Nature seemed altogether sentient, and willing to speak directly to a man in my own receptive mood. The Seer-woman evidently knew this, for she gave fully a minute of silence for the natural charm to work before she spoke. Then in a solemn warning voice she said:

"Time is flying by us; Lammas-tide is nigh." The words impressed me, why I know not; for though I had heard of Lammas-tide I had not the smallest idea of what was meant by it. Gormala was certainly quick with her eyes—she had that gypsy quality in remarkable degree—and she seemed to read my face like an open book. There was a suppressed impatience in her manner, as of one who must stop in the midst of some important matter to explain to a child whose aid is immediately necessary:

"Ye no ken why? Is it that ye dinna heed o' Lammas-tide, or that ye no ken o' the prophecy of the Mystery of the Sea and the treasures that lie hid therein." I felt more than ever abashed, and that I should have known long ago those things of which the gaunt woman spoke, towering above me as I leaned on my wheel. She went on:

"An' ye no ken, then listen and learn!" and she spoke the following rune in a strange, staccato cadence which seemed to suit our surroundings and to sink into my heart and memory so deep that to forget would be impossible:

> "To win the Mystery o' the Sea,
> "An' learn the secrets that there be,
> "Gather in one these weirds three:
>
> "A gowden moon on a flowin' tide,
> "And Lammas floods for the spell to bide;
> "And a gowden mon wi' death for his bride."

There was a long pause of silence between us, and I felt very strangely. The sea before me took odd, indefinite shape. It seemed as though it was of crystal clearness, and that from where I gazed I could see all its mysteries. That is, I could see so as to know there were mysteries, though what they were individually I could not even dream. The past and the present and the future seemed to be mingled in one wild, chaotic, whirling dream, from the mass of which thoughts and ideas seemed now and again to fly out unexpectedly on all sides as do sparks from hot iron under the hammer. Within my heart grew vague indefinite yearnings, aspirations, possibilities. There came a sense of power so paramount that instinctively I drew myself up to my full height and became conscious of the physical vigour within me. As I did so I looked around and seemed to wake from a dream.

Naught around me but the drifting clouds, the silent darkening land and the brooding sea. Gormala was nowhere to be seen.

IV

LAMMAS FLOODS

When I got to Cruden it was quite dark. I had lingered by the way thinking of Gormala MacNiel and all the queer kind of mystery in which she seemed to be enmeshing me. The more I thought, the more I was puzzled; for the strangest thing of all to me was that I understood part of what seemed to be a mystery. For instance I was but imperfectly acquainted with the Seer-woman's view of what was to be the result of her watching of Lauchlane Macleod. I knew of course from her words at our first conversation that in him she recognised a man doomed to near death according to the manifestation of her own power of Second Sight; but I knew what she did not seem to, that this was indeed a golden man. From the momentary glimpse which I had had in that queer spell of trance, or whatever it was which had come to me on the pier head, I had seemed to *know* him as a man of gold, sterling throughout. It was not merely that his hair was red gold and that his eyes might fairly be called golden, but his whole being could only be expressed in that way; so that when Gormala spoke, the old rhyme seemed at once a prime factor in the group of three powers which had to be united before the fathoming of the Mystery of the Sea. I accordingly made up my mind to speak with the Seer-woman and to ask her to explain. My own intellectual attitude to the matter interested me. I was not sceptical, I did not believe; but I think my mind hung in poise. Certainly my sympathies tended towards the mysterious side, backed up by some kind of understanding of the inner nature of things which was emotional or unintentional rather than fixed.

All that night I seemed to dream, my mind working eternally round the data of the day; hundreds of different relationships between Gormala, Lauchlane Macleod, Lammas-tide, the moon and the secrets of the sea revolved before me. It was grey morning before I fell asleep to the occasional chirping of the earliest birds.

As sometimes happens after a night of uneasy dreaming of some disturbing topic, the reaction of the morning carried oblivion with it. It was well into the afternoon when all at once I remembered the existence of the witch-woman—for as such I was beginning to think of Gormala.

The thought came accompanied by a sense of oppression which was not of fear, but which was certainly of uneasiness. Was it possible that the woman had in some way, or to some degree, hypnotised me. I remembered with a slightly nervous feeling how the evening before I had stopped on the roadway obedient to her will, and how I had lost the identity of my surroundings in her presence. A sudden idea struck me; I went to the window and looked out. For an instant my heart seemed to be still.

Just opposite the house stood Gormala, motionless. I went out at once and joined her, and instinctively we turned our steps toward the sand-hills. As we walked along I said to her:

"Where did you disappear to last night?"

"About that which is to be done!" Her lips and her face were set; I knew it was no use following up that branch of the subject, so I asked again:

"What did you mean by those verses which you told me?" Her answer was given in a solemn tone:

"Them that made them alone can tell; until the time shall come!"

"Who made them?"

"Nane can now tell. They are as aud as the rocky foundations o' the isles themselves."

"Then how did you come to know them?" There was a distinct note of pride in her answer. Such a note as might be expected from a prince speaking of his ancestry:

"They hae come doon to me through centuries. Frae mither to dochter, and from mither to dochter again, wi' never a break in the lang line o' the tellin'. Know ye, young master, that I am o' a race o' Seers. I take my name from that Gormala o' Uist who through long years foresaw the passing o' mony a one. That Gormala who throughout the islands of the west was known and feared o' all men; that Gormala whose mither's mither, and mither's mither again, away back into the darkness o' time when coracles crept towards the sunset ower the sea and returned not, held the fates o' men and women in their han's and ruled the Mysteries o' the Sea." As it was evident that Gormala must have in her own mind some kind of meaning of the prophecy, or spell, or whatever it was, I asked her again:

"But you must understand something of the meaning, or you would not attach so much importance to it?"

"I ken naught but what is seen to ma een, and to that inner e'e which telleth tae the soul that which it seeth!"

"Then why did you warn me that Lammas-tide was near at hand?" The grim woman actually smiled as she replied:

"Did ye no hearken to the words spoken of the Lammas floods, which be of the Powers that rule the Spell?"

"Well, the fact is that I don't know anything of 'Lammas-tide!' We do not keep it in the Church of England," I added as an afterthought, explanatory of my ignorance. Gormala was clever enough to take advantage of having caught me in a weak place; so she took advantage of it to turn the conversation into the way she wished herself:

"What saw ye, when Lauchlane Macleod grew sma' in yer een, and girt again?"

"Simply, that he seemed to be all at once a tiny image of himself, seen against a waste of ripe corn." Then it struck me that I had not as yet told her or any one else of what I had seen. How then did she know it? I was annoyed and asked her. She answered scornfully:

"How kent I it, an' me a Seer o' a race o' Seers! Are ma wakin' een then so dim or so sma' that I canna read the thochts o' men in the glances o' their een. Did I no see yer een look near an' far as quick as thocht? But what saw ye after, when ye looked rapt and yer een peered side to side, as though at one lyin' prone?" I was more annoyed than ever and answered her in a sort of stupor:

"I saw him lying dead on a rock, with a swift tide running by; and over the waters the broken track of a golden moon." She made a sound which was almost a cry, and which recalled me to myself as I looked at her. She was ablaze. She towered to her full height with an imperious, exultant mien; the light in her eyes was more than human as she said:

"Dead, as I masel' saw him an' 'mid the foam o' the tide race! An' gowd, always gowd ahint him in the een of this greater Seer. Gowden corn, and gowden moon, and gowden sea! Aye! an' I see it now, backiebird that I hae been; the gowden mon indeed, wi' his gowden een an' his gowden hair and all the truth o' his gowden life!" Then turning to me she said fiercely:

"Why did I warn ye that Lammas-tide was near? Go ask those that value the months and days thereof, when be Lammas and what it means to them that hae faith. See what they are; learn o' the comin' o' the moon and o' the flowin' o' the tides that follow!"

Without another word she turned and left me.

I went back to the hotel at once, determined to post myself as to Lammas-tide; its facts and constitutions, and the beliefs and traditions that hung around it. Also to learn the hours of the tides, and the age of the moon about the time of Lammas-tide. Doubtless I could have found out all I wanted from some of the ministers of the various houses of religion which hold in Cruden; but I was not wishful to make public, even so far, the mystery which was closing around me. My feeling was partly a saving sense of humour, or the fear of ridicule, and partly a genuine repugnance to enter upon the subject with any one who might not take it as seriously as I could wish. From which latter I gather that the whole affair was becoming woven into the structure of my life.

Possibly it was, that some trait, or tendency, or power which was individual to me was beginning to manifest itself and to find its means of expression. In my secret heart I not only believed but knew that some instinct within me was guiding my thoughts in some strange way. The sense of occult power which is so vital a part of divination was growing within me and asserting its masterdom, and with it came an equally forceful desire of secrecy. The Seer in me, latent so long, was becoming conscious of his strength, and jealous of it.

At this time, as the feeling of strength and consciousness grew, it seemed to lose something of its power from this very cause. Gradually it was forced upon me that for the full manifestation of such faculty as I might possess, some kind of abstraction or surrender of self was necessary. Even a few hours of experience had taught me much; for now that my mind was bent on the phenomena of Second Sight the whole living and moving world around me became a veritable diorama of possibilities. Within two days from the episode at the Pier head I had had behind me a larger experience of effort of occult force than generally comes to a man in a lifetime. When I look back, it seems to me that all the forces of life and nature became exposed to my view. A thousand things which hitherto I had accepted in simple faith as facts, were pregnant with new meanings. I began to understand that the whole earth and sea, and air—all that of which human beings generally ordinarily take cognisance, is but a film or crust which hides the deeper moving powers or forces. With this insight I began to understand the grand guesses of the Pantheists, pagan and christian alike, who out of their spiritual and nervous and intellectual sensitiveness began to realise that there was somewhere a purposeful cause of universal action. An action which in its special or concrete working appeared like the sentience of nature in general, and of the myriad items of its cosmogony.

I soon learned that Lammas day is the first of August and is so often accompanied by heavy weather that Lammas floods are almost annually recurrent. The eve of the day is more or less connected with various superstitions.

This made me more eager for further information, and by the aid of a chance friend, I unearthed at Aberdeen a learned professor who gave me offhand all the information which I desired. In fact he was so full of astronomical learning that I had to stop him now and again in order to elucidate some point easily explainable to those who understood his terminology, but which wrapped my swaddling knowledge in a mystery all its own. I have a sneaking friendliness even now for anyone to whom the word 'syzygy' carries no special meaning.

I got at the bases of facts, however, and understood that on the night of July 31, which was the eve of Lammas-tide, the moon would be full at midnight. I learned also that from certain astronomical reasons the tide which would ostensibly begin its flow a little after midnight would in reality commence just on the stroke. As these were the points which concerned me I came away with a new feeling of awe upon me. It seemed as though the heavens as well as the earth were bending towards the realisation or fulfillment of the old prophecy. At this time my own connection with the mystery, or how it might affect me personally, did not even enter my head. I was content to be an obedient item in the general scheme of things.

It was now the 28th July so, if it were to take place at the Lammas-tide of the current year, we should know soon the full measure of the denouêment. There was but one thing wanting to complete the conditions of the prophecy. The weather had been abnormally dry, and there might after all be no Lammas floods. To-day, however, the sky had been heavily overcast. Great black clouds which seemed to roll along tumbling over and over, as the sail of a foundered boat does in a current, loomed up from the west. The air grew closer, and to breathe was an effort. A sort of shiver came over the wide stretch of open country. Darker and darker grew the sky, till it seemed so like night that the birds in the few low-lying coppices and the scanty hedgerows ceased to sing. The bleat of sheep and the low of cattle seemed to boom through the still air with a hollow sound, as if coming from a distance. The intolerable stillness which precedes the storm became so oppressive that I, who am abnormally susceptible to the moods of nature, could almost have screamed out.

Then all at once the storm broke. There was a flash of lightning so vivid that it lit up the whole country away to the mountains which encircle Braemar. The fierce crash and wide roll of the thunder followed with incredible quickness. And then the hot, heavy-dropped summer rain fell in torrents.

All that afternoon the rain fell, with only a few brief intervals of glowing sunshine. All night, too, it seemed to fall without ceasing, for whenever I woke—which I did frequently with a sense over me of something impending—I could hear the quick, heavy patter on the roof, and the rush and gurgle of the overcharged gutters.

The next day was one of unmitigated gloom. The rain poured down ceaselessly. There was little wind, just sufficient to roll north-eastwards the great masses of rain-laden clouds piled up by the Gulf Stream against the rugged mountains of the western coast and its rocky islands. Two whole days there were of such rain, and then there was no doubt as to the strength of the Lammas floods this year. All the wide uplands of Buchan were glistening with runnels of water whenever the occasional glimpses of sunshine struck them. Both the Water of Cruden and the Back Burn were running bank high. On all sides it was reported that the Lammas floods were the greatest that had been known in memory.

All this time my own spiritual and intellectual uneasiness was perpetually growing. The data for the working of the prophecy were all fixed with remarkable exactness. In theatrical parlance 'the stage was set' and all ready for the action which was to come. As the hours wore on, my uneasiness changed somewhat and apprehension became merged in a curious mixture of superstition and exaltation. I was growing eager to the coming time.

The afternoon of July 31 was fine. The sun shone brightly; the air was dry and, for the time of year, cool. It seemed as though the spell of wet weather was over and that fiery August was coming to its own again. The effects of the rainstorm were, however, manifest. Not only was every rill and stream and river in the North in spate but the bogs of the mountains were so saturated with wet that many days must elapse before they could cease to send their quota to swell the streams. The mountain valleys were generally lakes in miniature. As one went through the country the murmur or rush of falling water was forever in the ears. I suppose it was in my own case partly because I was concerned in the mere existence of Lammas floods that the whole of nature seemed so insistent on the subject. The sound of moving water in its myriad gamut was so perpetually in my ears that I could never get my mind away from it. I had a long walk that afternoon through roads still too wet and heavy for bicycling. I came back to dinner thoroughly tired out, and went to bed early.

V

The Mystery of the Sea

I do not remember what woke me. I have a vague idea that it was a voice, but whether outside the house or within myself I know not.

It was eleven o'clock by my watch when I left the Kilmarnock Arms and took my way across the sandhills, heading for the Hawklaw which stood out boldly in the brilliant moonlight. I followed the devious sheep track amongst the dunes covered with wet bent-grass, every now and again stumbling amongst the rabbit burrows which in those days honeycombed the sandhills of Cruden Bay. At last I came to the Hawklaw, and, climbing the steep terraced edge near the sea, sat on the top to breathe myself after the climb.

The scene was one of exquisite beauty. Its natural loveliness was enhanced by the softness of the full yellow moonlight which seemed to flood the heavens and the earth alike. To the south-east the bleak promontory of Whinnyfold stood out stark and black as velvet and the rocks of the Skares were like black dots in the quivering sea of gold. I arose and went on my way. The tide was far out and as I stumbled along the rude path above the waste of boulders I had a feeling that I should be late. I hurried on, crossed the little rill which usually only trickled down beside the fishers' zigzag path at the back of Whinnyfold but which was now a rushing stream—again the noise of falling water, the voice of the Lammas floods—and took the cart track which ran hard by the cliff down to the point which looked direct upon the Skares.

When I reached the very edge of the cliff, where the long sea-grass and the deep clover felt underfoot like a luxurious carpet, I was not surprised to see Gormala seated, looking out seawards. The broad track of the moon lay right across the outmost rock of the Skares and falling across some of the jagged rocks, which seemed like fangs rising from the deep water as the heave of the waveless sea fell back and the white water streamed down, came up to where we stood and seemed to bathe both the Seer-woman and myself in light. There was no current anywhere, but only the silent rise and fall of the water in the everlasting movement of the sea. When she heard me behind her Gormala turned round, and the patient calmness of her face disappeared. She rose quickly, and as she did so pointed to a small boat which sailing up from the south was now drawing opposite to us and appeared to be making a course as close to shore as possible, just clearing the outer bulwark of the Skares.

"Look!" she said, "Lauchlane Macleod comes by his lanes. The rocks are around him, and his doom is at hand!"

There did not appear any danger in such a course; the wind was gentle, the tide was at the still moment between ebb and flow, and the smoothness of the water beyond the rock seemed to mark its great depth.

All at once the boat seemed to stand still,—we were too far off to hear a sound even on such a still night. The mast bent forward and broke short off, the sails hung limp in the water with the peak of the lug sail sticking up in a great triangle, like the fin of a mammoth shark. A few seconds after, a dark speck moved on the water which became agitated around it; it was evident that a swimmer was making for the land. I would have gone to help him had it been of use; but it was not, the outer rock was half a mile away. Indeed, though I knew it was no use, I was yet about to swim to meet him when Gormala's voice behind me arrested me:

"Do ye no see that gin ye meet him amid yon rocks, ye can, when the tide begins to race, be no help to any. If he can win through, ye may help him if ye bide here." The advice was good and I stayed my feet. The swimmer evidently knew the danger, for he hurried frantically to win some point of safety before the tide should turn. But the rocks of the Skares are deadly steep; they rise from the water sheer everywhere, and to climb them from the sea is a hopeless task. Once and again the swimmer tried to find a chink or cranny where he could climb; but each time he tried to raise himself he fell back into the water. Moreover I could see that he was wounded, for his left hand hung idle. He seemed to realise the hopelessness of the task, and turning, made desperately for the part where we stood. He was now within the most dangerous spot in the whole region of the Skares. The water is of great depth everywhere and the needlepoints of rocks rise almost to the very surface. It is only when the waves are rough at low water that they can be seen at all, when the dip of the waves leaves them bare; but from the surface in calm weather they cannot be seen as the swirl of the tide around them is invisible. Here, too, the tide, rounding the point and having the current broken by the masses of the great rock, rolls with inconceivable rapidity. I had too often watched from the headland where my home was to be the set of the tide not to know the danger. I shouted as loudly as I could, but for some reason he did not hear me. The moments ere the tide should turn seemed like ages; and yet it was with a sudden shock that I heard the gurgle of moving water followed by the lap, lap, lap, getting quicker each second. Somewhere inland a clock struck twelve.

The tide had turned and was beginning to flow.

In a few seconds the swimmer felt its effects, though he did not seem to notice them. Then he was swept towards the north. All at once there was a muffled cry which seemed to reach slowly to where we stood, and the swimmer rolled over for an instant. It was only too apparent what had happened; he had struck his arm against one of the sunken rocks and injured it. Then he commenced a mad struggle for life, swimming without either arm in that deadly current which grew faster and faster every moment. He was breathless, and now and again his head dipped; but he kept on valiantly. At last in one of these dips, borne by the momentum of his own strength and the force of the current, he struck his head against another of the sunken rocks. For an instant he raised it, and I could see it run red in the glare of the moonlight.

Then he sank; from the height where I stood I could see the body roll over and over in the fierce current which made for the outmost point to the north-east of the promontory. I ran over as fast as I could, Gormala following. When I came to the rock, which here shelved, I plunged in and after a few strokes met by chance the body as it rolled upward. With a desperate effort I brought it to land.

The struggle to lift the body from the water and to bear it up the rock exhausted me, so that when I reached the top of the cliff I had to pause for a few seconds to breathe hard. Since the poor fellow's struggle for life had begun I had never for an instant given the prophecy a thought. But now, all at once, as I looked past the figure, lying limp before me with the poor arms twisted unnaturally and the head turned—away past the moonlit sea and the great, golden orb whose track was wrinkled over the racing tide, the full force of it burst upon me, and I felt a sort of spiritual transformation. The air seemed full of fluttering wings; sea and land alike teemed with life that I had not hitherto dreamed of. I fell in a sort of spiritual trance. But the open eyes were upon me; I feared the man was dead, but Briton-like I would not accept the conviction without effort. So I raised the body to my shoulders, determined to make with what speed I could for Whinnyfold where fire and willing hands could aid in restoration. As I laid the limp body across my shoulders, holding the two hands in my right hand to steady the burden whilst with the left I drew some of the clothing tight, I caught Gormala's eye. She had not helped me in any possible way, though more than once in distress I had called to her. So now I said angrily:

"Get away woman! You should be ashamed of yourself never to help at such a time," and I took my way unaided. I did not heed at the time her answer, spoken with a certain measure of deprecation, though it afterwards came back to me:

"Am I to wark against the Fates when They have spoken! The Dead are dead indeed when the Voice has whispered in their ears!"

Now, as I passed along with the hands of the dead man in mine— the true shell of a man whose spirit could be but little space away whilst the still blood in the veins was yet warm—a strange thing began to happen. The spirits of earth and sea and air seemed to take shape to me, and all the myriad sounds of the night to have a sentient cause of utterance. As I panted and struggled on, my physical effort warring equally with the new spiritual experience so that nothing remained except sentience and memory, I could see Gormala walking abreast me with even steps. Her eyes glared balefully with a fierce disappointment; never once did she remit the vigilant, keen look which seemed to pierce into my very soul.

For a short space of time there was something of antagonism to her; but this died away imperceptibly, and I neither cared nor thought about her, except when my attention would be called to her. I was becoming wrapped in the realisation of the mightier forces around me.

Just where the laneway from the cliff joins Whinnyfold there is a steep zigzag path running down to the stony beach far below where the fishers keep their boats and which is protected from almost the wildest seas by the great black rock—the Caudman,—which fills the middle of the little bay, leaving deep channels on either hand. When I was come to this spot, suddenly all the sounds of the night seemed to cease. The very air grew still so that the grasses did not move or rustle, and the waters of the swirling tide ceased to run in grim silence on their course. Even to that inner sense, which was so new to me that the change in everything to which it was susceptible became at once noticeable, all things stood still. It was as though the spirits of earth and air and water were holding their breath for some rare portent. Indeed I noticed as my eye ranged the surface of the sea, that the moon track was for the time no longer rippled, but lay in a broad glistening band.

The only living thing in all the wide world was, it seemed to me, the figure of Gormala as, with lowering eyes and suspended breath, she stood watching me with uncompromising, persistent sternness.

Then my own heart seemed to stand still, to be a part of the grim silence of the waiting forces of the world. I was not frightened; I was not even amazed. All seemed so thoroughly in keeping with the prevailing influence of the time that I did not feel even a moment of surprise.

Up the steep path came a silent procession of ghostly figures, so misty of outline that through the grey green of their phantom being the rocks and moonlit sea were apparent, and even the velvet blackness of the shadows of the rocks did not lose their gloom. And yet each figure was defined so accurately that every feature, every particle of dress or accoutrement could be discerned. Even the sparkle of their eyes in that grim waste of ghostly grey was like the lambent flashes of phosphoric light in the foam of moving water cleft by a swift prow. There was no need for me to judge by the historical sequence of their attire, or by any inference of hearing; I knew in my heart that these were the ghosts of the dead who had been drowned in the waters of the Cruden Skares.

Indeed the moments of their passing—and they were many for the line was of sickening length—became to me a lesson of the long flight of time. At the first were skin-clad savages with long, wild hair matted; then others with rude, primitive clothing. And so on in historic order men, aye, and here and there a woman, too, of many lands, whose garments were of varied cut and substance. Red-haired Vikings and black-haired Celts and Phoenicians, fair-haired Saxons and swarthy Moors in flowing robes. At first the figures, chiefly of the barbarians, were not many; but as the sad procession passed along I could see how each later year had brought its ever-growing tale of loss and disaster, and added more and faster to the grim harvest of the sea. A vast number of the phantoms had passed when there came along a great group which at once attracted my attention. They were all swarthy, and bore themselves proudly under their cuirasses and coats of mail, or their garb as fighting men of the sea. Spaniards they were, I knew from their dress, and of three centuries back. For an instant my heart leapt; these were men of the great Armada, come up from the wreck of some lost galleon or patache to visit once again the glimpses of the Moon. They were of lordly mien, with large aquiline features and haughty eyes. As they passed, one of them turned and looked at me. As his eyes lit on me, I saw spring into them, as though he were quick, dread, and hate, and fear.

Hitherto I had been impressed, awed, by the indifference of the passing ghosts. They had looked nowhere, but with steady, silent, even tread had passed on their way. But when this one looked at me it was a glance from the spirit world which chilled me to the very soul.

But he too passed on. I stood at the head of the winding path, having the dead man still on my shoulders and looking with sinking heart at the sad array of the victims of the Cruden Skares. I noticed that most who came now were seamen, with here and there a group of shoresmen and a few women amongst them. The fishermen were many, and without exception wore great sea boots. And so with what patience I could I waited for the end.

At length it came in the shape of a dim figure of great stature, and both of whose arms hung limp. The blood from a gash on his forehead had streamed on to his golden beard, and the golden eyes looked far away. With a shudder I saw that this was the ghost of the man whose body, now less warm, lay upon my shoulders; and so I knew that Lauchlane Macleod was dead. I was relieved when I saw that he did not even look at me; though as I moved on, following the procession, he walked beside me with equal steps, stopping and moving as I stopped and moved.

The silence of death was upon the little hamlet of Whinnyfold. There was not a sign of life; not a dog barked as the grim procession had moved up the steep path or now filed across the running stream and moved along the footpath toward Cruden. Gormala with eager eyes kept watching me; and as the minutes wore on I began to resume my double action of thought, for I could see in her face that she was trying to reason out from my own expression something of what I was looking at. As we moved along she now began to make suggestions to me in a fierce whisper, evidently hoping that she might learn something from my acquiescence in, or negation of, her thought. Through that ghostly silence her living voice cut with the harshness of a corncrake.

"Shearing the silence of the night with ragged edge."

Perhaps it was for the best; looking back now on that awful experience, I know that no man can say what his mind may suffer in the aftertime who walks alone with the Dead. That I was strung to some amazing pitch was manifested by the fact that I did not seem to feel the great weight which lay upon my shoulders. I have naturally vast strength and the athletic training of my youth had developed it highly. But the weight of an ordinary man is much to hold or carry for even a short time, and the body which I bore was almost that of a giant.

The path across the neck of land which makes the Skares a promontory is flat, with here and there a deep cleft like a miniature ravine where the water from the upland rushes in flood time down to the sea. All these rills were now running strong, but I could hear no sound of murmuring water, no splash as the streams leapt over the edge of the cliff on the rocks below in whitening spray. The ghostly procession did not pause at any of these streams, but moved on impassively to the farther side where the path trends down to the sands of Cruden Bay. Gormala stood a moment watching my eyes as they swept the long line passing the angle so that I could see them all at once. That she guessed something was evident from her speech:

"They are many; his eyes range wide!" I started, and she knew that she had guessed aright. This one guess seemed to supply her with illimitable data; she evidently knew something of the spirit world, though she could not see into its mysteries. Her next words brought enlightenment to me:

"They are human spirits; they follow the path that the feet o' men hae made!"

It was so. The procession did not float over the surface of field or sand, but took its painful way down the zigzag of the cliff and over the rocky path through the great boulders of the foreshore. When the head of it reached the sand, it passed along the summit of the ridge, just as every Sunday night the fishermen of Whinnyfold and Collieston did in returning to their herring boats at Peterhead.

The tramp across the sands was long and dreary. Often as I had taken that walk in rain or storm, with the wind almost sweeping me off my feet whilst the sand drift from the bent-covered hills almost cut my cheeks and ears, I had never felt the way to be so long or so hard to travel. Though I did not realise it at the time, the dead man's weight was beginning to tell sorely upon me. Across the Bay I could see the few lights in the village of Port Erroll that were to be seen at such a time of night; and far over the water came the cold grey light which is the sign of the waning of the night rather than of the coming of the morning.

When we came to the Hawklaw, the head of the procession turned inward through the sandhills. Gormala, watching my eyes, saw it and an extraordinary change came over her. For an instant she was as if stricken, and stood stock still. Then she raised her hands in wonder, and said in an awed whisper:

"The Holy Well! They gang to St. Olaf's well! The Lammas floods will aye serve them weel."

With an instinct of curiosity strong upon me I hurried on so as to head the procession. As I moved along the rough path amongst the sandhills I felt the weight of the burden on my shoulders grow heavier and heavier, so that my feet dragged as do the feet of one in a nightmare. As I moved on, I looked round instinctively and saw that the shade of Lauchlane Macleod no longer kept pace with me, but retained its place in the procession. Gormala's evil eye was once more upon me, but with her diabolical cunning she guessed the secret of my looking round. She moved along, not with me but at the rate she had been going as though she liked or expected to remain in juxtaposition to the shade of the dead man; some purpose of her own was to be fulfilled.

As I pressed on, the shades around me seemed to grow dimmer and dimmer still; till at the last I could see little more than a film or haze. When I came to St. Olaf's well—then merely a rough pool at the base of the high land that stretches back from the Hawklaw—the ghostly mist was beginning to fade into the water. I stood hard by, and the weight upon my shoulders became dreadful. I could hardly stand; I determined, however, to hold on as long as I could and see what would happen. The dead man, too, was becoming colder! I did not know whether the dimming of the shadows was from this cause, or because the spirit of the man was farther away. It was possibly both, for as the silent, sad procession came on I could see more distinctly. When the wraith of the Spaniard turned and looked at me, he seemed once more to look with living eyes from a living soul. Then there was a dreary wait whilst the rest came along and passed in awesome stillness down into the well and disappeared. The weight upon my shoulders now became momentarily more intolerable. At last I could bear it no longer, and half bending I allowed the body to slip to the ground, I only holding the hands to steady the descent. Gormala was now opposite to me, and seeing what I had done leaped towards me with a loud cry. For one dim moment the wraith of the dead man stood above its earthly shell; and then I saw the ghostly vision no more.

At that instant, just as Gormala was about to touch the dead body, there was a loud hiss and murmur of waters. The whole pool burst up in a great fountain, scattering sand and water around for a wide space. I rushed back; Gormala did the same.

Then the waters receded again, and when I looked, the corpse of Lauchlane Macleod was gone. It was swallowed up in the Holy Well.

Overcome with physical weariness and strange horror of the scene I sank down on the wet sand. The scene whirled round me. . . I remember no more.

VI

The Ministers of the Doom

When at last I looked around me I was not surprised at anything I saw; not even at the intense face of Gormala whose eyes, bright in the full moonlight, were searching my face more eagerly than ever. I was lying on the sand, and she was bending over me so closely that her face almost touched mine. It was evident, even to my half-awake sensibilities, that she was listening intently, lest even a whispered word from me should be missed.

The witch-woman was still seemingly all afire, but withal there was manifested in her face and bearing a sense of disappointment which comforted me. I waited a few minutes until I felt my brain clear, and my body rested from the intolerable strain which it had undergone in carrying that terrific burden from Whinnyfold.

When I looked up again Gormala recognised the change in me, and her own expression became different. The baleful glitter of her eyes faded, and the blind, unreasoning hate and anger turned to keen inquiry. She was not now merely baffled in her hopes, and face to face with an unconscious man; there was at least a possibility of her gaining some knowledge, and all the energy of her nature woke again as she spoke:

"So ye are back wi' the moon and me. Whither went ye when ye lay down upon the sand. Was it back ye went, or forrart; wi' the ghaists into the Holy Well and beyond in their manifold course; or back to their comin' frae the sea and all that could there be told? Oh! mon, what it is to me that any ither can gang like that into spirit land, and me have to wait here by my lanes; to wring my hands an' torture my hairt in broken hopes!" I answered her question with another:

"How do you mean that ghosts go into the well and beyond?" Her answer was at the first given in a stern tone which became, however, softer, as she went on.

"Knew ye not, that the Lammas Floods are the carriers o' the Dead; that on Lammas nicht the Dead can win their way to where they will, under the airth by wherever there is rinnin' watter. Happy be they that can gain a Holy Well, an' so pass into the bowels o' the airth to where they list."

"And how and when do they return?"

"Dinna jest wi' Fate an' the Dead. They in their scope can gang and return again; no een, save your ain, o' man or Seer has seen the method o' their gangin'. No een, even yours, can see them steal out again in the nicht, when the chosen graves that they hae sought hae taken from them the dross o' the airth." I felt it was not wise to talk further, so without a word I turned and walked home by the sheep tracks amongst the sand hills. Now and again I stumbled in a rabbit hole, and as I would sink forward the wet bent would brush against my face.

The walk back in the dark dawn seemed interminable. All this time my mind was in a turmoil. I did not even seem to remember anything definitely, or think consecutively; but facts and fancies swept through my mind in a chaotic whirl. When I got to the house, I undressed quickly and got into bed; I must have instantly fallen into a deep sleep.

Next afternoon I walked by the shore to Whinnyfold. It was almost impossible to believe that I was looking at the same place as on last night. I sat on the cliff where I had sat last night, the hot August sun and the cool breeze from the sea being inconceivably soothing. So I thought and thought. . . The lack of sufficient sleep the night before and the tired feeling of the physical strain I had undergone—my shoulders still ached—told upon me, and I fell asleep.

When I waked Gormala stood in front of me.

After a long pause she spoke:

"I see that ye remember, else would ye ha' spoken to me. Will ye no tell me all that ye saw? Then, wi' your Seer's een an' my knowledge o' the fact we may thegither win oot the great Secret o' the Sea." I felt stronger than ever the instinctive conviction that I must remain keenly on guard with her. So I said nothing; waiting thus I should learn something, whether from her words or her silence. She could not stand this. I saw her colour rise till her face was all aglow with a red flush that shamed the sunset; and at last the anger blazed in her eyes. It was in a threatening tone which she spoke, though the words were themselves sufficiently conciliatory:

"The Secrets o' the Sea are to be won; and tae thee and me it is given to win them. What hae been is but an earnest of what will be. For ages ithers have tried to win but hae failed; and if we fail too for lack o' purpose or because ye like me not, then to ithers will come in time the great reward. For the secrets are there, and the treasures lie awaiting. The way is open for those to whom are the Gifts. Throw not away the favour of the Fates. For if they be kind to give where they will, they are hard to thwart, and their revenge is sure!" I must confess that her words began to weaken my purpose. In one way inexorable logic was on her side. Powers such as were mine were surely given for some purpose. Might I not be wrong in refusing to use them. If the Final Cause of my powers were purposeful, then might not a penalty be exacted from me because I had thwarted the project. Gormala, with that diabolical cunning of hers, evidently followed the workings of my mind, for her face lit up. How she knew, I know not, but I do know that her eyes never left mine. I suppose it may be that the eyes which have power to see at times the inwardness of things have some abnormal power also of expressing the thoughts behind them. I felt, however, that I was in danger. All my instincts told me that once in Gormala's power I should rue it, so I spoke out on the instant strongly:

"I shall have nothing to do with you whatever. Last night when you refused to help me with the wounded man—whom you had followed, remember, for weeks, hoping for his death—I saw you in your true colours; and I mean to have nothing to do with you." Fierce anger blazed again in her eyes; but again she controlled herself and spoke with an appearance of calm, though it was won with great effort, as I could see by the tension of her muscles:

"An' so ye would judge me that I would not help ye to bring the Dead to life again! I knew that Lauchlane was dead! Aye! and ye kent it too as weel as I did masel'. It needed no Seer to tell that, when ye brocht him up the rocks oot o' the tide. Then, when he was dead, for why wad ye no use him? Do the Dead themselves object that they help the livin' to their ends while the blood is yet warm in them? Is it ye that object to the power of the Dead? You whose veins have the power o' divination of the quick; you to whom the heavens themselves opened, and the airth and the watters under the airth, when the spirit of the Dead that ye carried walked beside ye as ye ganged to St. Olaf's Well. An' as for me, what hae I done that you should object. I saw, as you did, that Lauchlane's sands were run. You and I are alike in that. To us baith was given to see, by signs that ages have made sacred, that Fate had spoken in his ears though he had himself not heard the Voice. Nay more, to me was only given to see that the Voice had spoken. But to you was shown how, and when, and where the Doom should come, though you yersel' that can read the future as no ither that is known, canna read the past; and so could na tell what a lesser one would ha' guessed at lang

syne. I followed the Doom; you followed the Doom. I by my cunnin';
you when ye waked frae yer sleep, followin' yer conviction, till we met
thegither for Lauchlane's death, amid Lammas floods and under the
gowden moon on the gowden sea. Through his aid—aye, young sir—for
wi'oot a fresh corp to aid, no Seer o' airth could hae seen as ye did, that
lang line o' ghaists ye saw last nicht. Through his aid the wonders o' the
heavens and the deep, o' airth and air, was opened till ye. Wha then be
ye that condemn me that only saw a sign an' followed? Gin I be guilty,
what be you?"

It would be impossible to describe the rude, wild, natural eloquence
with which this was spoken. In the sunset, the gaunt woman seemed to
tower above me; and as she moved her arms, the long shadows of them
stretched over the green down before us and away over the wrinkled sea
as though her gestures were, giant like, appealing to all nature.

I was distinctly impressed, for all that she said was quite true. She
had in reality done nothing that the law would call wrong. Lauchlane's
death was in no possible way due to any act of hers. She had only
watched him; and as he did not even know that she watched he could
not have been influenced in any way by it or by her. As to my own part!
Her words gave me a new light. Why had I risen in the night and come
out to Whinnyfold? Was it intuition, or a call from the witch-woman,
who in such case must have had some hypnotic influence over me? Or
was it—?

I stood appalled at the unspoken thought. Could it be that the
powers of Nature which had been revealed to me in the dread hour had
not only sentience but purpose!

I felt that my tone was more conciliatory as I answered her:

"I did not mean to blame you for anything you had done. I see now
that your wrong was only passive." I felt that my words were weak, and
my feeling was emphasised by the scorn of her reply:

"My wrang was only passive! My wrang! What wrang hae I done that
you should sit in judgment on me. Could I hae helpit it when Lauchlane
met his death amang the rocks in the tide. Why you yoursel' sat here
beside me, an' ye no helpit him or tried to, strong man though ye be,
that could carry his corp frae here to St. Olaf's Well; for ye kenned that
no livin' arm could aid him in that hour o' doom. Aye! laddie, the Fates
know their wark o'er weel to hae ony such betterment o' their plans! An'
div ye think that by any act o' yer ain, or by any refusal o' act or speech,
ye can baffle the purpose o' the Doom. Ye are yet young and ye must

learn; then learn it now whiles ye can, that when the Word is spoken all follows as ordained. Aye! though the Ministers o' the Doom be many an' various, an' though they hae to gather in ane from many ages an' frae the furthermost ends o' the airth!"

Gormala's logic and the exactness of her statement were too much for me. I felt that I owed her some reparation and told her so. She received it in her gaunt way with the dignity of an empress.

But there her dignity stopped; for seeing that she had got a lever in her hands she began at once, womanlike, to use it. Without any hesitation or delay she asked me straightly to tell her what I had seen the night before. The directness of her questioning was my best help; my heart hardened and my lips closed. She saw my answer before I had spoken it, and turned away with an eloquent, rugged gesture of despair. She felt that her last hope was gone; that her last bolt had been sped in vain.

With her going, the link with last night seemed to break, and as she passed up the road the whole of that strange experience became dimmer and dimmer.

I walked home by Cruden sands in a sort of dream. The chill and strain of the night before seemed to affect me more and more with each hour. Feeling fatigued and drowsy I lay down on my bed and sank into a heavy, lethargic sleep.

The last thing I remember is the sounding of the dinner-gong, and a dim resolution not to answer its call. . .

It was weeks after, when the fever had passed away, that I left my bed in the Kilmarnock Arms.

VII

FROM OTHER AGES AND THE
ENDS OF THE EARTH

The last week in June of next year, 1898, found me back in Cruden. My own house was in process of building. I had purposely arranged with the builders that the fitting up and what the conveyancers call "beautifyings" should not be done until I should be on the spot myself next year, to be consulted about everything. Every day I went over to see the place and become familiar with it before the plans for decoration should be taken in hand. Still there was no enjoyment in getting wet every time I went and came, or in remaining in wet clothes, so that my day was mainly spent at home.

One of my first visits was to Peterhead which seemed to be in a state of absolute activity, for the herring fishing had been good and trade of all kinds was brisk. At the market place which was half full of booths, could be had almost everything required for the needs or comfort of life such as it can be on a fishing boat. Fruit and all sorts of summer luxuries were abundant. Being Saturday the boats had returned early and had got their nets away to the drying-grounds, and the men had been able to shave and dress tidily. The women, too, had got their dressing done early—the fish first and themselves afterwards.

For awhile I wandered about aimlessly amongst the booths, with that sort of unsatisfaction upon me which had of late been the prelude to many of the manifestations of the power of Second Sight. This used to be just as if something within me was groping or searching unsuccessfully for something unknown, the satisfaction coming with the realization of the objective of the search.

Presently I came to an itinerant auctioneer who was dealing with a small cart-load of odds and ends, evidently picked up in various places. His auction or "roup" was on the "Dutch" plan; an extravagant price, according to his own idea, being placed on each article, and the offer decreasing in default of bidders. The auctioneer was ready with his tongue; his patter showed how well he understood the needs and ideas of the class whom he addressed.

"Here's the works of the Reverend Robert William McAlister of

Trottermaverish in twal volumes, wantin' the first an' the last twa; three damaged by use, but still full of power in dealing with the speeritual necessities o' men who go down to the great deep in ships. A sermon for every day in the year, in the Gaelic for them as has na got the English, an' in good English for them as has. How much for the twal volumes, wantin' but three? Not a bawbee less than nine shellin', goin' goin'. Wha says eight shellin' for the lot. Seven shellin' an' no less. Goin' for six. Five shellin' for you sir. Any bidder at four shellin'. Not a bawbee less than three shellin'; Half a croon. Any bidder at twa shellin'. Gone for you sir!" the nine volumes were handed over to a grave-looking old man, and the two shillings which he produced from a heavy canvas bag duly pocketed by the auctioneer.

Everything he had, found some buyer; even a blue-book seemed to have its attraction. The oddness of some of the odd lots was occasionally amusing. When I had been round the basins of the harbour and had seen the dressings and barrelling of the fish, I again came across the auctioneer in the market place. He had evidently been using his time well, for the cart was almost empty. He was just putting up the last article, an old oak chest which up to now he had used as a sort of table on which to display the object for sale. An old oak chest has always charms for me, and I was about furnishing a house. I stepped over, opened the lid and looked in; there were some papers tossed on the bottom of it. I asked the auctioneer if the contents went with the chest, my real object being to get a look at the lock which seemed a very old one of steel, though it was much damaged and lacked a key. I was answered with a torrent of speech in true auctioneer fashion:

"Aye, good master. Take the lot just as it stands. An oaken kist, hundreds of years aud and still worthy a rest in the house-place of any man who has goods to guard. It wants a key, truth to tell; but the lock is a fine aud one and you can easy fit a key. Moreover the contents, be they what they may, are yours also. See! aud letters in some foreign tongue—French I think. Yellow in age an' the ink faded. Somebody's love letters, I'm thinkin'. Come now, young men here's a chance. Maybe if ye're no that fameeliar in writin' yer hairts oot to the lassies, ye can get some hints frae these. They can learn ye, I warrant!"

I was not altogether unaccustomed to auctions, so I affected a nonchalance which I did not feel. Indeed, I was unaccountably excited. It might have been that my feelings and memories had been worked up by the seeing again the pier where first I had met Lauchlane Macleod, and the moving life which then had environed him. I felt coming over me that strange impalpable influence or tendency which had been a part of my nature in the days immediately before the drowning of the Out-islander. Even as I looked, I seemed to feel rather than see fixed upon me the baleful eyes of the man in the ghostly procession on that Lammas eve. I was recalled to myself by the voice of the auctioneer:

"The kist and its contents will be sold for a guinea and not a bawbee less."

"I take it!" I cried impulsively. The auctioneer who in his wildest dreams had no hope of such a price seemed startled into momentary comparative silence. He quickly recovered himself and said: "The kist is yours, good master; and that concludes the roup!"

I looked around to see if there was present any one who could even suggest in any way the appearance of the man in the ghostly procession. But there was no such person. I met only *mirabile dictu*, the greedy eyes of Gormala MacNiel.

That evening in my room at the Kilmarnock Arms, I examined the papers as well as I could by lamplight. They were in an old-fashioned style of writing with long tails and many flourishes which made an added difficulty to me. The language was Spanish, which tongue I did not know; but by aid of French and what little Latin I could remember I made out a few words here and there. The dates ranged between 1598 and 1610. The letters, of which there were eight, were of manifest unimportance, short notes directed: "Don de Escoban" and merely arranging meetings. Then there were a number of loose pages of some printed folio, used perhaps as some kind of tally or possibly a cipher, for they were marked all over with dots. The lot was completed by a thin, narrow strip of paper covered with figures—possibly some account. Papers of three centuries ago were valuable, were it only for their style of writing. So I locked them all up carefully before I went to bed, with full intention to examine them thoroughly some day. The appearance of Gormala just at the time when I had become possessed of them seemed to connect them in some mysterious way with the former weird experiences in which she had so prominent a part.

That night I dreamed as usual, though my dreaming was of a scattered and incoherent character. Gormala's haunting presence and all that had happened during the day, especially the buying of the chest with the mysterious papers, as well as what had taken place since my arrival at Cruden was mixed up in perpetually recurring images with the beginning of my Second Sight and the death of Lauchlane Macleod. Again, and again, and again, I saw with the eyes of memory, in fragmentary fashion, the grand form of the fisherman standing in a blaze of gold, and later fighting his way through a still sea of gold, of which the only reliefs were the scattered piles of black rock and the pale face patched with blood. Again, and again, and again, the ghostly procession came up the steep path from the depths of the sea, and passed in slow silent measure into St. Olaf's Well.

Gormala's words were becoming a truth to me; that above and around me was some force which was impelling to an end all things of which I could take cognizance, myself amongst the rest. Here I stopped, suddenly arrested by the thought that it was Gormala herself who had set my mind working in this direction; and the words with which she had at once warned and threatened me when after the night of Lauchlane's death we stood at Witsennan point:

"When the Word is spoken all follows as ordained. Aye! though the Ministers of the Doom may be many and various, and though they may have to gather in one from many ages and from the furthermost ends of the earth!"

The next few days were delightfully fine, and life was one long enjoyment. On Monday evening there was a sunset which I shall never forget. The whole western sky seemed ablaze with red and gold; great masses of cloud which had rolled up seemed like huge crimson canopies looped with gold over the sun throned on the western mountains. I was standing on the Hawklaw, whence I could get a good view; beside me was a shepherd whose flock patched the steep green hillside as with snow. I turned to him and said:

"Is not that a glorious sight?"

"Aye! 'Tis grand. But like all beauty o' the warld it fadeth into naught; an' is only a mask for dool."

"You do not seem to hold a very optimistic opinion of things generally." He deliberately stoked himself from his snuff mull before replying:

"Optimist nor pessimist am I, eechie nor ochie. I'm thinkin' the optimist and the pessimist are lears alike; takin' a pairt for the whole, an' so guilty o' the logical sin o' *a particulari ad universale.* Sophism they misca' it; as if there were anything but a lee in a misstatement o' fac'. Fac's is good eneuch for me; an' that, let me tell ye, is why I said that the splendour o' the sunset is but a mask for dool. Look yon! The clouds are all gold and glory, like a regiment goin' oot to the battle. But bide ye till the sun drops, not only below the horizon but beyond the angle o' refraction. Then what see ye? All grim and grey, and waste, and dourness and dool; like the army as it returns frae the fecht. There be some that think that because the sun sets fine i' the nicht, it will of necessity rise fine i' the morn. They seem to no ken that it has to traverse one half o' the warld ere it returns; and that the averages of fine and foul, o' light and dark hae to be aye maintained. It may be that the days o' fine follow ane anither fast; or that the foul times linger likewise. But in the end, the figures of fine and foul tottle up, in accord wi' their ordered sum. What use is it, then, to no tak' heed o' fac's? Weel I ken, that the fac' o' the morrow will differ sair frae the fac's o' this nicht. Not in vain hae I seen the wisdom and glory o' the Lord in sunsets an' dawns wi'oot learnin' the lessons that they teach. Mon, I tell ye that it's all those glories o' pomp and pageantry—all the lasceevious luxuries o' colour an' splendour, that are the forerinners o' disaster. Do ye no see the streaks o' wind rinnin' i' the sky, frae the east to the west? Do ye ken what they portend? I'm tellin' ye, that before the sun sets the morrow nicht there will be ruin and disaster on all this side o' Scotland. The storm will no begin here. It is perhaps ragin' the noo away to the east. But it will come quick, most likely wi' the risin' o' the tide; and woe be then to them as has no made safe wi' all they can. Hark ye the stillness!" Shepherd-like he took no account of his own sheep whose ceaseless bleating, sounding in every note of the scale, broke the otherwise universal silence of nature. "I'm thinkin' it's but the calm before the storm. Weel sir, I maun gang. The yowes say it is time for the hame comin'. An' mark ye, the collie! He looks at me reproachful, as though I had forgot the yowes! My sairvice to ye, sir!"

"Good night" I answered, "I hope I shall meet you again."

"I'm thinkin' the same masel'. I hae much enjoyed yer pleasin' converse. I hope it's mony a crack we yet may hae thegither!" And so my philosophical egoist moved homewards, blissfully unconscious of the fact that my sole contribution to the "pleasing converse" was the remark that he did not seem optimistic.

The whole mass of his charge moved homewards at an even footpace, the collie making frantic dashes here and there to keep his flock headed in the right direction. Presently I saw the herd pouring like a foam-white noisy river across the narrow bridge over the Water of Cruden.

The next morning was fine, very hot, and of an unusual stillness. Ordinarily I should have rejoiced at such a day; but the warning of the erudite and philosophical shepherd made me mistrust. To me the worst of the prophecy business was that it became a disturbing influence. To-day, perforce, because it was fine, I had to expect that it would end badly. About noon I walked over to Whinnyfold; it being Saturday I knew that the workmen would have gone away early, and I wanted to have the house to myself so that I could go over it quietly and finally arrange the scheme of colouring. I remained there some hours, and then, when I had made up my mind as to things, I set off for the hotel.

In those few hours the weather had changed marvellously. Busy within doors and thinking of something else, I had not noticed the change, which must have been gradual however speedy. The heat had increased till it was most oppressive; and yet through it all there was now and then a cold shiver in the air which almost made me wince. All was still, so preternaturally still that occasional sounds seemed to strike the ear as disturbances. The screaming of the seagulls had mainly ceased, and the sound of breaking waves on rocks and shore was at variance with the silence over the sea; the sheep and cattle were so quiet that now and again the "moo" of a cow or the bleat of a sheep seemed strangely single. As I stood looking out seaward there seemed to be rising a cold wind; I could not exactly feel it, but I knew it was there. As I came down the path over the beach I thought I heard some one calling—a faint far-away sound. At first I did not heed it, as I knew it could not be any one calling to me; but when I found it continued, I looked round. There is at least a sufficient amount of curiosity in each of us to make us look round when there is a calling. At first I could not locate it; but then sight came to aid of sound, and I saw out on a rock two women waving handkerchiefs. The calling manifestly came from them. It was not good for any one to be isolated on a rock at a time when a storm was coming up; and I knew well the rocks which these women were amongst. I hurried on as quickly as I could, for there was a good way to go to reach them.

Near the south end of Cruden Bay there is a cluster of rocks which juts out from shore, something like a cock's spur. Beyond this cluster are isolated rocks, many of them invisible at high tide. These form part of the rocky system of the Skares, which spread out fan-like from the point of Whinnyfold. Amongst these rocks the sea runs at change of tide with great force; more than once when swimming there I had been almost carried away. What it was to be carried away amongst the rocks of the Skares I knew too well from the fate of Lauchlane Macleod. I ran as fast as I could down the steep pathway and along the boulder-strewn beach till I came to the Sand Craigs. As I ran I could see from the quick inrush of waves, which though not much at present were gathering force every instant, that the storm which the shepherd had predicted was coming fast upon us. In such case every moment was precious. Indeed it might mean life; and so in breathless haste I scrambled over the rocks. Behind the main body of the Sand Craigs are two isolated rocks whose tops are just uncovered at high tide, but which are washed with every wave. The near one of these is at low water not separated from the main mass, but only joined by a narrow isthmus a few feet long, over which the first waves of the turning tide rush vigourously, for it is in the direct sweep of the flowing tide. Beyond this, some ninety or a hundred feet off and separated by a deep channel, is the outer rock, always in island form. From this spot at low water is the best view of the multitudinous rocks of the Skares. On all sides they rise round you as you stand, the granite seeming yellow with the washing of the sea between the lines of high and low water; above the latter the black seaweed ceases growing. This island is so hidden by the higher rocks around it that it cannot be seen from any part of Cruden Bay or from Port Erroll across it; it can only be seen from the path leading to Whinnyfold. It was fortunate that some one had been passing just then, or the efforts of the poor women to attract attention might have been made in vain.

When I reached the Sand Craigs I scrambled at once to the farthest point of the rocks, and came within sight of the isolated rock. Fortunately it was low water. The tide had only lately turned and was beginning to flow rapidly through the rocks. When I had scrambled on the second last rock I was only some thirty yards from the outermost one and could see clearly the two women. One was stout and elderly, the other young and tall and of exceeding beauty. The elderly one was in an almost frantic condition of fright; but the younger one, though her face was deadly pale—and I could see from the anxious glances which she kept casting round her that she was far from at ease—was outwardly calm. For an instant there was a curious effect as her pale face framed in dark hair stood out against the foam of the tide churning round the far off rocks. It seemed as though her head were dressed with white flowers. As there was no time to lose, I threw off my coat and shoes and braced myself for a swim. I called as I did so: "What has become of your boat?" The answer came back in a clear, young voice of manifestly American intonation:

"It drifted away. It has gone off amongst those rocks at the headland."

I had for a moment an idea that my best plan might be to fetch it first, but a glance at the distance and at the condition of the sea made me see the futility of any such hope. Already the waves were rising so fast that they were beginning to sweep over the crest of the rocks. Even that in front of me where the women stood was now topped by almost every wave. Without further delay I jumped into the sea and swam across. The girl gave me a hand up the rock, and I stood beside them, the old lady holding tight to me whilst I held the younger one and the rising waves washing round our feet. For a moment or two I considered the situation, and then asked them if either of them could swim. The answer was in the negative. "Then," I said decisively, "you must leave yourselves to me, and I shall swim across with each of you in turn." The old lady groaned. I pointed out that there was no other way, and that if we came at once it would not be difficult, as the distance was short and the waves were not as yet troublesome. I tried to treat the matter as though it were a nice holiday episode so that I might keep up their spirits; but all the same I felt gravely anxious. The distance to swim was only some thirty yards, but the channel was deep, and the tide running strong. Moreover the waves were rising, and we should have to get a foothold on the slippery seaweed-covered rock. However there was nothing to be done but to hasten; and as I was considering how best I should take the old lady across I said:

"What a pity it is that we haven't even a strong cord, and then we could pull each other across." The girl jumped at the idea and said:

"There was plenty in the boat, but of course it is gone. Still there should be a short piece here. I took care to fasten the painter to a piece of rock; but like a woman forgot to see that the other end was fixed to the boat, so that when the tide turned she drifted away with the stream. The fast end should be here still." When the coming wave had rolled on she pointed to a short piece of rope tied round a jutting piece of rock; its loose end swayed to and fro with every wave. I jumped for it at once, for I saw a possible way out of our difficulty; even if the rope were short, so was the distance, and its strands ravelled might cover the width of the channel. I untied the rope as quickly as I could. It was not an easy task, for the waves made it impossible to work except for a few seconds at a time; however, I got it free at last and pulled it up. It was only a fragment some thirty feet in length; but my heart leaped for I saw my way clear now. The girl saw it too and said at once:

"Let me help you." I gave her one end of the rope and we commenced simultaneously to ravel the piles. It was a little difficult to do, standing as we did upon the uneven surface of the rock with the waves rushing over our feet and the old lady beside us groaning and moaning and imploring us to hasten. Mostly she addressed herself to me, as in some way the *deus ex machina* and thus superior to the occasion where helpless women were concerned; but occasionally the wail was directed to her companion, who would then, even in that time of stress and hurry, spare a moment to lay a comforting hand on her as she said:

"Hush! oh hush! Do not say anything, dear. You will only frighten yourself. Be brave!" and such phrases of kindness and endearment. Once the girl stopped as a wave bigger than the rest broke over her feet. The old lady tried to still her shriek into a moan as she held on to her, saying "Oh Miss Anita! Oh Miss Anita!" plaintively over and over again.

At last we had ravelled the four strands of the rope and I began to knot them together. The result was a rope long enough to reach from rock to rock, though it was in places of very doubtful strength. I made a big loop at one end of it and put it over the stout lady's head and under her armpits. I cautioned both women not to tax the cord too severely by a great or sudden strain. The elder lady protested against going first, but was promptly negatived by the young lady, whose wishes on the subject were to me a foregone conclusion. I took the loose end of the rope and diving into the water swam across to the other rock upon the top of which I scrambled with some little trouble, for the waves, though not as yet in themselves dangerous, made difficult any movement which exposed me to their force. I signed to the old lady to slide into the sea which, assisted by the girl, she did very pluckily. She gasped and gurgled a good deal and clutched the loop with a death grip; but I kept a steady even strain on the rope whose strength I mistrusted. In a few seconds she was safely across, and I was pulling her up by the hands up the rock. When she was firmly fixed I gave her the loose end of the cord to hold and swam back with the loop. The girl did not delay or give any trouble. As she helped me up the rock I could not but notice what strength she had; her grip of my wet hand was firm and strong, and there was in it no quiver of anxiety. I felt that she had no care for herself, now that her companion was safe. I signalled to the old lady to be ready; the girl slipped into the water, I going in at the same time and swimming beside her. The old lady pulled zealously. So absorbed was she in her work that she did not heed my warning cry not to pull too hard. She pulled as though on her strength rested the issue of life and death; with the result that before we were a third of the way across the rope broke and she fell sitting on the rock behind her. For an instant the girl was submerged and came up gasping. In the spasmodic impulse common at such moments she gripped me so hard round the neck that I felt we were both in danger. Before we sank I wrenched, though with some difficulty her hands away from me, so that when we rose I had her at arm's length. For a few seconds I held her so that she could get her breath; and as I did so I could hear the old lady screaming out in an agonised way:

"Marjory! Marjory! Marjory!" With her breath came back the girl's reason, and she left herself to me passively. As I held her by the shoulder, a wave sweeping over the rock took us, and in my sudden effort to hold her I tore away the gown at her throat. It was quite evident her wits were all about her now for she cried out suddenly:

"Oh, my brooch! my brooch!" There was no time to waste and no time for questions. When a man has to swim for two in a choppy sea, and when the other one is a fully clothed woman, there is little to waste of strength or effort. So I swam as I had never done, and brought her up to the rock where the old lady helped her to scramble to her feet. When I had got my breath I asked her about her brooch. She replied:

"I would not have lost it for all the world. It is an heirloom."

"Was it gold?" I asked, for I wanted to know its appearance as I intended to dive for it.

"Yes!" she said, and without another word I jumped into the channel again to swim to the outer rock, for it was close there it must have been lost and I could dive from there. The channel between the rocks has a sandy bottom, and it would be easy to see the gold. As I went she called out to me to come back, not to mind, that she would rather lose it a thousand times than have me run any risk, and so forth; things mightily pleasant to hear when spoken by such lips. For myself I had only exultation. I had got off both the women without accident, and the sea was as yet, not such as to give any concern to a good swimmer. I dived from the rock and got bottom easily, the depth being only ten or twelve feet; and after a few seconds looking round me I saw the gleam of gold. When I had risen and swam to the inner rock the two women pulled me up to my feet.

When I gave her the brooch the young lady pressed it to her lips, and turning to me with tears in her eyes said:

"Oh you brave man! You kind, brave man! I would not have lost this for anything I call mine. Thank you that you have saved our lives; and that you have saved this for me." Then with girlish impulsiveness and unpremeditation she put up her face and kissed me.

That moment, with her wet face to mine, was the happiest of my life.

VIII

A Run on the Beach

The girl's kiss was so spontaneous and so natural that it could not convey any false impression to me. It was a manifest expression of gratitude, and that only. Nevertheless it set my heart beating and my veins tingling with delight. From that instant I did not feel quite a stranger to the giver; nor could I ever feel as quite a stranger again. Something of the same idea may have passed through the girl's mind, for she blushed and looked around her shyly; but, with a proud lifting of her head and a slight stamp of her foot on the rock, she put the matter behind her, for the present. The old lady, in the midst of her concern for her companion and herself, was able to throw a glance of disapproval on me, as though I had done something wrong; from which I gathered that the younger lady was not only very dear to her, but held in some sort of unusual respect as well. It was peculiar that she should in the midst of her present condition be able to give a thought to so trivial a thing. For though death did not now stare her in the face, she was cold and wet; the rock she stood on was hard and slippery, and the foam of the breaking waves was even now curling around her feet.

She looked about her apprehensively; she did not know whether or no we were on another isolated rock. I reassured her on this subject, and we scrambled as quickly as we could over the rocks on our way shoreward. The elder lady took up most of my time. Here and there in a difficult place, for the wind by now blew so strongly that one found it hard to balance oneself as is necessary when walking on rocks, I offered the younger my hand. At first she firmly declined; but then, manifestly thinking it churlish, she relented and let me help her. That kiss was evidently rankling in her mind.

Both the women breathed more freely when we had reached the shore and stood secure from the sea. And indeed by this time the view, as we looked back, was enough to frighten one. Great waves topped with white were rolling in from as far as we could see; dashing over the rocks, sending up here and there white towers of spray, or rolling in on the flat shore in front of us with an ominous roar. Woe betide any one who might be isolated now on any rock beyond; he would be swept off, and beaten on the rocks. The old lady groaned as she saw it, and then said audibly a prayer of thankfulness. Even the girl grew white for a moment; then, to my secret joy, unconsciously she drew closer to me. I took control of the party.

"Come," I said, "you mustn't stand here in your wet clothes. Hurry to the hotel and get dried. You will get your death of cold. We must all run! Or hasten, at all events!" I added, as I took in the dimensions of the elder lady.

"We have left our trap at the hotel" said the younger lady as we began to walk quickly in the direction of Port Erroll.

As we were moving off it suddenly struck me that Gormala might have seen the episode of the rescue. The very thought of such a thing filled me with such dismay that I groaned aloud. Not for all the world would I have had her have a hand in this; it was too sacred—too delightful—too much apart from ordinary things! Whilst I was lost in a reverie of inexpressible sweetness for perhaps two or three seconds altogether, I was recalled to myself by the voice of the girl who came close to me:

"Are you hurt? Please tell me if you are. I am a First Aid."

"Hurt?" I asked, surprised "not at all. What on earth makes you think so?"

"I heard you groan!"

"Oh that—" I began with a smile. Then I stopped, for again the haunting fear of Gormala's interference closed over my heart like a wet mist. With the fear, however, came a resolution; I would not have any doubt to torment me. In my glance about the shore, as we came off the rocks on to the beach, I had not seen a sign of anyone. At this part of the shore the sandhills have faded away into a narrow flat covered with bent-grass, beyond which the land slopes up directly to the higher plain. There was not room or place for any one to hide; even one lying amongst the long bents could be seen at a glance from above. Without a word I turned to the left and ran as quickly as I could across the beach and up the steep bank of the sandy plateau. With a certain degree of apprehension, and my heart beating like a trip-hammer—I had certainly taken this matter with much concern—I looked around. Then I breathed freely; there was not a sign of anyone as far as I could see. The wind, now coming fiercely in from the sea, swept the tall bent-grass till it lay over, showing the paler green of its under side; the blue-green, metallic shimmer which marks it, and which painters find it so hard to reproduce, had all vanished under the stress.

I ran back to join the ladies. The elder one had continued walking stolidly along the shore, leaving a track of wet on the half dry sand as she went; but the younger one had lingered and came towards me as I approached.

"I hope there was nothing wrong?" she asked in a most natural way.

"No," I said it without thinking, for there was something about the girl which made me feel as if we were old friends, and I spoke to her unconsciously in this strain. "It's all right. She's not there!"

"Who?" she asked with unconsciousness of any *arrière pensée*, an unconsciousness similar to my own.

"Gormala!" I answered.

"And who is Gormala?" For quite a minute or two I walked on without speaking, for I wanted to think before I answered. I felt that it would be hard to explain the odd way in which the Seer-woman seemed to have become tangled up in my life; and yet I wanted to tell this girl. I feared that she might laugh at me; that she might think me ridiculous; that she might despise me; or even that she might think me a lunatic! Then again Gormala might come and tell things to her. There was no accounting for what the woman might do. She might come upon us at any moment; she might be here even now! The effect of her following or watching me had begun to tell on my mind; her existence haunted me. I looked around anxiously, and breathed freely. There was no sign of her. My eyes finally fetched up on the face of the girl. . . Her beautiful, dark eyes were fixed on me with interest and wonder.

"Well!" she said, after a pause, "I don't suppose I'm more inquisitive than my neighbours, but I should just like to know, right here, what's wrong with you. You looked round that time just as if you were haunted! Why did you run away that time and search round as if some one had taken a pot-shot at you and you wanted to locate him? Why did you groan before you went, and come back humming? Who is Gormala, anyhow; and why were you glad that you didn't see her? Why didn't you answer me when I asked you who she was? Why did you walk along with your head up and your eyes staring, as though you were seeing visions? And why—"

All at once she stopped, and a swift blush swept over her face and even her neck. "Oh," she said in a low tone with a note of pathos in her voice, "I beg your pardon! my unruly tongue ran away with me. I have no right to ask so many questions—and from a stranger too!" She stopped as suddenly as she had begun.

"You might have spared me that!" I said "I know I have been rude in delaying to answer your question about Gormala; but the fact is that there are so many odd things in connection with her that I was really considering whether you would think me a fool or a lunatic if I told them to you. And you certainly would not understand why I didn't want to see her, if I didn't. And perhaps not even if I did," I added as an afterthought. The girl's awkwardness slipped from her like a robe; the blush merged into a smile as she turned to me and said:

"This is most interesting. O! do tell me—if you don't mind."

"I shall be delighted" I said, and I only expressed my thought. "Gormala" I began; but just then the stout lady in front of us, who was now a considerable way ahead, turned round and called to us. I could only hear "Miss Anita;" but the girl evidently understood, for she called out:

"All right! We are coming at once!" and she hurried on. It gave me a thrill of pleasure that she said "we" not "I;" it was sweet to have a part in such a comprehension. As we went she turned to me and said:

"You must tell me all about it; I shan't be happy till I hear the whole story, whatever it is. This is all too lovely and exciting. I hadn't an idea when we went out sleepily this morning that there would be so much in the day to think of afterwards." I felt that I had taken my courage in both hands as I said:

"You'll both dine with me at the hotel, won't you. You have missed lunch and must be hungry, so we can dine early. It will be such a true pleasure to me; and I can tell you all about everything afterwards, if we can manage to get a moment alone."

She paused, and I waited anxiously. Then she spoke with a delightful smile:

"That must be as Mrs. Jack says. But we shall see!" With this I had to be content for the present.

When we came up to her, Mrs. Jack said in a woeful way:

"Oh, Miss Anita, I don't know what to do. The sand is so heavy, and my clothes are so weighty with the wet, and my boots squish so with the water in them that I'm beginning to think I'll never be able to get warm or dry again; though I'm both warm enough and dry enough in other ways." As she spoke she moved her feet somewhat after the manner of a bear dancing, so as to make her wet boots squeak. I would have liked to have laughed, though I really pitied the poor thing; but a glance at the concern on Miss Anita's face checked me. Very tenderly she began to help and comfort the old lady, and looked at me pleadingly to help her. "Why dear" she said "no wonder it is hard walking for you with your clothes so wringing wet," and she knelt down on the wet sand and began to wring them out. I looked around to see what I could do to help. Just opposite, where we were the outcrop of rock on which the Hawklaw is based sent up a jagged spur of granite through the sand, close under the bent-covered hillocks. I pointed to this and we led the old lady over to it and made her sit down on a flat rock. Then we proceeded to wring her out, she all the while protesting against so much trouble being taken about her. We pulled off her spring-side boots, emptied them out and, with considerable difficulty, forced them on again. Then we all stood up, and the girl and I took her arms and hurried her along the beach; we all knew that nothing could be done for real comfort till we should have reached the hotel. As we went she said with gratitude in every note of her voice, the words joggling out of her as she bumped along:

"Oh, my dears, you are very good to me."

Once again the use of the plural gave me pleasure. This time, however, it was my head, rather than my heart, which was affected; to be so bracketted with Miss Anita was to have hope as well as pleasure.

Things were beginning to move fast with me.

When we got to Cruden there was great local excitement, and much running to and fro on the part of the good people of the hotel to get dry clothes for the strange ladies. None of us gave any detail as to how the wetting took place; by some kind of common consent it was simply made known for the time that they had been overtaken by the tide. When once the incomplete idea had been started I took care not to elaborate it. I could see plainly enough that though the elder lady had every wish to be profuse in the expression of her gratitude to me, the younger one not only remained silent but now and again restrained her companion by a warning look. Needless to say, I let things go in their own way; it was too sweet a pleasure to me to share anything in the way of a secret with my new friend, to imperil such a bliss by any breach of reticence. The ladies were taken away to bedrooms to change, and I asked that dinner for the three of us might be served in my room. When I had changed my own clothes, over which operation I did not lose any time, I waited in the room for the arrival of my guests. Whilst the table was being laid I learned that the two ladies had come to the hotel early in the day in a dogcart driven by the younger one. They had given no orders except that the horse should be put up and well cared for.

It was not long before the ladies appeared. Mrs. Jack began to express her gratitude to me. I tried to turn it aside, for though it moved me a little by its genuineness, I felt somewhat awkward, as though I were accepting praise under false pretences. Such service as I had been able to render, though of the utmost importance to them, had been so easy of execution to me that more than a passing expression of thanks seemed out of place. After all I had only accepted a wetting on behalf of two ladies placed in an awkward position. I was a good swimmer; and my part of the whole proceeding was unaccompanied by any danger whatever, I thought, of course, had it been later in the coming of the storm, things might have been very different. Here I shuddered as my imagination gave me an instantaneous picture of the two helpless women in the toils of the raging sea amongst those grim rocks and borne by that racing tide which had done poor Lauchlane Macleod to death. As if to emphasise my fears there now came a terrific burst of wind which seemed to sweep over the house with appalling violence. It howled and roared above us, so that every window, chimney and door, seemed to bear the sound right in upon us. Overhead was heard, between the burst which shook the windows and doors, that vague, booming sound, which conveys perhaps a better sense of nature's forces when let loose, than even the concrete expression of their violence. In this new feeling of the possibilities of the storm, I realised the base and the truth of the gratitude which the ladies felt; and I also realised what an awful tragedy might have come to pass had I or some one else not come down the path from Whinnyfold just when I did.

I was recalled to myself by an expression of concern by Mrs. Jack:

"Look how pale he has got. I do hope he has not been hurt." Mechanically I answered:

"Hurt! I was never better in my life," then I felt that my pallor must have left me and that I grew red with pleasure as I heard Miss Anita say:

"Ah! I understand. He did not have any fear for himself; but he is beginning to feel how terrible it was for us." The fulness of understanding on the part of the beautiful girl, her perfect and ready sympathy, the exactness of her interpretation of my mind, made for me an inexpressible pleasure.

When I told Mrs. Jack that I had ventured to claim them both as my guests, and hoped that they would honour me by dining with me, she looked at her companion in the same inquiring way which I had already noticed. I could not see the face of the younger lady at the moment as it was turned away from me, but her approval was manifest; the answer was made gladly in the affirmative. Then I put forth a hope that they would allow me to have a carriage ready to take them home, whenever they might desire, so that they might feel at ease in remaining till they had been thoroughly restored after their fatigue. I added that perhaps it would be good for Miss Anita. Mrs. Jack raised her eyebrows slightly, and I thought there was a note of distance in her voice, as though she resented in a quiet way my mentioning the name:

"Miss Anita!" she said; and there was that unconscious stiffening of the back which evidences that one is on guard. I felt somewhat awkward, as though I had taken a liberty. The younger lady saw my difficulty, and with a quick smile jumped to the rescue.

"Oh Mrs. Jack" she said "I quite forgot that we were never introduced; but of course he heard you mention my name. It was rather hurried our meeting; wasn't it? We must set it right now." Then she added very demurely:

"Dear Mrs. Jack, will you present to Miss Anita, Mr.—" she looked at me interrogatively.

"Archibald Hunter" I said, and the presentation was formally made. Then Miss Anita answered my question about the carriage:

"Thank you for your kind offer, Mr. Archibald Hunter" I thought she dwelt on the name, "but we shall drive back as we came. The storm will not be quite so bad inland, and as it does not rain the cart will be all right; we have plenty of wraps. The lamps are good, and I know the road; I noted it well as we came. Is not that right?" she added, turning to her companion.

"Quite right, my dear! Do just as you like," and so the manner of their going was arranged.

Then we had dinner; a delightful, cosy meal. The fire leaped whenever the wind roared; and as the darkness of the storm made a sort of premature nightfall, it gave a pleasant, homely look to everything. After dinner we sat round the fire, and I think for a time we were all content. To me it was so like a dream. To sit there close to the beautiful stranger, and to think of the romantic beginning of our acquaintance, was enjoyment beyond words. As yet I did not dare to cast a glance forwards; but I was content to wait for that. I had a conviction that my own mind was made up.

After a little while we all became silent. Mrs. Jack was beginning to doze in her chair, and we two young folk instinctively banded ourselves together with our youthful superiority over sleep and fatigue. I sat quite still; there was something so sweet in this organised companionship of silence that it enraptured me. I did not need Miss Anita's look of caution to remain quiet; there was something in her face, some power or quality which was as eloquent as speech. I began to think of it; and the habit of introspection, which had now become a part of my nature, asserted itself. How much of this quality I thought, was in her face, how much in my own eyes and the brain that lay behind them. I was recalled to myself by a whisper:

"I thought for a moment you were going to sleep too. Hsh!" she placed a finger on her lip a moment and then tiptoed over to the sofa; taking a soft cushion she placed it under Mrs. Jack's head, which had now fallen over sideways upon the arm of the chair. Then she sat beside me again, and bending over said softly:

"While she is asleep would you mind walking down to the beach, I want to see the waves. They must be big by now; I can hear their roaring from here."

"I will go with delight;" I said "but you must wrap up properly. It will not do to run any chance of a chill."

"All right, oh wise man! I obey, King Solomon! I shall wait to put on my own clothes till I get back; and you can lend me a mackie-coat if you will." I got one of mine for her, the newest; and we walked over the sandhills to the beach.

The wind was blowing furiously. It never left off for a moment; but occasionally there were bursts of such added violence that we found it difficult to keep our feet. We clung to each other at such moments, and the very sense of the strength which enabled me to shield her somewhat from the violence of the storm, made a new feeling of love—I could not now disguise it from myself. Something went out from me to her; some subtle feeling which must, I suppose, have manifested itself in some way, how I know not, for I kept guard upon myself. For one blissful moment, possibly of forgetfulness, she clung to me as the weak cling to the strong, the clinging of self-surrender which is equally dear to the weak and the strong, to the woman and the man. And then she drew herself sharply away from me.

There was no misunderstanding the movement; it was an intentional and conscious one, and the motive which lay behind both was her woman's mystery. I did not know much about women, but I could make no mistake as to this. Inasmuch as Providence has thought fit in its wisdom to make men and women different, it is just as well that each sex should at critical times use its own potentialities for its protection and advancement. Herein comes, in the midst of an unnatural civilisation, the true utility of instinct. Since we have lost the need of early information of the presence of game or of predatory animals or hostile men, even our instincts adapt themselves to our surroundings. Many an act which may afterwards seem the result of long and careful premeditation is, on reflection, found to be simply the result of that form of momentary impulse which is in reality a blind obedience to some knowledge of our ancestors gained through painful experience. Some protective or militant instinct whose present exercise is but a variant of its primal use. For an instant the man and the woman were antagonistic. The woman shrank, therefore it was the man's interest to advance; all at once the man in me spoke through the bashfulness and reticence of years:

"Why do you shrink from me? Have I done anything?"

"Oh no!"

"Then why?" A hot blush mantled her face and neck. Had she been an English girl I should not probably have had a direct answer; she would have switched conversation on some safer track, or have, after some skirmishing, forbidden the topic altogether. This girl's training, however, had been different. Her equal companionship in study with boys in school and college had taught her the futility of trying to burke a question when her antagonist was masculine; and the natural pluck and dominance—the assertion of individuality which is a part of an American woman's birthright—brought up her pride. Still blushing, but bearing herself with additional dignity, she spoke. Had she been more self-conscious, and could she have seen herself at the moment, she would have recognised to the full that with so much pride and so much dignity she could well afford to discuss any topic that she chose.

"The fault is not yours. It is, or it was, my own."

"You mean when I gave you back your brooch?" The blood deepened and deepened to a painful intensity. In a low voice, in the tone of speech, but with only the power of a whisper she answered me:

"Yes!" This was my chance and I said with all the earnestness I had, and which I felt to the full:

"Let me say something. I shall not ever allude to it again unless you wish. I took that sweet acknowledgment of your gratitude exactly as it was meant. Do believe that I am a gentleman. I have not got a sister, I am sorry to say, but if I had, I should not mind her giving a kiss to a stranger under such circumstances. It was a sweet and womanly act and I respect—and—like you more for it. I wouldn't, of course, for all the world you hadn't done it; and I shall never forget it. But believe me I shall never forget myself on account of it. If I did I should be a howling cad;—and—that's all."

As I spoke her face brightened and she sighed with an expression of relief. The blush almost faded away, and a bright smile broke over her face. With a serious deep look in the eyes which glistened through her smile she held out her hand and said:

"You are a good fellow, and I thank you with all my heart."

I felt as if I walked on air as we forced our way through the storm which roared around us, over the sandhills towards the sea. It was with an exultation that made my head swim that I noticed that she kept step with me.

IX

CONFIDENCES AND SECRET WRITING

The shore was a miracle of wild water and white foam. When the wind blows into Cruden Bay there is no end or limit to the violence of waves, which seem to gather strength as they rush over the flat expanse of shore. The tide was now only half in, and ordinarily there would have been a great stretch of bare sand between the dunes and the sea. To-night, however, the piling up of the waters sent in an unnatural tide which swept across the flat shore with exceeding violence. The roaring was interminable, and as we stood down on the beach we were enveloped in sheets of flying foam. The fierce blasts came at moments with such strength that it was physically impossible for us to face them. After a little we took shelter behind one of the wooden bathing-boxes fastened down under the sandhills. Here, protected from the direct violence of the storm, the shelter seemed like a calm from which we heard the roaring of wind and wave as from far off. There was a sense of cosiness in the shelter which made us instinctively draw close together. I could have remained happy in such proximity forever, but I feared that it would end at any moment. It was therefore, with delight that I heard the voice of Miss Anita, raised to suit the requirements of the occasion:

"Now that we are alone, won't you tell me about Gormala and the strange occurrences?" I tried to speak, but the storm was too great for the purposes of narrative. So I suggested that we should come behind the sandhill. We went accordingly, and made a nest in a deep hollow behind the outer range of hillocks. Here crouched among the tall bent, which flew like whip lashes when the wilder bursts of the storm came, and amid a never-ending scourge of fine sand swept from the top of the sandhills, I told her of all my experiences of Gormala and Second Sight.

She listened with a rapt attention. At times I could not see her face, for the evening was closing in and the driving clouds overhead, which kept piling up in great masses along the western horizon, shut out the remnants of the day. When, however, in the pauses of drifting sand and flying foam I could see her properly, I found her face positively alight with eager intelligence. Throughout, she was moved at times, and now and again crept a little closer to me; as for instance when I told her of the dead child and of Lauchlane Macleod's terrible struggle for life in the race of the tide amongst the Skares. Her questions were quite illuminating to me at moments, for her quick woman's intuition grasped possibilities at which my mere logical faculties had shied. Beyond all else, she was interested in the procession of ghosts on Lammas Eve. Only once during my narrative of this episode she interrupted me; not an intentional interruption but a passing comment of her own, candidly expressed. This was where the body of armed men came along; at which she said with a deep hissing intake of her breath through her teeth:

"Spaniards! I knew it! They were from some lost ship of the Armada!" When I spoke of the one who turned and looked at me with eyes that seemed of the quick, she straightened her back and squared her shoulders, and looking all round her alertly as though for some hidden enemy, clenched her hands and shut her lips tightly. Her great dark eyes seemed to blaze; then she grew calm again in a moment.

When I had finished she sat silent for a while, her eyes fixed in front of her as with one whose mind is occupied with introspection. Suddenly she said:

"That man had some secret, and he feared you would discover it. I can see it all! He, coming from his grave, could see with his dead eyes what you could see with your living ones. Nay, more; he could, perhaps, see not only that you saw, and what you saw, but where the knowledge would lead you. That certainly is a grand idea of Gormala's, that of winning the Secret of the Sea!" After a pause of a few moments she went on, standing up as she did so and walking restlessly to and fro with clenched hands and flashing eyes:

"And if there be any Secrets of the Sea why not win them? If they be of Spain and the Spaniard, why not, a thousand times more, win them. If the Spaniard had a secret, be sure it was of no good to our Race. Why—" she moved excitedly as she went on: "Why this is growing interesting beyond belief. If his dead eyes could for an instant become quick, why should not the change last longer? He might materialise altogether." She stopped suddenly and said: "There! I am getting flighty as usual. I must think it all over. It is all too wonderful and too exciting for anything. You will let me ask you more about it, won't you, when we meet again?"

When we meet again! Then we would meet again: The thought was a delight to me; and it was only after several rapturous seconds that I answered her:

"I shall tell you all I know; everything. You will be able to help me in discovering the Mystery; perhaps working together we can win the Secret of the Sea."

"That would be too enchanting!" she said impulsively, and then stopped suddenly as if remembering herself. After a pause she said sedately:

"I'm afraid we must be going back now. We have a long way to drive; and it will be quite late enough anyhow."

As we moved off I asked her if I might not see her and Mrs. Jack safely home. I could get a horse at the hotel and drive with them. She laughed lightly as she answered:

"You are very kind indeed. But surely we shall not need any one! I am a good driver; the horse is perfect and the lamps are bright. You haven't any 'hold-ups' here as we have Out West; and as I am not within Gormala's sphere of influence, I don't think there is anything to dread!" Then after a pause she added:

"By the way have you ever seen Gormala since?" It was with a queer feeling which I could not then analyse, but which I found afterwards contained a certain proportion of exultation I answered:

"Oh yes! I saw her only two days ago—" Here I stopped for I was struck with a new sense of the connection of things. Miss Anita saw the wonder in my face and drawing close to me said:

"Tell me all about it!" So I told her of the auction at Peterhead and of the chest and the papers with the mysterious marks, and of how I thought it might be some sort of account—"or," I added as a new idea struck me—"secret writing." When I had got thus far she said with decision:

"I am quite sure it is. You must try to find it out. Oh, you must, you must!"

"I shall," said I, "if you desire it." She said nothing, but a blush spread over her face. Then she resumed her movement towards the hotel.

We walked in silence; or rather we ran and stumbled, for the fierce wind behind us drove us along. The ups and downs of the surface were veiled with the mist of flying sand swept from amongst the bent-grass on the tops of the sandhills. I would have liked to help her, but a judicious dread of seeming officious—and so losing a step in her good graces—held me back. I felt that I was paying a price of abstinence for that kiss. As we went, the silence between us seemed to be ridiculous; so to get over it I said, after searching in my mind for a topic which would not close up her sympathies with me:

"You don't seem to like Spaniards?"

"No," she answered quickly, "I hate them! Nasty, cruel, treacherous wretches! Look at the way they are treating Cuba! Look at the *Maine*!" Then she added suddenly:

"But how on earth did you know I dislike them." I answered:

"Your voice told me when you spoke to yourself whilst I was telling you about the ghosts and the man with the eyes."

"True," she said reflectively. "So I did. I must keep more guard on myself and not let my feelings run away with me. I give myself away so awfully." I could have made a reply to this, but I was afraid. That kiss seemed like an embodied spirit of warning, holding a sword over my head by a hair.

It was not long before I found the value of my silence. The lady's confidence in my discretion was restored, and she began, of her own initiative, to talk. She spoke of the procession of ghosts; suddenly stopping, however, as if she had remembered something, she said to me:

"But why were you so anxious that Gormala should not have seen you saving us from the rock?"

"Because," I answered, "I did not want her to have anything to do with this."

"What do you mean by 'this'?" There was something in the tone of her query which set me on guard. It was not sincere; it had not that natural intonation, even, all through, which marks a question put in simple faith. Rather was it in the tone of one who asks, knowing well the answer which will or may be given. As I have said, I did not know much about women, but the tone of coquetry, no matter how sweet, no matter how ingenuous, no matter how lovable, cannot be mistaken by any man with red blood in his veins! Secretly I exulted, for I felt instinctively that there rested some advantage with me in the struggle of sex. The knowledge gave me coolness, and brought my brain to the aid of my heart. Nothing would have delighted me more at the moment than to fling myself, actually as well as metaphorically, at the girl's feet. My mind was made up to try to win her; my only thought now was the best means to that end. I felt that I was a little sententious as I replied to her question:

"By 'this' I mean the whole episode of my meeting with you."

"And Mrs. Jack," she added, interrupting me.

"And Mrs. Jack, of course," I went on, feeling rejoiced that she had given me an opportunity of saying something which I would not otherwise have dared to say. "Or rather I should perhaps say, my meeting with Mrs. Jack and her friend. It was to me a most delightful thing to meet with Mrs. Jack; and I can honestly say this day has been the happiest of my life."

"Don't you think we had better be getting on? Mrs. Jack will be waiting for us!" she said, but without any kind of reproach in her manner.

"All right," I answered, as I ran up a steep sandhill and held out my hand to help her. I did not let her hand go till we had run down the other side, and up and down another hillock and came out upon the flat waste of sand which lay between us and the road, and over which a sort of ghostly cloud of sand drifted.

Before we left the sand, I said earnestly:

"Gormala's presence seems always to mean gloom and sorrow, weeping and mourning, fear and death. I would not have any of them come near you or yours. This is why I thanked God then, and thank Him now, that in our meeting Gormala had no part!"

She gave me her hand impulsively. As for an instant her soft palm lay in my palm and her strong fingers clasped mine, I felt that there was a bond between us which might some day enable me to shield her from harm.

When Mrs. Jack, and 'her friend', were leaving the hotel, I came to the door to see them off. She said to me, in a low voice, as I bade farewell:

"We shall, I daresay, see you before long. I know that Mrs. Jack intends to drive over here again. Thank you for all your kindness. Good night!" There was a shake of the reins, a clatter of feet on the hard road, a sweeping round of the rays of light from the lamp as the cart swayed at the start under the leap forward of the high-bred horse and swung up the steep inland roadway. The last thing I saw was a dark, muffled figure, topped by a tam-o'-shanter cap, projected against the mist of moving light from the lamp.

Next morning I was somewhat *distrait*. Half the night I had lain awake thinking; the other half I had dreamt. Both sleeping and waking dreams were mixed, ranging from all the brightness of hope to the harrowing possibilities of vague, undefined fear.

Sleeping dreams have this difference over day dreams, that the possibilities become for the time actualities, and thus for good and ill, pleasure or pain, multiply the joys or sufferings. Through all, however, there remained one fixed hope always verging toward belief, I should see Miss Anita—Marjory—again.

Late in the afternoon I got a letter directed in a strange hand, fine and firm, with marked characteristics and well formed letters, and just enough of unevenness to set me at ease. I am never quite happy with the writer whose hand is exact, letter by letter, and word by word, and line by line. So much can be told by handwriting, I thought, as I looked at the letter lying beside my plate. A hand that has no characteristics is that of a person insipid; a hand that is too marked and too various is disconcerting and undependable. Here my philosophising came to an end, for I had opened the envelope, and not knowing the writing, had looked at the signature, "Marjory Anita."

I hoped that no one at the table d'hote breakfast noticed me, for I felt that I was red and pale by turns. I laid the letter down, taking care that the blank back page was uppermost; with what nonchalance I could I went on with my smoked haddie. Then I put the letter in my pocket and waited till I was in my own room, secure from interruption, before I read it.

That one should kiss a letter before reading it, is conceivable, especially when it is the first which one has received from the girl he loves.

It was not dated nor addressed. A swift intuition told me that she had not given the date because she did not wish to give the address; the absence of both was less marked than the presence of the one alone. It addressed me as "Dear Mr. Hunter." She knew my name, of course, for I had told it to her; it was on the envelope. The body of the letter said that she was asked by Mrs. Jack to convey her warm thanks for the great service rendered; to which she ventured to add the expression of her own gratitude. That in the hurry and confusion of mind, consequent on their unexpected position, they had both quite forgotten about the boat which they had hired and which had been lost. That the owner of it would no doubt be uneasy about it, and that they would both be grateful if I would see him—he lived in one of the cottages close to the harbour of Port Erroll—and find out from him the value of the boat so that Mrs. Jack might pay it to him, as well as a reasonable sum for the loss of its use until he should have been able to procure another. That Mrs. Jack ventured to give him so much trouble, as Mr. Hunter had been already so kind that she felt emboldened to trespass upon his goodness. And was "yours faithfully, 'Marjory Anita.'" Of course there was a postscript—it was a woman's letter! It ran as follows:

Have you deciphered those papers? I have been thinking over them as well as other things, and I am convinced they contain some secret. You must tell me all about them when I see you on Tuesday.

M.

I fear that logic, as understood in books, had little to do with my kiss on reading this; the reasoning belonged to that higher plane of thought on which rests the happiness of men and women in this world and the next. There was not a thought in the postscript which did not give me joy—utter and unspeakable joy; and the more I thought of it and the oftener I read it the more it seemed to satisfy some aching void in my heart, "Have you deciphered the papers"—the papers whose existence was only known to her and me! It was delightful that we should know so much of a secret in common. She had been 'thinking over them'— and other things! 'Other things!'—I had been thinking of other things; thinking of them so often that every detail of their being or happening was photographed not only on my memory but seemingly on my very soul. And of all these 'other things' there was one!! . . .

To see her again; to hear her voice; to look in her eyes; to see her lips move and watch each varying expression which might pass across that lovely face, evoked by thoughts which we should hold in common; to touch her hand. . .

I sat for a while like one in a rapturous dream, where one sees all the hopes of the heart fulfilled in completeness and endlessly. And this was all to be on Tuesday next—Only six days off! . . .

I started impulsively and went to the oak chest which stood in the corner of my room and took out the papers.

After looking over them carefully I settled quietly down to a minute examination of them. I felt instinctively that my mandate or commission was to see if they contained any secret writing. The letters I placed aside, for the present at any rate. They were transparently simple and written in a flowing hand which made anything like the necessary elaboration impossible. I knew something of secret writing, for such had in my boyhood been a favourite amusement with me. At one time I had been an invalid for a considerable period and had taken from my father's library a book by Bishop Wilkins, the brother-in-law of Oliver Cromwell, called "Mercury: or the Secret and Swift Messenger." Herein were given accounts of many of the old methods of secret communication, ciphers, string writing, hidden meanings, and many of the mechanical devices employed in an age when the correspondence of ambassadors, spies and secret agents was mainly conducted by such means. This experience had set my mind somewhat on secret writing, and ever after when in the course of miscellaneous reading I came across anything relating to the subject I made a note of it. I now looked over the papers to see if I could find traces of any of the methods with which I was acquainted; before long I had an idea.

It was only a rudimentary idea, a surmise, a possibility; but still it was worth going into. It was not any cause of undue pride to me, for it came as a corollary to an established conclusion, rather than as a fine piece of reasoning from acute observation. The dates of the letters gave the period as the end of the sixteenth century, when one of the best ciphers of that time had been conceived, the "Biliteral Cipher" of Francis Bacon. To this my attention had been directed by the work of John Wilkins and I had followed it out with great care. As I was familiar with the principle and method of this cipher I was able to detect signs of its existence; and this being so, I had at once strong hopes of being able to find the key to it. The Biliteral cipher has as its great advantage, that it can be used in any ordinary writing, and that its forms and methods are simply endless. All that it requires in the first instance is that there be some method arranged on between the writer and the reader of distinguishing between different forms of the same letter. In my desk I had a typewritten copy of a monograph on the subject of the Biliteral cipher, in which I half suggested that possibly Bacon's idea might be worked out more fully so that a fewer number of symbols than his five would be sufficient. Leaving my present occupation for a moment I went and got it; for by reading it over I might get some clue to aid me. Some thought which had already come to me, or some conclusion at which I had already arrived might guide me in this new labyrinth of figures, words and symbols.[1]

When I had carefully read the paper, occasionally referring to the documents before me, I sat down and wrote a letter to Miss Anita telling her that I had undertaken the task at once on her suggestion and that I surmised that the method of secret writing adopted if any, was probably a variant of the Biliteral cipher. I therefore sent her my own monograph on the subject so that if she chose she might study it and

---

1. See Appendix A.

be prepared to go into the matter when we met. I studiously avoided saying anything which might frighten her or make any barrier between us; matters were shaping themselves too clearly for me to allow myself to fall into the folly of over-precipitation. It was only when I had placed the letter with its enclosure in the envelope and written Marjory's— Miss Anita's—name that I remembered that I had not got her address. I put it in my pocket to keep for her till we should meet on Tuesday.

When I resumed my work I began on the two remaining exhibits. The first was a sheaf of some thirty pages torn out of some black-letter law-book. The only remarkable thing about it was that every page seemed covered with dots—hundreds, perhaps thousands on each page. The second was quite different: a narrow slip of paper somewhat longer than a half sheet of modern note paper, covered with an endless array of figures in even lines, written small and with exquisite care. The paper was just such a size as might be put as marker in an ordinary quarto; that it had been so used was manifest by the discolouration of a portion of it that had evidently stuck out at the top of the volume. Fortunately, in its long dusty rest in the bookshelf the side written on had been downward so that the figures, though obscured by dust and faded by light and exposure to the air, were still decipherable. This paper I examined most carefully with a microscope; but could see in it no signs of secret writing beyond what might be contained in the disposition of the numbers themselves. I got a sheet of foolscap and made an enlarged copy, taking care to leave fair space between the rows of figures and between the figures themselves.

Then I placed the copy of figures and the first of the dotted pages side by side before me and began to study them.

I confined my attention at first chiefly to the paper of figures, for it struck me that it would of necessity be the simpler of the two systems to read, inasmuch as the symbols should be self-contained. In the dotted letters it was possible that more than one element existed, for the disposition of significants appeared to be of endless variety, and the very novelty of the method—it being one to which the eyes and the senses were not accustomed—made it a difficult one to follow at first. I had little doubt, however, that I should ultimately find the dot cipher the more simple of the two, when I should have learned its secret and become accustomed to its form. Its mere bulk made the supposition likely that it was in reality simple; for it would be indeed an endless task, to work out in this laborious form two whole sheets of a complicated cipher.

Over and over and over again I read the script of numbers. Forward and backward; vertically; up and down, for the lines both horizontal and vertical were complete and exact, I read it. But nothing struck me of sufficient importance to commence with as a beginning.

Of course there were here and there repetitions of the same combination of figures, sometimes two, sometimes three, sometimes four together; but of the larger combinations the instances were rare and did not afford me any suggestion of a clue!

So I became practical, and spent the remainder of my work-time that day in making by aid of my microscope an exact but enlarged copy, but in Roman letters, of the first of the printed pages.

Then I reproduced the dots as exactly as I could. This was a laborious task indeed. When the page was finished, half-blinded, I took my hat and went out along the shore towards Whinnyfold. I wanted to go to the Sand Craigs; but even to myself I said 'Whinnyfold' which lay farther on.

"Men are deceivers ever," sang Balthazar in the play: they deceive even themselves at times. Or they pretend they do—which is a new and advanced form of the same deceit.

X

A Clear Horizon

If any ordinary person be afflicted with ennui and want something to take his thoughts away from a perpetual consideration of his own weariness let me recommend him to take up the interpretation of secret writing. At first, perhaps, he may regard the matter lightly and be inclined to smile at its triviality. But after a little while, if he have in him at all any of the persistence or doggedness which is, and should be, a part of a man's nature, he will find the subject take possession of him to the almost entire exclusion of all else. Turn from it how he will; make he never so many resolutions to put the matter behind him; try he never so hard to find some more engrossing topic, he will still find the evasive mystery ever close before him. For my own part I can honestly say that I ate, drank, slept and dreamed secret writing during the entire of the days and nights which intervened between my taking up the task and the coming of Miss Anita to Cruden Bay. All day long the hidden mystery was before me; wherever I was, in my room, still or contorting myself; walking on the beach; or out on the headlands, with the breezes singing in my ears, and the waves lapping below my feet. Hitherto in my life my only experience of haunting had been that of Gormala; but even that experience failed before the ever-hopeful, ever-baffling subject of the cryptograms. The worst of my feeling, and that which made it more poignant, was that I was of the firm belief not only that there was a cryptogram but that my mind was already on the track of it. Every now and again, sometimes when the Ms. or its copy was before me and sometimes when I was out in the open, for the moment not thinking of it at all, a sort of inspiration would come to me; some sort of root idea whose full significance I felt it difficult to grasp.

My first relief came on Tuesday when at noon I saw the high dog-cart dash past the gate and draw up short opposite the post-office.

I did not lose any time in reaching the cart so as to be able to help the ladies down. Marjory gave me both her hands and jumped lightly, but the elder lady required a good deal of help. It is always thus; the experience of every young man is the same. Every woman, old or young, except the one whom he likes to lift or carry tenderly, is willing to be lifted or carried in the most leisurely or self-denying manner.

When Mrs. Jack and 'her friend' had come into the hotel sitting-room the latter said to me:

"I hope you forgive us for all the trouble we have put you to."

"No trouble at all," I answered—and oh! it sounded so tame—"only a pleasure!" "Thank you," she continued gravely, "that is very nice of you. Now we want you to add to your kindness and take us out again on that rock. I have not yet finished my sketch, and I don't like to be baffled."

"Finished your sketch, my dear," said Mrs. Jack, in a tone which manifestly showed that the whole thing was new to her. "Why, Marjory, it was washed into the sea before Mr. Hunter came to help us!" The slight, quick blush which rose to her face showed that she understood the false position in which the maladroit remark placed her; but she went on pluckily:

"Oh, yes, dear, I know! What I mean is, that having set my heart on making that sketch, I want to do it; even if my first effort went wrong. That is, dear Mrs. Jack, if you do not mind our going out there again."

"Oh, my dear," said the elder lady, "of course I will do just whatever you wish. But I suppose it will do if I sit on the rock near at hand? Somehow, since our experience there, I seem to prefer the mainland than any place where you may have to swim to get away from it." Marjory smiled at me as she said to her:

"That will do capitally. And you can keep the lunch basket; and have your eye on me and the rising of the tide all the time."

So I sent to Whinnyfold to have a boat ready when we should drive over. Whilst the ladies were preparing themselves for the boating trip I went to my room and took in my pocket the papers from the chest and my rescripts. I took also the letter which I had not been able to deliver.

At Whinnyfold Miss Anita and I took the steep zigzag to the beach, piloted by one of John Hay's boys whilst the other took Mrs. Jack across the neck of the headland to the Sand Craigs.

As we went down the steep path, the vision of the procession of ghosts moving steadily up it on Lammas Eve, came back to me; instinctively I looked round to see if Gormala was watching. I breathed more freely when I saw she was not about.

I should dearly have liked to take Miss Anita alone in the boat, but I feared that such was not safe. Rowing amongst the rocks of the Skares is at the best of times no child's play, and I was guardian of too great a treasure to be willing to run any risks. Young Hay and I pulled, the boy being in the bow and doing the steering. This position of affairs suited me admirably, for it kept me close to my companion and facing her. It was at all times a pleasure to me as it would have been to any man, to watch her face; but to-day her eager joy at the beauty of all around her made me thrill with delight. The day was ideal for the place; a bright, clear day with just a ripple of wind from the water which took the edge from the July heat. The sea quivered with points of light, as though it were strewn with diamonds, and the lines of the racing tide threading a way amongst the rocks below were alone an endless source of interest. We rowed slowly which is much the safest way of progression in these waters, and especially when, as now, the tide was running towards the end of the ebb. As the boy seemed to know every one of the myriad rocks which topped the water, and by a sort of instinct even those that lay below, we steered a devious course. I had told him to take us round by the outer rocks from which thousands of seabirds rose screaming as we approached; and as we crept in under the largest of them we felt that mysterious sense of unworthiness which comes to one in deep water under the shadow of rocks. I could see that Marjory had the sense of doubt, or of possible danger, which made her clutch hard at each gunwale of the boat till her knuckles grew white. As we rounded the Reivie o' Pircappies, and found the tide swirling amongst the pointed rocks, she grew so deadly pale that I felt concerned. I should have liked to question her, but as I knew from my experience of her courage that she would probably prefer that I remained silent, I pretended not to notice. Male pretence does not count for much with women. She saw through me at once, and with a faint smile, which lit the pallor of her face like sunshine on snow, she said in so low a whisper that it did not reach the fisher boy:

"I was thinking what it would have been for us that day—only for you."

"I was glad," I answered in an equally low voice, "to be able to render any help to—to Mrs. Jack and her friend."

"Mrs. Jack—and her friend—are very much obliged to you," she answered gaily in her natural voice and tone. I could see that she had fully regained her courage, as involuntarily she took her hands from the sides of the boat. We kept now well out from the rocks and in deep water, and shortly sighted the Sand Craigs. As we could see Mrs. Jack and her escort trudging leisurely along the sand, and as we did not wish to hurry her, I asked young Hay with my companion's consent, to keep round the outermost of the Sand Craigs, which was now grey-white with sea-gulls. On our approach the birds all rose and wheeled round with myriad screaming; the wonder and admiration of the girl's eyes as they eagerly followed the sweep of the cloud of birds was good to see.

We hung around the great pointed rock till we saw Mrs. Jack making her way cautiously along the rocks. We rowed at once to the inner rock and placed the luncheon basket in a safe place. We then prepared a little sheltered nook for Mrs. Jack, with rugs and cushions so that she might be quite at ease. Miss Anita chose the place herself. I am bound to say it was not just as I should have selected; for when she sat down, her back was towards the rock from which she had been rescued. It was doubtless the young girl's thoughtfulness in keeping her mind away from a place fraught with such unpleasant memories.

When she was safely installed we dismissed the boys till the half tide. Mrs. Jack was somewhat tired with her trudge over the sand, and even when we left her she was nodding her head with coming sleep. Then Miss Anita got out her little easel which I fixed for her as she directed; when her camp stool was rightly placed and her palette prepared I sat down on the rock at her feet and looked at her whilst she began her work. For a little while she painted in silence: then turning to me she said suddenly:

"What about those papers? Have you found anything yet?" It was only then I bethought me of the letter in my pocket. Without a word I took it out and handed it to her. There was a slight blush as well as a smile on her face as she took it. When she saw the date she said impulsively:

"Why did I not get it before?"

"Because I had not got your address, and did not know how to reach you."

"I see!" she answered abstractedly as she began to read. When she had gone right through it she handed it to me and said:

"Now you read it out loud to me whilst I paint; and let me ask questions so that I may understand." So I read; and now and again she asked me searching questions. Twice or three times I had to read over the memorandum; but each time she began to understand better and better, and at last said eagerly:

"Have you ever worked out such reductions?"

"Not yet, but I could do so. I have been so busy trying to decipher the secret writing that I have not had time to try any such writing myself."

"Have you succeeded in any way?"

"No!" I answered. "I am sorry to say that as yet I have nothing definite; though I am bound to say I am satisfied that there is a cipher."

"Have you tried both the numbers and the dots?"

"Both," I answered; "but as yet I want a jumping-off place."

"Do you really think from what you have studied that the cipher is a biliteral one, or on the basis of a biliteral cipher?"

"I do! I can't say exactly how I came to think so; but I certainly do."

"Are there combinations of five?"

"Not that I can see."

"Are there combinations of less than five?"

"There may be. There are certainly."

"Then why on earth don't you begin by reducing the biliteral cipher to the lowest dimensions you can manage? You may light on something that way."

A light began to dawn upon me, and I determined that my task—so soon as my friends had left Cruden—would be to reduce Bacon's biliteral. It was with genuine admiration for her suggestion that I answered Miss Anita:

"Your woman's intuition is quicker than my man's ratiocination. 'I shall in all my best obey you, Madam!'" She painted away steadily for some time. I was looking at her, covertly but steadily when an odd flash of memory came to me; without thinking I spoke:

"When I first saw you, as you and Mrs. Jack stood on the rock, and away beyond you the rocks were all fringed with foam, your head looked as if it was decked with flowers." For a moment or two she paused before asking:

"What kind of flowers?"

Once again in our brief acquaintance I stood on guard. There was something in her voice which made me pause. It made my brain whirl, too, but there was a note of warning. At this time, God knows, I did not want any spurring. I was head over heels in love with the girl, and my only fear was lest by precipitancy I should spoil it all. Not for the wide world would I have cancelled the hopes that were dawning in me and filling me with a feverish anxiety. I could not help a sort of satisfied feeling as I answered:

"White flowers!"

"Oh!" she said impulsively, and then with a blush continued, painting hard as she spoke:

"That is what they put on the dead! I see!" This was a counter-stroke with a vengeance. It would not do to let it pass so I added:

"There is another 'first-column' function also in which white flowers are used. Besides, they don't put flowers on the head of corpses."

"Of whom then?" The note of warning sounded again in the meekness of the voice. But I did not heed it. I did not want to heed it. I answered:

"Of Brides!" She made no reply—in words. She simply raised her eyes and sent one flashing glance through me, and then went on with her work. That glance was to a certain degree encouragement; but it was to a much greater degree dangerous, for it was full of warning. Although my brain was whirling, I kept my head and let her change the conversation with what meekness I could.

We accordingly went back to the cipher. She asked me many questions, and I promised to show her the secret writings when we should go back to the hotel. Here she struck in:

"We have ordered dinner at the hotel; and you are to dine with us." I tried not to tremble as I answered:

"I shall be delighted."

"And now," she said "if we are to have lunch here to-day we had better go and wake Mrs. Jack. See! the tide has been rising all the time we have been talking. It is time to feed the animals."

Mrs. Jack was surprised when we wakened her; but she too was ready for lunch. We enjoyed the meal hugely.

At half-tide the Hay boys came back. Miss Anita thought that there was enough work for them both in carrying the basket and helping Mrs. Jack back to the carriage. "You will be able to row all right, will you not?" she said, turning to me. "You know the way now and can steer. I shall not be afraid!"

When we were well out beyond the rock and could see the figures of Mrs. Jack and the boys getting further away each step, I took my courage in both hands; I was getting reckless now, and said to her:

"When a man is very anxious about a thing, and is afraid that just for omitting to say what he would like to say, he may lose something that he would give all the rest of the world to have a chance of getting—do—do you think he should remain silent?" I could see that she, too, could realise a note of warning. There was a primness and a want of the usual reality in her voice as she answered me:

"Silence, they say, is golden." I laughed with a dash of bitterness which I could not help feeling as I replied:

"Then in this world the gold of true happiness is only for the dumb!" she said nothing but looked out with a sort of steadfast introspective eagerness over the million flashing diamonds of the sea; I rowed on with all my strength, glad to let go on something. Presently she turned to me, and with all the lambency of her spirit in her face, said with a sweetness which tingled through me:

"Are you not rowing too hard? You seem anxious to get to Whinnyfold. I fear we shall be there too soon. There is no hurry; we shall meet the others there in good time. Had you not better keep outside the dangerous rocks. There is not a sail in sight; not one, so far as I know, over the whole horizon, so you need not fear any collision. Remember, I do not advise you to cease rowing; for, after all, the current may bear us away if we are merely passive. But row easily; and we may reach the harbour safely and in good time!"

Her speech filled me with a flood of feeling which has no name. It was not love; it was not respect; it was not worship; it was not, gratitude. But it was compounded of them all. I had been of late studying secret writing so earnestly that there was now a possible secret meaning in everything I read. But oh! the poverty of written words beside the gracious richness of speech! No man who had a heart to feel or a brain to understand could have mistaken her meaning. She gave warning, and hope, and courage, and advice; all that wife could give husband, or friend give friend. I only looked at her, and without a word held out my hand. She placed hers in it frankly; for a brief, blissful moment my soul was at one with the brightness of sea and sky.

There, in the very spot where I had seen Lauchlane Macleod go down into the deep, my own life took a new being.

XI

IN THE TWILIGHT

It was not without misgiving that I climbed the steep zigzag at Whinnyfold, for at every turn I half expected to see the unwelcome face of Gormala before me. It seemed hardly possible that everything could go on so well with me, and that yet I should not be disturbed by her presence. Miss Anita, I think, saw my uneasiness and guessed the cause of it; I saw her follow my glances round, and then she too kept an eager look out. We won the top, however, and got into the waiting carriage without mishap. At the hotel she asked me to bring to their sitting-room the papers with the secret writing. She gave a whispered explanation that we should be quite alone as Mrs. Jack always took a nap, when possible, before dinner.

She puzzled long and anxiously over the papers and over my enlarged part copy of them. Finally she shook her head and gave it up for the time. Then I told her the chief of the surmises which I had made regarding the means by which the biliteral cipher, did such exist, might be expressed. That it must be by marks of some sort was evident; but which of those used were applied to this purpose I could not yet make out. When I had exhausted my stock of surmises she said:

"More than ever I am convinced that you must begin by reducing the biliteral cipher. Every time I think of it, it seems plainer to me that Bacon, or any one else using such a system, would naturally perfect it if possible. And now let us forget this for the present. I am sure you must want a rest from thinking of the cipher, and I feel that I do. Dinner is ready; after it, if you will, I should like another run down to the beach."

"*Another*" run to the beach! then she remembered our former one as a sort of fixed point. My heart swelled within me, and my resolution to take my own course, even if it were an unwise one, grew.

After dinner, we took our way over the sandhills and along the shore towards the Hawklaw, keeping on the line of hard sand just below high-water mark.

The sun was down and the twilight was now beginning. In these northern latitudes twilight is long, and at the beginning differs little from the full light of day. There is a mellowed softness over everything, and all is grey in earth and sea and air. Light, however, there is in abundance at the first. The mystery of twilight, as Southerns know it, comes later on, when the night comes creeping up from over the sea, and the shadows widen into gloom. Still twilight is twilight in any degree of its changing existence; and the sentiment of twilight is the same all the world over. It is a time of itself; between the stress and caution of the day, and the silent oblivion of the night: It is an hour when all living things, beasts as well as human, confine themselves to their own business. With the easy relaxation comes something of self-surrender; soul leans to soul and mind to mind, as does body to body in moments of larger and more complete intention. Just as in the moment after sunset, when the earth is lit not by the narrow disc of the sun but by the glory of the wide heavens above, twin shadows merge into one, so in the twilight two natures which are akin come closer to the identity of one. Between daylight and dark as the myriad sounds of life die away one by one, the chirp of birds, the lowing of cattle, the bleating of sheep, the barking of dogs, so do the natural sounds such as the rustle of trees, the plash of falling water, or the roar of breaking waves wake into a new force that strikes on the ear with a sense of intention or conscious power. It is as though in all the wide circle of nature's might there is never to be such a thing as stagnation; no moment of poise, save when the spirits of nature proclaim abnormal silence, such as ruled when earth stood "at gaze, like Joshua's moon on Ajalon."

The spirits of my companion and myself yielded to this silent influence of the coming night. Unconsciously we walked close together and in step; and were silent, wrapt in the beauty around us. To me it was a gentle ecstasy. To be alone with her in such a way, in such a place, was the good of all heaven and all earth in one. And so for many minutes we went slowly on our way along the deserted sand, and in hearing of the music of the sounding sea and the echoing shore.

But even Heaven had its revolt. It seems that whether it be on Earth or in Heaven intelligence is not content to remain in a condition of poise. Ever there are heights to be won. Out of my own very happiness and the peace that it gave me, came afresh the wild desire to scale new heights and to make the present altitude which I had achieved a stepping-off place for a loftier height. All arguments seemed to crowd in my mind to prove that I was justified in asking Marjory to be my wife. Other men had asked women whom they had known but a short time to marry them; and with happy result. It was apparent that at the least she did not dislike me. I was a gentleman, of fair stock, and well-to-do; I could offer her a true and a whole heart. She, who was seemingly only companion to a wealthy woman, could not be offended at a man's offering to her all he had to give. I had already approached the subject, and she had not warned me off it; she had only given me in a sweetly artful way advice in which hope held a distinct place. Above all, the days and hours and moments were flying by. I did not know her address or when I should see her again, or if at all. This latest thought decided me. I would speak plainly to-night.

Oh, but men are dull beside women in the way of intuition. This girl seemed to be looking over the sea, and yet with some kind of double glance, such as women have at command, she seemed to have been all the time looking straight through and through me and getting some idea of her own from my changing expression. I suppose the appearance of determination frightened her or set her on guard, for she suddenly said:

"Ought we not to be turning home?"

"Not yet!" I pleaded, all awake in a moment from my dreams. "A few minutes, and then we can go back."

"Very well," she said with a smile, and then added demurely; "we must not be long." I felt that my hour had come and spoke impulsively:

"Marjory, will you be my wife?" Having got out the words I stopped. My heart was beating so heavily that I could not speak more. For a few seconds, which seemed ages to me, we were both silent. I daresay that she may have been prepared for something; from what I know now I am satisfied that her own intention was to ward off any coming difficulty. But the suddenness and boldness of the question surprised her and embarrassed her to silence. She stopped walking, and as she stood still I could see her bosom heave—like my own. Then with a great effort, which involved a long breath and the pulling up of her figure and the setting back of her shoulders, she spoke:

"But you know nothing of me!"

"I know all of you that I want to know!" This truly Hibernian speech amused her, even through her manifest emotion and awkwardness, if one can apply the word to one compact of so many graces. I saw the smile, and it seemed to set us both more at ease.

"That sounds very rude," she said "but I understand what you mean, and take it so." This gave me an opening into which I jumped at once. She listened, seeming not displeased at my words; but on the whole glad of a moment's pause to collect her thoughts before again speaking:

"I know that you are beautiful; the most beautiful and graceful girl I ever saw. I know that you are brave and sweet and tender and thoughtful. I know that you are clever and resourceful and tactful. I know that you are a good comrade; that you are an artist with a poet's soul. I know that you are the one woman in all the wide world for me; that having seen you there can never be any one else to take your place in my heart. I know that I would rather die with you in my arms, than live a king with any other queen!"

"But you have only seen me twice. How can you know so many nice things about me. I wish they were all true! I am only a girl; and I must say it is sweet to hear them, whether they be true or not. Anyhow, supposing them all true, how could you have known them?"

Hope was stepping beside me now. I went on:

"I did not need a second meeting to know so much. To-day was but a repetition of my joy; an endorsement of my judgment; a fresh rivetting of my fetters!" She smiled in spite of herself as she replied:

"You leave me dumb. How can I answer or argue with such a conviction." Then she laid her hand tenderly on my arm as she went on:

"Oh, I know what you mean, my friend. I take it all in simple truth; and believe me it makes me proud to hear it, though it also makes me feel somewhat unworthy of so much faith. But there is one other thing which you must consider. In justice to me you must." She paused and I felt my heart grow cold. "What is it?" I asked. I tried to speak naturally but I felt that my voice was hoarse. Her answer came slowly, but it seemed to turn me to ice:

"But I don't know you!"

There was a pity in her eyes which gave me some comfort, though not much; a man whose soul is crying out for love does not want pity. Love is a glorious self-surrender; all spontaneity; all gladness, all satisfaction, in which doubt and forethought have no part. Pity is a conscious act of the mind; wherein is a knowledge of one's own security of foothold. The two can no more mingle than water and oil.

The shock had come, and I braced myself to it. I felt that now if ever I should do my devoir as a gentleman. It was my duty as well as my privilege to shield this woman from unnecessary pain and humiliation. Well I knew, that it had been pain to her to say such a thing to me; and the pain had come from my own selfish impulse. She had warned me earlier in the day, and I had broken through her warning. Now she was put in a false position through my act; it was necessary I should make her feelings as little painful as I could. I had even then a sort of dim idea that my best plan would have been to have taken her in my arms and kissed her. Had we both been older I might have done so; but my love was not built in this fashion. Passion was so mingled with respect that the other course, recognition of, and obedience to, her wishes seemed all that was open to me. Besides it flashed across me that she might take it that I was presuming on her own impulsive act on the rock. I said with what good heart I could:

"That is an argument unanswerable, at present. I can only hope that time will stand my friend. Only" I added and my voice choked as I said it "Do, do believe that I am in deadly earnest; that all my life is at stake; and that I only wait, and I will wait loyally with what patience I can, in obedience to your will. My feelings and my wish, and—and my request will stand unaltered till I die!" She said not a word, but the tears rose up in her beautiful eyes and ran down her blushing cheeks as she held out her hand to me. She did not object when I raised it to my lips and kissed it with all my soul in the kiss!

We turned instinctively and walked homewards. I felt dejected, but not broken. At first the sand seemed to be heavy to my feet; but when after a little I noticed that my companion walked with a buoyancy unusual even to her, I too became gay again. We came back to the hotel much in the spirit in which we had set out.

We found Mrs. Jack dressed, all but her outer cloak, and ready for the road. She went away with Marjory to finish her toilet, but came back before her younger companion. When we were alone she said to me after a few moments of 'hum'ing and 'ha'ing and awkward preparation of speech:

"Oh Mr. Hunter, Marjory tells me that she intends to ride on her bicycle down to Aberdeen from Braemar where we are going on Friday. I am to drive from Braemar to Ballater and then go on by train so that I shall be in before her, though I am to leave later. But I am fearful about the girl riding such a journey by herself. We have no gentleman friend here, and it would be so good of you to take charge of her, if you happened to be anywhere about there. I know I can trust you to take care of her, you have been so good to her, and to me, already."

My heart leaped. Here was an unexpected chance come my way. Time was showing himself to be my friend already.

"Be quite assured," I said as calmly as I could "I shall be truly glad to be of the least service. And indeed it will just suit my plans, as I hoped to go to Braemar on my bicycle one day very soon and can arrange to go just as may suit you. But of course you understand that I must not go unless Miss Anita wishes it. I could not presume to thrust myself upon her."

"Oh that is all right!" she answered quickly, so quickly that I took it that she had already considered the matter and was satisfied about it. "Marjory will not object." Just then the young lady entered the room and Mrs. Jack turning to her said:

"I have asked Mr. Hunter my dear to ride down with you from Braemar; and he says that as it just suits his plans as he was going there he will be very happy if you ask him." She smiled as she said:

"Oh since you asked him and he had said yes I need not ask him too; but I shall be very glad!" I bowed. When Mrs. Jack went out, Marjory turning to me said:

"When did you plan to go to Braemar?"

"When Mrs. Jack told me you were going" I answered boldly.

"Oh! I didn't mean that," she said with a slight blush "but at what time you were to be there." To which I said:

"That will be just to suit your convenience. Will you write and let me know?" She saw through my ruse of getting a letter, and smilingly held up a warning finger.

As we strolled up the road, waiting for the dog-cart to be got ready, she said to me:

"Now you can be a good comrade I know; and you said that, amongst other things, I was a good comrade. So I am; and between Braemar and Aberdeen we must both be good comrades. That and nothing more! Whatever may come after, for good or ill, that time must be kept apart."

"Agreed!" I said and felt a secret exultation as we joined Mrs. Jack. Before they started Marjory said:

"Mrs. Jack I also have asked Mr. Hunter to come on the ride from Braemar. I thought it would please him if we both asked him, since he is so diffident and unimpulsive!"

With a smile she said good-bye and waved it with her whip as they started.

XII

THE CIPHER

I went straight to my own room and commenced to work afresh on the biliteral cipher. More than ever had I the conviction upon me that the reading of the secret writing would be the first step to the attainment of my wishes regarding Marjory. It would have been strange therefore if I had not first attempted the method which she had herself suggested, the reducing the Baconian cipher to its lowest elements.

For many hours I laboured at this work, and finally when I had reduced the Baconian five symbols to three I felt that I had accomplished all that was possible in that way.[1]

When I had arrived at this result, and had tested its accuracy in working, I felt in a position to experiment with my new knowledge on the old number cipher. First I wrote out my method of reduction as a sort of addendum to the paper which I had prepared for Marjory. Then I made a key to cipher and one to de-cipher.[2] By this time the night was well on and the grey of early morning was beginning to steal in by the edges of the blinds; I was not sleepy, however; I was too much excited to think of sleep, for the solving of the problem seemed almost within my grasp. Excited to a state which almost frightened me by its intensity, I got ready my copy of the number cipher and my newly prepared key. With an effort which took me all my resolution I went on steadily writing its proper letter under each combination without once looking back; for I knew that even should some of the letters be misplaced in the key the chance of recognising the right ones would be largely increased by seeing a considerable number of letters together.

Then I glanced over the whole and found that many of the symbols made up letters. With such a basis to work on, the rest was only labour. A few tentative efforts and I had corrected the key to agreement with some of the combinations in the cipher.

I found, however, that only here and there were letters revealed; try how I would, I could not piece out the intervening symbols. At last it

1. See Appendix B.
2. See Appendix C.

occurred to me that there might be in the paper two or more ciphers. On trying to follow out the idea, it became apparent that there were at least a quantity of impeding numbers scattered through the cipher. These might be only put in to baffle pursuit, as I had surmised might be done when I made the cipher; or they might have a more definite purpose. At any rate they hampered my work, so I struck them out as I went along. That I continued till I had exhausted the whole list of numbers in the script.

When I looked back over the letters translated from the cipher thus depleted, I found to my inexpressible joy that the sequence and sense were almost complete. The translation read as follows:

"To read the history of the Trust use cipher of Fr. Bacon. The senses and the figures are less worthy than the Trinity B. de E."

One step more and my work was done. I set the discarded numbers in sequence on another sheet of paper, and found to my intense satisfaction they formed an inner record readable by the same key. The "encloased" words, to use Bacon's phrase, were:

"Treasure Cave cliff one and half degree Northe of East from outer rock."

Then and then only did I feel tired. The sun was well up but I tumbled into bed and was asleep in a moment.

The gong was sounding for breakfast when I awoke. After breakfast when I resumed my work I set myself to construct a variant of my number key to suit the dotted letters, for my best chance, now that I was on the track was to construct rather than to decipher. After some hard work I at last constructed a cipher on this plan.[3]

I then began therefore to apply my new key to the copy of the cipher in the printed pages.

I worked steadily and completed the whole of the first page, writing down only the answer to those combinations which fitted into my scheme, and leaving all doubtful matters blank. Then I laid aside my key, and with a beating heart glanced over the result.

It more than satisfied me, for in the scattered letters though there were many blanks, was manifestly a connected narrative. Then I took the blanks and worked at them altering my key to suit the scheme of the original writer, till by slow degrees I had mastered the secret of the cipher construction.

---

3. See Appendix D.

From that hour on, till I had translated the cipher writing from beginning to end I knew no rest that I could avoid. I had to take my meals, and to snatch a few hours of sleep now and again; for the labour of translation was very arduous and slow, and the strain on my eyes was too great to be kept up continuously; with each hour, however, I acquired greater facility in the work. It was the evening of the fourth day, however, before my work was complete. I was then absolute master of the writer's intent.

All this time I had not heard from Marjory, and this alone made excessive work a necessary anodyne. Had I not had the long and overwhelming preoccupation to keep my mind from dwelling on the never ending disappointment, I do not know what I should have done. I fully expected a letter by the last post that night. I knew Marjory was staying somewhere in the County; it was by that post that we received local letters. None came, however, and that night I spent in making a fair transcript of the whole translation.

The first part of it was in the shape of a letter, and ran as follows:

My deare Sonne, These from the towne of Aberdeyne in Scotland wherin I lie sick, and before I go on my quest for the fullfillment of my Trust. I have written, from time to time during my long sickness, a full narrative of what has been; so that you may know all as though your own ears had heard and your own eyes had seen. All that I have written is to the one end—that you my eldest sonne and the rest of my children, may, should I fail—and I am weak in bodie to so strive—carry on the Trust to which I have pledged you as well as myself; so that untill that Trust be yielded up complete, neither I nor you nor they are free to any that may clash with the purpose to which our race is henceforth now devoted. But that mine oath may not press overhard on my children, and if need be on their children and their children's children to the end, it will suffice if one alone at all times shall hold himself or herself pledged to the fullfillment of the Trust. To this end I charge herewith all of my blood and race that the eldest sonne of each generation do hold himself pledged to the purpose of the Trust, unless some other of the direct lineage do undertake it on his behalf. In default of which, or if such undertaken Trust shall fail, then the duty reverteth back and back till one be found whose duty it is by priority of inheritance, unless by some other of the direct lineage the Trust be undertaken on his behalf. And be mindful one and all to whom is this sacred duty that secrecy is of its very essence. The great Trust was to me in the first instance in that His Holiness Pope Sixtus Fifth and my good kinsman known as the Spanish Cardinal held gracioslly that I was one in whose heart the ancient honour of our dear Spain had a place of lodgement so secure that time alone could not efface it nor its continuance in the hearts of my children. To the purpose then of this great Trust His Holiness hath himself given to me and mine full powers of all kinds so to deal with such circumstances as may arise that the labour which we have undertaken may in all cases be brought to a successful issue. To the which His Holiness hath formulated a Quittance which shall be co-existent with the Trust and which shall purge the natural sin of any to whom in the discharge of the duties of the Trust any necessity may arise. But inasmuch as the Trust is a secret one and the undue publication of such Quittance might call the attention of the curious to its existence, such Document is filed in the secret record of the Vatican, where, should necessity hereafter arise, it may be found by the Holy Father who may then occupy the Chair of St. Peter on application made to him on behalf of any who may so offend against law or the rules of well-being which govern the children of Christ. And I charge you, oh! my sonne to ever bear in mind that though there be some strange things in the narrative they are in mine own eyes true in all ways, though it may appear to you that they accord not with what may be said hereafter of these time's by other men.

"And oh, my sonne, and my children all, take this my last blessing and with it my counsel that ye walk always in Faith and Righteousness, in Honour and in Good Report, with your duty ever to Holy Church and to the King in loyal service. Farewell! God and the Blessed Virgin and the Saintes and Angels watch over you and help you that your duty be done.

Your father in all love,
BERNARDINO DE ESCOBAN

"These will be brought by a trusty hand, for I fear lest they shall fall into the hands of the English Queene, or any of her hereticall surroundings. If it be that you fail at the first in the speedy fullfillment of the Trust—as may be, now that the purpose of our great Armada hath been checked—it may be well that whoso to whom is the Trust may come hither and dwell upon these shores so that he may watch over the purpose of the Trust and be at hand for its fullfillment when occasion may serve. But be mindful ever, oh my sonne, that who so guardeth the Trust will be ever surrounded by enemies, heathenish and without remorse, whose greed should it ever be awakened to this purpose would be fatal to all which we cherish. Dixi."

Following this came:

Narrative of Bernardino de Escoban, Knight of the Cross of the Holy See and Grandee of Spain.

In this was set out at full length[4] the history of the great Treasure gathered by Pope Sixtus Fifth for the subjugation of England, and which he entrusted to the writer of the narrative who had at his own cost built and manned one of the vessels of the Armada the *San Cristobal* flagship of the Squadron of the Galleons of Castile. The Pope, wearied by the demands of Philip of Spain and offended by his claim to appoint bishops under the new domain and further incensed by the incautious insolence of Count de Olivares the Spanish ambassador to Rome, has chosen to make this a secret trust and has on the suggestion of the Spanish Cardinal chosen Don Bernardino de Escoban for the service. In furtherance of his design he has sent him for his new galleon a "figurehead" wrought in silver and gold for his own galley by Benvenuto Cellini. Also he has given him as a souvenir a brooch wrought by the same master-hand, the figurehead wrought *in petto*. Don Bernardino gives account of the defeat of the Armada and tells how his vessel being crippled and he being fearful of the seizure of the treasure entrusted to him buries

---

4. See Appendix E.

it and the coveted figurehead in a water cave at the headland of a bay on the coast of Aberdeyne. He has blown up the opening of the cave for safety. In the narrative were certain enlightening phrases such as when the Pope says:

"'To which end I am placing with you a vastness of treasure such as no nation hath ever seen." Which was to be applied to only the advancement of the True Faith, and which was in case of failure of the enterprise of the Armada to be given to the custody of whatever King should, after the death of Sixtus V, sit upon the throne. And again:

"'The Cave was a great one on the south side of the Bay with many windings and blind offsets. . .'The black stone on one hand and the red on the other giving back the blare of the lantern.'"

The memoranda which follow give the future history of the Trust:

The narrative of my father, the great and good Don Bernardino de Escoban, I have put in the present form for the preservation of the secret. For inasmuch as the chart to which he has alluded is not to be found, though other papers and charts there be, it may be necessary that a branch of our house may live in this country in obedience to the provision of the Trust and so must learn to speak the English as though it were the mother tongue. As I was but a youth when my father wrote, so many years have elapsed that death has wrought many changes and the hand that should have carried the message and given me the papers and the chart is no more, lying as is thought beside my father amongst the surges of the Skyres. So that only a brief note pointing to the contents of an oaken chest wherein I found them, though incomplete, was all that I had to guide me. The tongue that might have spoken some added words of import was silent for ever

FRANCISCO DE ESCOBAN
23, October, 1599

The narrative of my grandfather, together with my father's note have I Englished faithfully and put in this secret form for the guidance of those who may follow me, and whose life must be passed in this rigorous clime untill the sacred Trust committed to us by Pope Sixtus the Fifth be fullfilled. When on the death of my elder brother, I being but the second son, I was sent to join my father in Aberdeyne, I made grave preparation for bearing worthily the burden laid upon us by the Trust and so schooled myself in the English that it is now as my mother tongue. Then when my father, having completed the building of his castle, set himself to the finding of the cave whereof the secret was lost, in which emprise he, like my grandfather lost his life amongst the waters of the Skyres of Crudene. Ye that may follow me in the trust regard well this secret writing, made for the confusion of the curious but to the preservation of our secret. Bear ever in mind that not all that is shows on the surface of even simple words. The cipher of my Grandfather devised by Fr. Bacon now High Chancellor of England has many mouths, all of which may speak if there be aught to say.

BERNARDINO DE ESCOBAN

4, July, 1620

In addition to the cipher narrative I found on close examination that there was a separate cipher running through the marginal notes on the earlier of the printed pages. When translated it ran as follows:

"Cave mouthe northe of outer rock one degree and half North of East. Reef lies from shore point three and half degrees South of South East."

XIII

A Ride Through the Mountains

I read Don Escoban's narrative over and over again, till I had thoroughly mastered every detail of it; then I studied the key of the number cipher till I had it by heart. I had an instinct that memory on this subject would be a help and a safety to me now or hereafter. For now new doubts had begun to assail me. What I had learned was in reality a State secret and had possible consequences or eventualities which, despite the lapse of three centuries, might prove far-reaching and dangerous. The treasure in question was so vast, its purpose so definite, and its guardianship so jealously protected against time and accident, that there was but little chance of forgetfulness regarding it. I was not assailed by moral scruples in any way. The treasure had been amassed and dedicated to the undoing of England; and for those who had gathered it and sent it forth I had no concern. That it had been hidden in Britain by Britain's enemies during time of war surely deprived them of all right to recover by legal means. What the law might be on the subject I did not know, and till I knew I cared little. It was a case of "finders keepers," and if I could find it first I held myself justified in using it to my own purposes. All the same I made up my mind to look up the law of Treasure Trove, which I had a hazy idea was in a pretty uncertain condition. At first none of these issues troubled me. They were indeed side issues till the treasure should be found; when they would become of prime importance. I had felt that my first step to winning the hand of Marjory Anita was to read the cipher. This I had done; and in the doing had made discovery of a secret of such a nature that it might place me beyond the dreams of avarice, and in a position to ask any girl in the world to marry me. I believe that I regarded the treasure as already my own; as much as though I had already recovered it from the bowels of the earth.

Early in the morning I took my way to Whinnyfold, bringing with me a pocket compass so that I could locate the exact spot where the mouth of the cave had been closed. I knew of course that even granite rocks cannot withstand untouched the beating of three centuries of stormy sea, the waste of three hundred summers and winters, and the thousands of nights of bitter frost and days of burning sun which had come to pass since the entrance of the cave had been so rudely shaken down. But I was, I confess, not prepared for the utter annihilation which had come to every trace of its whereabouts. Time after time the sea had bitten into the land; and falling rocks, and creeping verdure, and drifting sand had changed the sea-front beyond all recognition.

I did what I could, however, to take the bearings of the place as laid down by Don de Escoban by walking along the top of the cliff, beginning at the very edge of Witsennan Point till I reached a spot where the south end of the outer rock of the Skares stood out.

Then to my surprise I found that it was as near as possible in the direction of my own house. In fact when I looked at the plan which the local surveyor had made of my house I found that the northern wall made a bee line for the south end of the main rock of the Skares. As it was manifest that what had originally been the front of the cave had fallen in and been partly worn and worked away, my remaining hope was that the cave itself lay under part of my ground if not under the house itself. This gave a new feature to the whole affair. If my surmise were correct I need not hurry at all; the safest thing I could do would be to quietly make an opening from my house into the cave, and explore at leisure. All seemed clear for this proceeding. The workmen who had done the building were gone, and the coming of the decorators had not yet been fixed. I could therefore have the house to myself. As I went back to the hotel, I planned out in my mind how I should get from Glasgow or Aberdeen proper implements for digging and cutting through the rock into the house; these would be sent in cases, so that no one would suspect what I was undertaking. The work would have to be done by myself if I wished to preserve secrecy. I had now so much to tell Marjory when we should meet that I felt I should hardly know where to begin, and the business side of my mind began to plan and arrange so that all things might come in due order and to the best effect.

When I got to the hotel I found awaiting me a letter from Marjory which had come by the last post. I took it away to my room and locked the door before opening it. It had neither address nor date, and was decidedly characteristic:

My dear Sir

Mrs. Jack asks me to write for her to say that we shall be leaving Braemar on Tuesday. We shall be staying at the Fife

Arms Hotel, and she will be very happy if you will breakfast with us at nine o'clock A. M. Room No. 16. This is all of course in case you care to ride down to Aberdeen. We are breakfasting so early as the ride is long, sixty miles, and Mrs. Jack thinks that I should have a rest at least twice on the way. As I believe you know the road, she will be glad if you will kindly arrange our stopping places. Mrs. Jack will leave Braemar at about three o'clock and drive down to Ballater to catch the half-past five train. She asks me to say that she hopes you will pardon her for the trouble she is giving you, and to impress on you that in case you would rather not come, or should anything occur to prevent you, she will quite understand a telegram with the single word 'regret.' By the way she will be obliged if you will kindly not mention her name—either her surname or her Christian name—before any of the people—strangers or hotel people, at Braemar or during the journey—or indeed during the day. Believe me,

Yours very truly,
Marjory Anita

"P.S.—How about the cipher; have you reduced the biliteral, or got any clue yet?

"P.P.S.—I don't suppose that anything, unless it be really serious, will prevent your coming. Mrs. Jack is so looking forward to my having that bicycle ride.

"P.P.P.S.—Have you second-sighted any ships yet? Or any more white flowers—for the Dead?"

For long I sat with the letter in my hand after I had read it over and over again many many times. Each time I read it its purpose seemed more luminous. It may have been that my old habit of a year ago of finding secret meanings in everything was creeping back to me. I thought and thought; and the introspective habit made me reason out causes even in the midst of imaginative flights. "Might not" I thought "it be possible that there be minor forms of Second Sight; Day Dreams based on some great effort of truth. In the real world there are manifestations of life in lower as well as higher forms; and yet all alike are instinct with some of that higher principle which divides the quick and the dead. The secret voices of the brain need not always speak in thunder; the Dream-Painter within us need not always have a full canvas for the exercise of his craft."

On Tuesday morning when at nine o'clock to the minute I went to the Fife Arms at Braemar, I found Marjory alone. She came forward with a bright, frank smile and shook hands. "It's real good to see you" was all she said. Presently she added:

"Mrs. Jack will be here in a minute or two. Before she comes, it is understood that between this and Aberdeen and indeed for to-day, you and I are only to be comrades."

"Yes!" said I, and then added: "Without prejudice!" She showed her pearly teeth in a smile as she answered:

"All right. Without prejudice! Be it so!" Then Mrs. Jack came in, and having greeted me warmly, we sat down to breakfast. When this was over, Marjory cut a good packet of sandwiches and tied them up herself. These she handed to me saying:

"You will not mind carrying these. It will be nicer having our lunch out than going to a hotel; don't you think so?" Needless to say I cordially acquiesced. Both our bicycles were ready at the door, and we lost no time in getting under weigh. Indeed my companion showed some anxiety to be off quickly, as though she wished to avoid observation.

The day was glorious. There was bright sunshine; and a sky of turquoise with here and there a flock of fleecy clouds. The smart easterly breeze swept us along as though we were under sail. The air was cool and the road smooth as asphalt, but with the springiness of well-packed gravel. With the least effort of pedalling we simply seemed to fly. I could see the exhilaration on my companion's face as clearly as I could feel it in my own nature. All was buoyancy, above, below, around us; and I doubt if in all the wide circle of the sun's rays there were two such glad hearts as Marjory's and my own.

As we flew along, the lovely scenery on either hand seemed like an endless panorama. Of high mountains patched with heather which here and there, early in the year as it was, broke out in delicate patches of pink; of overarching woods whose creaking branches swaying in the wind threw kaleidoscopic patterns of light along our way; of a brown river fed by endless streams rushing over a bed of stones which here and there lifted their dark heads through the foam of the brown-white water; of green fields stretching away on either side of the river or rising steeply from our feet to the fringes of high-lying pines or the black mountains which rose just beyond; of endless aisles of forest where, through the dark shade of the brown trunks, rose from the brown mass of long-fallen pine needles which spread the ground below, and where patches of sunlight fell in places with a seemingly intolerable glare! Then out into the open again where the sunlight seemed all natural and even the idea of shade unreal. Down steep hills where the ground seemed to slide back underneath our flying wheels, and up lesser hills, swept without effort by the wind behind us and the swift impetus of our pace.

After a while the mountains before us, which at first had seemed like an unbroken line of frowning giants barring our course, seemed to open a way to us. Round and round we swept, curve after curve yielding and falling back and opening new vistas; till at the last we passed into the open gap between the hills around Ballater. Here in the face of possible danger we began to crawl cautiously down the steep hill to the town. Mrs. Jack had proposed that we should make our first halt at Ballater. As, however, we put on pace again at the foot of the hill Marjory said:

"Oh do not let us stop in a town. I could not bear it just after that lovely ride through the mountains."

"Agreed!" I said "let us push on! That twenty miles seems like nothing. Beyond Cambus-o-May there is a lake on the northern side; we can ride round it and come back to the road again at Dinnet. If you like we can have our lunch in the shelter of a lovely wood at the far side of it."

"That will be enchanting!" she said, and the happy girlish freshness of her voice was like a strain of music which suited well the scene. When we had passed Ballater and climbed the hill up to the railway bridge we stopped to look back; and in sheer delight she caught hold of my arm and stood close to me. And no wonder she was moved, for in the world there can be few places of equal beauty of a similar kind. Right above us to the right, and again across the valley, towered mountains of rich brown with patches of purple and lines of green; and in front of us in the centre of the amphitheatre, two round hills, looming large in a delicate mist, served as portals to the valley which trended upward between the hills beyond. The road to Braemar seemed like a veritable road of mystery, guarded by an enchanted gate. With a sigh we turned our backs on all this beauty, and skirting the river, ran by Cambus-o-May and between woods of pine in an opening vista of new loveliness. Eastward before us lay a mighty sweep of hill and moor, backed on every side by great mountains which fell away one behind the other into misty distance of delicate blue. At our feet far below, lay two spreading lakes of sapphire hue, fringed here and there with woods, and dotted with little islands whose trees bent down to the water's edge. Marjory stood rapt for awhile, her breast heaving and her face glowing. At last she turned to me with a sigh; her beautiful eyes were bright with unshed tears as she said:

"Oh, was there ever in the world anything so beautiful as this Country! And was there ever so exquisite a ride as ours to-day!"

Does ever a man love a woman more than when she shows herself susceptible to beauty, and is moved to the fulness and simplicity of emotion which is denied to his own sex? I thought not, as Marjory and I swept down the steep road and skirted by the crystal lakes of Ceander and Davan to the wood in which we were to have our *al fresco* lunch. Here, sheltered from the wind, the sunshine seemed too strong to make sitting in the open pleasant; and we were glad to have the shade of the trees. As we sat down and I began to unpack the luncheon, Marjory said:

"And now tell me how you have been getting on with the cipher." I stood still for so long that she raised her head and took a sharp glance of surprise at me.

In the charm of her presence I had absolutely forgotten all about the cipher and what might grow from it.

XIV

A SECRET SHARED

There is so much to tell" I said "that I hardly know where to begin. Perhaps I had better tell you all here, where we are alone and not likely to be disturbed. We have come so fast that we have lots of time and we need not hurry. When you have had your lunch I shall tell you all."

"Oh please don't wait till then," she said, "I am all impatience. Let me know right away."

"Young woman" I said sternly "you are at present insincere. You *know* you are ravenously hungry, as you should be after a twenty mile ride; and you are speaking according to your idea of convention and not out of your heart. This is not convention; there is nothing conventional in the whole outfit. Eat the food prepared for you by the thoughtfulness of a very beautiful and charming girl!" She held up a warning finger and said:

"Remember '*Bon Camarade*—without prejudice.'"

"All right" I answered "so it shall be. But if the lady wants to hold me up for criminal libel I shall undertake to repeat the expression when, and where, and how she will. I shall repeat the assertion and abide by the consequences." She went on eating her sandwiches, not, I thought, displeased. When we had both finished she turned to me and said:

"Now!" I took from my pocket the rescript of Don Bernardino de Escoban's narrative and handed it to her. She looked at it, turned over the pages, and glanced at them as she went. Then she returned to the beginning, and after reading the first few lines, said to me with an eager look in her eyes:

"Is this really the translation of the secret writing? Oh, I am so glad you have succeeded. You are cute!" She took out her watch, and having looked at it, went on: "We have loads of time. Won't you read it for me? It will be so much nicer! And let me ask you questions."

"Delighted!" I answered, "But would it not be better if I read it right through first, and then let you ask questions! Or better still you read it yourself right through, and then ask." I had a purpose in this. If I had to read it, my eyes must be wholly engrossed in my work; but if she read, I need never take them off her face. I longed to see the varying expression with which she would follow every phase of the strange story. She thought for a few seconds before answering, and as she thought looked me straight in the eyes. I think she read my secret, or at any rate enough of it to fathom my wish; nothing else could account for the gentle blush that spread over her face. Then she said in quite a meek tone:

"I shall read it myself if you think it best!"

I shall never forget that reading. Her face, always expressive, was to me like an open book. I was by this time quite familiar with de Escoban's narrative, as I had with infinite patience dug it out letter by letter from the cipher in which it had been buried for so long. As also I had written it out fair twice over, it was little wonder that I knew it well. As she read I so followed that I could have told to a sentence how far she had got in the history. Once she unconsciously put her hand to her throat and felt the brooch; but immediately drew it away again, glancing for a moment at me from under her eyelashes to see whether I had observed. She saw I had, shook her head with a smile, and read on.

When she had finished reading, she gave a long sigh and then held out her hand to me saying:

"Bravo! I congratulate you with all my heart!" Her touch thrilled me; she was all on fire, and there was a purposeful look in her face which was outside and beyond any joy that she could have with regard to any success of mine. This struck me so much that I said impulsively:

"Why are you so glad?" She answered instinctively and without thought:

"Because you will keep it from the Spaniards!" Then she stopped suddenly, with a gesture of self repression.

I felt a little piqued. I would have thought that her concern would have been rather individual than political. That in such a matter even before racial hatred would have come gladness at the well-doing of even such a friend—without prejudice—as I was. Looking at me, she seemed to see through me and said

"With her two white hands extended, as if praying one offended:"

"Oh, I am sorry! I did not mean to hurt you. I can't explain yet; not to-day, which is for comradeship only.—Yes without prejudice"—for she saw my look and answered it "But some day you will understand." She was so evidently embarrassed and pained at having for some reason which I did not comprehend to show reticence to me who had been so open with her, that I felt it my duty to put her at ease. This I tried to do by assuring her that I quite understood that she had some good reason, and that I was quite content to wait. I could not help adding before I stopped: "This is a small thing to have to wait for after all; when I have to wait for something so much more important." The warning finger was held up again with a smile.

Then we went over the whole of the narrative again, I reading this time and she stopping to ask me questions. There was not much to ask; all the story was so plain that the proceeding did not take very long. Then she asked me to explain how I had come to decipher the cryptogram. I took out my pocket book and proceeded to make a key to the cipher, explaining as I went on the principle. "To me," I said, "it is very complete, and can be used in an infinity of ways. Any mode of expression can be used that has two objects with five varieties of each." Here she interrupted me. As I was explaining I was holding out my hands with the fingers spread as a natural way of expressing my meaning. She saw at once what had escaped me, and clasping her hands exclaimed impulsively:

"Like your two hands! It is delightful! Two hands, and five fingers on each. We can talk a new deaf and dumb alphabet; which no one but ourselves can understand!" Her words thrilled through me. One more secret to share with her; one more secret which would be in perpetual exercise, in pursuance of a common thought. I was about to speak when she stopped me with a gesture. "Sorry!" she said. "Go on; explain to me! We can think of variety later!" So I continued:

"So long as we have means that are suitable, we have only to translate into the biliteral, and we who know this can understand. Thus we have a double guard of secrecy. There are some who could translate into symbols with which they are familiar, symbols with which they are not; but in this method we have a buffer of ignorance or mystery between the known and the unknown. There is also this advantage; the cipher as it stands is sufficiently on a basis of science or at any rate of order, that its key is easily capable of reproduction. As you have seen, I can make a key without any help. Bacon's biliteral cipher is scientifically accurate. It can, therefore, be easily reproduced; the method of exclusions is also entirely rational, so that we need have no difficulty in remembering it. If two people would take the trouble to learn the symbols of the biliteral, as kept after the exclusions and which are used in this cipher, they might with very little practice be able to write or read off-hand. Indeed the suggestion, which you have just made, of a deaf-and-dumb alphabet is capital. It is as simple as the daylight! You have only to decide whether the thumb or the little finger means 1 or 2; and then reproduce by right hand or left, and using the fingers of each hand, the five symbols of the amended biliteral, and you can talk as well and as easily as do the deaf mutes!" Again she spoke out impulsively:

"Let us both learn off by heart the symbols of our cipher; and then we shan't want even to make a key. We can talk to each other in a crowd, and no one be the wiser of what we are saying."

This was very sweet to me. When a man is in love, as I was, anything which links him to his lady, and to her alone, has a charm beyond words. Here was a perpetual link, if we cared to make it so, and if the Fates would be good to us.

"The Fates!" With the thought came back Gormala's words to me at the beginning. She had told me, and somehow I seemed to have always believed the same, that the Fates worked to their own end and in their own way. Kindness or unkindness had no part in their workings; pity had no place at the beginning of their interest, no more than had remorse at the end. Was it possible that in the scheme of Fate, in which Gormala and I and Lauchlane Macleod had places, there was also a place for Marjory? The Witch-woman had said that the Fates would work their will, though for the doing of it came elements out of past centuries and from the ends of the earth. The cipher of Don de Escoban had lain hidden three centuries, only to be revived at its due time. Marjory had come from a nation which had no existence when the Don had lived, and from a place which in his time was the far home of the red man and the wolf and the bison and the bear.

But yet what was there to connect Marjory with Don de Escoban and his secret? As I thought, I saw Marjory who had turned her back to me, quietly take something from her throat and put it into her pocket. Here was the clue indeed.

The brooch! When I had taken it up from the sea at the Sand Craigs I had returned it to her with only a glance; and as I had often seen it since, without any mystery, I had hardly noticed it. It rushed in on my mind that it was of the same form as that described by Don de Escoban as having been given by the Pope. I had only noticed a big figure and a little one; but surely it could be none other than a figure of St. Christopher. I should have liked to have asked Marjory about it at once; but her words already spoken putting off explanation, and her recent act, of which I was supposed to know nothing, in putting it out of sight, forbade me to inquire. All the more I thought, however; and other matters regarding it crowded into my mind.

The chain was complete, the only weak link being the connection between Marjory and the St. Christopher brooch. And even here there was a mystery, acknowledged in her concealment, which might explain itself when the time came.

Matters took such a grave turn for me with my latest surmise, that I thought it would be well to improve the occasion with Marjory, in so far as it might be possible to learn something of her surroundings. I was barred from asking questions by her own wish; but still I did not like to lose the chance without an effort, so I said to her:

"We have learned a lot to-day, haven't we?"

"Indeed we have. It hardly seems possible that a day could make such a change!"

"I suppose we should take it that new knowledge should apply new conditions to established fact?" I said this with some diffidence; and I could see that the change in my tone, much against my will, attracted her attention. She evidently understood my wish, for she answered with decision:

"If you mean by 'new conditions' any alteration of the compact made between us for to-day—yes, I remember 'without prejudice'—there is nothing in our new knowledge to alter the old ones. Do remember, sir, that this day is one set apart, and nothing that is not a very grave matter indeed can be allowed to alter what is established regarding it."

"Then," said I, "at all events let us learn the cipher—our cipher as you very properly called it."

"Oh no! surely?" this was said with a rising blush.

"Indeed, yes—I am glad to say!"

"Take care!" she replied, meaningly, then she added:

"Very well! Ours let it be. But really and truly I have no right to its discovery; it makes me feel like a fraud to hear you say so."

"Be easy," I replied. "You helped me more than I can say. It was your suggestion to reduce the terms of the biliteral; and it was by that means that I read the cipher. But at any rate when we call it 'ours' it will content me if the word 'ours'"—I could not help repeating the word for it was delight to me; it did not displease her either, though it made her blush—"is applied not to invention but to possession!"

"All right," she said. "That is good of you. I cannot argue with you. Amendment accepted! Come, let us get on our wheels again. You have the key of *our* cipher with you; you can tell me the items one by one, and we will learn them as we go along."

And so as we swept round Davan Lake, with the wind behind us driving us along except just before we regained the high road at Dinnet, I repeated the symbols of the reduced biliteral. We went over and over them again and again, till we were unable to puzzle each other questioning up and down, 'dodging' as the school-boys say.

Oh, but that ride was delightful! There was some sort of conscious equality between us which I could see my comrade felt as well as myself. Down the falling road we sped almost without effort, our wheels seeming to glide on air. When we came to the bridge over the railway just above Aboyne, where the river comes north and runs in under a bank of shale and rock, we dismounted and looked back. Behind us was our last view of the gorge above Ballater, where the two round hills stood as portals, and where the cloud rack hanging above and beyond made a mystery which was full of delightful fascination and no less delightful remembrance. Then with a sigh we turned.

There, before us lay a dark alley between the closing pines. No less mysterious, but seemingly dark and grim.

XV

A Peculiar Dinner-Party

We did not stop at Aboyne, but ran on beyond Kincardine O'Neill, and took our second rest close to the Bridge of Potarch where we had tea at the little hotel on the right bank of the river. Then for a while we leaned over the parapet and looked at the water flowing swiftly far below as the river narrows from its pebbly bed to the gorge of rock on which the bridge rests. There is something soothing, perhaps something hypnotic, in the ceaseless rush of water. It unconsciously takes one's thoughts on and on, till the reality of the present is in some measure lost and the mind wanders towards imagination through the regions of the unknown. As I looked at Marjory, with the afternoon sun falling on her superb figure and showing up her clear-cut profile with all the finish of a cameo, I could not but be struck with the union of gentleness and independence which was so clearly manifested in her. Without thinking, I spoke out my mind. It is a privilege of those who understand each other, or of the very young, to give voice to the latter portion of a train of thought without feeling it necessary to enlighten the hearer as to what has gone to make up the conclusion. The feeling was hourly growing upon me that, even if I could not quite understand Marjory, at least she understood me.

"But then all you American girls are so independent!" She did not seem a bit surprised by this fag end of reasoning; she had evidently been following up some train of thought of her own, and by some happy instinct my words fitted in with it. Without turning towards me, but still keeping her eyes fixed down the stream to where far away it swayed to the right through a gap between pine clad hills she answered:

"Yes! We are as a rule brought up to be independent. It seems to be a part of what our people call the 'genius' of the country. Indeed for many, women as well as men, it is a sort of necessity. Our nation is so vast, and it expands so quickly, that there is nearly everywhere a family separation. In the main, all the children of one generation become the heads of families of the next. Somehow, the bulk of our young people still follow the sunset; and in the new life which comes to each, whether in the fields or in the city or in the reclamation of the wilderness, the one thing which makes life endurable is this independence which is another form of self-reliance. This it is which enables them to brave hunger and thirst and all danger which comes to pioneers; which in the cities makes the solitude of lonely life bearable to the young as well as to the old; which makes them work and study in patience; which makes them self-sacrificing, and thrifty, and long enduring. I tell you it is this which makes a race of patriots, whose voices swell in unison till the great voice of the nation, raised in some good cause, can ring and echo through the world!" As she spoke she got more and more earnest, more and more enthusiastic, till her voice began to vibrate and her face to flush. When she turned towards me at the end, her eyes were full of spiritual light. I looked at her, and I suppose my love as well as my admiration must have expressed itself, for her eyes fell and the flush on her face melted into a soft blush. She turned, looked at the water again, and then went on speaking:

"This is the good side of our independence and *faute de mieux* it serves; those who know no better do not miss what might be. But oh! it has to be paid for. The little sufferings of day by day can grow into a mass which in the end outweighs those seemingly far greater ills which manifest themselves all at once. No one knows, no one ever will know, how much quiet, dull pain goes to tame a woman's heart to the solitude of life. I have not seen so much of it as some others; my life has been laid in pleasant places, and only through the small accidents of life have I come to know of the negative pain which other girls have to endure. It is so much to have round one the familiar faces of our youth; to meet sympathy at every turn of life, and to know that there is understanding for us always. We women have to give something in order to be happy. The stronger-minded ones, as we call them, blame the Creator for this disposition of things—or else I do not know who or what they blame; but the rest of us, who are wise enough to accept what cannot be altered, try to realise what can be done for the best. We all want to care for some one or something, if it is only a cat or a dog. For myself, so far back as I can remember, I longed to have a brother or sister, but I think that in my secret heart it was a brother I wanted. Of course as I merged into my actual surroundings I grew out of this; but once it was brought home to me with new force. We were staying for a few days in one of those great English houses where there was a growing family of boys and girls. There was one sweet young girl, just about my own age, who seemed idolised by all her brothers. When we arrived they were all going in to evening prayers. The last of the sunlight was falling through the old stained glass window of the great baronial hall, and lit up the little family group. The girl sat between two of her young brothers, great stalwart lads who had all the characteristics of a family of soldiers. During prayers each of them held one of her hands; and when they all knelt, her arms went round their necks. I could not help feeling deeply—down into the very depths of my soul—how good it was for them all. I would have given everything I have, or am ever likely to have, that mine had been such an upbringing. Think, how in after years it will come back to those boys in hours of trial, or pain, or prosperity, or passion; in all times when their manhood or their honour or their worth is to be tried; how they will remember the words which were spoken to them as those were spoken, and were listened to as those were listened to, in the midst of sympathy and love. Many and many a time in years to come those boys will bless such hours, and God Himself will surely rejoice that His will was being wrought in so sweet a way. And the same thing is going on in a thousand English homes!" She paused and turned to me and the feeling in her heart found expression in the silent tears that ran down her cheeks. Again she turned her eyes to the running water and gazed awhile before speaking again. Then looking at me, she went on:

"And the girl, too, how good it was for her! What an antidote to selfishness! How much of self-control, of sympathy, of love, of toleration was begun and fostered and completed in those moments of the expression of her heart! What place can there really be for selfish want and sorrows in the heart of a woman so trained to sympathise with and help others? It is good! good! good! and I pray that in the later development of my own dear country, all such things may have a part. Expansion at its present rate must soon cease; and then some predominant idea must take the place of the eternal self-independence. We shall, I trust, moult no feather of our national feeling of personal duty; but I am sure that our people, and more especially our women, will lead happier as well as healthier lives."

This present phase of Marjory's character was new to me, fresh and enchanting. Every hour seemed to bring out new worths and beauties of the girl's character, of her intellectual gifts, of the endless wealth of her heart.

When she ceased speaking I took her hand in mine, she not resenting, and kissed it. I said only one word "Marjory!" but it was enough. I could see that in her eyes which made my heart leap.

Then a new life seemed to come to both of us. With one accord we moved towards our bicycles, and mounted in silence. After a few minutes of rapid spin down the sloping road from the bridge, we began to chat again gaily. For myself I was in wildly joyous spirits. Even a self-doubting lover could not fail to understand such a look in his mistress's eyes. If ever love spoke out in eloquent silence it was then, all doubt melted from my heart, as the night shadows pale before the dawn. I was content to wait now, illimitably and in silence. She, too, seemed altogether happy, and accepted in unquestioning faith all the little pleasures which came in the progress of our journey. And such pleasures are many. As we drew down the valley of the Dee, with the mountains falling back and the dark pinewoods running up them like tongues of flame and emphasising by their gloom the brightness of grass and heather which cropped up amongst the rocks beyond, every turn of the road brought us to some new scene of peaceful beauty. From under the splendid woods of Crathes Castle we saw the river running like a blue ribbon far to the east and on either side of it fields and gardens and woods spreading wide. On we sped with delight in every moment, till at last through miles of shady woods we came to the great stone bridge, and ended our jaunt over the rough granite cobblestones of Aberdeen.

We were a little before the time the train was due; so leaving our wheels in the Palace Hotel we went down on the platform to meet Mrs. Jack on her arrival.

We met her in due course, and brought her up to the hotel. At the stairway Marjory, who had lingered half a flight behind her companion, whispered to me:

"You have been a good boy to-day, a real good boy; and you shall before long have your reward." As she gave me her hand, I whispered:

"I am content to wait now Marjory; dear Marjory!" She blushed and smiled, and fled upstairs with a warning finger laid upon her lips.

It had been understood that I was to dine with Mrs. Jack and her friend, so I went up to the room which I had secured, to change my clothes. When I came down, in what I thought was a reasonable time, I went to the private sitting-room and knocked. As there was no answer I knocked again; then receiving no reply I took it for granted that the ladies had not yet come from their rooms and entered.

The room was empty but on the table which was laid for dinner for three was a note in Marjory's hand directed to me. With a sinking of the heart I opened it, and stood for a few minutes amazed. It had no apostrophe and ran as follows:—

"We have had to leave suddenly, but Mrs. Jack wants you to oblige her very much if you will be so good. Stay in the room, and when dinner is served sit down by yourself and eat it. Please, please do not think hardly of Mrs. Jack's request; and do not fail to carry it out. There is good reason for it, as you will very soon know. More depends on your doing as Mrs. Jack"—the "Mrs. Jack" was written over an obliterated "I"—"asks than you may think. I am sure that by this time you know you can trust me.

MARJORY

The situation was disappointing and both humiliating and embarrassing. To be a guest under such conditions was almost ridiculous; and under ordinary circumstances I should have refused. But then I remembered that last look of Marjory's eyes at the bridge of Potarch! Without a word, or another thought, of revolt I sat down to the dinner which the waiter was just now bringing into the room.

As it was evident to me that my staying in the room was for some purpose of delay, I lingered over my wine and had two cigars before I came away.

XVI

REVELATIONS

In the hall I met together two men whom I knew well. The first was Adams of the American Embassy in London; the second Cathcart of the British Embassy at Washington, now on leave. I had not seen either for two years, and it was with mutual pleasure that we met. After our preliminary handshaking, and the inevitable drink at the American's request, Adams slapped me on the shoulder and said heartily:

"Well, old fellow, I congratulate you; or rather am I to congratulate you?"

"What do you mean?" I asked in feeble embarrassment.

"All right, old chap!" he said heartily. "Your blush is enough. I see it hasn't come off yet at all events!" A man never lets well alone when he is in an awkward position. If I had only held my tongue I might not have made a guy of myself; but as I was in doubt as to what might be the issue of my suit to Marjory, I felt additionally constrained to affect ignorance of his meaning. So I floundered on:

"'Come off yet'? What on earth do you mean?" Again he slapped me on the back as he said in his chaffing way:

"My dear boy I saw you come in over the bridge. You had had a long ride I could see by your wheels; and I am bound to say that you did seem on excellent terms with each other!" This was getting dangerous ground, so I tried to sheer off. "Oh," I said, "you mean my bike ride with Miss Anita"—I was interrupted by his sudden whistle.

"Oh," he said in exact imitation of my own manner. "You mean Miss Anita! So it has come to that already! Anyhow I congratulate you heartily, whether it has come, or may come, or will come to anything else."

"I don't see," I said, with a helpless feeling of having been driven into a corner, "that there is anything especially remarkable in a man having a bicycle ride with a young lady of his acquaintance."

"Keep your hair on, old man!" he said with a smile. "There is nothing remarkable about a man riding with a young lady; but there is something very remarkable about any man riding with this particular young lady. Why, man alive, don't you know that there isn't a man in America, or out of it, that wouldn't give the eyes out of his head to take your place on such an occasion. To ride alone with Marjory Drake—"

"With whom?" I said impulsively; and having spoken could have bitten out my tongue. Adams paused; he was silent so long that I began to grow uneasy. His face grew very grave, and there spread over it that look between cunning and dominance which was his official expression. Then he spoke, but his words had not the same careless ring in them. There was a manifest caution and a certain indefinable sense of distance.

"Look here, Archie Hunter! Is it possible that you don't know who it is that you were with. All right! I know of course that you are acquainted with her personally," for he saw I was about to protest, "the very fact of your being with her and your knowing the name that she seldom uses answer for that; and you may take it from me that the lady needs no character for discretion from me. But how is it that you are on such good terms with her, and yet don't seem even to know her name?" For fully a minute there was silence between us. Cathcart had as yet said not a word, and Adams was thinking. For myself I was in a sea of multitudinous concerns; whichever way I turned I was face to face with some new difficulty. It would not do to leave these men under the impression that there was any social irregularity in my friendship with Marjory; I was too jealous of her good name to allow such a thing to be possible. And yet I could not explain at length how we had come to be such good friends. Already there were so many little mysteries; right up to this very evening when she and Mrs. Jack had gone away so strangely, leaving me in the ridiculous position of a guest with no host. It was not easy to explain these things; it was impossible to avoid them. In the midst of this chaotic whirl of thoughts Adams spoke:

"I think I had better say no more, anyhow. After all, if Miss Drake chooses to keep a secret, or to make one, it is not my business to give it, or her, away. She knows what she's doing. You will excuse me, old fellow, won't you; but as it is manifestly a lady's wish, I think I can do best by holding my tongue."

"Any wish of that lady's," said I, and I felt that I must seem to speak grandiloquently, "can only have my most loyal support."

There was an awkward silence which was relieved by Cathcart, who said to me:

"Come up to my room, Archie; I want to tell you something. You'll join us, too, Sam, won't you?"

"All right, Billy," said Adams, "I'll come in a few minutes. I want to give some directions about a horse for to-morrow."

When we were in Cathcart's room, he closed the door and said to me with the most genuine good feeling:

"I didn't like to say a word downstairs, old chap; but I could see you were in some difficulty. Of course I know it's all right; but ought you not to know something of the lady? With any one else but Sam and myself such a thing might have conveyed a false impression. Surely you can best protect the lady by knowing how to avoid anything that might embarrass her!" This was all good sound common sense. For a moment I weighed up the matter against the possibility of Marjory's wishing to keep her name a secret. Looking back, however, I could see that any concealment that had been was rather positive than negative. The original error had been mine; she had simply allowed it to pass. The whole thing had probably been the passing fancy of a bright, spirited young girl; to take it too seriously, or to make too much of it might do harm. Why, even these men might, were I to regard it as important, take it as some piece of deliberate deceit on her part. Thus convinced of the wisdom of Cathcart's proposition I spoke:

"You are quite right! and I shall be much obliged if you will—if you will enlighten me." He bowed and smiled, and went on genially:

"The lady you called Miss Anita, you so far called quite correctly. Her name is Anita; but it is only her second Christian name. She is known to the world as Miss Marjory Drake, of Chicago."

"Known to the world." Was this a mere phrase, or the simple expression of a fact! I asked directly:

"How known to the world? Do you mean that is the name known amongst her circle of acquaintances? Is—is there any cause why the great world outside that circle should know her at all?" He smiled and laid his hand on my shoulder in a very brotherly way as he answered:

"Yes, old fellow. There is a reason, and a good one, why the great world should know her. I see you are all in the dark; so I had better tell you what I know. Marjory Anita Drake is an heiress, a great heiress, a very great heiress; perhaps a long way the greatest heiress in America, or out of it. Her father, who died when she was a baby, left her a gigantic fortune; and her trustees have multiplied it over and over again." He paused; so I said—it seeming necessary to say something:

"But being an heiress is not sufficient reason why a girl should be known to the world."

"It is a pretty good one. Most people wouldn't want any better. But this is not the reason in her case. She is the girl who gave the battle ship to the American Government!"

"Gave the battle ship! I don't understand!"

"It was this way. At the time the reports kept crowding in of the Spanish atrocities on the *reconcentrados*; when public feeling was rising in the United States, this girl got all on fire to free Cuba. To this end she bought a battle ship that the Cramp's had built for Japan. She had the ship armed with Krupp cannon which she bought through friends in Italy; and went along the Eastern coast amongst the sailors and fishermen till she had recruited a crew. Then she handed the whole thing over to the Government as a spur to it to take some action. The ship is officered with men from the Naval Academy at Annapolis; and they tell me there isn't one of the crew—from the cabin boy to the captain—that wouldn't die for the girl to-morrow."

"Bravo!" I said instinctively! "That's a girl for a nation to be proud of!"

"She is all that!" said Cathcart enthusiastically. "Now you can understand why Adams congratulated you; and why he was so surprised when you did not seem to know who she was." I stood for a moment thinking, and all the clouds which wrapped Marjory's purpose in mystery seemed to disperse. This, then, was why she allowed the error of her name to pass. She had not made an *incognita*; chance had done this for her, and she had simply accepted it. Doubtless, wearied with praise and with publicity and notoriety in all its popular forms, she was glad to get away and hide herself for a while. Fortune had thrown in her way a man who was manifestly ignorant of her very existence; and it was a pleasure to play with him at hide-and-seek!

It was, after all, an up-to-date story of the Princess in disguise; and I was the young man, all unknowing, with whom she had played.

Here a terrible doubt assailed me. Other Princesses had played hide-and-seek; and, having had their sport, had vanished; leaving desolation and an empty heart behind them. Was it possible that she too was like this; that she had been all the while playing with me; that even whilst she was being most gracious, she was taking steps to hide even her whereabouts from me? Here was I, who had even proposed marriage; and yet who did not even know when or where I should see her again—if indeed I should ever see her again at all. I could not believe it. I had looked into her eyes, and had seen the truth. Here was no wanton playing at bowls with men's hearts. My life upon her faith!

I seemed to have lost myself in a sort of trance. I was recalled from it by Cathcart, who seeing me in a reverie had gone over to the fireplace and stood with his back to me, filling his pipe at the mantel-piece:

"I think I hear Adams coming. Pardon me, old fellow, but though I am sure he knows I have told you about Miss Drake, and though he probably made an excuse for delay so that I might have an opportunity to do so, he wants to appear not to enter on the subject. He is *diplomat* all over. Remember he is of the U. S. Embassy; and Miss Drake, as an American citizen, is theoretically under his care in this foreign country. Let us be talking of something else when he comes in!" Sam came along the passage softly whistling a bar of "Yankee Doodle." Cathcart nodded to me and whispered:

"I told you so! He takes good care that he may not surprise us." When he came in we were talking of the prospects of the Autumn fishing on the Dee.

When we left Cathcart's room, after a cigar, I, being somewhat tired with my long ride, went at once to my room. Adams came with me as far as the door.

I was just getting into bed when I heard a slight tap at the door. I unlocked it and found Adams without. He raised a warning hand, and said in a whisper:

"May I come in? I want to say something very privately." More than ever mystified—everything seemed a mystery now—I opened the door. He came in and I closed it softly and locked it.

XVII

Sam Adams's Task

Adams began at once: "Archie I want to tell you something; but it is in the strictest confidence. You must promise me not to mention to any one, mind *any one*, what I say; or even that I have spoken to you on the subject." I thought for a moment before replying. It flashed across me that what he had to say must concern Marjory, so I answered:

"I fear I cannot make such a promise, if the matter is regarding some one other than myself." A shade of annoyance passed across his face as he said:

"Well, it is about some one else; but really you must trust me. I would not for the world, old fellow, ask you to do anything that was not correct."

"I know that" I said "I know it right well; but you see it might be regarding some one with whom my relations might be peculiar—not fixed you know. It might be necessary for me to speak. Perhaps not now; but later on." I was stumbling blindly, so sought refuge in fact and query, "Tell me" I said "does it relate to Miss Drake?"

"It does; but I thought that you who are a friend of hers might like to do her a service."

"Of course I would." I answered. "There is nothing I would not do for her if it were in my power."

"Except hold your tongue!" he said with a touch of bitterness unusual with him. I could see that anxious as I was to hear he was still more anxious to tell me; so I was able to keep my temper and not make matters worse by answering back sarcastically. I said:

"Yes, old chap, even by holding my tongue. If I could see that I would benefit her by holding my tongue, or by cutting out my tongue, I would do it. What I must refuse is to *promise* to hold my tongue. Come, old fellow, don't put me in a wrong position. You don't know all that I do, or exactly how I am placed. Why don't you trust me? I am willing to promise that I won't speak at all of the matter unless it be necessary; and that I won't speak at all in any case of having been told anything by you." He brightened up at once and said:

"All right, then we can drive on. I take it that since we met last"—that was a few minutes ago, but he was a diplomatist—"you have learned more about Miss Drake, or rather of her history and her position and importance, than you knew at that time?"

"Yes," I answered, and I could not help smiling.

"Then we needn't go into that. We take facts for granted. Well, that fine act of hers—you know what I mean—has brought her, or may bring her, a peck of trouble. There are, or there were, a certain lot of Spaniards—Copperheads—at home who look on her as a sort of embodiment of the American antagonism to their own nation. They are the low lot; for mind you, though we are at war with them I say it, the good Spaniard is a fine fellow. It came to the ears of the authorities in Washington that there was some sort of plot on foot to do her a harm. The Secret Service was a little at fault, and couldn't get accurate or full information; for naturally enough the Spaniards didn't trust any but themselves in such a matter. We know enough, however, to be somewhat concerned for her; and it was arranged that a secret watch should be kept on her, so that no harm should come that could be prevented. The proper men had been detailed off for the work; when to our surprise, and a little to our consternation, it turned out that the young lady had disappeared. We knew of course that her going was voluntary; she had left word to that effect, so that there might not be any bother made about her. But the trouble was that she did not know of the danger which threatened her; and as our people didn't know where she was, no step could be taken to protect or warn her. It is clear that my lady got tired of fireworks and of the Joan of Arc business, and bolted. It was considered necessary at headquarters that we should in the meantime all keep our heads shut. But we were advised at the Embassy in London that the plot was on, and that we should hump ourselves a bit to look after her in case she was in England. The matter was handed over to me, and I have been on the run ever since; but I have not been able to hear tale or tiding of her. Two days ago we got a cable in our cipher which told us that, from information received and the rest of it, they suspected she was in England, or probably in Scotland; and that there was later evidence that the plot was more active than ever. Unfortunately we have as yet no details, and not even a clue. That is why I am here. I came down with Cathcart, who fortunately was bound for the North, as it covered up my purpose. I have been in a regular stew for days past. Marjory Drake is too good to have any trouble come to her that any American can help.

You can imagine my delight when I saw her this evening; for now that I have located her, I can take steps to look after her safety if necessary. You two went so fast on your wheels that I lost you at the Bridge; but I surmised that you would be coming here anyhow after your ride. So I came up as quickly as I could, and saw you two and the old lady come up from the railway station. I couldn't get to see Miss Drake to-night; but I expect to look her up pretty early in the morning."

Here was a new entanglement. It seemed to me as more than likely that Marjory, having seen Adams and knowing his diplomatic position, suspected some interference with her liberty, and made an escape at once. This, then, was the reason why she had asked me to stay and eat dinner alone; I was to cover up her tracks and secure her a night's delay. Thus, even to Adams, my tongue was tied as to her movements. I did not wish to seem to deceive him, so avoided the subject. In answer to him I asked:

"But tell me, old fellow, how and where do I come into your story? Why do you tell me this?" He answered very gravely:

"Because I want your help. This is, or rather may be, a very serious matter to Miss Drake. The whole business is entrusted by our government to my chief, who has detailed me on the service. It is of so delicate and secret a nature that I cannot make confidence with many people, and I am loth to trust any one but a gentleman. Besides Miss Drake is a very peculiar girl. She is absolutely independent, thoroughly determined, and more than plucky. If she knew there was a plot on foot, as likely as not she would try to encourage it out of mere recklessness; and would try to counterplot all by herself. Her enemies know this, and will avail themselves of every chance and of every false move of hers; so that she might help to work out herself the evil intended for her. This we cannot permit; and I am quite sure that you, who are a friend of hers, are at one with me here. Now, if you want to know exactly how you can help I will tell you; and you will, I am sure, pardon me if I say too much—or too little. If she were to know that the matter of her protection was a Government one, nothing on earth would make her yield herself to our views. But if it were suggested by a—a friend whom she—she valued, her action would probably be quite the opposite. She is a girl all heart and soul. When she is taken rightly you can lead her with a thread; but you can't drag her with gun-ropes. From what I saw yesterday, I am inclined to think that you might have more influence with her than any one else I could pick out."

I could not say anything to this, either positive or negative, so I remained silent. He went on:

"There is one other reason why I ask you to help, but it is secondary to the other one, believe me, and one I only use to fortify a better one. I ask you as an old friend to help me in a matter which, even if you are not concerned in it, may be of the utmost importance to me in my diplomatic career. This matter has been placed in my hands, and it would not do for me to fail. There is not much κυδος to be got out of it if all be well—except with my immediate chiefs; but if I failed it would go far against me. If Marjory Drake should suffer from this Spanish plot, she who had, so to speak, fired the torch of the nation in the war, it would be formal, official ruin to me. There wouldn't be a man from Maine to California, from the Lakes to the Gulf, who wouldn't look on me as an imbecile, or worse!" Whilst he was speaking I was thinking, and trying to make up my mind as to what I should do. Manifestly, I could not tell him of the dawning relations between Marjory and myself. I was not yet prepared to speak of the Pope's treasure. I could not in honour give away Marjory's confidence in me in asking me to cover up her escape, or the implied promise of my acceptance of it. Still, Adams's confidence required some measure of frankness from me. His last appeal to me as an old friend to help him as an individual in an important work, which might mar if it could not make him, demanded that I should stretch every point I could in his favour. So I said:

"Sam, I shall do all I honestly or honourably can. But I must ask you to wait a while and trust me. The fact is I am not at liberty just at present to turn any way I choose. I am already committed to certain confidences, which were made before I saw you or had any knowledge of what you tell me. Moreover, I am in certain ways ignorant in matters that you would not expect. I shall at once take every step I can to be in a position to speak to you more freely. I am more deeply stirred, old fellow, by what you have told me than I can say; and out of the depths of my heart I am grateful to you and your Government for your care for Miss Anita—Miss Drake. I may say this, that until to-morrow at all events, I am unable to help you in any possible way. Were I to try to do anything till a certain thing happens, it would hinder rather than help your purpose. So wait patiently and do please try to understand me."

He replied with unwonted sarcasm:

"Try to understand you! Why man alive I've been trying whilst you were speaking, until my brain reels. But I'm blamed if I can make head or tail of what you say. You seem to be snarled up in more knots than a conjuror. What the hell does it all mean? You don't seem to be able to turn anywhere or do anything, even when the safety or the life of such a girl as Marjory Drake is in question. On my faith Mr. Hunter I hope I don't make any mistake about you!"

"Yes, you do, Sam!" I said quietly, for I could not but feel that he had good cause for disappointment or even anger. "At the first moment I am free to do so, I shall tell you all I can; and you shall then see that I am only doing what you would under similar circumstances do yourself. Won't you trust me, old friend!" He gazed at me steadily for a few seconds, and then his look softened.

"By God I will!" he said, as he held out his hand.

"Now tell me," I said "what can I do to keep in touch with you. I must go back to Cruden in the morning. It is necessary." This was in answer to his questioning look. "It is the first step in my doing as you wish." I knew that Marjory would send to me, if at all, to Cruden. "But tell me how or where I can wire you in case we are not within hail." For answer he pulled out of his pocket a bundle of "priority" telegrams addressed to the United States Embassy in London.

"Take them and use them as may be required. I am in constant touch with the Embassy and they will know where to find me. How will I find you?"

"Send to me care of Post-office, Cruden Bay," I said, "I shall keep you advised of wherever I may be." With that we said good night.

"I shall see you in the morning," he said as he went out.

XVIII

Fireworks and Joan of Arc

For some time I did not sleep. Things were hurrying on so fast; and so many new events and facts and dangers were coming to light, that I hardly knew where to begin to think. Of course all things concerning Marjory, principally her safety, took the first place. What could be this Spanish plot; what could be its method or its purpose? At first when Adams had told me of it, I had not been much concerned; it seemed so far away, so improbable, that I fear I did not take it with sufficient gravity. I had not thought at the time that the two nations were actually at war, and that already, both before the war and during it, deeds of desperate treachery had been done, the memory of which were not even obliterated by the valour and chivalry which had been shown by the nobler of America's foes. *"Remember The Maine"* was still a watchword and war cry. There were many scoundrels, such as chiefly come to the surface in war time, who would undertake any work, however deadly, however brutal, however dangerous. Such villains might be at work even now! With a bound I was out upon the floor. In that moment of concrete thought of danger to Marjory I realised to the full the danger of my own ignorance of her situation, and even of the locality where she might be. This impotence to do anything was simply maddening; when I felt it I could not but understand the annoyance of Adams in feeling a measure of the same impotence, with what looked like my obstinacy added. But think how I would, I could do nothing till I should see Marjory or hear from her. With this thought, which, under the circumstances, was more than harrowing, I went back to bed.

I was waked by the knocking of Adams who in reply to my "Come," slipped in and shut the door behind him.

"They are gone!"

"Who?" I asked mechanically, though I well knew.

"Miss Drake and her friend. They went away last night, just after you came back from the station. By the way, I thought you dined with them?" he said interrogatively, and with a dash of suspicion in his tone.

"I was to dine with them;" I answered "but they were not there." He made a long pause.

"I don't understand!" he said. I felt that as the time which I was to cover had passed, I might speak; for all sakes I wanted to avoid collision with Adams or the appearance of deceiving him. So I said:

"I can tell you now, Sam. I was asked to dine last night with Mrs. Jack and Miss Anita—Miss Drake. When I came down to the room I found a letter saying that they had to go away and making a special request that I would dine alone, just as though they were there. I was not to say a word to any one about their being away. Please understand, my dear fellow—and I must ask you to take it that this is only a hint which you must accept and not attempt to follow up—that there are reasons why I should act on any request of Miss Drake's, blindfold. I told you last night that my hands were tied; this was one of the cords. To-day I hold myself free to explain I may now also tell you more. Last night I could do nothing. I could take no step myself, nor could I help you to take one; simply for the reason that I do not know where Miss Drake is staying. She is I know stopping, or was till lately, somewhere on the eastern side of Aberdeen County; but where the place is I have not the faintest idea. I expect to know very shortly; and the moment I know I will try to inform you, unless I am forbidden. You will know in time that I have spoken exact truth; though you may have found my words or meaning hard to understand. I am more than anxious to put Marjory on guard. When you left me last night, the whole deadly seriousness of the matter grew on me, till I was as miserable as a man can be." His face lightened as I spoke.

"Well," he said "at least we are one in the matter; that is something. I feared you were, and would be, working against me. Now look here, I have been thinking the matter over, and I daresay I have come nearer to understanding your position than you imagine. I don't want to limit or hamper you in working in your own way for Miss Drake's good; but I may tell you this. I mean to find her if I can, and in my own way. I am not fettered anywhere, except by the necessary secrecy. Outside of this I am free to act. I shall keep you advised at Cruden."

Before I was dressed I had another visitor. This time it was Cathcart who, with considerable diffidence and all the shamefaced embarrassment of an Englishman when doing a kindly action in which he may be taken as intruding, offered me his services. I tried to set him at ease by the heartiness of my thanks. Upon which he expanded enough to say:

"From something Adams let drop—in all confidence believe me—I gather you are or may be in trouble about some friend. If this should be, and from my heart I trust it may not, I hope you will bear in mind that I am a friend, and unattached. I am pretty well alone in the world so far as family is concerned, and there is no one to interfere with me. Indeed there are some who would be happy, for testamentary reasons, to attend my funeral. I hope you will remember this, old chap, if there is any fun going." Then he went away, easy of carriage and debonair as usual. It was in such wise that this gallant gentleman made me a proffer of his life. It moved me more than I can tell.

I went down to Cruden by the next train, and arranged with the postmaster to send on to me at once by messenger or wire any telegram that might come directed as I had told Adams.

Towards dusk a letter was brought to me. It was in Marjory's hand, and on my asking at once how it had come, I was told that it was brought by a mounted man who on handing it in had said "no answer" and had ridden away.

With hope and joy and misgiving mingled I opened it. All these feelings were justified by the few words it contained:

"Meet me to-morrow at eleven at Pircappies."

I passed the night with what patience I could, and rose early. At ten I took a light boat and rowed by myself from Port Erroll across the bay. I hung round outside the Skares, ostensibly fishing but keeping watch for any sign of Marjory; for from this point I could see the road to Whinnyfold and the path by the beach. A little before eleven I saw a woman wheeling a bicycle down the Whinnyfold laneway. Taking in my lines, I pulled, quietly and avoiding any appearance of hurry, for I knew not whether any one might see us, into the tiny harbour behind the jutting rock. Marjory arrived just at the same time, and I rejoiced to see that her face bore no mark or sign of care. As yet nothing had happened. We met with a slight hand shake; but there was a look in her eyes which made my heart leap. For the past thirty-six hours my anxiety for her had put aside every other feeling. I had not thought of myself, and therefore not of my love for her; but now my selfish instinct woke again in full force. In her presence, and in the jubilance of my own heart, fear in all forms seemed as impossible to realise as that the burning sun above us should be blotted out with falling snow. With one of her mysterious signs of silence she pointed to the rock that here stretches out into the sea, and whose top is crowned with long sea grass. Together we climbed the face of the cliff, and bearing across the narrow promontory passed over the top of the rock. We found a cosy nest hidden behind it. Here we were absolutely isolated from the world; out of earshot of every one, and out of sight except from beyond the stretch of rocky sea. In a demure way she acknowledged my satisfaction.

"Isn't it a nice place. I chose it out yesterday when I was here!" For an instant I felt as though she had struck me. Just to think that she had been here yesterday, whilst I was waiting for her only across the bay, eating my heart out. However, there was no use looking back. She was with me now, and we were alone. The whole delight of the thing swept away every other feeling. With a pretty little motion of settling herself comfortably, and which to me seemed to prelude a long talk, she began:

"I suppose you know a lot about me now?"

"How do you mean?"

"Come now, don't prevaricate. I saw Sam Adams in Aberdeen, and of course he told you all about me." I interrupted:

"No he didn't." The very tone of my voice enlightened her. With a smile she said:

"Then some one else did. Answer me some questions. What is my name?"

"Marjory Anita Drake."

"Am I poor?"

"In the way of money, no."

"Right! Why did I leave America?"

"To run away from the fireworks and the Joan of Arc business."

"Right again; but that sounds mighty like Sam Adams. Well, that's all right; now we may begin. I want to tell you something which you don't know." She paused. Half in delight and half in fear, for her appearance of purpose alarmed me, I set myself to listen.

XIX

ON CHANGING ONE'S NAME

With a smile Marjory began:

"You are satisfied that it was because of the fireworks and Joan of Arc business that I came away?"

"Oh yes!"

"And that this was the final and determining cause?"

"Why certainly!"

"Then you are wrong!" I looked at her in wonder and in some secret concern. If I were wrong in this belief, then why not in others? If Adams's belief and my acceptance of it were erroneous, what new mystery was there to be revealed? Just at present things had been looking so well for the accomplishment of my wishes that any disturbance must be unwelcome. Marjory, watching me from under her eyelashes, had by this time summed me up. The stern look which she always had when her brows were fixed in thought, melted into a smile which was partly happy, partly mischievous, and wholly girlish.

"Make your mind easy, Archie" she said, and oh! how my heart leaped when she addressed me by my Christian name for the first time. "There isn't anything to get uneasy about. I'll tell you what it was if you wish."

"Certainly I wish, if you don't dislike telling me."

So she went on:

"I did not mind the fireworks; that is I did mind them and liked them too. Between you and me, there has to be a lot of fireworks for one to object to them. People may say what they please, but it's only those who have not tasted popular favour that say they don't like it. I don't know how Joan of Arc felt, but I've a pretty cute idea that she was like other girls. If she enjoyed being cheered and made much of as well as I did, no wonder that she kept up the game as long as she could. What broke me all up was the proposals of marriage! It's all very well getting proposed to by people you know, and that you don't dislike. But when you get a washing basket full of proposals every morning by the post; when seedy looking scallywags ogle you; when smug young men with soft hats and no chins wait outside your door to hand you their own poems; and when greasy cranks stop your carriage to proffer their hearts to you before your servants, it becomes too much. Of course you can burn the letters, though there are some of them too good and too honest not to treat their writers with respect. But the cranks and egotists, and scallywags and publicans and sinners, the loafers that float round one like an unwholesome miasma; these are too many and too various, and too awful to cope with. I felt the conviction so driven in to me that the girl, or at any rate her personality, counts for so little, but that her money, or her notoriety, or celebrity or whatever it is, counts for so much, that I couldn't bear to meet strangers at all. Burglars and ghosts and tigers and snakes and all kinds of things that dart out on you are bad enough; but I tell you that proposers on the pounce are a holy terror. Why, at last I began to distrust everyone. There wasn't an unmarried man of my acquaintance that I didn't begin to suspect of some design; and then the funny part of it was that if they didn't come up to the scratch I felt aggrieved. It was awfully unfair wasn't it? But I could not help it. I wonder if there is a sort of moral jaundice which makes one see colours all wrong! If there is, I had it; and so I just came away to get cured if I could.

"You can't imagine the freedom which it was to me not to be made much of and run after. Of course there was a disappointing side to it; I'm afraid people's heads swell very quick! But, all told, it was delightful. Mrs. Jack had come with me, and I had covered up my tracks at home so that no one would be worried. We ran up to Canada, and at Montreal took a steamer to Liverpool. We got out, however, at Moville. We had given false names, so that we couldn't be tracked." Here she stopped; and a shy look grew over her face. I waited, for I thought it would embarrass her less to tell things in her own way than to be asked questions. The shy look grew into a rosy blush, through which came that divine truth which now and again can shine from a girl's eyes. She said in quite a different way from any in which she had spoken to me as yet; with a gentle appealing gravity:

"That was why I let you keep the wrong impression as to my name. I couldn't bear that you, who had been so good to me, should, at the very start of our—our friendship, find me out in a piece of falsity. And then when we knew each other better, and after you had treated me with so much confidence about the Second Sight and Gormala and the Treasure, it made me feel so guilty every time I thought of it that I was ashamed to speak." She stopped and I ventured to take her hand. I said in as consolatory a way as I could:

"But my dear, that was not any deceit—to me at any rate. You took another name to avoid trouble before ever I even saw you; how then could I be aggrieved. Besides" I added, feeling bolder as she did not make any effort to draw away her hand, "I should be the last person in the world to object to your changing your name!"

"Why?" she asked raising her eyes to mine with a glance which shot through me. This was pure coquetry; she knew just as well as I did what I meant. All the same, however, I said:

"Because I too want you to change it!" She did not say a word, but looked down.

I was now sure of my ground, and without a word I bent over and kissed her. She did not draw back. Her arms went round me; and in an instant I had a glimpse of heaven.

Presently she put me away gently and said:

"There was another reason why I did not speak all that time. I can tell it to you now."

"Pardon me" I interrupted "but before you tell me, am I to take it that—well, what has just been between us—is an affirmative answer to my question?" Her teeth flashed as well as her eyes as she answered:

"Have you any doubt? Was there any imperfection in the answer? If so, perhaps we had better read it as 'no.'"

My answer was not verbal; but it was satisfactory to me. Then she went on:

"I can surely tell you now at all events. Have you still doubts?"

"Yes" said I, "many, very many, hundreds, thousands, millions, all of which are clamouring for instant satisfaction!" She said quietly and very demurely, at the same time raising that warning hand which I already well knew, and which I could not but feel was apt to have an influence on my life, though I had no doubt but that it would always be for good:

"Then as there are so many, there is not the slightest use trying to deal with them now."

"All right" I said "we shall take them in proper season and deal with them seriatim." She said nothing, but she looked happy.

I felt so happy myself that the very air round us, and the sunshine, and the sea, seemed full of joyous song. There was music even in the screaming of the myriad seagulls sweeping overhead, and in the wash of the rising and falling waves at our feet. I kept my eyes on Marjory as she went on to speak:

"Oh, it is a delight to be able to tell you now what a pleasure it was to me to know that you, who knew nothing of me, of my money, or my ship, or all the fireworks and Joan of Arc business—I shall never forget that phrase—had come to me for myself alone. It was a pleasure which I could not help prolonging. Even had I had no awkwardness in telling my name, I should have kept it back if possible; so that, till we had made our inner feelings known to each other, I should have been able to revel in this assurance of personal attraction;" I was so happy that I felt I could interrupt:

"That sounds an awfully stilted way of putting it, is it not?" I said. "May I take it that what you mean is, that though you loved me a little—of course after I had shown you that I loved you a great deal—you still wished to keep me on a string; so that my ignorance of your extrinsic qualities might add a flavour to your enjoyment of my personal devotion?"

"You talk" she said with a joyful smile "like a small book with gilt edges! And now, I know you want to know more of my surroundings, where we are living and what are our plans."

Her words brought a sort of cold shiver to me. In my great happiness I had forgotten for the time all anxiety for her safety. In a rush there swept over me all the matters which had caused me such anguish of mind for the last day and a half. She saw the change in me, and with poetic feeling put in picturesque form her evident concern:

"Archie, what troubles you? your face is like a cloud passing over a cornfield!"

"I am anxious about you" I said. "In the perfection of happiness which you have given me, I forgot for the moment some things that are troubling me." With infinite gentleness, and with that sweet tenderness which is the sympathetic facet of love, she laid her hand on mine and said:

"Tell me what troubles you. I have a right to know now, have I not?" For answer I raised her hand and kissed it; then holding it in mine I went on:

"At the same time that I learned about you, I heard of some other things which have caused me much anxiety. You will help to put me at ease, won't you?"

"Anything you like I shall do. I am all yours now!"

"Thank you, my darling, thank you!" was all I could say; her sweet surrender of herself overwhelmed me. "But I shall tell you later; in the meantime tell me all about yourself, for that is a part of what I wait for." So she spoke:

"We are living, Mrs. Jack and I, in an old Castle some miles back in the country from here. First I must tell you that Mrs. Jack is my old nurse. Her husband had been a workman of my father's in his pioneer days. When Dad made his own pile he took care of Jack—Jack Dempsey his name was, but we never called him anything but Jack. His wife was Mrs. Jack then, and has been so ever since to me. When mother died, Mrs. Jack, who had lost her husband a little while before, came to take care of me. Then when father died she took care of everything; and has been like a mother to me ever since. As I dare say you have noticed, she has never got over the deferential manner which she used to have in her poorer days. But Mrs. Jack is a rich woman as women go; if some of my proposers had an idea of how much money she has they would never let her alone till she married some one. I think she got a little frightened at the way I was treated; and there was a secret conviction that she might be the next to suffer. If it hadn't been for that, I doubt if she would ever, even to please me, have fallen in with my mad scheme of running away under false names. When we came to London we saw the people at Morgan's; and the gentleman who had charge of our affairs undertook to keep silence as to us. He was a nice old man, and I told him enough of the state of affairs for him to understand that I had a good reason for lying dark. I thought that Scotland might be a good place to hide in for a time; so we looked about amongst the land agents for a house where we would not be likely to be found. They offered us a lot; but at last they told us of one between Ellon and Peterhead, way back from the road. We found it in a dip between a lot of hills where you would never suspect there was a house at all, especially as it was closely surrounded with a wood. It is in reality an old castle, built about two or three hundred years ago. The people who own it—Barnard by name, are away, the agent told us, and the place was to let year after year but no one has ever taken it. He didn't seem to know much about the owners as he had only seen their solicitor; but he said they might come some time and ask to visit the house. It is an interesting old place, but awfully gloomy. There are steel trellis gates, and great oak doors bound with steel, that rumble like thunder when you shut them. There are vaulted roofs; and windows in the thickness of the wall, which though they are big enough to sit in, are only slits at the outside. Oh! it is a perfect daisy of an old house. You must come and see it! I will take you all over it; that is, over all I can, for there are some parts of it shut off and locked up."

"When may I go?" I asked.

"Well, I had thought," she answered, "that it would be very nice if you were to get your wheel and ride over with me to-day."

"Count me in every time! By the way what is the name of the place?"

"Crom Castle. Crom is the name of the little village, but it is a couple of miles away." I paused a while thinking before I spoke. Then with my mind made up I said:

"Before we leave here I want to speak of something which, however unimportant you may think it, makes me anxious. You will let me at the beginning beg, won't you, that you do not ask me who my informant is, or not to tell you anything except what I think advisable." Her face grew grave as she said:

"You frighten me! But Archie, dear, I trust you. I trust you; and you may speak plainly. I shall understand."

XX

COMRADESHIP

I want you to promise me that you will not hide yourself where I cannot find you. I have grave reason for the request. Also, I want you, if you will, to let some others know where you are." At first there was instinctive defiance in her mouth and nostrils. Then her brows wrinkled in thought; the sequence was an index to character which I could not but notice. However the war was not long; reason, whatever was the outcome of its dominance, triumphed over impulse. I thought I could understand the logical process which led to her spoken conclusion:

"You want to report me to 'Uncle Sam'."

"That's about it!" I answered, and hurried on to give her a reason before she made up her mind to object.

"Remember, my dear, that your nation is at war; and, though you are at present safe in a country friendly to both belligerents, there are evil-minded people in all countries who will take advantage of anything unusual, to work their own ends. That splendid gift of yours to the nation, while it has made you a public favourite and won for you millions of friends—and proposals—has yet made for you a host of enemies. It is not as if you had given a hospital-ship or an ambulance. Your gift belongs to the war side and calls out active hatred; and no doubt there are men banded together to do you harm. This cannot be allowed. Your friends, and the nation as a whole, would take any step to prevent such a thing; but they might all be powerless if you were hidden anywhere where they could not find you." As I spoke, Marjory looked at me keenly, not with hostility, but with genuine interest. When I had finished she said quietly:

"That is very well; but now tell me, dear"—how the word thrilled me; it was the first time she had used it to me—"did Sam Adams fill you up with that argument, or is it your own? Don't think me nasty; but I want to know something of what is going on. Believe me, I am willing to do all *you* wish if it is your own will; and I am grateful for your thought for me. But I don't want you to be a mere mouthpiece for any party moves by the politicians at home."

"How do you mean?"

"My dear boy, I don't suppose you know enough of American politics to see how a certain lot would use to their own advantage anything that came in their way. Anybody or anything which the public takes an interest in would be, and is, used by them unscrupulously. Why, if the hangers-on to the war party wanted to make a show, they might enroll my proposers and start a new battalion."

"But," I remonstrated, "you don't think the Government is like that?" In reply she smiled:

"I don't altogether know about that. Parties are parties all the world over. But of course the Washington people wouldn't do things that are done by local politicians. And one other thing. Don't imagine for a moment that I think Sam Adams is anything of the kind. He belongs to the service of the nation and takes his orders from his chief. How can he, or any one fixed like him, know the ins and outs of things; except from what he hears privately from home, or gathers from what goes on around him if he is cute?" It appeared to me that all this was tending to establish an argument against taking the American Embassy into confidence, so I struck in before it should be complete. As I was not at liberty to take Marjory into confidence with regard to my source of information, I had to try to get her to agree to what I thought right or necessary on other grounds:

"My dearest, can you not leave out politics, American or otherwise. What on earth have politics to do with us?" She opened her eyes in wonder; she was reasoning better than I was. With an air of conviction she said:

"Why, everything! If any one wants to do me harm, it must be on the grounds of politics. I don't believe there is any one in the world who could want to injure me on private grounds. Oh! my dear, I don't want to talk about it, not even to you; but all my life I have tried to help other people in a quiet way. My guardians would tell you that I have asked them for too much money to give to charities; and personally I have tried to do what a girl can in a helpful way to others. I have been in hospitals and homes of all kinds; and I have classes of girls in my own house and try to make them happier and better. Archie, don't think poorly of me for speaking like this; but I couldn't bear that *you* should think I had no sense of the responsibility of great wealth. I have always looked on it as a trust; and I hope, my dear, that in time to come you will help me to bear the burden and to share the trust!" I had thought up to now that I couldn't love her more than I did. But when I heard her words, and recognised the high purpose that lay behind them, and saw the sweet embarrassment which came to her in speaking them to me, I felt that I had been mistaken. She looked at me lovingly, and, holding my hand in both of hers, went on:

"What then could hurt me except it came from the political side. I could quite understand it if Spaniards wished to harm me, for I have done what I can to hinder them from murdering and torturing other victims. And I could understand if some of our own low-down politicians would try to use me as a stalking horse, though they wouldn't harm me. I want to keep clear of politics; and I tell you frankly that I shall if I can."

"But Marjory dear, there may be, I believe there are, Spaniards who would try to harm you. If you were in America you would be safer from them; for there at present, whilst the war is on, every stranger is a marked man. Here, on neutral ground, foreigners are free; and they are not watched and observed in the same way. If there were such fiends, and I am told there are, they might do you a harm before any one could know their intention or have time to forestall them."

All the native independence of Marjory's race and nature stood out in strong relief as she answered me:

"My dear Archie, I come from a race of men who have held their lives in their hands from the cradle to the grave. My father, and my grandfather, and my great grandfather were pioneers in Illinois, in Kentucky, in the Rockies and California. They knew that there were treacherous foes behind them every hour of their lives; and yet they were not afraid. And I am not afraid either. Their blood is in my veins, and speaks loudly to me when any sense of fear comes near me. Their brains, as well as their hands, kept guard on their lives; and my brains are like theirs. I do not fear any foe, open or secret. Indeed, when I think of a secret foe all the keenness of my people wakes in me, and I want to fight. And this secret work is a way in which a woman can fight in an age like ours. If my enemies plot, I can counter-plot; if they watch without faltering to catch me off guard, I can keep guard unflinchingly. A woman can't go out now-a-days, except at odd times, and fight with weapons like Joan of Arc, or the Maid of Saragossa; but she can do her fighting in her own way, level with her time. I don't see that if there is to be danger around me, why I shouldn't do as my ancestors did, fight harder than their foes. Here! let me tell you something now, that I intended to say later. Do you know what race of men I come from? Does my name tell you nothing? If not, then this will!"

She took from her neck, where again it had been concealed by a lace collar, the golden jewel which I had rescued from the sea. As I took it in my hand and examined it she went on:

"That came to me from my father, who got it from his, and he from his, on and on till our story of it, which is only verbal, for we have no records, is lost in the legend that it is a relic of the Armada brought to America by two cousins who had married, both being of the family to which the great Sir Francis Drake belonged. I didn't know, till lately, and none of us ever did, where exactly in the family the last owners of the brooch came in, or how they became possessed of such a beautiful jewel. But you have told me in your translation of Don de Escoban's narrative. That was the jewel that Benvenuto Cellini made in duplicate when he wrought the figurehead for the Pope's galley. The Pope gave it to Bernardino de Escoban, and he gave it to Admiral Pedro de Valdes. I have been looking up the history of the time since I saw you, and I found that Admiral de Valdes when he was taken prisoner by Sir Francis Drake at the fight with the Armada was kept, pending his ransom, in the house of Richard Drake, kinsman of Sir Francis. How the Drake family got possession of the brooch I don't know; but anyhow I don't suppose they stole it. They were a kindly lot in private, any of them that I ever knew; though when they were in a fight they fought like demons. The old Spanish Dons were generous and free with their presents, and I take it that when Pedro de Valdes got his ransom he made the finest gift he could to those who had been kind to him. That is the way I figure it out."

Whilst she was speaking, thoughts kept crowding in upon me. Here was indeed the missing link in the chain of Marjory's connection with the hidden treasure; and here was the beginning of the end of Gormala's prophecy, for as such I had come to regard it. The Fates were at work upon us. Clotho was spinning the thread which was to enmesh Marjory and myself and all who were in the scheme of the old prophecy of the Mystery of the Sea and its working out.

Once more the sense of impotence grew upon me. We were all as shuttlecocks, buffeted to and fro without power to alter our course. With the thought came that measure of resignation which is the anodyne to despair. In a sort of trance of passivity I heard Marjory's voice run on:

"Therefore, my dear Archie, I will trust to you to help me. The comradeship which has been between us, will never through this grow less; though nearer and dearer and closer ties may seem to overshadow it."

I could not answer such reasoning; but I took her in my arms and kissed her. I understood, as she did, that my kisses meant acquiescence in her wishes. After a while I said to her:

"One thing I must do. I owe it as a duty of honour to tell my informant that I am unable to give your address to the American Embassy, and that I cannot myself take a part in anything which is to be done except by your consent. But oh! my dear, I fear we are entering on a dangerous course. We are all staying deliberately in the dark, whilst there is light to be had; and we shall need all the light which we can get." Then a thought struck me and I added, "By the way, I suppose I am free to give information how I can, so long as you are not committed or compromised?" She thought for quite a few minutes before she answered. I could see that she was weighing up the situation, and considering it from all points of view. Then she said, putting both her hands in mine:

"In this, as in all ways, Archie, I know that I can trust you. There is so much more than even this between us, that I should feel mean to give it a thought hereafter!"

XXI

The Old Far West and the New

Presently Marjory jumped up and said:

"Now you must get your wheel and come over to Crom. I am burning to show it to you!" We crossed the little isthmus and climbed the rocks above the Reivie o' Pircappies. As we topped the steep path I almost fell back with the start I gave.

There sat Gormala MacNiel, fixed and immovable as though she were of stone. She looked so unconcerned that I began to suspect her. At first she seemed not to notice us; but I could see that she was looking at us under her eyelashes. I was anxious to find out how long she had been there, so I said, mentioning her name in order that Marjory might know who she was:

"Why, Gormala, what has become of you? I thought you were off again to the Islands. We haven't seen you for a long time." She replied in her usual uncompromising way:

"I hae nae doot that ye thocht me far, gin ye did na see me. Aye! Aye! the time has been lang; but I could wait: I could wait!"

"What were you waiting for?" Marjory's voice seemed almost as that of a being from another world. It was so fresh, so true, so independent that it seemed at variance with Gormala and her whole existence. As a man beside two women, I felt more as a spectator than as a participant, and my first general impression was that the New World was speaking to the Old. Gormala seemed to me absolutely flabbergasted. She stared, and looked in a dazed way, at the girl, standing up as she did so with the instinctive habit, ingrained through centuries of custom, of an inferior to a superior. Then she moved her hand across her forehead, as though to clear her brain, before she replied:

"What was I waitin' for? I'll tell ye, an ye will. I was waitin' for the fulfillment o' the Doom. The Voices hae spoken; and what they hae said, will be. There be them that would stand in the way o' Fate, and would try to hinder the comin' that must be. But they will fail; they will fail! They can no more block the river o' time wi' ony deeds o' mon, than they can dam the spate wi' a bairn's playtoy." Again came Marjory's searching question, with all the mystery-dispelling freshness of her unfettered youth; and indeed it seemed as if the Old-world mystery could not hold its dignity in the face of overt, direct questioning:

"By the way, what was it that the Doom said? Was it anything that an American girl can understand?" Gormala gazed at her in manifest wonder. To her, reared in the atmosphere of the Old Far West, this product of the New Far West seemed like a being of another world. Had Marjory been less sweet in her manner than she was, or less fair to look upon, less dignified, or less grave, the old woman would probably have shown hostility at once. But it seemed to me impossible that even a witch-woman could be hostile to Marjory to-day. She looked so sweet, and kind and happy; so bright and joyous; so much like the incarnation of ideal girlhood, that criticism was disarmed, and hostility could not force a way into the charmed circle of that radiant presence. To me, her attitude towards Gormala was incomprehensible. She knew Gormala, for I had told her of who and what the Seer was, and of the prophecies and warnings that she had already uttered; and yet from her manner she appeared ignorant of all concerning both her and them. She was not conciliatory after the manner of the young who wish to please the old, or to ingratiate themselves with them. She was not hostile, as would be one who had determined on opposition. About her or her manner there was nothing hard, or frivolous or contradictory. And yet it was apparent to me that she had some fixed, determined purpose of her own; and it became before long apparent to me also, that the other woman knew, or at any rate suspected, such an existence, though she could neither comprehend nor locate it. Gormala seemed once, twice, as though she were about to speak, but hesitated; at last with an effort she spoke out:

"The Voice o' the Doom no sounds in words such as mortals can hear. It is spoken in sounds that are heard of the inner ear. What matter the words, when the ear that hearkens can understan'!"

"But," said Marjory, "could I not be told the words, or if there were no actual words, could you not give me in your own words what the sounds uttered seemed to you to mean?" To anyone but a Seer such a request would seem reasonable enough; but visionaries who have a receptive power of their own, and who learn by means whose methods are unconscious to them, can hardly undertake to translate the dim, wide-stretching purpose of the powers of the Unknown into bald, narrow, human speech. Gormala's brows wrinkled up in thought; then a scowl of disappointment swept over her face. In an angry tone she turned to me and said:

"Wha be yon lassie that questions so blithely the truth o' the Voice that is kent by ye an' me? Why dinna ye tak her awa' before she mocks me, an' in me the Doom; an' I speak oot to her?" Marjory spoke up for herself.

"Please do not think it a liberty to ask you; but I should like so much to know exactly what was said. It is so easy for people to confuse ideas when words are loosely used. Don't you find it so?" I do not think Gormala MacNiel had any humour at all; if she had, I had certainly never seen any trace of it. Had it been there it would have surely saved her from anger; for there was something delicious in the way in which Marjory put her question, as though to one of her own kind and holding the same views as herself on general matters. Gormala did not like it. Though there was a blank in her mind as to the existence of humour, she must have felt conscious of the blank. She could not understand the other woman; and for a little while sought refuge in a silence composed of about equal parts of sulk and dignity. But Marjory was not content with silence; she pressed home her question in the most polite but most matter of fact way, till I could see the Witch-woman mentally writhe. I should have interfered, for I did not want any unpleasant scene in which Marjory must have a part; but I felt that the girl had some purposeful meaning in her persistence. Had Gormala had a pause in the attack she would, I felt, have gone away and bided her time: but in such a pushing of the matter as Marjory braced herself to, there could be no withdrawal, unless under defeat. Gormala looked round now and again, as one, man or animal, does when hunted; but each time she restrained herself by an effort. At last her temper began to rise; her face flushed, and the veins, of passion stood out on her forehead. Her eyes flashed, and white marks began to come and go about the face, especially round the nose. I could see from the leap of fire in Marjory's eyes that this was what she was waiting for. She lowered her voice, and the tone of her speaking, till both matter and manner were icily chill; but all the time she persisted in her matter-of-fact questioning.

At last Gormala's temper broke, and she turned on the girl in such a fury that for a few seconds I thought she was going to attack her physically. I stood ready to hold her off if necessary. At the first moment the passion in her was so great that she spoke in Gaelic; blind, white-hot fury will not allow a choice of tongues. The savage in her was speaking, and it spoke in the tongue it knew best. Of course neither of us could understand it, and we only stood smiling. Marjory smiled deliberately as though to exasperate her; I smiled because Marjory was smiling. Presently, through the tumult of her passion, Gormala began to realise that we did not understand her; and, with an effort which shook her, began to speak in English. With the English which she had, came intention and the restraint which it implies. Her phrases were not common curses, but rather a picturesque half prophecy with a basis of hate. The gravamen of her charge was that Marjory had scoffed against the Doom and Fate and the Voices. To me, who had suffered the knowledge to which she appealed, the attack was painful. What was charged was a sort of natural sacrilege; and it wounded me and angered me to see Marjory made the subject of any attack. I was about to interfere, when with a gesture, which the Witch-woman did not see, she warned me to silence. She struck into the furious woman's harangue with quiet, incisive, cultured voice which made the other pause:

"Indeed you do me a wrong; I scoffed at nothing. I should not scoff at your religion any more than I should at my own. I only asked you a few questions as to facts which seemed to touch a friend of mine." The point of this speech which, strange to say, affected the woman most was regarding her religion:

"Wha be ye, ye hizzie, that wad daur to misca' me that is a Christian woman all my days. What be your releegion, that ye try to shame me wi' mine." Marjory said deliberately, but with all the outward appearance of courtesy:

"But I did not know that in the scheme of the Christian belief there were such things as the Doom and the Voice and Fate!" The old woman towered up; for a moment she was all Seer and Prophet. Her words thrilled through me; and I could see through Marjory also. Though she held herself proudly, her lips grew pale:

"Then learn while ye may that there be lesser powers as well as greater in the scheme o' God's warld, and o' His working o' the wonders therein. Ye may scoff at me wha' am after all but an aud wife; though one to whom are Visions given, and in whose ears the Voice has spoken. Ye may pride yersel' that yer ignorance is mair than the knowledge o' ithers. Ye may doot the truths that hae been garnered oot o' centuries o' dour experience, an' tak' the cloak o' yer ignorance as an answer to a' the mysteries that be. But mark me weel! the day will come—it is no far aff the noo—when ye will wring yer honds, and pray wi' all the power an' bitter grief o' yer soul for some licht to guide ye that ye no hae had yet!" She paused and stood in a sort of trance, stiffening all over like a pointer at mark. Then she raised one hand high over her head, so that the long arm seemed to extend her gaunt form to an indefinite length. With a far-away solemn voice she spoke:

"I see ye too, though no by yer lanes, in the wild tide-race amang the rocks in the dark nicht, mid leaping waves. An' lo! o'er the waste o' foam is a floatin' shroud!" Then she stopped, and in a few seconds came back to herself. In the meantime Marjory, whose lips had grown white as death, though she never lost her proud bearing, groped blindly for my hand and held it hard. She never for a moment took her eyes off the other.

When Gormala was quite her own woman again, she turned without a word and walked away in her gaunt, stately manner, feeling I am sure, as we did, that she did not go without the honours of war. Marjory continued to watch her until she had passed up the track, and had disappeared behind the curve of the hill.

Then, all at once, she seemed to collapse in a faint; and had I not held her hand, and so was able to draw her into my arms, she must have fallen to the ground.

In a wonderfully short time she recovered her senses, and then with a great effort stood up; though she still had to steady herself by my hand. When she was all right again she said to me:

"I suppose you wonder why I attacked her like that. Oh! yes, I did attack her; I meant to," for she saw the question in my eyes. "It was because she was so hostile to you. What right had she to force you to do anything? She is harmful to you, Archie. I know it! I know it! I know it! and I determined not to let her have her way. And besides,"—this with a shy loving look at me, "as she is hostile to you she must be to me also. I want to be with you, even in the range of the hate and the love of others. That is to be one; and as we are to fight together I must share your lot in all!" I took her in my arms, and for some divine moments, our hearts beat together.

In those moments my mind was made up as to the wishes of Adams. How could I refuse in any way to fight the battle, as she might wish it fought, of a girl who so loyally shared my lot!

Then we arranged that I should go home for my bicycle, and meet Marjory at the bridge by the Parish Church.

XXII

CROM CASTLE

When I rejoined Marjory, we went up the high road and then turned off by a by-way which took us round innumerable slopes and mounds, so characteristic of this part of Aberdeen. The entire county, seen from high places, looks bare and open; but it has its hills and hollows in endless variety. From the cross road we turned up another and still another, till I lost my bearings entirely.

The part of the country where we now were was a sort of desolation of cultivation; endless low hills clad with fields of wheat and barley with never a house to be seen, except some far off cottage or the homestead of a laird perched on the top of a hill. At last we entered through an open gateway with broken pillars, still bearing the remains of some armorial device in statuary. There was an avenue, fringed with tall trees on either side, and beyond a broad belt of undergrowth. The avenue wound round and round in an endless series of curves. From the gate where we entered was a thick, close wood nearly a quarter of a mile in width. Here the trees stood so close, and their locking branches made such a screen, that it was quite gloomy within. Here too the road was made in perpetual curves, so that it was not possible to see far ahead. Indeed I remarked to Marjory as we rode along:

"No wonder you chose this as a place to hide in; it looks as if it was made for concealment. It is a regular Rosamund's Bower!"

When we had passed through the wood, we came out on a great piece of level ground with a wide mound some twenty feet high, in the midst of it. On this was built of granite, a crenelated castle. It was not very high, but extended wide in a square, with a low arched doorway in front of us through which it might be possible to drive with care. The doorway was closed by two gates; first a massive network of interlocking steel bars of seemingly foreign workmanship, and secondly great gates of oak fortified with steel bands and massive bosses of hammered iron. Before going in, Marjory took me right round the castle and I saw that it was the same on all four sides. It was built by the points of the compass; but there was no gateway except on one side. The ordinary way of entering was by a more modern door on the south side. From inside the castle it was not possible to see anywhere beyond the wood. Even from the stone roof, made for defence, where Marjory took me, it was only possible to get a glimpse through the tree tops here and there of round-topped hills yellow with ripening grain or crowned with groves of scanty wind-swept pine trees. Altogether it was as gloomy a place as I had ever seen. It was cut off altogether from the outer world; one might remain in it for a life-time unknown.

Inside it was, if possible, more gloomy. Small rooms almost everywhere, except the great hall, and one room at the top facing the south side which lay just under the roof and which was lined with old oak. Here there were quite a number of windows such as Marjory had described, all of them, though wide on the inner side, narrowed to mere slits on the outer. In castles and houses built, like this, for defence, it did not do to allow opportunities to an attacking force to send missiles within.

Mrs. Jack and Marjory had made this their living room, and here were all the pretty treasures and knick-knacks which they had gathered on their travels. The old lady welcomed me warmly. Then Marjory took her aside and told her something in whispers. I could guess what it was; but any doubts I might have had were dispelled when she came over and kissed me and said:

"Indeed, I congratulate you with all my heart. You have won the best, and sweetest, and dearest girl that ever drew breath. I have been with her all my life; and I have not found a flaw in her yet. And I am glad that it is you whom she has chosen. Somehow, I wished it from the first moment I saw you. That you may both be happy, I pray the good Lord God! And I know you will; for you are true, and Marjory has a heart of gold."

"A heart of gold!" Her words had given me more than pleasure; but the last phrase pulled my joy up short. A cold shiver ran through me. A golden man had been a part of the prophecy of the Mystery of the Sea; and only a little while ago Gormala had in her vision seen Marjory struggling in the tide-race with a shroud in the air.

I think Marjory felt something of the same kind, for she looked at me anxiously and grew a little pale. She said nothing, however, and I thought it better to pass the matter by. Although Marjory had heard the expression of the Witch-woman's vision, and though I had told her of my first experience of the old rhyming prophecy, the former was at a time when neither I myself nor the whole mystery was of any special importance to her. She might not have remembered it; I trusted that this was so.

However, we could not either of us be sad for long to-day. Our joy was too fresh to be dimmed by any thought of gloom, except momentarily as a mirror is by a passing breath.

Tea in the old oak room was a delight, with the afternoon sun coming in slantwise through the narrow windows and falling in lines of light across the floor. Marjory made the tea and served me; and each time I took anything from her hand our fingers met, she no more than myself avoiding the touch. Then, leaving the old lady upstairs, she took me through the various rooms; and in her pretty, impulsive way she told me all the romances which she had already woven about them in her brain. She came and saw me off; with her kiss of good-bye on my lips I rode back through the gloomy wood, feeling as proud and valiant as a knight of old.

I found my way to Ellon and went on the train to Aberdeen, for I felt it due to Adams that I should see him at once. It was impossible to write all I had to say; and besides I wanted to retain his good will, and to arrange for securing his aid, if he would consent to do so under our altered conditions.

I found him in his room hard at work. He was writing something which I suppose he considered important, for he put it carefully away and locked his despatch box before we began to talk. Of course it might have been only his diplomatic habit; but he seemed grave over it. I entered at once on the matter between us, for I thought to get the disagreeable side over first and let concessions and alterations follow:

"I am sorry, Sam, I shall not be able to help you with information regarding Miss Drake."

"Why? Haven't you heard from her?"

"It is not that; but I am not free to do what you wish." Adams looked at me for a long time. Then he said quietly:

"I see. You have your orders! Well, I am sorry for it; it may bring dreadful harm to her, and I daresay to you too, now. Say, old chap, is that decision of yours final? The matter is more grave than I thought when I saw you last. We have had more information, and they are pressing us from Washington to take all precautions we can. Come, won't you help me—help her?"

"I can't, the way you say. Sam Adams, you know I would do anything I could for you; but in this matter I am pledged. I have been given a secret, and I must keep it honourably at all hazards. But look here, I am anxious all the same. Can't you trust me a little bit and tell me what to look for. I won't give you away; and I may be able to carry out your wishes as to helping to guard her, though I have to do it in my own way." He smiled, though very bitterly and ironically. I was glad to see the smile anyhow, for we were old and tried friends and I should not like there to be any break between us. Besides I wanted his help; his knowledge now, and his resources later on, if need should be. He was an official, and the matter was an official one though his heart was in it; it was not as if his personal feelings or his honour had been involved.

"Well," he said, "you have a fine gall anyhow! You refuse point blank to give me the slightest help, though I ask it on all grounds, official for America, personal as I am in charge, and for the sake of your own girl; and then you expect me to tell you all I can. Well, look here, I'll tell you anything that will help you as soon as I know it, if you will keep me advised of exactly where you are—so—so that I may be able to find you if I wish."

I told him heartily that I would keep him posted as to my movements. Then, as there was nothing to remain for, I said good-bye—a good-bye, I am glad to say, given and taken with our old heartiness. Before I went I said:

"Sam, you know how a message can find me if there is anything you should think it well to tell me." To which he replied:

"All right, Archie, I'll remember. You understand that as I shall have to work this racket alone I must do it in my own way: otherwise we shall have complications. But if there is anything I can do on your side, I shall do it all the same. You know how to reach me. If you send for me I shall come any hour of the day or night. And say, old chap, I go heeled!" he pointed to his pistol pocket. "Let me advise you to do the same just at present!"

I took his advice and bought in Aberdeen, before returning to Cruden, two of the finest revolvers I could get. One of them was made for a lady; the other I always carried myself from that day forward.

XXIII

SECRET SERVICE

Next morning after breakfast I wheeled over to Crom, bringing in my bicycle bag the revolver and ammunition for Marjory. I could not but feel alarmed for her safety as I rode through the wood which surrounded the house. It would need a regiment to guard one from a stray assassin. For myself I did not have any concern; but the conviction grew and grew on me to the point of agony that harm which I should be powerless to prevent might happen here to Marjory. When I was inside the house the feeling was easier. Here, the place was to all intents and purposes fortified, for nothing short of cannon or dynamite could make any impression on it.

Marjory received my present very graciously; I could see from the way that she handled the weapon that she had little to learn of its use. I suppose the thought must have crossed her that I might think it strange to find her so familiar with a lethal weapon, for she turned to me and said with that smoothness of tone which marks the end rather than the beginning of a speech:

"Dad always wished me to know how to use a gun. I don't believe he was ever without one himself, even in his bed, from the time he was a small boy. He used to say 'It never does any one any harm to be ready to get the drop first, in case of a scrap!' I have a little beauty in my dressing-case that he got made for me. I am doubly armed now."

I stayed to lunch, but went away immediately after as I was anxious to find if Adams had sent me any message. Before going, I asked Marjory to be especially careful not to be out alone in the woods round the house, for a few days at any rate. She demurred at first; but finally agreed—'to please you' as she put it—not to go out at all till I had come again. I told her that as I was coming to breakfast the next morning if I might, it was not a very long time of imprisonment.

When I asked for telegrams at the post-office, which was in the hotel, I was told that a gentleman was waiting to see me in the coffee room. I went in at once and found Sam Adams reading an old newspaper. He started up when he saw me and straightway began:

"I hurried over to tell you that we have had further news. Nothing very definite to-day; but the Washington people hope to have a lot of detail by to-morrow night. So be ready, old chap!" I thanked him, but even in the act of doing so it struck me that he had taken a deal of trouble to come over when he could have sent me a wire. I did not say so, however; doubts of an act of this kind can always wait.

Sam had tea with me, and then we smoked a cigar outside on the little terrace before the hotel. There were some fishermen and workmen, as usual sitting on or leaning against the wall across the road, and three men who were lounging about, evidently trippers waiting for their tea to be served. When we came out and had passed them, the little group went into the coffee room. They were, all three, keen-looking, alert men, and I had a passing wonder what they were doing in Cruden as they had no golf bags with them. Sam did not remain long but caught the six-ten train back to Aberdeen.

I cannot say that my night was an easy one. Whilst I lay awake I imagined new forms of danger to Marjory; and when I fell asleep I dreamt them. I was up early, and after a sharp ride on my bicycle came to Crom in time for breakfast.

As we had a long forenoon, Marjory took me over the house. It was all of some interest, as it represented the life and needs of life in the later days of Queen Elizabeth in a part of the country where wars and feuds had to be prepared for. The Castle was arranged for siege, even to the water supply; there was a well of immense depth situated in a deep dungeon under the angle of the castle which they called the Keep. They did not, however, ordinarily depend on this, as there was otherwise an excellent water supply. In the dungeon were chains and manacles and some implements of torture, all covered with the rust of centuries. We hoped that they had not been used. Marjory consoled herself with the thought that they had been placed there at the time of the building as part of the necessary furnishing of a mediæval castle. One room, the library, was of great interest. It had not been built for the purpose, for there was no provision of light; but it must have been adapted to this use not long after the place was built. The woodwork of carved oak was early seventeenth century. I did not have time to look over the books, and there was no catalogue; but from the few which I glanced at I could see that whoever had gathered the library must have been a scholar and an enthusiast.

In the course of our survey of the castle, Marjory showed me the parts which were barred up and the rooms which were locked. That such a thing should be in a house in which she lived was a never-ending source of curiosity. There was a dozen times as much room as she could possibly want; but here was something unknown and forbidden. She being a woman, it became a Tree of Knowledge and a Bluebeard's Chamber in one. She was so eager about it that I asked if she could not get permission from the agent to go through the shut rooms and places so as to satisfy herself. She replied that she had already done so, the very day after she had arrived, and had had an answer that the permission could not be given without the consent of the owner; but that as he was shortly expected in Scotland her request would be forwarded to him and his reply when received would be at once communicated to her. Whilst we were talking of the subject a telegram to Mrs. Jack came from the agent, saying that the owner had arrived and was happy to give permission required and that further he would be obliged if the tenant would graciously accord him permission to go some day soon through the house which he had not seen for many years. A telegram was at once sent in Mrs. Jack's name, thanking him for the permission and saying that the owner would be most welcome to go through the house when he pleased.

As I was anxious to hear if there was any news from Adams I said good-bye at the door, and rode back on my bicycle. I had asked Marjory to renew her promise of not going out alone for another day, and she had acceded; 'only to please you,' she said this time.

I found a wire from Adams sent at six o'clock:

"Important news. Come here at once." I might catch the train if I hurried, so jumped on my bicycle and got to the station just in time.

I found Adams in his room at the Palace Hotel, walking up and down like a caged panther. When I came in he rushed over to me and said eagerly as he handed me a sheet of note paper:

"Read that; it is a translation of our cipher telegram. I thought you would never come!" I took it with a sinking heart; any news that was so pressing could not be good, and bad must affect Marjory somehow. I read the document over twice before I fully understood its meaning. It ran as follows:

"Secret Service believe that Drake plot is to kidnap and ransom. Real plotters are understood to be gang who stole Stewart's body. Are using certain Spanish and other foreigners as catspaw. Heads of plot now in Europe, Spain, England, Holland. Expect more details. Use all precautions."

"What do you think of that?" said Adams when I had taken my eyes off the paper.

"I hardly know yet. What do you make of it? You have thought of it longer than I have."

"Just what I have thought all along. The matter is serious, very serious! In one way that wire is something of a relief. If that kidnapping gang are behind it, it doesn't mean political vengeance, but only boodle; so that the fear of any sudden attack on her life is not so imminent. The gang will take what care they can to keep from killing the goose that lays the golden eggs. But then, the political desperadoes who would enter on such a matter are a hard crowd; if they are in power, or at any rate in numerical force, they may not be easy to keep back. Indeed, it is possible that they too may have their own game to play, and may be using the blackmailers for their own purpose. I tell you, old man, we are in a very tight place, and must go to work pretty warily. The whole thing swings so easily to one side or the other, that any false move on the part of any of us may give the push to the side we would least care should win. By the way, I take it that you are of the same mind still regarding Miss Drake's wishes."

"Now and always! But as you can guess I am anxious to know all I can that can help me to guard her." Somewhat to my astonishment he answered heartily:

"All right, old chap, of course I will tell you; but I will depend on your letting me know of anything you are free to tell which might serve me in my work."

"Certainly! I say," I added, "you don't mind my not having worked with you about finding her address."

"Not a bit! I have to find it in my own way; that is all!" There was a sort of satisfaction, if not of triumph, in his tone which set me thinking.

"Then you know it already?" I said.

"Not yet; but I hope to before the night is over."

"Have you a clue?" He laughed.

"Clue? a hundred. Why, man, none of us were born yesterday. There isn't a thing on God's earth that mayn't be a clue now and again if it is properly used. You are a clue yourself if it comes to that." In a flash I saw it all. Adams had come to Cruden to point me out to his detectives. These were the keen-looking men who were at Cruden when he was. Of course they had followed me, and Marjory's secret was no secret now. I said nothing for a little while; for at the first I was angry that

Adams should have used me against my will. Then two feelings strove for mastery; one of anxiety lest my unconscious betrayal of her secret might hurt me in Marjory's eyes, the other relief that now she was in a measure protected by the resources of her great country. I was easier in my mind concerning her safety when I thought of those keen, alert men looking after her. Then again I thought that Adams had done nothing which I could find fault with. I should doubtless have done the same myself had occasion arisen. I was chagrined, however, to think that it had all been so childishly simple. I had not even contemplated such a contingency. If I couldn't plot and hide my tracks better than that, I should be but a poor ally for Marjory in the struggle which she had voluntarily undertaken against her unknown foes.

Before I left Adams, I told him that I would come back on the to-morrow evening. I went to bed early in the Palace hotel, as I wanted to catch the first train back to Cruden.

XXIV

A Subtle Plan

It was now a serious matter of thought to me how I could take Marjory into proper confidence, without spoiling things and betraying Adams's confidence. As I pondered, the conviction grew upon me that I had better be quite frank with her and ask her advice. Accordingly when I saw her at Crom at noon I entered on the matter, though I confess with trepidation. When I told her I wanted to ask her advice she was all attention. I felt particularly nervous as I began:

"Marjory, when a man is in a hole he ought to consult his best friend; oughtn't he?"

"Why certainly!"

"And you are my best friend; are you not?"

"I hope so! I should certainly like to be."

"Well, look here, dear, I am in such a tangle that I can't find a way out, and I want you to help me." She must have guessed at something like the cause of my difficulty, for a faint smile passed over her face as she said:

"The old trouble? Sam Adams's diplomacy, eh?"

"It is this. I want to know how you think I should act so as to give least pain to a very dear friend of mine, and at the same time do a very imperative duty. You may see a way out that I don't."

"Drive on dear; I'm listening."

"Since we met I have had some very disturbing information from a source which I am not at liberty to mention. I can tell you all about this, though you must not ask me how I know it. But first there is something else. I believe, though I do not know for certain, that your secret is blown; that the detectives have discovered where you live." She sat up at once.

"What!" I went on quickly:

"And I am sorry to say that if it is discovered it has been through me; though not by any act or indeed by any fault of mine." She laid her hand on mine and said reassuringly:

"If you are in it, I can look at it differently. May I ask how you came into that gallery?"

"Certainly! I am not pledged as to this. It was by the most simple and transparent of means. You and I were seen together. They did not know where to look for you or follow you up, when they had lost the scent; but they knew me and watched me. Voila!"

"That's simple enough anyhow!" was her only comment. After a while she asked:

"Do you know how far they have got in their search?"

"I do not; I only know that they expected to find where you lived two days ago. I suppose they have found it out by this."

"Sam Adams is getting too clever. They will be making him President, or Alderman or something, if he doesn't look out. But do you know yet why all this trouble is being taken about me."

"I can tell you," I answered "but you must not tell any one, for it would not do for the sake of others if it got about. There is a plan got up by a gang of blackmailers to kidnap you for a ransom." She jumped up with excitement and began to clap her hands.

"Oh, that is too delicious!" she said. "Tell me all you know of it. We may be able to lead them on a bit. It will be an awful lark!" I could not possibly share her mirth; the matter was really too grave. She saw my feeling in my face and stopped. She thought for a minute or two with her brows wrinkled and then she said:

"Are you really serious, Archie, as to any danger in the matter?"

"My dear, there is always danger in a conspiracy of base men. We have to fear, for we don't know the power or numbers of the conspiracy. We have no idea of their method of working, or where or how we may expect attack. The whole thing is a mystery to us. Doubtless it will only come from one point; but we must be ready to repel, all round the compass."

"But, look here, it is only danger."

"The danger is to you; if it were to me, I think I could laugh myself. But, my darling, remember that it is out of my love for you that my fear comes. If you were nothing to me, I could, I suppose, bear it easily enough. You have taken new responsibilities on you, Marjory, since you let a man love you. His heart is before you to walk on; so you have to tread carefully."

"I can avoid treading on it, can't I?" she said falling into the vein of metaphor. "Surely, if there is anything in the world that by instinct I could know is in danger, it would be your heart!"

"Ah, my dear, it does not stay still. It will keep rolling along with you wherever you go; hopping back and forward and sideways in every conceivable way. You must now and again tread on it for all your care; in the dark or in the light."

"I had no idea," she said "that I had taken such a responsibility on my shoulders when I said I would marry you."

"It is not the marrying" I said "but the loving that makes the trouble!"

"I see!" she replied and was silent for a while. Then she turned to me and said very sweetly:

"Anyhow Archie, whatever we may settle about what we are to do, I am glad you came to consult me and to tell me frankly of your trouble. Do this always, my dear. It will be best for you, and best for me too, to feel that you trust me. You have given me a pleasure to-day that is beyond words."

Then we spoke of other things, and we agreed to wait till the next day before arranging any fixed plan of action. Before I went away, and whilst the sentiment of parting was still on her, she said to me—and I could see that the thought had been in her mind for some time:

"Archie, you and I are to live together as man and wife. Is it not so? I think we both want to be as nearly one as a man and a woman can be—flesh of each other's flesh, and bone of bone, and soul of soul. Don't you think we shall become this better by being joined, us two, against all comers. We have known each other only a short time as yet. What we have seen of each other has been good enough to make us cling together for life. But, my dear, what has been, has been only the wishing to cling; the clinging must be the struggle that is to follow. Be one with me in this fight. It is my fight, I feel, begun before I ever knew you. When your fight comes, and I can see you have it before you with regard to that treasure, you will know that you can count on me. It may be only a fancy of mine, but the comradeship of pioneers, when the men and women had to fight together against a common foe, runs in my blood! Let me feel, before I give myself altogether to your keeping, or you to mine, that there is something of this comradeship between us; it will make love doubly dear!"

What could a man in love say to this? It seemed like the very essence of married love, and was doubly dear to me on that account. Pledged by my kisses I came away, feeling as if I had in truth left my wife behind.

When I got back to Cruden I took up the matter of the treasure whilst I was waiting for news from Adams. In the stir of the events of the last few days I had almost forgotten it. I read the papers over again, as I wished to keep myself familiar with the facts; I also went over the cipher, for I did not wish to get stale in it. As I laboured through it, all Marjory's sweetness to me on that day of the ride from Braemar came back to me; and as I read I found myself unconsciously drumming out the symbols on the table with the fingers of my right hand and my left after the fashion of Marjory's variant. When I was through, I sat pondering, and all sorts of new variants kept rising before me in that kind of linked succession when the mind runs free in day-dreaming and one idea brings up another. I was not altogether easy, for I was now always expecting some letter or telegram of a disconcerting kind; anxiety had become an habitual factor in my working imagination. All sorts of possibilities kept arising before me, mostly with reference to Marjory. I was glad that already we understood in common one method of secret communication; and I determined then and there that when I went over to Crom on the next day I would bring the papers with me, and that Marjory and I would renew our lesson, and practice till we were quite familiar with the cipher.

Just then a message was brought to me that a gentleman wished to see me, so I asked the maid to bring him up. I do not think that I was altogether surprised to find that he was one of the three men whom I had seen at Cruden before. He handed me in silence a letter which I found to be from Adams. I read it with a sinking heart. In it he told me that it was now ascertained that two members of the blackmail gang had come to England. They had been seen to land at Dover, but got out between there and London; and their trace was lost. He said he wished to advise me at once, so that I might be on the alert. He would himself take his own steps as I understood. The messenger, when he saw I had read the letter, asked me if there was any answer. I said "only thanks" and he went away. It was not till afterwards that I remembered that I might have asked the man to tell me something of the appearance of the suspected men, so that I might know them if I should come across them. Once again I fell in my own esteem as a competent detective. In the meantime I could do nothing; Marjory's last appeal to me made it impossible for me to take steps against her wishes. She manifestly wanted the fight with the kidnappers to go on; and she wanted me to be with her in it heart and soul. Although this community of purpose was sweet, there grew out of our very isolation a new source of danger, a never-ending series of dangers. The complications were growing such that it would soon be difficult to take any step at all with any prospect of utility. Marjory would now be watched with all the power and purpose of the American Secret Service. That she would before long infallibly find it out, and that she would in such case endeavour at all hazards to escape from it, was apparent. If she did escape from their secret surveillance, she would be playing into the hands of her enemies; and so might incur new danger. I began to exercise my brain as to how I could best help her wishes. If we were to fight together and alone, we would at least make as good a battle as we could.

I thought, and thought, and thought till my head began to spin; and then an idea all at once sprang into my view. It was so simple, and so much in accord with my wishes; so delightful, that I almost shouted out with joy.

I did not lose a minute, but hurried a change of clothes into a bag and caught the train for Aberdeen *en route* for London.

I did not lose any time. Next morning I was in London and went with my solicitor to Doctor's Commons. There I got a license of the Archbishop of Canterbury entitling Archibald Hunter and Marjory Anita Drake to be married anywhere in England—there being no similar license in Scotland. I returned at once, stopping at Carlisle to make arrangements with a local clergyman to be ready to perform a marriage service at eight o'clock of the second morning.

XXV

Inductive Ratiocination

I think Marjory must have suspected that I had something strange to say, for almost as soon as I came in the morning room I saw that queer little lift of her eyebrows and wrinkle in her brows which I was accustomed to see when she was thinking. She held out her two hands towards me so that I could see them without Mrs. Jack being able to. She held up her fingers in the following succession:

Left index finger, right middle finger, left little finger, right little finger, left thumb, right fourth finger, right index finger, left thumb, right index finger; thus spelling "wait" in her own variant of our biliteral cipher. I took her hint, and we talked commonplaces. Presently she brought me up to the long oak-lined room at the top of the Castle. Here we were all alone; from the window seat at the far end we could see that no one came into the room unknown to us. Thus we were sure of not being overhead. Marjory settled herself comfortably amongst a pile of cushions, "Now" she said "go on and tell me all about it!"

"About what?" said I, fencing a little.

"The news that you are bursting to tell me. Hold on! I'll guess at it. You are elated, therefore it is not bad; but being news and not bad it must be good—from your point of view at any rate. Then you are jubilant, so there must be something personal in it—you are sufficiently an egoist for that. I am sure that nothing business-like or official, such as the heading off the kidnappers, would have such a positive effect on you. Then, it being personal, and you having rather more of a dominant air than usual about you—Let me see—Oh!" she stopped in confusion, and a bright blush swept over her face and neck. I waited. It frightened me just a wee bit to see the unerring accuracy with which she summed me up; but she was clearing the ground for me rapidly and effectively. After a pause she said in a small voice:

"Archie show me what you have got in your waistcoat pocket." It was my turn to blush a bit now. I took out the tiny case which held the gold ring and handed it to her. She took it with a look of adorable sweetness and opened it. I think she suspected only an engagement ring, for when she saw it was one of plain gold she shut the box with a sudden "Oh!"

and kept it hidden in her hand, whilst her face was as red as sunset. I felt that my time had come.

"Shall I tell you now?" I asked putting my arms round her.

"Yes! if you wish." This was said in a low voice "But I am too surprised to think. What does it all mean? I thought that this—this sort of thing came later, and after some time was mutually fixed for—for—*it*!"

"No time like the present, Marjory dear!" As she was silent, though she looked at me wistfully, I went on:

"I have made a plan and I think you will approve of it. That is as a whole; even if you dislike some of the details. What do you think of an escape from the espionage of both the police and the other fellows. You got hidden before; why not again, when once you have put them off the scent. I have as a matter of fact planned a little movement which will at any rate try whether we can escape the watchfulness of these gentlemen."

"Good!" she said with interest.

"Well, first of all" I went on, getting nervous as I drew near the subject "Don't you think that it will be well to prevent anyone talking about us, hereafter, in an unpleasant way?"

"I'm afraid I don't quite understand!"

"Well, look here, Marjory. You and I are going to be much thrown together in these matters that seem to be coming on; if there is any escaping to be done, there will be watchful eyes on us before it, and gossiping tongues afterwards; and inquiries and comparing of notes everywhere. We shall have to go off together, often alone or under odd circumstances. You can't fight a mystery in the open, you know; and you can't by walking out boldly, bamboozle trained detectives who have already marked you down."

"Not much; but it doesn't need any torturing of our brains with thinking to know that."

"Well then my suggestion is that we be married at once. Then no one can ever say anything in the way of scandal; no matter what we do, or where we go!" My bolt was sped, and somehow my courage began to ooze away. I waited to hear what she would say. She waited quite a while and then said quietly:

"Don't be frightened, Archie, I am thinking it over. I must think; it is all too serious and too sudden to decide on in a moment. I am glad, anyhow, that you show such decision of character, and turn passing circumstances into the direction in which you wish them to work. It argues well for the future!"

"Now you are satirical!"

"Just a little. Don't you think there is an excuse?" She was not quite satisfied; and indeed I could not be surprised. I had thought of the matter so unceasingly for the last twenty-four hours that I did not miss any of the arguments against myself; my natural dread of her refusal took care of that. As, however, I almost expected her to begin with a prompt negative, I was not unduly depressed by a shade of doubt. I was, however, so single-minded in my purpose—my immediate purpose—that I could endure to argue with her doubts. As it was evident that she, naturally enough, thought that I wanted her to marry me at once out of the ardour of my love, I tried to make her aware as well as I could of my consideration for her wishes. Somehow, I felt at my best as I spoke; and I thought that she felt it too:

"I'm not selfish in the matter, Marjory dear; at least I don't wish to be. In this I am thinking of you altogether; and to prove it let me say that all I suggest is the formal ceremony which will make us one in form. Later on—and this shall be when you choose yourself and only then—we can have a real marriage, where and when you will; with flowers and bridesmaids and wedding cake and the whole fit out. We can be good comrades still, even if we have been to church together; and I will promise you faithfully that till your own time I won't try to make love to you even when you're my wife—of course any more than I do now. Surely that's not too much to ask in the way of consideration."

My dear Marjory gave in at once. It might have been that she liked the idea of an immediate marriage; for she loved me, and all lovers like the seal of possession fixed upon their hopes:

"Time goes on crutches, till love have all his rites."

But be this as it may, she wished at any rate to believe in me. She came to me and put both her hands in mine and said with a gentle modesty, which was all tenderness in fact, and all wifely in promise:

"Be it as you will, Archie! I am all yours in heart now; and I am ready to go through the ceremony when you will."

"Remember, dear" I protested "it is only on your account, and to try to meet your wishes at any sacrifice, that I suggested the interval of comradeship. As far as I am concerned I want to go straight to the altar—the real altar—now." Up went her warning finger as she said lovingly:

"I know all that dear; and I shall remember it when the time comes. But what have we to do to prepare for—for the wedding. Is it to be in a church or at a registry. I suppose it doesn't matter which under the circumstances—and as we are to have the real marriage later. When do you wish it to be, and where?"

"To-morrow!" She started slightly as she murmured:

"So soon! I did not think it could be so soon."

"The sooner the better" said I "If we are to carry out our plans. All's ready; see here" I handed her the license which she read with glad eyes and a sweet blush. When she had come to the end of it I said:

"I have arranged with the clergyman of St. Hilda's Church in Carlisle to be ready at eight o'clock to-morrow morning." She sat silent a while and then asked me:

"And how do you suggest that I am to get there without the detectives seeing me?"

"That is to be our experiment as to escape. I would propose that you should slip out in some disguise. You will of course have to arrange with Mrs. Jack, and at least one servant, to pretend that you are still at home. Why not let it be understood that you have a headache and are keeping your room. Your meals can be taken to you as would be done, and the life of the household seem to go on just as usual."

"And what disguise had you thought of?"

"I thought that if you went dressed as a man it would be best."

"Oh that would be a lark!" she said. Then her face fell. "But where am I to get a man's dress? There is not time if I am to be in Carlisle to-morrow morning."

"Be easy as to that, dear. A man's dress is on its way to you now by post. It should be here by now. I am afraid you will have to take chance as to its fit. It is of pretty thick cloth, however, so that it will look all right."

"What sort of dress is it?"

"A servant's, a footman's. I thought it would probably avoid suspicion easier than any other."

"That goes! Oh this is too thrilling;" she stopped suddenly and said:

"But how about Mrs. Jack?"

"She will go early this afternoon to Carlisle and put up at a little hotel out of the way. I have got rooms in one close to the station. At first I feared it would not be possible for her to be with us; but then when I thought it over, I came to the conclusion that you might not care to let the matter come off at all unless she were present. And besides you would want her to be with you to-night when you are in a strange place." Again she asked after another pause of thought:

"But how am I to change my clothes? I can't be married as a footman; and I can't go to a strange hotel as one, and come out as a young lady."

"That is all thought out. When you leave here you will find me waiting for you with a bicycle in the wood on the road to Ellon. You will have to start about half past five. No one will notice that you are using a lady's wheel. You will come to Whinnyfold where you will find a skirt and jacket and cap. They are the best I could get. We shall ride into Aberdeen as by that means we shall minimise the chance of being seen. There we will catch the eight train to Carlisle where we shall arrive about a quarter to two. Mrs. Jack will be there ready for you and will have the dress you will want to-morrow."

"Oh, poor dear won't she be flustered and mystified! How lucky it is that she likes you, and is satisfied with you; otherwise I am afraid she would never agree to such precipitancy. But hold on a minute! Won't it look odd to our outside friends on the watch if a footman goes out and doesn't return."

"You will return to-morrow late in the evening. Mrs. Jack will be home by then; she must arrange to keep the servants busy in some distant part of the house, so that you can come in unobserved. Besides, the detectives have to divide their watches; the same men will not be on duty I take it. Anyhow, if they do not consider the outgoing of a footman as sufficiently important to follow him up they will not trouble much about his incoming."

This all seemed feasible to Marjory; so we talked the matter over and arranged a hundred little details. These things she wrote down for Mrs. Jack's enlightenment, and to aid her memory when she would be alone to carry out the plans as arranged.

Mrs. Jack was a little hard to convince; but at last she came round. She persisted to almost the end of our interview in saying that she could not understand the necessity for either the hurry or the mystery. She was only convinced when at last Marjory said:

"Do you want us to have all the Chicago worry over again, dear? You approve of my marrying Archie do you not? Well, I had such a sickener of proposals and all about it, that if I can't marry this way now, I won't marry at all. My dear, I want to marry Archie; you know we love each other."

"Ah, that I do, my dears!"

"Well then you must help us; and bear with all our secrecy for a bit; won't you dear?"

"That I will, my child!" she said wiping tears from the corners of her eyes.

So it was all settled.

XXVI

A Whole Wedding Day

Fortune favoured us admirably in our plans. Mrs. Jack, taking only her dressing bag and a few odd parcels, went by the afternoon train from Ellon to Aberdeen. In hearing of the household she regretted that she had to go alone, as Miss Marjory was unable to leave her room. About five o'clock I was in the wood as appointed; and in about half an hour Marjory joined me in her footman's livery. I had a flannel coat in my bag which we exchanged for that which she wore and which we hid in the wood. We were thus less noticeable. We reached Whinnyfold a little after six, and Marjory went into the house and changed her dress which was left ready. She was not long; and we were soon flying on our road to Aberdeen. We arrived a little before eight and caught the mail; arriving at Carlisle at ten minutes to two o'clock. In the hotel we found Mrs. Jack anxiously awaiting us.

In the early morning we were ready; and at eight o'clock we all went together to St. Hilda's Church, where the clergyman was waiting as had been arranged. All formalities were gone through and Marjory and I were made one. She looked oh! so sweet in her plain white frock; and her manner was gentle and solemn. It all seemed to me like a dream of infinite happiness; from which every instant I feared I should wake, and find in its stead some grim reality of pain, or terror, or unutterable commonplace.

When we went back to breakfast at the hotel, we did not even go through the form of regarding it as in any way a wedding feast. Marjory and I had each our part to play, and we determined—I certainly did— to play it well. Mrs. Jack had been carefully coached by Marjory as to how she should behave; and though now and again she looked from one to the other of us wistfully, she did not make any remark.

After a little shopping we got the 12:53 train, arriving at Aberdeen at 6:20. Mrs. Jack was to go on by the 7 train to Ellon where the carriage was to meet her. My wife and I got our bicycles and rode to Whinnyfold by Newburgh and Kirkton so as to avoid observation. When she had changed her clothes in our own house, we started for Crom. In the wood she changed her coat and left her bicycle.

Before we parted she gave me a kiss and a hug that made my blood tingle.

"You have been good" she said "and that is for my husband!" Once again she held up that warning finger which I had come to know so well, and slipped away. She then went on alone to the Castle, whilst I waited in nervous expectancy of hearing the whistle which she was to blow in case of emergency. Then I rode home like a man in a dream.

I left my bicycle at the hotel, and after some supper walked by the sands to Whinnyfold, stopping to linger at each spot which was associated with my wife. My wife! it was almost too much to think of; I could hardly realise as yet that it was all real. As I sat on the Sand Craigs I almost fancied I could see Marjory's figure once again on the lonely rock. It seemed so long ago, for so much had happened since then.

And yet it was but a few days, all told, since we had first met. Things had gone in a whirl indeed. There seemed to have been no pause; no room for a pause. And now I was married. Marjory was my wife; mine for good or ill, till death did us part. Circumstances seemed to have driven us so close together that we seemed not new lovers, not bride and groom, but companions of a lifetime.

And yet. . . There was Marjory in Crom, compassed round by unknown dangers, whilst I, her husband of a few hours, was away in another place, unable even to gaze on her beauty or to hear her voice. Why, it was not like a wedding day or a honeymoon at all. Other husbands instead of parting with their wives were able to remain with them, free to come and go as they pleased, and to love each other unfettered as they would. Why. . .

I brought myself up sharp. This was grumbling already, and establishing a grievance. I, who had myself proposed the state of things to Marjory, to my wife. She was my wife; mine against all the rest of the world. My love was with her, and my duty was to her. My heart and soul were in her keeping, and I trusted her to the full. This was not my wedding day in the ordinary sense of the word at all. This was *not* my honeymoon. Those things would come later, when our joy would be unfettered by circumstances. Surely I had reason to rejoice. Already Marjory had called me her husband, she had kissed me as such; the sweetness of her kiss was still tingling on my lips. If anything but love and trust could come to me from sitting still and sentimentalising and brooding, then the sooner I started in to do some active work the better! . . .

I rose straightway and went across the headland to my house, unpacked the box of tools which had come from Aberdeen, and set about my task of trying to make an opening into the cave.

I chose for various reasons the cellar as the spot at which to make the first attempt. In the first place it was already dug down to a certain depth, so that the labour would be less; and in the second, my working could be kept more secret. In clearing the foundations of the house the workmen had gone down to the rock nearly all round. Just at the end of Witsennan point there seemed to be a sort of bowl-like hollow, where the thin skin of earth lay deeper than elsewhere. It was here that the cellar was dug out, and the labour of cutting or blasting the rock saved. With a pick-axe I broke and stripped away a large patch of the concrete in the centre of the cellar, and in a short time had dug and shovelled away the earth and sand which lay between the floor level and the bed rock. I cleared away till the rock was bare some four or five feet square, before I commenced to work on it. I laboured furiously. What I wanted was work, active work which would tire my muscles and keep my thoughts from working into channels of gloom and disintegration.

It took me some time to get into the way of using the tools. It is all very well in theory for a prisoner to get out of a jail or a fortress by the aid of a bit of scrap iron. Let any one try it in real life; under the most favourable conditions, and with the best tools available, he will come to the conclusion that romancing is easy work. I had the very latest American devices, including a bit-and-brace which one could lean on and work without stooping, and diamond patent drills which could, compared with ordinary tools of the old pattern, eat their way into rock at an incredible rate. My ground was on the gneiss side of the geological division. Had it been on the granite side of the line my labour and its rapidity might have been different.

I worked away hour after hour, and fatigue seemed to come and go. I was not sleepy, and there was a feverish eagerness on me which would not let me rest. When I paused to ease my muscles cramped with work, thought came back to me of how different this night might have been. . . And then I set furiously to work again. At last I took no heed of the flying hours; and was only recalled to time by the flickering of my lamp, which was beginning to go out. When I stood up from my task, I was annoyed to see how little I had done. A layer of rock of a few inches deep had been removed; and that was all.

When I went up the steps after locking the cellar door behind me and taking away the key, I saw the grey light of dawn stealing in through the windows. Somewhere in the village a cock crew. As I stepped out of the door to return home, the east began to quicken with coming day. My wedding night had passed.

As I went back to Cruden across the sands my heart went out in love without alloy to my absent wife; and the first red bolt of dawn over the sea saw only hope upon my face.

When I got to my room I tumbled into bed, tired beyond measure. In an instant I was asleep, dreaming of my wife and all that had been, and all that was to be.

Marjory had arranged that she and Mrs. Jack were for the coming week at least, to come over to Cruden every day, and lunch at the hotel; for my wife had set her heart on learning to swim. I was to be her teacher, and I was enthusiastic about the scheme. She was an apt pupil; and she was strong and graceful, and already skilled in several other physical accomplishments, we both found it easy work. The training which she had already had, made a new accomplishment easy. Before the week was over she was able to get along so well, that only practice was needed to make her a good swimmer. All this time we met in public as friends, but no more; we were scrupulously careful that no one should notice even an intimacy between us. When we were alone, which was seldom and never for long, we were good comrades as before; and I did not venture to make love in any way. At first it was hard to refrain, for I was wildly in love with my wife; but I controlled myself in accordance with my promise. I soon began to have a dawning feeling that this very obedience was my best means to the end I wished for. Marjory grew to have such confidence in me that she could be more demonstrative than before, and I got a larger share of affection than I expected. Besides I could see with a joy unspeakable that her love for me was growing day by day; the tentative comradeship—without prejudice—was wearing thin!

All this week, whilst Marjory was not near, I worked in the cellar at Whinnyfold. As I became more expert with the tools, I made greater progress, and the hole in the rock was becoming of some importance. One day on coming out after a spell of afternoon work, I found Gormala seated on a stone against the corner of the house. She looked at me fixedly and said:

"Be yon a grave that ye thole?" The question staggered me. I did not know that any one suspected that I was working in the house, or even that I visited it so often as I did. Besides, it did not suit my purpose that any one should be aware, under any circumstances, that I was digging a hole. I thought for a moment before answering her:

"What do you mean?"

"Eh! but I'm thinkin' ye ken weel eneuch. I'm no to be deceived i' the soond. I've heard ower mony a time the chip o' the pick, not to ken it though there be walls atween. I wondered why ye came by yer lanes to this dreary hoose when ye sent yon bonnie lassie back to her hame. Aye she is bonnie though her pride be cruel to the aud. Ah, weel! The Fates are workin' to their end, whatsoe'er it may be. I maun watch, so that I may be nigh when the end cometh!"

There was no use arguing with her; and besides anything that I could say would only increase her suspicion. Suspicion abroad about my present task was the last thing I wished for.

She was round about the headland the next morning, and the next, and the next. During the day I never saw her; but at night she was generally to be found on the cliff above the Reivie o'Pircappies. I was glad of one thing; she did not seem to suspect that I was working all the time. Once I asked her what she was waiting for; she answered without looking at me:

"In the dark will be a struggle in the tide-race, and a shrood floatin' in the air! When next death an' the moon an' the tide be in ane, the seein' o' the Mystery o' the Sea may be mine!"

It made me cold to hear her. This is what she foretold of Marjory; and she was waiting to see her prophecy come to pass.

XXVII

Entrance to the Cavern

One night, when I had got down a considerable depth into the rock, I took the pick to loosen out some stone which I had drilled. As I struck, the sound of the rock was hollower than I had before noticed. My heart leaped into my mouth, and I had to pause. Then I struck again harder, and the sound was more hollow still. Whether or no it was the place I was looking for, there was some cave in the rock below me. I would have gone on working straightway had there been anyone with me; but being alone I had to be careful. I was now standing on, evidently, only a layer of rock, over an opening of whose depth I was in ignorance. Should this piece of stone break away, as was quite possible from my working on it, I might be precipitated into a living tomb. The very secrecy in which I had kept my work, might tend to insure my death. Therefore I made all preparation for such a casualty. Henceforth I worked with round my waist a short rope the other end of which was fastened to a heavy staple in the wall. Even if the rock should give way underneath me, a foot or two would limit my fall. This precaution taken, I worked more furiously than ever. With a large hammer I struck the rock at the bottom of the shaft, again and again, with all my might. Then I heard a dull sound of something rattling below me; the top of the cave was falling in. I redoubled my efforts; and all at once a whole mass of rock sunk beneath my hammer and disappeared into a black chasm which sent up a whiff of cold air. I had seized my rope to scramble out, fearing asphyxiation; but when I smelled salt water I did not fear. Then I knew that I had got an opening into a sea cave of some sort. I stuck to my work till I had hammered an irregular hole some three feet square. Then I came up to rest and think. I lowered a rope with a stone at the end, and found that the depth was some thirty feet. The stone had gone into water before it touched bottom. I could hear the "plop" as it struck the surface. As I thought it better not to descend by myself, lest there should be any danger of returning, I spent the rest of my stay for that evening in rigging up a pulley in the roof over the hole so that I might be lowered down when the time should come. Then I went home, for

I feared lest the fascinating temptation to make the descent at once would overcome me.

After breakfast I rode over to Crom, and when I was alone with Marjory told her of my discovery. She was wild with excitement, and I rejoiced to find that this new pleasure drew us even closer together. We agreed that she should come to help me; it would not do to take any one else into our confidence, and she would not hear of my going down into the cave alone. In order to avoid comment we thought it better that she should come late in the evening. The cave being dark, it was of course immaterial whether day or night was appointed for the experiment. Then it was, I could not help it, that I said to her:

"You see now the wisdom of our being married. We can go where we like; and if we should be found out no one can say a word!" She said nothing; there was nothing to say. We decided that she had better slip out, as she had done before, in the footman's dress. I went off and made preparation for her coming, bringing in food for supper and plenty of candles and matches and lamps and rope; for we did not know how long the exploration might take.

A little before nine o'clock I met her as before in the wood. She changed her livery coat for the flannel one, and we rode off to Whinnyfold. We got into the house without being noticed.

When I took her down to the cellar and turned into the hole the reflector of the strong lamp, she held on to me with a little shiver. The opening did certainly look grim and awesome. The black rock was slimy with sea moisture, and the rays of the light were lost far below in the gloom. I told her what she would have to do in lowering me down, and explained the rude mechanism which I had constructed. She was, I could see, a little nervous with the responsibility; and was anxious to know any detail so thoroughly that no accident of ignorance could occur.

When the rope was round me and I was ready to descend, she kissed me more fondly than she had ever done yet, and held on to me as though loth to part. As I sank into the opening, holding the gasoline bicycle lamp which I had elected to take with me, I saw her pretty forehead wrinkled up in anxiety as she gave all her mind to the paying out of the rope. Even then I was delighted with the ease and poise of her beautiful figure, fully shown in the man's dress which she had not changed, as it was so suitable for the work she had to do.

When I had been lowered some twenty feet, I turned my lantern down and saw through the sheen of water a bottom of rock with here and there a cluster of loose stones; one big slab which stuck up endwise, was evidently that which had fallen from the roof under my hammer. It was manifest that there was, in this part of the cave at any rate, not sufficient water to make it a matter of any concern. I called to Marjory to lower slowly, and a few seconds later I stood in the cave, with the water just above my knees. I moved the new-fallen slab to one side lest it might injure any one who was descending. Then I took the strong rope from me, and knotted round my waist the end of the thin rope which I had brought for the purpose. This formed a clue, in case such should be necessary, and established a communication with Marjory which would tend to allay her anxiety. With the cord running through her fingers, she would know I was all right. I went cautiously through the cave, feeling my way carefully with the long stick which I had brought with me. When I had got some distance I heard Marjory's voice echoing through the cave:

"Take care there are no octopuses!" She had been thinking of all sorts of possible dangers. For my own part the idea of an octopus in the cave never crossed my mind. It was a disconcerting addition to my anxieties; but there was nothing to do. I was not going to abandon my project for this fear; and so I went on.

Further inland the cave shelved down on one side, following the line of the rock so that I passed through an angular space which, though wide in reality, seemed narrow by comparison with the wide and lofty chamber into which I had descended. A little beyond this again, the rock dipped, so that only a low tunnel, some four feet high, rose above the water. I went on, carefully feeling my way, and found that the cave ended in a point or narrow crevice.

All this time I had been thinking that the appearance of the place did not quite tally with the description in de Escoban's narrative. No mention had been made of any such difficulties; as the few men had carried in what must have been of considerable bulk and weight there would have been great difficulties for them.

So I retraced my steps, intending to see if there was any other branch nearer to the sea. I kept the line taut so that Marjory might not be alarmed. I think I was as glad as she was when I saw the light through the opening, and the black circle of her head as she looked down eagerly. When underneath, I told her of my adventure, and then turned seawards to follow the cave down. The floor here was more even, as though it had been worn smooth by sea wash and the endless rolling of pebbles. The water deepened only a few inches in all. As I went, I threw the rays of my lamp around, anxiously looking for some opening. The whole distance from the place where I had made the entry to the face of the cliff was not very great; but distance in the open seems very different from that within an unknown cavern. Presently I came to a place where the floor of the cave was strewn with stones, which grew bigger and more as I went on; till at last I was climbing up a rising pile of rocks. It was slippery work, for there seemed some kind of ooze or slime over the stones which made progress difficult. When I had climbed up about half way towards the roof, I noticed that on my left side the slope began to fall away. I moved over and raising my lamp saw to my inexpressible joy that there was an opening in the rock. Getting close I found that though it was nearly blocked with stones there was still a space large enough to creep through. Also with pleasure I saw that the stones here were small. With a very slight effort I dislodged some of them and sent them rolling down, thus clearing the way. The clatter of the stones evidently alarmed Marjory for I heard her calling to me. I hurried back under the opening—the way seemed easy enough now I knew it—and told her of my fresh discovery.

Then I went back again and climbed down the slope of fallen stones; this was evidently the debris of the explosion which had choked the mouth of the cave. The new passage trended away a little to the right, making a sharp angle with the cave I had left. Then after deflecting to the left it went on almost straight for a considerable distance, thus lying, as I made it out, almost parallel to the first cave. I had very little anxiety as to the safety of the way. The floor seemed more level than even that of the entrance to the first cave. There was a couple of feet of water in the deepest part, but not more; it would not have been difficult to carry the treasure here. About two hundred feet in, the cave forked, one arm bending slightly to the left and the other to the right. I tried the former way and came to a sheer dip in the rock such as I had met with before. Accordingly I came back and tried the second. When I had gone on a little way, I found my line running out; so I went back and asked Marjory to throw me down the end. I was so sure of the road now that I did not need a clue. At first she demurred, but I convinced her; taking the rope I fixed one end of it within the cave before it branched. Then I started afresh on my way, carrying the coil of rope with me.

This branch of the cave went on crookedly with occasionally strange angles and sharp curves. Here and there, on one side or the other and sometimes on both, the rock walls bellied out, making queer chambers or recesses, or narrowing the cave to an aperture only a few feet wide. The roof too was raised or fell in places, so that I had now and again to bend my head and even to stoop; whilst at other times I stood under a sort of high dome. In such a zigzag course I lost my bearings somewhat; but I had an idea that the general tendency was inland to the right. Strange to say, the floor of the cave remained nearly level. Here again, ages of tide and rolling pebbles had done their work effectively. My cord ran out again and I had to lose the far end and bring it on, fixing it afresh, as I did not like to proceed without keeping a clue behind me. Somewhat further on, the cave dipped and narrowed so that I had to bend nearly double to pass, my face being just above the water as I went. It was with difficulty that I kept the lamp from touching the water below or knocking against the rock above. I was much chagrined to find this change in the structure of the cave, for since I had entered on this branch of it I had completely made up my mind that I was on the right road and that only a short time and a little distance lay between me and the treasure. However there was nothing to do but to go on.

A few feet more and the roof began to rise; at first in a very gentle slope, but then suddenly. Stretching my cramped back and raising my head, I looked around. I raised my lamp high, turning it so that its rays might let me take in a wide circle.

I stood at the side of a large, lofty cave, quaint of outline, with here and there smooth walls from which great masses of red rock projected ominously. So threatening did these overhanging masses look, that for a few seconds I feared to stir lest some of them should topple over on me. Then, when my eyes had become accustomed to the greater glare, I saw that they were simply masses of the rugged rock itself. The whole cave, so far as I could see, was red granite, formed of the great rock flung upward in the pristine upheaval which had placed the Skares in the sea.

XXVIII

Voices in the Dark

I looked round the cave with mingled feelings. The place itself was, as a natural wonder, superb; but to me as a treasure hunter it was a disappointment. In no way did it answer the description of Don de Escoban. However I did not despair; there were many openings, and some one of them might bring me to the required spot. I passed to the centre of the cavern and looked round. As I did so, I got a momentary fright, for several of the openings were so much alike that only for my rope I would not have been able to distinguish that by which I had come in. The lesson of this shock should not be lost; I must make a mark by which I could distinguish this entrance from the others. No matter where the other openings might lead to, this alone, so far as I could tell, was the one which could lead me to safety. With a heavy pebble I hammered away at the right side of the entrance till I had chipped off a piece of rock. I could tell this place again by sight or by touch. Then I went round the cave examining the various branches. It was here that I began to feel the disadvantage of my imperfect light. I wanted some kind of torch which would give sufficient light to see the whole place at once. One could get no fit idea of proportion by merely making the little patch of dim light from the bicycle lamp travel along the rocky walls. I felt that all this time Marjory must be anxious about me, doubly so since she had no clue to where I had gone. So I determined to come back at once, and postpone the thorough examination of the place until I should have proper appliances. Accordingly I made my way back to the place where Marjory anxiously awaited me.

Her reception of me was sweet and tender. It was so natural that its force was hardly manifest. It may have been that my mind was so full of many things that I did not receive her caress with the same singleness of devotion as was my wont. Now that I was assured of her love for me, and since I had called her my wife, my love lost its element of anxiety. It is this security which marks the difference of a husband's love from that of a lover; doubt is an element of passion, but not of true conjugal love. It was only afterwards, when I was alone, and Marjory's enchanting presence was not with me, that I began to realise through the lenses of memory and imagination the full sweetness of my wife's greeting in her joy at the assurance of my safety. It took a very few moments to tell her all the details of my adventure, and of the conclusion which I had come to as to the need for postponement. She thoroughly agreed with me in the necessity; and we then and there settled that it would be wiser for her to go back to Crom to-night. We were to settle later, when all preparations had been made, when we should again attempt the investigation of the cave.

When I had put on dry clothes, we set out for Crom. We walked our bicycles past Whinnyfold, and were grateful for the unique peculiarity of that village, an absence of dogs. We did not light our lamps till we got on the Peterhead road; and we put them out when we got into the mesh of crossroads near Crom. In the wood Marjory once more resumed her footman's coat, and we set out for the castle. On our way we had agreed that it would be best to try the other side of the castle where it was not likely that any stranger would attempt to approach, as there was only the mossy foot track through the wood by the old chapel. In the later days both Marjory and I had used our opportunities of finding new paths through the wood round the castle; and we had already marked down several tracks which we could follow even in the dark with a little care. This was almost a necessity, as we had noticed of late traces of the watchers round the main gateway through which all in the castle were accustomed to come and go.

The path which we took to-night required a long detour of the wood, as it lay right on the other side from the entrance gate. It was only a narrow grass path, beginning between two big trees which stood closely together not very far from one of the flanking mounds or hillocks which here came closer down to the castle than any of the others. The path wound in and out among the tree trunks, till finally it debouched at the back of the old chapel which stood on a rising rock, hidden in the wood, some three hundred feet from the west side of the castle. It was a very old chapel, partly in ruins and antedating the castle by so many centuries that it was manifestly a relic of the older castle on whose site Crom was built. It may have been used for service early in the sixteenth century; but it could not even have been in repair, or even weather-proof, for there were breaches at the end of it in which had taken root seedlings which were now forest trees. There was one old oak whose girth and whose gnarled appearance could not have been achieved within two centuries. Not merely the roots but the very trunk and branches had pushed aside the great stones which lay firmly and massively across the long low windows peculiar to the place. These windows were mere longitudinal slits in the wall, a sort of organised interstices between great masses of stone. Each of the three on either side of the chapel was about two feet high and some six feet in length; one stone support, irregularly placed, broke the length of each. There was some kind of superstition amongst the servants regarding this place. None of them would under any circumstances go near it at night; and not even in daytime if they could decently excuse themselves.

In front of the chapel the way was very much wider. Originally there had been a clear space leading through the wood: but centuries of neglect had done their work. From fallen pine-cone, and beech-mast, and acorn, here and there a tree had grown which now made of the original broad alleyway a number of tortuous paths between the towering trunks. One of the reasons why we had determined to use this path was that it was noiseless. Grass and moss and rusty heaps of pine needles betrayed no footfall; with care one could come and go unheard. If once she could get through the wood unnoticed, Marjory might steal up to the doorway in the shadow of the castle and let herself in, unobserved.

We went hand in hand slowly and cautiously, hardly daring to breathe; and after a time that seemed endless came out at the back of the chapel. Then we stole quietly along by the southern wall. As we passed the first window, Marjory who was ahead of me stopped and gripped my hand so hard that I knew there must be some good cause for her agitation. She pressed back so that we both stood away from the window opening which we could just see dimly outlined on the granite wall, the black vacancy showing against the lichen-covered stone. Putting her lips close to my ear she whispered:

"There are people there. I heard them talking!" My blood began to run cold. In an instant all the danger in which Marjory stood rushed back upon me. Of late we had been immune from trouble, so that danger which we did not know of seemed to stand far off; but now the place and the hour, the very reputation of the old chapel, all sent back in a flood the fearful imaginings which had assailed me since first I had known of the plot against Marjory. Instinctively my first act was to draw my wife close to me and hold her tight. Even in that moment it was a joy to me to feel that she let herself come willingly. For a few moments we stood silent, with our hearts beating together; then she whispered to me again:

"We must listen. We may perhaps find out who they are, and what they intend."

Accordingly we drew again close to the opening, Marjory standing under the aperture, and I beside it as I found I could hear better in this position. The stooping made the coursing of my own blood sound in my ears. The voice which we first heard was a strong one, for even when toned to a whisper it was resonant as well as harsh and raucous:

"Then it's settled we wait till we get word from Whiskey Tommy. How long is it likely to be?" The answering voice, also a whisper, was smooth and oily, but penetrating:

"Can't say. He has to square the Dutchy: and they take a lot of sugar, his kind. They're mighty pious when they're right end up; but Lordy! when they're down they're holy terrors. This one is a peach. But he's clever—I will say that; and he knows it. I'm almost sorry we took him in now, though he is so clever. He'd better mind out, though, for none of us love him; and if he goes back on us, or does not come up to the mark—" He stopped, and the sentence was finished by a click which I knew was the snapping of the spring of a bowie knife when it is thrown open.

"And quite right too. I'm on if need be!" and there was another click. The answering voice was strong and resolute, but somehow, for all the wicked intent spoken, it did not sound so evil as the other. I looked at Marjory, and saw through the darkness that her eyes were blazing. My heart leaped again; the old pioneer spirit was awake in her, and somehow my dread for her was not the same. She drew close to me and whispered again:

"Be ready to get behind the trees at the back, I hear them rising." She was evidently right, for now the voices were easier to hear since the mouths of the speakers were level with the window. A voice, a new one, said:

"We must git now. Them boys of Mac's 'll be on their round soon." With a quick movement Marjory doubled under the window and came to me. She whispered as before:

"Let us get behind trees in front. We may see them coming through the door, and it will be well to know them." So motioning to her to go on the side we were on, I slipped round the back, and turning by the other side of the chapel, and taking care to duck under the windows, hid myself behind one of the great oak trees in front, to the north of the original clearing. From where I stood I could see Marjory behind a tree across the glade. From where we were we could see any one who left the chapel; for one or other of us commanded the windows, and we both commanded the ruined doorway. We waited, and waited, and waited, afraid to stir hand or foot lest we should give a warning to our foes. The time seemed interminable; but no one came out and we waited on, not daring to stir.

Presently I became conscious of two forms stealing between the trees up towards the chapel. I glided further round behind my sheltering tree, and, throwing an anxious glance toward Marjory, was rejoiced to see that she was doing the same. Closer and closer the two forms came. There was not the faintest sound from them. Approaching the doorway from either side they peered in, listened, and then stole into the darkness between the tree trunks which marked the breach in the wall. I ventured out and slipped behind a tree somewhat nearer; Marjory on her side did the same, and at last we stood behind the two nearest trees and could both note the doorway and each of us the windows on one side. Then there was a whisper from within; somehow I expected to hear a pistol shot or to see a rush of men out through the jagged black of the doorway. Still nothing happened. Then a match was struck within. In the flash I could see the face of the man who had made the light—the keen-eyed messenger of Sam Adams. He held up the light, and to our amazement we could see that, except for the two men whom we had seen go in, the chapel was empty.

Marjory flitted over to me and whispered:

"Don't be afraid. Men who light up like that aren't likely to stumble over us, if we are decently careful." She was right. The two men, seeing that the place was empty, seemed to cast aside their caution. They came out without much listening, stole behind the chapel, and set off along the narrow pathway through the wood. Marjory whispered to me:

"Now is my chance to get in before they come back. You may come with me to the edge of the wood. When I get in, dear, go back home as fast as you can. You must be tired and want rest. Come to-morrow as soon as you can. We have lots to talk over. That chapel must be seen to. There is some mystery there which is bigger than anything we have struck yet. It's no use going into it now; it wants time and thinking over!" We were whispering as we walked along, still keeping carefully in the shadow of the trees. Behind the last tree Marjory kissed me. It was her own act, and as impulsively I clasped her tight in my arms, she nestled in to me as though she felt that she belonged there. With a mutual 'good-night' and a whispered blessing she stole away into the shadow. I saw her reach the door and disappear through it.

I went back to Cruden with my mind in a whirl of thoughts and feelings. Amongst them love was first; with all the unspeakable joy which comes with love that is returned.

I felt that I had a right to call Marjory my very own now. Our dangers and hopes and sympathies made a tie which seemed even closer than that tied in the church at Carlisle.

XXIX

The Monument

For the remainder of that night, whether rushing home on my bicycle, preparing for rest, lying awake, or even in my sleep, I thought over the mystery of the disappearance of the speakers in the old chapel. Certainly I went to sleep on the thought, and woke with it. It never left me even after breakfast as I rode out towards Crom. It was manifest that there must be some secret vault or hiding place in the chapel; or it might be that there was some subterranean passage. If the latter, where did it lead to? Where else, unless to the castle; such would be the natural inference. The very thought made my blood run cold; it was no wonder that it overspread my mind to the exclusion of all else. In such case Marjory's enemies were indeed dangerous, since they held a secret way to her at all times; once within the castle it would not be hard to work evil to her.

I thought that this morning I would do a little prospecting on my own account. Accordingly I left my bicycle in the wood and went a long circuit, keeping in the shadow of the woods where possible, and elsewhere stealing behind the hedgerows, till I got to the far side of the hill or spur which came nearest to the old chapel. This was one of the hills up whose base the trees ran in flame-shaped patches. Half way up, the woods ceased, and there was a belt of barrenness—outcropping rock fringed with green grass. The top, like most of the hills or mounds around the castle, was covered with woods, close-growing masses of pine which made a dusk even in the noonday.

I took my way up the back of the hill and stole through the wood, carefully keeping a watchful look out all round me, for I feared the presence of either of the sets of spies. At the very top I came upon a good sized circle of masonry, low but heavily built of massive stones completely covered with rich green lichen. The circle was some fifteen feet diameter, and the top was slightly arched as though forming a roof. Leaning over it I could hear a faint trickle of water; this was evidently the source of the castle supply.

I walked round it, examining it carefully; anything which had any direct communication with the castle was at present of possibly the supremest importance. There was no flaw or opening anywhere; and from the unbroken covering of the stones by the lichen, it was apparent that there had been no disturbance for years.

I sat down on the edge of the stonework and for a long time thought over matters of probability. If underneath me, as was almost to be taken for granted, lay the reservoir of the castle, it must have been made coevally with Crom itself, or even with the older castle on whose ruins it was built. It must be fed by springs in the rock which formed the base of the hill and cropped out all over it; and if it was not approachable from without, there must be some way of reaching the water from within. It might be that the chamber which contained the reservoir had some other entrance from the hill top, or from some lower level. Accordingly I made as I conceived a bee line for the castle, till I came to the very base of the hill, for I knew that in matters of water conduit the direct way is always chosen where work has to be done. As I went, I conned the ground carefully; not merely the surface for that was an uniform thick coating of brown pine needles, but the general conformation. Where a trench has been made, there is ever after some trace of it to be found. Even if the workmen level the trench most carefully there and then, the percolation of rain through the softer broken earth will make discovery of the change by shrinkage. Here, however, there was no such sign; the ground, so far as one could judge, had never been opened. The trees grew irregularly, and there was no gap such as would be, had one ever been removed. Here and there particles of rock cropped out amongst the pine needles just as anywhere else. If any opening existed it was not on the direct line between the reservoir and the castle.

Back again I went to the reservoir, and, using it as a base, began to cast around for some opening or sign. I made circles in all directions, just as a retriever does when looking for a fallen partridge in a dry stubble when the scent is killed by heat.

At last I came upon something, though whether or no it might have any point of contact with my purpose, I could not at once decide. It was a rude monument of some kind, a boulder placed endwise on a slab of rock roughly hewn to form a sort of square plinth. This again was surrounded on the outside, for the whole monument was on the very edge of a steeply-dipping crag, by a few tiers of rough masonry. The stones were roughly cut and laid together without mortar; or if mortar or cement there had ever been, time and weather had washed it away. In one respect this structure was in contrast to that above the reservoir, there was not a sign of moss or lichen about it. The trees of the wood came close up behind it; in front it was shut out from view below by the branches of a few pine trees which grew crookedly from a precarious foothold amongst the ledges of rock beneath. As I stood in front of it, I could see nothing immediately below me; however, when I had scrambled to a ledge a few feet lower down, the back wall of the old chapel became visible, though partly obscured by trunks and branches of intervening trees. I searched all over the monument for some inscription, but could see none. Then I stood on the plinth to see if there might be any inscription on the top of the boulder. As I stood, looking over the top of it from the bank, I could just see through a natural alleyway amongst the tree tops, the top of one corner of the castle, that on the side of, and farthest from the old chapel. As I looked, a bright thought struck me. Here was a place from which one might correspond with the castle, unseen by any one save at the one spot. I determined then and there, that Marjory and I should arrange some method of signalling to one another.

Somehow this place impressed me, possibly because it was the only thing, except the reservoir, which seemed to have a purpose in the whole scheme of the hill top. Where there was labour and manifest purpose, there must surely be some connection. I examined all round the place minutely, scrambling down the rocks below and on either side, but always keeping a bright look out in case of spies. The only thing I noticed was that there seemed a trace of some kind of a pathway through the wood here. It was not sufficiently marked to allow one to accept it with certainty as a pathway; but there is something about a place which is even occasionally trodden, which marks it from its surroundings virgin of footsteps. I could not find where the path ended or where it began. It seemed to grow from the monument, but here underfoot was stone and hard gravel; and the wind coming over the steep slope swept the fallen pine needles back amongst the shelter of the trees. After a few hundred yards any suggestion of a pathway disappeared, lost in the aisles of the pine trees spreading round on every side. There was no need of a pathway here where all was open. Once or twice as I searched the thought came to me that there might be some opening here to a secret way or hiding place; but look how I would, I could not find the faintest trace or suggestion of any opening. In the end I had to take it that the erection was merely a monument or mark of some kind, whose original purpose was probably lost in time.

At last, as the day was well on, I made my way back to where my bicycle was hidden, always taking care to keep from observation. Then emerging on the road, I went as usual through the old ruined gateway and the long winding avenue to the castle.

Marjory met me with an anxious look, and hung on to my arm lovingly as she said:

"Oh, you are late! I have been quite nervous all the morning lest anything should have happened to you!" Mrs. Jack, after we had greeted, discreetly left us alone; and I told my wife of all that I had thought since we had parted, and of what I had seen on the hill top. She was delighted at the idea of a means of signalling; and insisted on my coming at once to the roof to make further arrangements and discoveries.

We found the spot which I had indicated admirably adapted for our purpose. One could sit on the stone roof, well back from the wall, and through one of the openings in the castellation see the top of the monument amongst the tree tops; and could yet be unobserved oneself from any other spot around. The angles of the castellation of the various walls shut out the tops of the other hills or mounds on every side. As the signs of our code were already complete we had only to fix on some means of signalling 'A' and 'B'. This we did by deciding that by daylight A should be signified by red and B by white and at night A by red and B by green. Thus by daylight two pocket handkerchiefs of red and white or two flowers of white and red; or a piece of paper and a red leaf or flower would suffice. We fixed on colour as the best representative, as the distance made simplicity necessary. By night an ordinary bicycle lamp with the lens covered could be used; the ordinary red and green side lights could be shown as required. Then and there we arranged that that very afternoon when I had left the castle I should steal back to the monument and we should make a trial of our signalling.

Then we talked of other things. Alone there on the roof we could talk freely; and the moments flew swiftly by in a sweet companionship. Even if the subjects which we had to discuss were grim ones of danger and intrigue; of secret passages and malignant enemies; of spies and possibilities of harm to one or both of us, still mutuality of our troubles and dangers made their existence to us sweet. That we shared in common even such matters was dear to us both. I could not but be conscious of Marjory's growing love for me; and if I had to restrain myself now and again from throwing my arms round her and pressing her beautiful body close to me and sweeping her face with kisses, I was repaid when, as we descended she put both her hands in mine and said:

"Oh Archie! you are good to me! and—and—I love you so!" Then she sank into my arms and our mouths met in a long, loving kiss.

We decided that as there must be some hidden opening in the old chapel, we should make search for it the next day. I was to come soon after sunrise, for this we judged would be the time when the spies of both kinds would least expect movement from the castle. I was to come by the grass path between the trees into the old chapel where she would meet me and we should make our investigations together.

After tea I came away. Marjory came out on the steps with me to see me off. As we bade each other good-bye she said aloud in case any one might be listening:

"Remember, you are to come to tea to-morrow and to bring me the book. I am quite anxious to know how it ends. It is too bad of the librarian not to send us all the volumes at once!"

When I got to the road I hid my bicycle in the old place, and took my way secretly to the monument. Marjory had been much struck by the suggestion of the footpath, and, woman-like, had made up her mind on the subject. She had suggested that we should test whether any one came or went by it, and to this end gave me a spool of the finest thread so that I might lay a trap. Before I should leave the place I was to stretch threads across it here and there between the tree trunks. If on the next visit I should find them broken, we might take it that some one had been there.

From the top of the boulder I made signal and was immediately answered. My own signal was simply the expression of my heart's feeling:

"I love you, my wife!" The answer came quickly back filling me with joy:

"I love you, my husband! Don't forget me! Think of me!"

XXX

The Secret Passage

That night was one of rest. I was physically tired out, and after I had posted a few letters to merchants in Aberdeen, giving orders for various goods to be sent at once to Whinnyfold, I went to bed and slept till the early morning. I got up at daylight, and after my morning swim rode off to Crom. Again I left my bicycle in the wood and took my way round to the back of the hill and up through the wood to the monument beyond the reservoir. It was still early morning, as it is counted in the cities, though the sun was well up. I went with extra caution, stealing from tree to tree; for I knew nothing of the locality of the watchers at this hour. I saw no sign of anyone; and coming at last to where the rudimentary pathway lay, examined carefully where I had placed the first thread. As I did so I straightened myself quickly and looked round with apprehension. The thread was broken across, though the two ends were tied where I had placed them!

With a beating heart I examined all the others in turn, with the same result. It was quite evident that some one, or some thing had passed along the track. In spite of my concern I rejoiced, for something had been found. It was at least probable that there was a regular route somewhere at hand. Accordingly I prepared my traps afresh, this time placing them in various directions, and at irregular distances along the path and all round the monument. I might thus be able to trace the exact route of anyone who might disturb them. This done, and it took some time, I went back to the wood, and thence rode to the castle.

Marjory was eager for news, but it thrilled me to see that her eagerness was not all from this cause; hour by hour I found myself growing in her affection. When I told her of the broken threads, she clapped her hands with delight; the hunter spirit hereditary in her was pleased. She gave her opinion that on the next morning I should be able to locate the entrance to the passage, if one there was. In the midst of her speaking thus she stopped; a bright, keen light came into her eyes, and her brows knitted.

"Why," she said, "how stupid I am. I never once thought of doing the same at my end. Yesterday, after you left, I spent an hour in the old chapel and went over every inch of it; but it never occurred to me to do there what you had gone to do at the monument. If I had done so, I might this morning have been able to discover the secret of the disappearance of the kidnappers. I shall take good care to do it this evening."

While she was speaking a fear grew upon me lest being alone in the ruin she might give her enemies the very opportunity they wanted. She saw my distress, and with her quick woman's wit guessed the cause of it. With a very tender movement she placed her hand on the back of mine, and without squeezing it held it there firmly as she said:

"Don't be frightened for me, dear. These are expert workmen that we are dealing with. They won't move till their plans are all ready. They don't wish to get hold of me for five minutes and let "Mac's men"—as lacking due respect for President McKinley, they call the Secret Service agents of my country—catch them red-handed. They are only laying their plans as yet. Perhaps we may have cause to be anxious when that is done; but as yet it's all right. Anyhow, my dear, as I know it will make you easier in your mind, when you are not at hand to protect me, I shall lay the traps whilst you are with me. There now! Am I good to my husband, or am I not?" I made her aware in my own way—I could not help it—that she was good! and she let the incident pass unrebuked. Even lovers, though they have not the status of the husband, must be allowed a little latitude now and again.

We talked over all the possibilities that we could either of us think of with regard to a secret passage between the castle and the monument. It was apparent that in old time such a hidden way might have been of the utmost importance; and it was more than possible that such a passage might exist. Already we had reason to believe that there was a way between the ruined chapel and the top of the reservoir hill, and we knew that there must be existing some secret hiding place gained from the interior of the chapel. What we had still to discover, and this was the most important of all, was whether there was a method of communication between the castle and the chapel. After tea we started out together; and as we had arranged between us before starting, managed in our strolling to go quite round the castle and through many of the grassy alleys between the woods. Then, lest there should be any listener, I said:

"Let us go into the old chapel. I haven't had a good look at it since I have been coming here!" So we went into the chapel and began to lay our traps. Of course we could not guard against any one spying upon us. There might be eyes of enemies bent on us through some secret chink or cranny or organised spy-hole. This we could not help, and had to take our chances of it; but if anyone were within ear-shot and unable to see us, we guarded our movements by our misleading remarks concerning history and art. Deftly Marjory stretched sections of her gossamer thread from place to place, so that if any one went in the chapel their course must be marked by the broken threads. We finished near the door, and our artless, innocent, archæological conversation stopped there, too. We strolled back to the castle, feeling sure that if there were any secret hiding place within the ruin we should have located the entrance to it in the morning.

That afternoon I went to the house at Whinnyfold. Most of the things which I had ordered had arrived, and when I had had the various boxes and bundles moved inside I felt able to start on my work.

First I rigged up a proper windlass over the hole into the cave; and fixed it so that any one could manipulate it easily and safely from above. It could be also worked from below by aid of an endless chain round the axle. I hammered the edges of the hole somewhat smoother, so that no chance friction might cut the rope; and I fixed candles and lanterns in various places, so that all the light which might be necessary could be had easily. Then I furnished a room with rugs and pillows, and with clothes for Marjory for changing. She would be sure to require such, when our search after the treasure should come off. I had ready some tins of provisions, and I had arranged at the hotel that as I might sometimes stay and work in my own home—I was supposed to be an author—some fresh provisions were to be sent over each morning, and left ready for me with Mrs. Hay at Whinnyfold. By the time my work was through, it was late in the evening, and I went to the hotel to sleep. I had arranged with Marjory to be with her early in the morning. It was hardly daylight when I woke, but I got up at once and took my way towards Crom, for the experience of the day before had shown me that whoever used the path near the monument used it in the grey of the dawn. As usual I hid my bicycle and took my way cautiously to the monument. By this time the sun was up and the day was bright; the dew lay heavy, and when I came on any of my threads I could easily distinguish them by the shimmering beads which made each thread look like a miniature rope of diamonds.

Again the strings across the path were broken. My heart beat heavily as I began to follow back towards the monument the track of the broken thread. It led right up to it, on the side away from the castle, and then stopped. The other threads all round the monument were intact. Having learned so much, my first act was to prevent discovery of my own plan. Accordingly I carefully removed all the threads, broken and unbroken. Then I began to make minute investigation of the monument itself. As it was evident that whoever had broken the threads had come straight from it, there was a presumption that there was an opening somewhere. The rock below was unbroken and the stonework was seemingly fixed on the rock itself. By a process of exclusions I came to the belief that possibly the monument itself might be moveable.

Accordingly I began to experiment. I pressed against it, this way and that. I tried to move it by exercising pressure top and bottom in turn; but always without avail. Then I began to try to move it sideways as though it might be on a pivot. At first there was no yielding, no answer of any kind to my effort; but suddenly I thought I perceived a slight movement. I tried again and again, using my strength in the same way; but with no result. Then I tried turning it in the suspected direction, holding both my hands low down on the corners of the boulder; then going gradually up higher I pursued the same effort; again no response. Still I felt I was on the track and began to make efforts in eccentric ways. All at once, whilst I was pressing with my left hand low down whilst I pulled with my right high up on the other edge, the whole great stone began to move in a slow easy way, as though in perfect poise. I continued the movement and the stone turned lazily over on one side, revealing at my very feet a dark opening of oval form some three feet across its widest part. Somehow I was not altogether surprised; my head kept cool in what was to me a wonderful way. With an impulse which was based on safety, lest the opening of the hole should make discovery of my presence, I reversed the action; and the stone rolled slowly over to its old position. Several times I moved it from its place and then back again, so that I might become accustomed to its use.

For a while I hesitated as to whether I should explore the opening immediately; but soon came to the conclusion that I had better begin at once. So I went back to my bicycle and took the lamp with me. I had matches in my case, and as I had the revolver which I always carried now, I felt equal to any emergency. I think I was finally influenced in my decision to attempt the passage at once by the remembrance of Marjory's remark that the kidnappers would make no effort until their plans were quite complete. They, more than I, might fear discovery; and on this hope I was strong as I lowered myself down through the narrow opening. I was glad to see that there was no difficulty in moving the stone from the inside; there were two iron handles let into the stone for the purpose.

I cannot say I was at ease in my mind, I was, however, determined to go on; and with a prayer to God for protection, and a loving thought of Marjory, I went on my way.

The passage was doubtless of natural origin, for it was evident that the seams in the rock were much like those on the coast where the strata of different geological formations joined. Art had, however improved the place wonderfully. Where the top had come too low it had been quarried away; the remnants still lay adjacent where the cave broadened out. The floor where the slope was steep was cut into rough steps. Altogether, there were signs of much labour in the making of the passage. As I went down, I kept an eye on the compass whenever I came to a turn, so that I might have a rough idea of the direction in which I was going. In the main the road, with counterbalancing curves and angles, led straight down.

When I had got to what I considered must be half way, allowing for the astounding magnitude which seems to be the characterisation of even a short way under ground; the passage forked, and at a steep angle another passage, lower and less altered than that along which I had come, turned away to the left. Going a few feet up it I could hear the sound of running water.

This was evidently the passage to the reservoir.

XXXI

Marjory's Adventure

As I felt that time, in which I had the passage all to myself, was precious, I turned back to the main way down. The path was very steep and low and the rock underfoot was cut in rude steps; as I held the lantern before me I had to droop it so that I could smell the hot metal where the flame touched the back. It was indeed a steep and difficult way, made for others than men of my own stature. As I went, I felt my first fears passing away. At first I had dreaded a lack of air, and all sorts of horrors which come to those who essay unknown passages. There came back to my recollection passages in Belzoni's explorations in the Pyramids when individuals had got lost, and when whole parties were stopped by the first to advance jamming in a narrow passage as he crawled along on his belly. Here, though the roof came down in places dangerously low, there was still ample room, and the air came up sweet and cool. To any one unused to deep burrows, whether the same be natural or artificial, there is a dread of being underground. One is cut off from light and air; and burial alive in all its potential horrors is always at hand. However, the unexpected clearness and easiness of the way reassured me; and I descended the steep passage with a good heart. All distance underground seems extravagantly long to those unaccustomed to it; and to me the mere depth I had descended seemed almost impossible when the way before me became somewhat level again. At the same time the roof rose so that I could stand upright. I guessed that I must be now somewhere at the foot of the hillock and not far from the old chapel; so I went forward carefully, keeping my hand ready to cover up the front of the lamp. As the ground was fairly level, I could in a way pace it; and as I knew that there was only about two hundred feet distance from the foot of the hill to the chapel, I was not surprised when after some eighty paces I found the passage end in a sort of rude chamber cut in the rock. At right angles to the place of my entry there was a regular stairway, partly cut in rock and partly built, leading upward. Before I ascended I looked around carefully and could see that sections of the walls of the chamber were built of great blocks of stone. Leaving further investigation for the future I went upward with a beating heart.

The stair was rudely circular, and I had counted thirty steps when I saw the way blocked by a great stone. For a few seconds I was in fear lest I should find this impossible; then I looked carefully for any means of moving the obstacle. I thought it more than likely that something of the same process would be adopted for both ends of the passage.

Luck was certainly on my side to-day! Here were two iron handles, much the same as those with which I had been enabled to move the monument from within. I grasped them firmly, and began to experiment as to which way the stone moved. It trembled under my first effort; so exerting a very little of my strength in the same direction the great stone began to move. I saw a widening line of open space through which a dim light shone in upon me. Holding the stone in poise with one hand, I covered the front of the lamp with my cap, and then resumed the opening process. Slowly, slowly, the stone rolled back till a clear way lay abreast of me through which, doubled up, I could pass. From where I stood I could see part of the wall of a building, a wall with long low windows in massive stone; and I knew that at last I had reached the old chapel. A joyous feeling rushed over me; after the unknown perils of the cavern passage at last I had reached safety. I bent low and began to step out through the narrow opening. There was fully four feet in the circumference of the stone so that two such steps as were possible to me were necessary to take me out. I had taken one and my foot was lifted for the second when a clear firm voice said in a whisper:

"Hands up! If you move you are a dead man!" I stopped of course, and raising my face, for my head was bent low in the necessary effort of stooping, I found myself opposite the muzzle of a revolver. For an instant I looked at it; it was firm as the rock around me, and I felt that I must obey. Then I looked beyond it, to the hand which held it, and the eyes which directed. These too were inflexible; but a great joy came over me when I recognised that the hand and eyes were those of Marjory. I would have sprung forward to her, but for that ominous ring of steel in front of me. I waited a few seconds, for it seemed strange that she did not lower the revolver on seeing who it was. As, however, the pistol still covered me unpleasantly, I said:

"Marjory!" In an instant her hand dropped to her side. I could not but notice with an admiration for her self-control and the strength of her resolution, that she still held the revolver in her grasp. With a glad cry she leaped towards me with a quick impulsive movement which made my heart bound, for it was all love and spontaneity. She put her left hand on my shoulder; and as she looked into my eyes I could feel the glad tremor that swept through her.

For several seconds she stood, and then with a sigh said in a voice of self-reproach:

"And *I* did not know *you*!" The way she spoke the words "I" "you" was luminous! Had I not already known her heart, she would in that moment have stood self-revealed.

We were manifestly two thoroughly practical people, for even in the rapture of our meeting—to me it was no less than rapture to come from so grim an aperture in the secret cavern passage—we had our wits about us. I think she was really the first to come to a sense of our surroundings; for just as I was opening my mouth to speak she held up a warning finger.

"Hush! Some one may come; though I think there is no one near. Wait dear, whilst I look!" she seemed to flit noiselessly out of the doorway and I saw her vanish amongst the trees. In a few minutes she returned carrying carefully a wicker basket. As she opened it she said:

"Some one might suspect something if they saw you in that state." She took from the basket a little bowl of water, soap, towel and a clothes-brush. Whilst I washed my face and hands she was brushing me down. A very short time completed a rough toilet. Then she poured the water carefully into a crack in the wall, and putting the things together with my lamp, back in the basket, she said:

"Come now! Let us get to the Castle before any one finds us. They will think that I have met you in the wood." We went as unobtrusively as we could to the Castle; and entered, I think, unobserved. I had a thorough clean up before I let any one see me; our secret was too precious to risk discovery by suspicion. When I had seen Mrs. Jack, Marjory took me to her boudoir in the top of the castle, and there, whilst she sat by me holding my hands, I told her every detail of my adventure. I could feel how my story moved her; when there was any passage of especial interest the pressure of her clasp grew tense. She, who had seemingly no fear for herself, was all in fear for me!

Then we talked matters over. We had now a good clue to the comings and goings of the kidnappers; and we felt that by a little thoughtful organisation we might find their hours, and be able to trace them one by one. By lunch time we had decided on our plan of action. We took our idea from one of the old "Tales of the Genii" where the conquered king was brought by his faithful vizier into a cavern and asked to cut a rope which was stretched before him, and which he soon discovered released the great rock which roofed the pavilion specially built by the vizier to be seen and occupied by the conqueror. We would fix a fine thread to the top of the monument and bring it secretly to the castle, where its breaking would apprise Marjory of the opening of the passage; thus she would discover the hour of the coming of the kidnappers to the chapel. We arranged another ingenious device, whereby a second thread, fastened to the stone in the old chapel, would be broken by the opening of the stone, and would cause a book to fall on Marjory's bed and wake her if she were asleep. The better part of the afternoon was taken up by us carrying out these ideas, for we went slowly and cautiously to work. Then I went home.

I was early at the monument in the morning, and getting behind the stone signalled to the Castle roof in case Marjory should happen to expect me and be there. But there was no answer. So I sat down to wait till it would be decent time to go to the Castle for an early breakfast.

As I sat waiting I thought I heard a sound, either close to me and muffled, or else distant; I could hardly tell which. Matters might be lively if I were discovered; so I got my revolver ready. With my heart beating so heavily that I mistook it at moments for the foreign sound, I listened and listened, all ears.

It was as I had suspected; the sound came from the tunnel beneath me. I hardly knew whether to stay or go. If I waited I could see who came from the opening; but on the other hand I should at once be known to have discovered the secret. Still as the stone might roll back at any moment, it was necessary that I should make up my mind; I should either go or stay. I decided that I would stay and make discovery at once. In any case should I succeed in capturing a blackmailer, or even in discovering or partially discovering his identity, I should be aiding in Marjory's safety. So I got my revolver ready; and standing back so that I could not be seen at once by any one emerging, waited.

No one came; but I could still hear a slight sound. Filled with a growing unrest, I determined to take the initiative, and began to move close to the stone. As I looked, it began to quiver, and then to move slowly. As it rolled softly back I kept behind it so that I might not be seen; and waited with revolver ready and what patience I could.

There was dead silence; and then a hand holding a revolver rested a moment on the edge of the opening.

I knew the hand, and I knew the revolver, and I knew the quickness of both. I did not say a word or make a sound, till Marjory with an alert movement seemed to sweep up out of the opening and whirled round with ready pistol, as though suspecting an enemy on every side.

Marjory, all covered with dust, her cheeks as white as snow, so that the smears of dust lay on them like soot; and eyes with pupils distended as in coming from the dark. For a few seconds she seemed hardly to recognise me; but when she did she sprang gladly into my arms.

"Oh! Archie, I am glad to see you. It was so terrible and lonely in the dark. I began to fear I might never find my way out!" In the dark! I began to fear, and asked her:

"But, dear one, how did you come; and why? Hadn't you got a light with you? Surely you didn't come unprepared, if you did venture into the cave!" Then in a rush she told me the whole story. How before dawn she had been waked by the dropping of the book and had hurried to the castle roof to watch the stone. With her field glass she had presently seen it move. She was then satisfied that the watchers had gone home; and had determined on a little adventure on her own account.

"I put on a grey tweed dress, and taking my revolver and bicycle lamp, stole out of the castle and reached the old chapel. Having lit my lamp, I rolled back the stone and set out to explore the tunnel. I followed from your description, the passage to its bifurcating, and determined to explore the other arm to the reservoir. I easily found it, a deep, dark tank cut in the rock and seemingly fed by springs which bubbled up from patches of fine sand, the accumulation of years of wasting rock. Whilst I was trying to look into the depth of the reservoir, holding my bicycle lamp so as to throw its light downwards, I saw something white at the bottom. Just then the lamp from its inverted position began to smoke, but as I looked in that last moment through the crystal pure water I recognised that the white object was a skull. In the sudden shock of the discovery, the lamp dropped from my hand and disappeared hissing and bubbling in the last flicker of light." As she told me this, I took her hand for I feared that the memory of such an appalling moment must have unnerved her; but to my surprise her nerves were as firm as my own. She let her hand remain in mine; but she had evidently understood my thought for she said:

"Oh! it's all right now, Archie. For a moment or two I do believe I was frightened. You can have the laugh on me there if you like! But then common sense came to my aid. I was in a tight place, and it would need all I knew to get out. I thought the matter over as coolly as I could; and do you know that coolness seemed to grow with the effort! I was in the dark, in a cave, deep underground, the entrance to which was secret; I had no means of getting a light even for an instant, for though I had taken plenty of wax matches they were all in my lamp. The only thing I could do was to try to grope my way out. I had noted the passage as I came along, but I found so soon as I had felt my way out of the reservoir chamber, how little use an abstract recollection is when every second there is a new detail. I found, too, the astonishing difference between sight and touch; what I had remembered had been with my eyes and not with my fingers. I had to guard all round me, my head, my feet, my sides. I am amazed, now when I think of it, how many different kinds of mistakes and calculations I made in a few yards. It seemed a terribly long time till I came to the place where the passage forks. There I weighed up the matter of whether it would be better to go back by the way I had come to the old chapel, or to go up the other passage to the monument of which you told me. Somehow the latter seemed to me the more feasible. I think it must have been that I trusted you more than myself. You had not shrunk from going into that passage; and I would not shrink from going out."

I squeezed her hands hard, I had got both by this time. She blushed a little and looked at me fondly and went on:

"There was something cheering in the mere fact of going up instead of down. It was like coming towards the air and light again; and the time did not seem so long till I came to the end of the passage, for so far as I could feel there was nothing but solid rock all round me. For a little bit my heart sank again; but I soon bucked up. I knew that this must be the way out; and I felt around for the iron handles of which you had told me. And then, Thank God for His goodness! when the stone began to turn I saw the light, and breathed fresh air again. They seemed to give me back all my courage and caution. Up to this I had not troubled about kidnappers; there was quite enough to think of in getting along the passage. But now I was my own woman again, and I determined to take no chances. When I saw it was your gun that was aimed at me I was glad!"

XXXII

THE LOST SCRIPT

After a little consideration of ways and means, we decided that the best thing we could do was to pass through the passage to the old chapel. It was still very early, so early that in all probability none of the household were yet awake; if Marjory could regain her room before being seen, it would avoid curiosity. She was certainly in a shocking condition of dust and dishevelment. Her groping in the dark through that long rugged passage had not been accomplished without many hardships. Her dress was torn in several places, and her hat was simply knocked to pieces; even her hair was tumbled about, and had been put up again and again with dusty fingers. She saw me smiling; I think it pained her a little for she suddenly said:

"Come along quick; it's simply awful standing here in the light of day in this filthy state. It won't feel half so bad in the dark passage!" Without more ado I lit my lamp, and having, of course, closed the entrance behind us, we went back into the cavern.

The tramp back through the tunnel did not seem nearly so long or so difficult as at first. It may have been that comparative familiarity made it easier; it certainly eased its terrors. Or it is possible that our companionship, each to the other, made the bearing of fears and difficulties lighter.

Anyhow, it was something of a surprise to both of us to find ourselves so quickly in the rude chamber whence the steps led up to the old chapel. Before we left this, we made a rough examination of it, turning the lantern over walls and floor and ceiling; for I had an idea that the passage from the castle, which I was satisfied must exist, made its exit here. We could not, however, see any external sign of an opening; the walls were built up of massive unmortared stones, and were seemingly as solid as the rock itself.

When we got into the chapel we found the utility of Marjory's foresight. In a corner was her little basket with soap and towel, water and clothes brush; and together we restored her to some semblance of decency. Then she went back to the castle and got in unobserved, as I, watching from the shelter of the trees, could see. I took my way back through the passage; and so to the wood where my bicycle was hidden. I washed my hands in the stream and lay down in the shelter of a thick grove of hazel, where I slept till breakfast time. When I rode up to the castle, I found Marjory with her kodak on the sweep outside, taking views of its various points.

The morning was intensely hot; and here, in the shelter of the little valley and the enclosing wood, the air was sultry, and the sun beat down pitilessly. We had a table set out under the shelter of the trees and breakfasted *al fresco*.

When we were alone in her boudoir I settled with Marjory that we would on that evening attempt to find the treasure, as the tide would be out at midnight. So we went down to the library and got out Don de Escoban's narrative and began to read it afresh, noting as we went every word and sign of the secret writing, in the hope that we might in thus doing stumble on some new secret or hidden meaning.

Whilst we were thus engaged a servant came looking for Mrs. Jack, for whom a stranger had brought a letter. Marjory told where she might be found, and for some time we went on with our work.

Suddenly the door opened, and Mrs. Jack entered, speaking over her shoulder as she came to a high-bred looking, dark man who followed her. As she saw us she stopped and said to Marjory:

"Oh! my dear, I didn't know you were here. I thought you were in the ladies' room." This was what they usually called the big room at the top of the castle. We both rose, seeing a stranger. For my own part there was something in his face which set me thinking; as to Marjory I could not help noticing that she drew herself up to her full height, and held herself at tension in that haughty way which now and again marked her high spirit and breeding. There seemed so little cause for this attitude that my own thinking of the new-comer was lost in the contemplation of hers. Mrs. Jack noticed that there was some awkwardness, and spoke hurriedly:

"This is the gentleman, my dear, that the agent wrote about; and as he wanted to look over the house I brought him myself." The stranger probably taking his cue from her apologetic tone spoke:

"I trust I have not disturbed the Senora; if I have, pardon! I have but come to renew my memory of a place, dear to me in my youth, and which through the passing of time and of some who were, is now my own heritage." Marjory smiled, and swept him a curtsey as she said, but still in her distant arm's-length manner:

"Then you are the owner of the castle, sir. I hope that we do not disturb you. Should you wish to be anywhere alone we shall gladly withdraw and wait your pleasure." He raised a hand of eloquent protest, a well-kept, gentleman's hand, as he said in tones sweet and deferent:

"Oh! I pray you, do not stir. May I say that when my house is graced with the presence of so much loveliness I am all too full of gratitude to wish for any change. I shall but look around me, for I have a certain duty to do. Alas! this my heritage comes not only as a joy, but with grave duties which I must fulfill. Well I know this room. Many a time as a boy I have sat here with my kinsman, then so old and distant from me in my race; and yet I am his next successor. Here has he told me of old times, and of my race of which we who have the name are so proud; and of the solemn duty which might some day come to me. Could I but tell. . ." Here he stopped suddenly.

His eyes had been wandering all over the room, up and down the bookshelves, and at the few pictures which the walls contained. When they rested on the table, a strange look came into them. Here lay the type-script which we had been reading, and the secret writing of the dotted printing. It was on the latter that his eyes were fixed absorbingly.

"Where did you get that?" he said suddenly, pointing to it. The question in its bald simplicity was in word rude, but his manner of asking it was so sweet and deferential that to me it robbed it of all offence. I was just about to answer when my eye caught that of Marjory, and I paused. There was such meaning in her eyes that my own began roving to find the cause of it. As I looked she put her hands on the table before her, and her fingers seemed to drum nervously. To me, however, it was no nervous trifling; she was speaking to me in our own cipher.

"Be careful!" she spelled out "there is some mystery! Let me speak." Then turning to the stranger she said:

"It is curious is it not?"

"Ah, Senora, though curious it be in itself, it is nothing to the strangeness of its being here. If you only knew how it had been searched for; how the whole castle had been ransacked from roof to dungeon to find it, and always without avail. Did you but understand the import of that paper to me and mine—if indeed the surmises of many generations of anxious men availed aught—you would pardon my curiosity. In my own youth I assisted in a search of the whole place; no corner was left untouched, and even the secret places were opened afresh." As he went on, Marjory's eyes were resting on his face unflinchingly, but her fingers were spelling out comments to me.

"There are secret places, then; and he knows them. Wait" the stranger went on:

"See, I shall convince you that I speak from no idle curiosity, but from a deep conviction of a duty that was mine and my ancestors' for ages." There was a sternness mingled with his grave sweetness now; it was evident that he was somewhat chagrined or put out by our silence. Leaving the table he went over to one of the bookshelves, and after running his eye over it for a moment, put his hand up and from a shelf above his head took down a thick leather-covered volume. This he laid on the table before us. It was a beautiful, old black letter law book, with marginal notes in black letter and headings in roman type. The pagination was, I could see as he turned it over, by folios. He turned to the title-page, which was an important piece of printing in many types, explanatory of the matter of the book. He began to read the paragraphs, placed in the triangular in form in vogue at that day; following the text with his forefinger he read:

"A collection in English of the Statutes now in force, continued from the beginning of Magna Charta made in the 9. yeere of the reigne of King H. 3. until the ende of the Session of Parliament holden in the 28 yeere of the reigne of our gracious Queene Elizabeth under Titles placed by order of Alphabet. Wherein is performed (touching the Statutes wherewith Justices of the Peace have to deale) so much as was promised in the Booke of their office lately published. For which purpose"—&c. &c.,—Then turning over the page he pointed to a piece of faded writing on the back of it which had been left blank of printing. We bent down and read in the ink, faded to pale brown by time:

"My sonnes herein you will find the law which binds the stranger in this land, wherein a stranger is a Vagabond. F. de E.

XXIII. X. MDLXLIX."

Then he turned rapidly over the leaves, till towards the end there was a gap. On the right hand page, where the folio number was all along placed was the number 528.

"See," he said, turning back and pointing to the bottom of the title page "Anno 1588. Three hundred years, since first my people used it."

Turning back he looked at the folio before the gap; it was 510. "See" he said, placing his hand on the pinmarked pages. "Folio 511 and the heading of 'Vagabonds, Beggars, et cetera.'" He folded his arms in a dignified way and stood silent.

All along I had been following my own train of thought, even whilst I had been taking in the stranger's argument, and at the same time noting Marjory's warning. If this man who owned the Castle knew of the existence of the secret writing; whose ancestors had owned the book in which was the clue signed F. de E., surely then this could be none other than the descendant of the Don Bernardino who had hidden the treasure. This was his castle; no wonder that he knew its secret ways.

Matters were getting complicated. If this man were now the hereditary guardian of the hidden treasure—and from his likeness to the ghostly Spaniard whom I had seen in the procession at Whinnyfold I saw no reason to doubt it—he might be an enemy with whom we should have to cope. I was all in a whirl, and for a few seconds I think quite lost my head. Then rushed over me the conviction that the mere lapse of time passed in these few minutes of agonised silence was betraying our secret. This brought me up with a round turn, and I looked about me. The strange man was standing still as marble; his face was set, and there was no sign of life in him except his eyes which blazed as they wandered around, taking everything in. Mrs. Jack saw that there was something going on which she did not understand, and tried to efface herself. Marjory was standing by the table, still, erect and white. Her fingers began to drum softly as she caught my eye, and spelled out:

"Give him the paper, from Mrs. Jack. Lately found in old oak chest. Say nothing of interpretation." This seemed such a doubtful move that with my eyes I queried it. She nodded in reply. So I gathered myself together and said:

"I'm afraid, sir, that there is some mystery here which I cannot undertake to understand. I think I may say, however, for my friend Mrs. Jack, that there will be no trouble in your having full possession of your book. I am told that these pages were lately found in an old oak chest. It is remarkable that they should have been missing so long. We were attracted by the funny marks. We thought that there might be some sort of cryptogram; and I suppose I may take it, from the fact of your looking for them so long, that this is so?"

He grew suspicious in a moment, and stiffened all over. Marjory saw, and appreciated the reason. She smiled at me with her eyes as she drummed on the table:

"The herring is across his path!" As the awkward pause was this time with the stranger, we waited with comparative ease. I saw with a feeling of wonder that there was, through all her haughtiness, a spice of malice in Marjory's enjoyment of his discomfiture. I looked at Mrs. Jack and said: "May I give these papers to Mr.—" She answered promptly:

"Why cert'nly! If Mr. Barnard wants them." Marjory turned round suddenly and in a surprised voice said:

"Mr. Barnard?"

"That is the name given in the letter which he brought, my dear!" The stranger at once spoke out:

"I am Mr. Barnard here; but in my own country I am of an older name. I thank you, sir, and Madam" turning to Mrs. Jack "for your courteous offer. But it will be time enough for me to consider the lost pages when through the unhappiness of your departure from my house, I am enabled to come hither to live. In the meantime, all I shall ask is that the pages be replaced in this book and that it be put in its place on the shelf where none shall disturb it." As he spoke in his sweet, deferential way there was something in his look or manner which did not accord with his words; a quick eager shifting of his eyes, and a breathing hard which were at variance with his words of patience. I did not pretend, however, to notice it; I had my own game to play. So without a word I placed the pages carefully in the book and put the latter back on the shelf from which he had taken it. There was an odd look in Marjory's face which I did not quite understand; and as she gave me no clue to her thoughts by our sign language, I waited. Looking at the stranger haughtily, and with a distinctly militant expression she said:

"The agent told us that the Barnard family owned this castle!" He bowed gravely, but a hot, angry flush spread over his face as he replied:

"He spoke what truth he knew." Marjory's reply came quickly:

"But you say you are one of the family, and the very memorandum you pointed out was signed F. de E." Again the hot flush swept his face; but passed in an instant, leaving him as pale as the dead. After a pause of a few moments he spoke in a tone of icy courtesy:

"I have already said, Senora, that in this country our name—my name, is Barnard. A name taken centuries ago when the freedom of the great land of England was not as now; when tolerance for the stranger was not. In my own land, the land of my birth, the cradle of my race, I am called Don Bernardino Yglesias Palealogue y Santordo y Castelnuova de Escoban, Count of Minurca and Marquis of Salvaterra!" As he rehearsed his titles he drew himself up to his full height; and pride of race seemed actually to shine or emanate from him. Marjory, too, on her side of the table drew herself up proudly as she said in a voice in which scorn struggled for mastery with dignity:

"Then you are a Spaniard!"

XXXIII

Don Bernardino

The stranger held himself with, if possible, greater hauteur as he answered:

"I have that great honour."

"And I, sir," said Marjory, with a pride rivalling his own, "am an American!" Issue was joined.

For a period which from its strain seemed very long, though it was probably but a few seconds, they stood facing each other; types of the two races whose deadly contest was then the interest of the world. The time was at any rate sufficiently long for me to consider the situation, and to admire the types. It would have been hard to get a better representative of either, of the Latin as well as of the Anglo-Saxon. Don Bernardino, with his high aquiline nose and black eyes of eagle keenness, his proud bearing and the very swarthiness which told of Moorish descent, was, despite his modern clothes, just such a picture as Velasquez would have loved to paint, or as Fortuny might have made to live again.

And Marjory! She looked like the spirit of her free race, incarnate. The boldness of her pose; her free bearing; her manifest courage and self belief; the absence of either prudery or self-consciousness; her picturesque, noble beauty, as with set white face and flashing eyes she faced the enemy of her country, made a vision never to be forgotten. Even her racial enemy had unconsciously to fall into admiration; and through it the dominance of his masculine nature spoke. His words were gracious, and the easy gracefulness of their delivery was no less marked because the calm was forced:

"Our nations alas! Senora are at war; but surely not even the courtesies of the battlefield need be strained when individuals, even of the most loyal each to their own, meet on neutral soil!" It was evident that even Marjory's quick wit did not grasp at a suitable reply. The forgiveness of enemies is not the strong point of any woman's nature, or of her education. The only remark she made was to again repeat:

"I am an American!" The Spaniard felt the strength of his position; again his masculinity came out in his reply:

"And all good women, as well as all men, should be loyal to their Flag. But oh Senora, before even your nationality comes your sex. The Spanish nation does not make war on women!" He seemed really to believe what he said; for the proud light in his face could not have been to either a dastard or a liar. I confess it was with a shock that I heard Marjory's words:

"In the *reconcentrados* were as many women as men. More, for the men were fighting elsewhere!" The passionate, disdainful sneer on her lips gave emphasis to the insult; and blood followed the stab. A red tide rushed to the Spaniard's swarthy face, over forehead and ears and neck; till, in a moment of quick passion of hate, he seemed as if bathed in red light.

And then in truth I saw the very man of my vision at Whinnyfold.

Marjory, womanlike, feeling her superiority over the man's anger, went on mercilessly:

"Women and children herded together like beasts; beaten, starved, tortured, mocked at, shamed, murdered! Oh! it is a proud thought for a Spaniard, that when the men cannot be conquered, even in half a century of furious oppression, their baffled foes can wreak their vengeance on the helpless women and children!"

The Spaniard's red became white; a deathly pallor which looked grey in the darkened room. With his coldness came the force of coldness, self-command. I had a feeling that in those few moments of change had come to him some grim purpose of revenge. It was borne in upon me by flashes of memory and instinct that the man was of the race and class from which came the rulers and oppressors of the land, the leaders of the Inquisition. Eyes like his own, burning in faces of deathly white, looked on deeds of torture, whose very memory after centuries can appal the world. But with all his passion of hate and shame he never lost the instinct of his dignity, or his grace of manner. One could not but feel that even when he struck to kill he would strike with easeful grace. Something of the feeling was in his speech, perhaps in the manner rather than the words, when after a pause he said:

"For such foul acts I have nought but indignation and grief; though in the history of a nation such things must be. It is the soldier's duty to obey; even though his heart revolt. I have memory of hearing that even your own great nation has exercised not so much care as might be"— how he sneered with polished sarcasm as he turned the phrase—"in the dealing with Indians. Nay more, even in your great war, when to kill was fratricidal, there were hardships to the conquered, even to the helpless women and children. Have I not heard that one of your most honoured generals, being asked what was to become of the women in a great march of devastation that he was about to make, replied, "The women? I would leave them nothing but their eyes to weep with!" But, indeed, I grieve that in this our mutual war the Senora grieves. Is it that she has suffered in herself, or through others dear to her?" Marjory's eyes flashed; pulling herself to full height she said proudly:

"Sir, I am not one who whines for pain of my own. I and mine know how to bear our own troubles, as our ancestors did before us. We do not bend before Spain; no more to-day than when my great ancestors swept the Spaniard from the Western Main, till the seas were lit with blazing masts and the shores were fringed with wreckage! We Americans are not the stuff of which you make *reconcentrados*. We can die! As for me, the three hundred years that have passed without war, are as a dream; I look on Spain and the Spaniard with the eyes, and feel with the heart, of my great uncle Francis Drake."

Whilst she was speaking Don Bernardino was cooling down. He was still deadly pale, and his eyes had something of the hollow glare of phosphorus in the sockets of a skull. But he was master of himself; and it seemed to me that he was straining every nerve to recover, for some purpose of his own, his lost ground. It may have been that he was ashamed of his burst of passion, with and before a woman; but anyhow he was manifestly set on maintaining calm, or the appearance of it. With the fullness of his grace and courtesy he said, turning to Mrs. Jack:

"I thank you for the permission, so graciously granted to me, to visit again this my house. You will permit me, however, I hope without any intention of offence, to withdraw from where my presence has brought so much of disturbance; the which I deplore, and for which I crave pardon."

To me he bowed stiffly with a sort of lofty condescension; and finally, looking towards Marjory, he said:

"The Senora will I trust believe that even a Spaniard may have pity to give pain; and that there are duties which gentlemen must observe because they are gentlemen, and because they reverence the trust that is reposed in them more than do common men. She can appreciate the call of duty I know; for she can be none other than the new patriot who restores in the west our glorious memories of the Maid of Saragossa. I pray that the time may come when she shall understand these things and believe!" Then, with a bow which seemed the embodiment of old-fashioned grace and courtesy, he bent almost to the ground. Marjory instinctively bowed. Her training as to good manners, here stood her in good stead; not even patriotic enthusiasm can at times break the icy barrier of social decorum.

When the Spaniard left the room, which he did with long strides but bearing himself with inconceivable haughtiness, Mrs. Jack, with a glance at us, went with him. Instinctively I started to take her place; in the first instance to relieve her from an awkward duty, and beyond this with a feeling that I was not quite satisfied with him. No one could be in antagonism with Marjory, and acquire or retain my good will. As I moved, Marjory held up her hand and whispered to me to stay. I did so, and waited for her to explain. She listened intently to the retreating footsteps; when we heard the echoing sound of the closing the heavy outer door, she breathed freely and said to me with relief in her voice:

"I know you two would have fought if you had got alone together just now!"

I smiled, for I was just beginning to understand that that was just how I felt. Marjory remained standing at the table, and I could see that she was buried in thought. Presently she said:

"I felt it was cruel to say such things to that gentleman. Oh! but he is a gentleman; the old idea seems embodied in him. Such pride, such haughtiness; such disdain of the commoner kind; such adherence to ideas; such devotion to honour! Indeed, I felt it very cruel and ungenerous; but I had nothing else to do. I had to make him angry; and I knew he couldn't quarrel with me. Nothing else would have taken us all away from the cipher." Her words gave me quite a shock. "Do you mean to say Marjory," I asked, "that you were acting a part all the time?"

"I don't know" she answered pensively, "I meant every word I said, even when it hurt him most. I suppose that was the American in me. And yet all the time I had a purpose or a motive of my own which prompted me. I suppose that was the woman in me."

"And what was the motive or purpose?" I asked again, for I wondered.

"I don't know!" she said naively. I felt that she was concealing something from me; but that it was a something so tender or so deep in her heart that its very concealment was a shy compliment. So I smiled happily as I said:

"And that is the girl in you. The girl that is American, and European, and Asiatic, and African, and Polynesian. The girl straight out of the Garden of Eden, with the fragrance of God's own breath in her mouth!"

"Darling!" she said, looking at me lovingly. That was all.

During the day, we discussed the visitor of the morning. Mrs. Jack said very little, but now and again implored Marjory to be cautious; when she was asked her reason for the warning her only reply was:

"I don't like a man who can look like that. I don't know which is worst, when he is hot or cold!" I gathered that Marjory in the main agreed with her; but did not feel the same concern. Marjory would have been concerned if the danger had been to anyone else; but she was not habituated to be anxious about herself. Besides, she was young; and the antagonist was a man; and haughty and handsome, and interesting.

In the afternoon we completed our arrangements for the visit to the treasure cave. We both felt the necessity for pressing on this matter, since the existence of the secret writing was known to Don Bernardino. He had not hesitated to speak openly, though he did not know of course the extent of our own knowledge of the subject, of a grave duty which he had undertaken from hereditary motives, or of the tragic consequences which might ensue. It was whilst we were speaking of the possibility of his being able to decipher the cryptogram, that Marjory suddenly said:

"Did you understand exactly why I asked you to give him the paper at once?"

"Far be it from me" I answered "to profess to understand *exactly* the motives of any charming woman."

"Not even when she tells you herself?"

"Ah! then the real mystery only begins!" I said bowing. She smiled as she replied:

"You and I are both fond of mysteries. So I had better tell you at once. That man doesn't know the secret. I am sure of it. He knows there is a secret; and he knows a part, but only a part. That eager look wouldn't have been in his eye if he had known already. I daresay there is, somewhere, some duplicate of what the original Don Bernardino put down in his story. And of course there must be some allusion to the treasure in the secret records at Simancas or the Quirinal or the Vatican. Neither the kings of Spain nor the Popes would let such a treasure pass out of mind. Indeed it is possible that there is some key or clue to it which he holds. Did you notice how he referred at once to the secret meaning of the memorandum in the beginning of the law book? If we had not given it up at once, he would have forced on the question and wished to take the paper away; and we could not have refused without letting him know something by our very refusal. Do you understand any more of my meaning now? And can you forgive me any more for my ill-mannered outbreak? That is what I am most sorry for, of all that has been in the interview to-day. Is that also any more light to you on the mystery of a woman's mind?"

"It is, you dear! it is!" I said as I took her for a moment in my arms. She came easily and lovingly to me, and I could not but be assured that the yielding even momentarily to tenderness helped to ease the strain which had been bearing upon her for so long. For my Marjory, though a strong and brave one, was but a woman after all.

At six o'clock I took my way back to Whinnyfold; for I wanted to have all ready for our enterprise, and take full advantage of the ebb tide. We arranged that on this occasion Marjory should come alone to join me at the house—our house.

XXXIV

The Accolade

When Marjory arrived, I had all ready for our exploration. There were several packages waiting for her, and when she emerged from the room where she had gone to change, their purpose was manifest. She appeared in a flannel tennis frock, short enough to show that she had put on her sand shoes on her bare feet. She saw that I noticed and said with a little blush:

"You see I am dressed for the part; you came back so wet the last time that I thought I had better prepare for it too."

"Quite right, my dear," I said. "That pretty head of yours is level." We went to the cellar at once where I had lamps and candles prepared and ready to light. I showed Marjory how to get up and down by herself, in case anything should happen to me. This made the gravity of our enterprise apparent. Her face grew a trifle anxious, though she did not change colour; I could see that all her anxiety was for me and none for herself. We took care to bring a plentiful supply of matches and candles, as well as an extra lamp and an oil can, and some torches and red and white lights. All these were in a tin box to insure their being kept dry. I had a meal of bread and meat packed ready; also a bottle of water and a flask of brandy, for the exploration might take a long time. The tide was not quite out, and there was still in places a couple of feet of water; but we decided to go on at once as it would give us more time if we started on a falling tide.

I took Marjory first up the passage inland, so that she might understand something of the lines of the cave system. There was, however, too much tide just then to show her where I surmised there might be some deep opening, perhaps permanently under water, into some of the other caves. Then we retraced our steps and gained the pile of debris of the explosion at the cave's mouth. I could not but notice how much Marjory was impressed by the stillness of the place. Here, the tide, filtering in by innumerable crevices and rifts between the vast pile of stones, showed no sign of the force of waves without. There was not time for the rise and fall of waves to be apparent; but the water maintained its level silently, except for that ceaseless gurgle which comes with the piling in of water anywhere, and is so constant that it does not strike one as a sound. It was borne in upon us that the wildest storm without, would make no impress upon us here in this cavern deep; and with it, as an inevitable corollary, came the depressing thought of our helplessness should aught go wrong in the fastnesses of this natural prison.

Marjory bounded over the slippery stones like a young deer, and when we passed through the natural archway into the cave beyond, her delight was manifest. She was hurrying on so quickly that I found it necessary to tell her she must go slow so as to be able to take stock of all around her as she went. It was needful to look back as well as forward, so that she might recognise the places when coming the other way. I reminded her of caution by holding up the great ball of stout cord which I carried, the end of which was attached to the rope of the windlass in the cellar. "Remember, dear," I said, "that you have to be prepared for all eventualities; if necessary to go back alone and in the dark." She shuddered a little and drew closer to me; I felt that the movement was one of protection rather than of fear.

When we went along the passage, where on the first occasion I had found the water rise nearly to the roof, we had to wait; a little way ahead of us, where the cave dipped to its lowest, the water was still touching the top. We possessed our souls with what patience we could, and in about half an hour's time we were able to pass. We were quite wet, however, for only our faces and our lamps were above water; with the exception, of course, of the tin box with the candles and matches and our provisions, which I took care to keep dry.

Marjory's delight at the sight of the huge red cave was unspeakable. When I lit one of the red lights the blinding glow filled the place, exposing every nook and corner, and throwing shadows of velvet blackness. The natural red of the granite suited the red light, the effect being intensely rich. Whilst the light lasted it was all like a dream of fairyland; and Marjory hung on to me in an ecstasy of delight. Then, when the light died down and the last sparks fell into the natural darkness, it seemed as if we and all around us were steeped in gloom. The little patches of faint light from our lamps seemed to our dazzled eyes to openly emphasise the surrounding blackness.

Marjory suggested that we should explore the great cavern before we did anything else. I acquiesced, for it was just as well that we should be thoroughly acquainted with the various ramifications of the cave. I was not by any means sure as yet that we should be able to get to the cave of the treasure. Here, all around us, was red; we were entirely within the sienite formation. When I had been first in the cave I had not seen it lit up. Only where the comparatively feeble light of my bicycle lantern had fallen had I seen anything at all. Of course it may have been that the red light which I had burned had misled me by overwhelming everything in its lurid glow. So this time I got a white light out of the box and lit it. The effect was more ghastly and less pleasant. In the revealing glare, the edges of everything stood out hard and cold, and so far repulsive that instinctively Marjory drew closer to me. While the light remained, however, I was able to satisfy myself of one thing; all around was only the red granite. Colour and form and texture all told the same thing; we had passed the stratification of gneiss and entered on that of the sienite. I began to wonder and to think, though I did not at once mention the matter to Marjory. The one guiding light as to locality in the Don's narrative was the description of the cave "the black stone on one hand and the red on the other." Now at Broad Haven the gneiss and the red sienite join, and the strata in places seem as if welded together or fused by fire. Here and there can be found patches in the cliff where it is hard to say where one class of rock ends and the other begins. In the centre bay, however, to the north of my house, there is a sort of dip in the cliff covered deep with clay, and bright with grass and wild flowers. Through this a tiny stream rushes in wet weather, or in dry trickles down the steep incline. This is the natural or main division between the geological formations; for on either side of it is a different kind of rock—it was here that I expected to find that the treasure cave was situated. It had been of course impossible for me, though I had had a compass with me, to fix exactly the windings of the cave. I knew, however, that the general trend was to the right; we must, therefore, have passed behind the treasure cave and come into the region of red granite. I began to have an idea, or rather the rudiment of one, that later on we should have to go back on our tracks. Inasmuch as my own house stood on the gneiss formation, we should have to find whereabout in the cave windings the red and the black rocks joined. From this point we might be able to make new and successful progress towards discovery of the treasure itself. In the meantime I was content to linger a few minutes in the great cavern. It was evident that Marjory was in love with it, and was at present in a whirl of delight. And, after all, she was my world, and her happiness my sunshine. I fully realised in the delightful passages of our companionship the truth of the lover's prayer in Herrick's pretty poem.

> *"Give me but what this Ribbon bound,*
> *Take all the rest the sun goes round."*

Every day, every hour, seemed to me to be revealing new beauties of my wife's character and nature. She was herself becoming reconciled to our new relationship; and in the confidence of her own happiness, and in her trust of her husband, the playful and sweet sides of her nature were gaining a new development. I could not help feeling at times that all was going on for the best; that the very restraint of the opening of our married life was formative of influence for good on us both. If all young husbands and wives could but understand the true use of the old-fashioned honeymoon, the minute knowledge of character coming in moments of unconscious self-revelation, there might be more answers in the negative to the all important nineteenth century philosophical query, "Is marriage a failure?" It was evident that Marjory was reluctant to leave the cave. She lingered and lingered; at last in obedience to a command of hers, conveyed—for she said nothing—in some of those subtle feminine ways, which, though I did not understand their methods, I was beginning to learn to obey, I lit a torch. Holding it aloft, and noticing with delight how the light danced in my wife's beautiful eyes as she clapped her hands joyously with the overt pleasure of a child, I said:

"Her Majesty wishes to inspect her new kingdom. Her slave awaits her pleasure!"

"Lead on!" she said. "Her Majesty is pleased with the ready understanding of her Royal Consort, and with his swift obedience to her wishes; and oh! Archie isn't this simply too lovely for anything!" The quick change into the vernacular made us both laugh; and taking hands like two children we walked round the cavern. At the upper end of it, almost at the furthest point from where we entered, we came across a place where, under an overhanging red wall which spread out overhead like a canopy, a great rock rose from the level floor. It was some nodule of especial hardness which in the general trituration had not been worn away by the wash of the water and the rolling of pebbles which at one time undoubtedly helped to smooth the floor. In the blinking light of the torch, the strength of which was dimmed in the vastness of the cavern, the isolated rock, standing as it did under the rocky canopy whose glistening surface sent down a patchy reflex of the glare, seemed like a throne. The idea occurred simultaneously to both of us; even as I spoke I could see that she was prepared to take her seat:

"Will not Her Majesty graciously take her seat upon the throne which the great Over-Lord, Nature, has himself prepared for her?"

She took the stick which she carried to steady her in the wading, and holding it like a sceptre, said, and oh, but her sweet voice sounded like far music stealing through the vastness of the cavern:

"Her Majesty, now that she has ascended her throne, and so, formally taken possession of her Kingdom, hereby decrees that her first act of power shall be to confer the honour of Knighthood on her first and dearest subject. Kneel therefore at the feet of your Queen. Answer me by your love and loyalty. Do you hereby promise and vow obedience to the wishes of your Queen? Shall you love her faithfully and truly and purely? Shall you hold her in your heart of hearts, yielding obedience to all true wishes of hers, and keeping the same steadfastly to the end? Do—you—love—me?"

Here she paused; the rising emotion was choking her words. The tears welled into her eyes and her mouth quivered. I was all at once in a fire of devotion. I could then, and indeed when I think of it I can now, realise how of old, in the days when loyalty was a passion, a young knight's heart flowered and blossomed in the moment of his permitted devotion. It was with all the truth of my soul and my nature that I answered:

"I do love you, oh, my gracious Queen. I hereby take all the vows you have meted to me. I shall hold you ever, as I do now, in my very heart of hearts. I shall worship and cherish you till death parts us. I shall reverence and obey your every true wish; even as I have already promised beside the sea and at the altar. And whithersoever my feet may go in obedience to your will, my Queen and my Love, they shall go on steadfast, to the end." Here I stopped, for I feared to try to say more; I was trembling myself and the words were choked in my throat. Marjory bent over as I knelt, laid her wand on my shoulder and said:

"Rise up, Sir Archibald, my own True Knight and Loyal Lover!" Before I rose I wanted to kiss her hand, but as I bent, her foot was temptingly near. I stooped lower to kiss it. She saw my intention and saying impulsively: "Oh, Archie dear, not that wet, dirty shoe," kicked it off. I stooped still lower and kissed her bare foot.

As I looked up at her face adoringly, a blush swept over it and left her pale; but she did not flinch. Then I stood up and she stepped down from her throne, and into my arms. She laid her head against my shoulder, and for a few moments of ecstasy our hearts beat together.

XXXV

The Pope's Treasure

N ow," said Marjory, at last disengaging herself from me, "let us get down to business. We've got to find the treasure, you know!" So we set ourselves down to a systematic search.

We explored one after another all the caves leading out of the main cavern. Some of them were narrow and tortuous; some were wide and low with roof dropping down, down, until it was impossible for anything in the shape of humanity to pass. All these, however, with one exception, ended in those fissure-like clefts, running somewhere to a point, which characterise cavern formations. The exception was at the north west side of the cavern where a high, fairly wide passage extended, with an even floor as though it too had been levelled by rolling pebbles. It kept on straight for a good length, and then curved round gently to the right, all the while fairly maintaining its proportions. Presently it grew so high that it was like a narrow way between tall houses. I lit a white light, and in the searching glare noticed that far overhead the rocky walls leaned together till they touched. This spot, just above us, was evidently the highest point; the roof thence fell rapidly till at last it was only some ten feet high. A little further on it came to a sudden end.

Here there was a great piled-up mass of huge, sharp-edged rocks, at the base of which were stones of all sizes, some round and some jagged. Scattered near and isolated were many stones rounded by constant friction.

As I looked, the whole circumstances seemed to come to me. "See," I cried to Marjory, "this was evidently another entrance to the cave. The tides, ebbing or flowing, drove in through one way and out at the other; and the floor was worn level in process of countless years by rolling pebbles like these. Then came some upheaval or wearing away by water drift of supporting walls of rock; and this mouth of the cave fell in. We must be by now somewhere at the Cruden side of Whinnyfold; we are facing almost due north."

As there was manifestly nothing to be done here, we took our way back to the main cavern. When we began to look around us for a new place to explore, Marjory said:

"There doesn't seem to be any treasure cave at all here. We have now tried everywhere." Then it was that my mind went back again to the Don's description "Black on the one hand and red on the other." "Come," I said, "let us go back till we find the joining of the gneiss and granite." As we went back the floor was almost dry; only a few pools of water here and there, lying in the depressions, called attention to the fact that we were under tidal influence. As we went we kept a careful look-out for the fusion of the rocks; and found it where the passage with the descending roof debouched into that which led from the blocked up entrance of the cave. There was here, however, no sign of another passage, and the main one outside was like that under my own house, entirely through the gneiss.

I could not help feeling a little disappointed. For many weeks my mind had been set on finding the Pope's treasure; and though I believe it was not greed which controlled me even to any great extent, I was deeply chagrined. I had a sort of unworthy fear that it might lower me in the eyes of Marjory. This feeling, however, was only momentary; and when it went, it went for good. Drawing in my note-book a rough outline of Whinnyfold, I dotted lines where I took the various branches of the cave to lie and then marked in the line of fusion of the gneiss and the granite as it was manifest on the cliffs and on the shore beyond. Marjory was at once convinced; indeed when I saw my surmise put down in black and white it seemed to me quite apparent that it must be correct. The treasure cave must be within that space which lay between the dismantled entrance on the side of the Skares, and that which had fallen in on the north side. The logical inference was that if there was an entrance to be found at all it would be close to the debris from the Don's explosion. So we took in silence, our way back to that point and began at once to examine the debris for any sign of an opening in the rock to the north side. Marjory scrambled up to the top of the pile whilst I explored the base. Turning my lantern on the rocky wall I began to examine it foot by foot and inch by inch.

Suddenly Marjory cried out. I raised my head and looked at her. Her face, lit by the rays of my own lamp which, with the habit of searching now familiar to me I had turned as my eyes turned, was radiant with joy and excitement.

"Look! look!" she cried. "Oh, Archie, there is the top of an opening here. The stones fill it up." As she spoke she pushed at a stone on the top of the pile; under her hand it moved and disappeared with a hollow rattle. By this time I had scrambled up the slippery pile and was beside her. The disappearance of the stone had enlarged the opening, and something like a foot square was discovered.

So we began to work at the heap of stones, only we pulled and threw them into the cave where we were so as not to block the place we aimed at. The top layer of stones was easy to move, as they were comparatively small, and were not interlocked, but below them we found a much more difficult task. Here the rocks were larger and more irregular in shape, and their points and edges interlocked. We did not mind, however, but toiled on. I could not but notice as we did so, a trait of Marjory's coolness of head in the midst of all her excitement, when she took from her pocket a pair of heavy gloves and put them on.

In some fifteen or twenty minutes we had unmasked a hole sufficiently large to pass through comfortably. I found that the oil of my lamp was running low; so I refilled it and Marjory's also. Then holding my own lamp carefully, whilst Marjory turned hers in the direction I was going, I passed over the top of the miniature moraine, and in a few seconds was on the floor of the other cave. Marjory threw me the ball of string and scrambling down joined me at once. We went along carefully, for the roof of the cave dipped very low and we had in more than one place to bend considerably; even then we were walking in a couple of feet of water as the floor dipped as well as the roof. When we had gone some distance, however, the roof rose as the cave turned sharp to the left, round a corner of very broken and jagged rock in which I could see signs of the fusion of the two geological formations. Our hearts beat high and we took hands instinctively; we were now confident that we were in the treasure house at last.

As we went up the cave, here running, so far as I could ascertain by the compass, straight in and from the sea, we could note, as we turned our lamps now and again to either side, that on our left was all black rock whilst on the right was all red. The cave was not a long one; nothing to compare with those we had left. It was not very many seconds, though we had to go slow as we did not know for certain as to the floor level, before the cave began to expand.

When, however, it widened and became more lofty, the floor rose in all some three feet and we went up a sharp incline though not of very great magnitude. This dipped a little again forming a pool which spread ahead of us so far as we could see by the dim light of our bicycle lamps. As we did not know the depth I waded in, Marjory enjoining me anxiously to be careful. I found it deepened very slowly; so she joined me and we went on together. By my advice, Marjory kept a few feet in the rear, so that in case I should stumble or meet with a deep hole and so lose my light, hers would still be safe. I was so intent on my feet, for I feared lest Marjory following so close might get into some trouble, that I hardly looked ahead, but kept cautiously on my way. Marjory, who was flashing her lamp all around as she went, suddenly called out:

"Look! look! There to the right, the figure of the San Cristobal with the golden Christ on his shoulder."

I turned my lantern to the angles of the cave to the right to which we were now close. The two lamps gave us light enough to see well.

There, rising from the water under the shelf of rock, was the figure that Benvenuto had wrought, as Don Bernardino had left it three centuries ago.

As I moved forwards I stumbled; in trying to save myself the lamp was shaken from my hand and fell hissing in the dark water. As it fell I saw by the flash of light the white bones of a skeleton under the San Cristobal. Instinctively I called out to Marjory:

"Stand still and take care of your lamp; I've dropped mine!"

"All right!" came back her answer coolly; she had quite command of herself. She turned the lamp downwards, so that we could see into the water, and I found I had stumbled against an iron box, beside which, in about two feet of water, lay my lamp. I picked this up first and shook the water from it and laid it on the shelf of rock. "Wait here a moment," I said, "I shall run back and get a torch." For I had left the tin box on the top of the heap of debris when we had scrambled through the hole. I was starting back at once when she said after me, and in that cave the voice came after me "monotonous and hollow like a ghost's:"

"Take my lamp with you dear. How can you find the box, or even the way to it, in the dark?"

"But I can't leave you alone here; all in the dark, too."

"Oh, I'm all right," she answered gaily, "I don't mind a bit! And besides it will be a new sensation to be here alone—with Olgaref and the treasure. You won't be long, will you, dear?" I felt that her query almost belied her brave words; but I knew that behind the latter lay her pride which I must not offend; so I took the lamp she was holding out to me and hurried on. In a few minutes I had found the box and brought it back; but I could see that even those minutes had been a trying time to Marjory, who was deathly white. When I came close, she clung to me; after a second or two she said, as she drew herself away, looking at me diffidently as though to excuse herself, or rather to account for her perturbation:

"The moment you had gone and I was alone in the dark with the treasure, all the weird prophecying of Gormala came back to me. The very darkness itself made light patches, and I saw shrouds floating everywhere. But it's all right now that you are here. Light a torch, and we shall look at the Pope's treasure." I took a torch out of the box and lit it; she laid it so that the lighted end projected well beyond the shelf of rock and gave a fine if fitful, light to all around. We found water about three feet deep at its worst; in the glare of the torch and because of its crystal purity, it did not look even so much. We stooped down to examine the box, which was only one of several lying in front of a great heap of something, all dark with rust and age, which filled up a whole corner of the cave.

The hasp was eaten through with rust, as well it might be after three centuries in the water, and only retained its form. This was doubtless due to the stillness of the water, for even the shock of my striking the box with my boot had broken it across. When I pulled at it, it crumbled to pieces in my fingers. In the same way the iron of the box itself was rusted right through; and as I tried to lift the lid which was annealed by corrosion to the sides of the box, it broke in my hands. I was able to tear it away like matchwood. The contents were not corroded, but were blackened by the sea. It was all money, but whether silver or gold we could not tell, and did not stop to see. Then we opened box after box in the same way, and in all but one found coins. This took a considerable time; but we did not in our excitement note its flying. The heap in the corner was composed of great ingots, to lift any of which took a distinct effort of strength. The one box unfilled with coins contained smaller boxes or caskets which were uncorroded and were, we presumed, of some superior metal, silver or gold. They were all locked; I lifted one of them and laid it on the shelf of rock whilst I searched for a key. It was a difficult matter to find any definite thing whilst stooping in the water, so I took my knife and tried with its point to prise open the casket. The lock must have been of iron and corroded; it gave way instantly under pressure, disclosing a glittering heap of stones which, even through all the cloudiness of the saline deposit of centuries, flashed red lights everywhere.

"Rubies!" cried Marjory who stood close to me, clapping her hands. "Oh! how lovely. Darling!" she added kissing me, for her expression of delight had to find a vent on something.

"Next!" I said as I bent to the iron chest to lift out another of the caskets.

I drew back with a shudder; Marjory looking anxiously at my face divined the cause and cried in genuine alarm:

"The tide! The tide is rising; and is shutting us in!"

XXXVI

The Rising Tide

I think there must be some provision of nature which in times of real danger keeps men's minds away from personal fears. I can honestly say that not a thought of danger for myself crossed my mind; though I was harrowed up and appalled by fears for Marjory. My mental excitement, however, took a practical shape, and thought after thought flashed through my brain as to how I could best serve my wife. The situation with its woeful possibilities came first; and afterwards, in quick succession, the efforts which might be made. But first I must see how we really stood. I did not know this cave and the lengths and levels of it well enough to be sure whether the tide could block us completely in. If there were but head-room the actual distance was not far to swim. This I could soon settle; taking Marjory's lamp which stood on the ledge of rock I ran down the cave calling out as I went:

"Stay here a minute, dear, I want to see how far the tide is in." The double winding of the cave made it hard for me to judge at a glance; it was only when I came to the piece of straight passage leading up from the sea that I could judge. From the time I left the treasure chamber of the cave the water got deeper and deeper as I went, but the difficulty was not in this way; I knew that so long as there was headway I could swim for it and take Marjory with me. But when I came down the straight, my hopes were altogether dashed. As the floor dipped towards the sea so did the roof in much greater degree. I knew that there was one place where at low water there was only barely headway even when we stooped low; but I was not prepared for what I saw. The water had already risen so far that this place was, from where I stood waist high in water, obliterated; the rocky roof sank into the still, level water. For a moment I considered whether it would not be best to dive through it. I had the cord to guide me, and I knew that towards its mouth the cave roof rose again. But then there was Marjory. She was not like myself an accomplished diver. It might be possible if the worst should come to the worst to draw her through the water-choked piece of tunnel by the guiding cord. But if the cord should break or anything go wrong... The thought was too dreadful!

I hurried back to Marjory to see how far it might be advisable to make the attempt, however dangerous, rather than be drowned in the deepening water of the cave, or asphyxiated if the space left were too small to allow us breathing till the falling of the tide.

I found Marjory standing on the shelf of rock, to which she had climbed by the aid of the San Cristobal figurehead. She was holding up the torch and examining carefully the walls and roof of the cave. When she heard the splash of my coming through the water, she turned; I could see that though her face was pale she was very calm and self-possessed. She said quietly:

"I have been looking for high-water mark, but I can hardly see any sign of it. I suppose in this dark cave, where neither seaweed nor zoophyte exists, there is no such thing. Unless of course it be that the whole cave is under the water line; in which case we must be ready for the worst." As she spoke she was raising the torch till its light illuminated, so far as was possible, the extreme angle of the cavern where it ran up to a sort of point. I scrambled up beside her, and making use of my greater height, took the torch and keeping it away at arm's length put my hand into the narrowing angle. I had a sort of secret hope that there might be some long crack or rift which, though it might be impossible for our bodies, might still give us air. Any such half-formed hope was soon shattered; the angle of the cave was in the solid rock, and there was no fissure or even crack beyond.

As there was no clue to the level reached by the tide, I tried back on the possibility of gauging it by measuring from low water, so far as my memory of the tides might serve. Judging by the depth of the water, so far as I had gone, the fall of the floor level must here have been some three feet. The floor level of the cave was almost that of low water, except where it dipped under the overhanging roof, or where was the ascending grade up to the pool in which the treasure boxes lay. As here on the border of the North Sea, with no estuary to increase tidage, the normal rise of the tide is between eleven and twelve feet, we had to account for another eight or nine feet for the rise of the tide. The ledge was about a foot above the surface of the water. If my calculations were correct there was head room and breathing space, for as I stood on the ledge the top of my head was still about two feet from the highest point of roof over us. I could not, however, be certain of my calculations, within a couple of feet. If, therefore, we could keep our place on the shelf of rock and endure the cold we might yet win through. The cold was a serious matter. At Cruden where the full sweep of the icy current from the North Sea runs in shore, the water is grievously cold, even in the hottest summer time. Already we were feeling the effects of our wet clothes, even in this silent cavern where the heat seemed to be much more than outside. When we had been looking at the jewels, I had myself felt the chill, and could feel Marjory shiver now and again. Indeed, I had been about to suggest our returning when I made the discovery of the rising tide.

It was no use regretting, however. We were caged in the cavern; and our only chance was to hold on somehow, till the tide should fall again. The practical side of Marjory's mind was all awake. It was she who quietly refilled the two lamps, and, with much spluttering of the wick at first, lighted again the one which I had let fall into the water. When both lamps were ready, she put out the torch and placed it in the tin box which she handed to me, saying:

"We may need all the air we can get for our breathing, and the torches would burn it up. We must have two lamps lest one should fail. Shove the box as far as it will go into the corner of the cave; it will be safe there—as safe as us at any rate, for it will be over our heads."

As she spoke a new idea occurred to me. I might raise the level of the ledge by piling the ingots on it! I did not lose any time, but jumping down began at once to lift them one by one on the ledge. It was heavy work, and no one but a very strong man could have lifted them from off the ground, much less have placed them on a ledge over where he stood. Moreover I had to bend into the water to reach them, and in the years which they had lain there in juxtaposition some deposit of salt or sea lime of some kind had glued them together. After the separation of the first, however, this difficulty grew less. Marjory aided me in placing the bars in position; when they were once fixed their great weight kept them in place.

It was odd how little in these moments the treasure counted for. The little heap of rubies lay on the shelf of rock unnoticed, and when in the strain of placing the ingots some of them were brushed off into the water, neither Marjory nor I took the trouble even to sweep them with a brush of the hand into a safer place. One of the metal caskets was tumbled bodily into the water without a thought.

When the ingots were all in place, and shaken into steady position, we got on the ledge together and began to test the security of our platform; it would be too late to find out any flaw of construction when the tide should have risen. We had made a foothold nearly two feet above the surface of the ledge, and this might give us at the last an additional chance. At any rate, even if we should not be so hard pressed as to have to raise our heads so high, it would give us a longer period of comparative dryness. We were already beginning to feel the chill of the tide. In those caves the air is all right, and we had not felt chilled, although we were more or less wet through; but I dreaded lest it might numb either of us so much as to prevent our taking every chance. When we stood together on the pile of gold and silver, our heads were so close to the roof that I felt safe so far as actually drowning or asphyxiation were concerned if the tide did not rise higher than I had computed. If we could only hold out till the tide had fallen sufficiently, we might get back.

And then we began the long, dreary wait for the rising tide. The time seemed endless, for our apprehension and suspense multiplied the real danger whatever it might be. We stood on the cave floor till the water had reached our waists, and all this time tried to keep moving, to dance up and down, to throw about arms and legs so as to maintain the circulation of the blood. Then we climbed up and sat on the platform of bullion till the water rose round our knees again. Then we stood on the ledge and took what exercise we could till the water climbed up over our feet and knees. It was a terrible trial to feel the icy, still water creep up, and up, and up. There was not a sound, no drip or ripple of water anywhere; only silence as deadly as death itself. Then came the time when we had to stand together on the pile of bullion which we had built up. We stood close, for there was merely foothold; I held Marjory up as well as I could, so as to lessen for her the strain of standing still. Our hearts beat together. We felt it, and we knew it; it was only the expression of both our thoughts when Marjory said:

"Thank God! dear, at the worst we can die together." In turn we held the lamp well over the water, and as we looked in aching suspense we saw the dark flood rise up to the sloping roof of the cave and steal towards us with such slow, relentless precision that for my own part I felt I must scream. I felt Marjory tremble; the little morsel of hysterics which goes to make up the sum total of every woman was beginning to assert itself. Indeed there was something hypnotic in that silent line of death creeping slowly towards us. At this time, too, the air began to feel less fresh. Our own breaths and the exhalations of the lamp was vitiating our breathing space. I whispered to Marjory:

"We must put out the light!" She shuddered, but said with as brave a voice as she could:

"All right! I suppose it is necessary. But, darling, hold me tight and do not let me away from you, or I shall die!"

I let the lantern fall into the water; its hissing for a moment drowned my own murmur of grief and Marjory's suppressed groan.

And now, in the darkness, the terror of the rising flood grew worse and worse. The chill water crept up, and up, and up; till at last it was only by raising her head that Marjory could breathe. I leaned back against the rock and bending my legs outward lifted her so that she rested her feet upon my knees. Up and up rose the chill water till it reached my chin, and I feared that the last moments had come.

There was one chance more for Marjory: and though it cut me to the soul to speak it, for I knew it would tear at her very heartstrings, I had to try it:

"Marjory, my wife, the end is close! I fear we may not both live. In a few minutes more, at most, the water will be over my mouth. When that time comes I shall sink over the pile of treasure on which we rest. You must then stand on me; it will raise you sufficiently to let you hold out longer." A dreadful groan broke from her.

"Oh, my God!" was all she said, but every nerve in her body seemed to quiver. Then without a word she seemed to become limp and was sliding out of my arms. I held her up strongly, for I feared she had swooned: she groaned out:

"Let me go, let me go! Either of us can rest on the other's body. I shall never leave this if you die."

"Dear one" I said "do as I wish, and I shall feel that even death will be a happy thing, since it can help you." She said nothing but clung to me and our mouths met. I knew what she meant; if die we must, we should die together in a kiss.

In that lover's kiss our very souls seemed to meet. We felt that the Gates of the Unknown World were being unbarred to us, and all its glorious mysteries were about to be unveiled. In the impassive stillness of that rising tide, where never a wave or ripple broke the dreadful, silent, calm, there was no accidental fall or rise which might give added uneasiness or sudden hope. We had by this time become so far accustomed to its deadly perfection as to accept its conditions. This recognition of inevitable force made for resignation; and I think that in those moments both Marjory and I realised the last limitations of humanity. When one has accepted the inevitable, the mere act of dying is easy of accomplishment.

But there is a contra to everything in the great ledgers of the Books of Life and Death, and it is only a final balance which counts for gain or loss. The very resignation which makes the thought of death easy to bear, is but a balance of power which may not be gainsayed. In the struggle of hope and despair the Winged One submits, and that is all. His wings are immortal; out of fire or water, or pestilence, or famine, or the red mist of battle they ever rise again, when once there is light of any kind to animate them.

Even when Marjory's mouth was bent to mine in a fond kiss of love and death, the wings of Hope fluttered around her head. For an instant or two she paused, as if listening or waiting, and then with a glad cry, which in that narrow space seemed to ring exultingly, she said:

"You are saved! You are saved! The water is falling; it has sunk below your lips." Even in that dread moment of life and death, I could not but be touched by her way of rejoicing in the possibility of our common safety. Her only thought was for me.

But her words were true. The tide had reached its full; the waters were falling. Minute by minute we waited, waited in breathless suspense; clinging to each other in an ecstasy of hope and love. The chill which had been upon us for so long, numbing every sense and seeming to make any idea of effort impossible, seemed to have lost its power. In the new quickening of hope, our hearts seemed to beat more warmly, till the blood tingled in our veins. Oh! but the time was long, there in the dark, with the silent waters receding inch by inch with a slowness which was inconceivable. The strain of waiting became after a while almost unbearable; I felt that I must speak to Marjory, and make her speak and keep speaking, lest we should both break down, even at the very last. In the time of our waiting for death we had held on to our determination, blindly resolute to struggle to the last; even though we had accepted the inevitable. But now there was impatience added to our apprehension. We did not know the measure of our own endurance; and Terror seemed to brood over us with flapping wings.

Truly, the moments of coming Life are longer than hours of coming Death.

XXXVII

Round the Clock

When the water had fallen so far that we could sit on the ledge, we rested for a few minutes to relieve the long and terrible strain of standing, cramped and chilled as we were. But we soon felt the chill of the water and stood again till the rocky ledge was quite free. Then we enjoyed a rest, if the word "enjoyment" could be applied to our wearied, teeth-chattering, exhausted condition. I made Marjory sit on my lap, so that we could get some warmth together, and that she might be saved from the benumbing coldness of the rock. We wrung out our clothes as well as we could, and with braver hearts set ourselves down to the second spell of our dark captivity. Well we knew that the tide had risen higher than the tin box in the corner of the cave, and tacitly put off the moment of assured knowledge. Presently when the chill had somewhat passed from her and she shivered less, she stood up and tried to get down the box. She could not reach it, so I rose and took it down. Then we resumed our places on the ledge, and, with the box beside us, began to investigate.

It was a sadly helpless performance. In the dark everything seemed strange, with regard to size as well as to shape. Our wet hands could not of themselves discriminate as to whether anything was wet or dry. It was only when we found that the box was quite full of water that we realised that there was no hope of light in this quarter, and that we must have patience through the darkness as well as we could. I think that Marjory cried a little. She covered it up for me in some womanly way. But there are eyes in the soul that can see even through cimmerian gloom; and I knew that she cried, though my senses could detect no sign. When I touched her face, my wet hands and my own wet face could tell me nothing. Still we were happy in a way. The fear of death had passed, and we were only waiting for light and warmth. We knew that every minute, every breath we drew, the tide was falling; and we knew too that we could grope our way through the cavern. We rejoiced now that there was no labyrinth of offshoots of the cave; and we were additionally glad that our clue, the cord which we had taken with us, remained. We could easily pick it up when we should begin to move, for there was no stir of water to shift it and draw it away.

When we thought that a sufficient time must have elapsed, even at the deadly slow pace at which it crawled, we kissed each other and began our first effort to escape.

We easily found the cord, and keeping hold of it, felt our way slowly along the rugged wall. I made Marjory keep close behind me, a little to the right, for I was feeling way by the left hand alone. I feared lest she should get bruised by the jagged rock which protruded here and there. It was well I did so, for in the first dozen yards I got some severe knocks that might have permanently scarred her tender skin. The experience made me careful, however, and after it I took care to feel my way all round before advancing a step. I found by experience that it was the cord which had misled me by straining where there was a curve or an angle, and so taking me close to the rock instead of in the middle of the passage where we had originally dropped it as we went along.

When we had passed the first two bends, the anxious time came; it was here that the roof dropped, and we did not know if the tide had fallen low enough to let us through. We pushed on however into the deepening water, Marjory still keeping close behind me, though I wished to go on alone and explore. We found that the rock dipped below the water level when we had gone some way into the tunnel. So we came back and waited a good while—it seemed a long, long time. Then we essayed again, and found that though the water was still high there were some inches of space between rock and water.

Joyfully we pushed on slowly; our hearts beat gladly when we could raise our heads from the stooping position and raise them freely in the air. It only took us a few minutes to reach the pile of rocks; then holding the cord as a clue to the narrow opening we scrambled up as well as we could. I helped Marjory as much as possible, but in this matter she was as good as I was; nay better, for all her woman's instinct came to aid, and it was she who first got through the narrow hole. Then very carefully we climbed down the other side, and, still holding our guiding cord, came at last to the tackle by which we had lowered ourselves into the cave. It was rather a surprise to us when we reached it, for we expected to see the welcome light through the opening before we had come under it.

At first, in the whirl of thoughts, I imagined that something had gone wrong, a rock fallen in, or some sort of general collapse. Then I fancied that we had been tracked down, and that some one had tried to bury us in the cave. It is wonderful what strange thoughts come to one in a prolonged spell of absolute darkness; no wonder that even low-grade, violent, unimaginative criminals break down in the black hole! Marjory said nothing; but when she spoke, it was evident from her words that she had some of the same ideas herself. There was a tone of relief in her voice which was unmistakable, and which must have followed some disconcerting thought:

"Of course not! It is only that the lamps and candles have burned out. We have forgotten the long time which has passed; but the lights haven't!" It was evident enough now. We had been so many hours in the cave that the lights were exhausted; and at no time was there a gleam of natural light in the cellar.

I found it a little difficult to work the tackle in the dark with my numbed hands. Hope, however, is a paramount force, and very soon Marjory was swinging up through the hole in the rock. I called to her to get light as soon as she could; but she refused point blank to do anything until I was beside her. When I got the rope round me, we both pulled; and in a very few seconds I too was up through the hole and in the cellar. I found the matches easily enough and oh! the glorious sight of the light even in this spluttering form. We did not linger an instant but moved to the door, which I unlocked, and we stepped out and ran up the steps. The lantern on the roof which lit the staircase was all ablaze with sunshine, and we felt bathed in light. For a second or two we could not realise it, and blinked under the too magnificent glare.

And then, with inconceivable rapidity, we came back to the serenity and confidence which comes with daylight. In less than a second we were again in the realities of life; and the whole long night of darkness and fear was behind us like a dream.

I hurried Marjory into the room where she had dressed, and where were a store of her clothes; and then I proceeded to make up a fire. The chimney place in the dining room was made after the old fashion, wide and deep, and had in the back a beautiful old steel rack with brackets on which to hang pots and kettles. I thought this would be the best place for a fire, as it was the biggest in the house. So I got from the fuel house off the kitchen an armful of dry furze and another of cut billets of pine which I dumped on top of it. A single match was sufficient, and in an instant, there was a large fire roaring up the chimney. I filled a great copper kettle with water and slung it in the blaze, and then, when I found myself in a cloud of steam from my wet clothes, ran into my own room. After a hard rub down which made my skin glow, and a wash which was exquisite, I put myself into dry clothes. When I came back to the dining room I found Marjory busy getting ready a meal—supper, breakfast, dinner, we did not know what to call it. One glad moment in each other's arms, and then kneeling together we thanked God for the great mercy which He had shown us. Then we resumed preparations to eat, for we were ravenous. The kettle was beginning to sing, and we soon had hot delicious tea, which sent a glow through us. There were plenty of cooked provisions, and we did not wait to warm them: such luxuries as hot food would come into our lives later. It was only when we had satisfied our appetites that we thought of looking at the time. My own watch had stopped when I had first tried the entrance to the great cave and had been waist high in water, but Marjory had left hers in her room when she had changed her dress for the expedition. It was now one o'clock and as the sun was high in the heavens it was—P. M. Allowing for the time of dressing and eating, we must have been in all in the caves some twelve hours. I looked amongst my books and found Whittaker's Almanach, from which I gathered that as the tide was full at half past six o'clock we must as the normal rise of the tide was between eleven and twelve feet have been immersed in the water some four hours. The very thought of it made us shudder; with an instinctive remembrance of our danger and misery we drew close together.

Then a heavy sleepiness seemed all at once to settle on us. Marjory would not leave me, and I did not wish her to. I felt, as she did, that we could not sleep easily if separated. So I got great armloads of rugs and cushions and made up two nests close to the fire which I built up with solid logs. I wrapped her in a great, warm plaid and myself in another, and we sank down on our couches, holding hands and with her head upon my shoulder.

When I woke it was almost pitch dark; only for a slight glow which came from the mass of red embers on the hearth the darkness would have been as complete as that of the cave. It is true that the sunblinds were down and the curtains drawn; but even so, when there was light outside some gleams of it even, if only reflected, found their way in. Marjory was still sleeping as I stole softly to the window and looked out.

All was dark. The moon was hidden behind a bank of cloud, only the edges of which tinged with light showed its place in the heavens. I looked at Marjory's watch which she had laid upon the table, having wound it up instinctively before the sleepiness had come upon her. It was now a few minutes past one.

We had slept right round the clock.

I began to make up the fire as softly as I could, for I did not wish to wake Marjory. I felt that sleep and plenty of it was the best thing for her after the prolonged strain and trial which she had undergone. I got ready clean plates and knives and forks, and put on the kettle again. Whilst I was moving about, she woke. For an instant or two she looked round in a dazed uncomprehending way; and then all at once the whole remembrance of the night swept across her. In a single bound, with the agility of a young panther, she sprang to her feet, and in an instant her arms were round me, half protectingly and whole lovingly.

We had another hearty meal. It was pic-nic-ing *in excelsis*, and I doubt if the whole world held two happier beings. Presently we began to talk of the cave and of the treasure, and I was rejoiced to find that all the trial and anxiety had left no trace on Marjory's courage. It was she herself who suggested that we should go back to the cave and take out what she called those dear little boxes. We put on once more our cave clothes, which were dry again but which had shrunk lamentably, and laughing at each other's grotesque appearance we went down into the cellar again. Having renewed the lamps and made all safe for our return, we took lamps and torches and matches and set out on our quest. I think we both felt a little awed—we were certainly silent—as we crept through the hole over the moraine and took our way up the treasure cave. I confess that my own heart sank within me when we saw the ledge, with the San Cristobal and the infant Christ seeming to keep guard upon it; and I felt a pity, which I had not felt before, for the would-be thief, Olgaref. Marjory I think felt the same way as I did, for she kept very close to me and now and again held on to me; but she said nothing. We lit a torch and renewed our search. Whilst I stooped over the box and took out other caskets containing gems, Marjory held the light with one hand whilst she gathered the little heap of rubies from the first box and put them in the pocket of my jacket. Her feminine care was shown in her searching for the box and the rubies which had fallen into the water so that none might be lost. There were not many of the little caskets—it is astounding what a small space will contain a many precious gems. They easily fitted into the bag which I had brought for the purpose. Then we took our way back to the house.

When we had ascended, we put out the lights and locked the cellar. We changed our clothes again, Marjory putting on her livery; it was now nearly four o'clock in the morning, and it was time to be getting back to Crom.

XXXVIII

The Duty of a Wife

Just as we were about to start Marjory said to me, half in jest but wholly in earnest:

"I wonder what has become of Gormala these times. If she knew of the last two nights, she would simply become desperate; and there is no knowing what she might prophecy!"

Strangely enough, I had been myself thinking of the Witch-woman. I suppose it was that the memory of the finding of the treasure, and of the hovering near us of death, had recalled her weirds. With the thought of her, came once more that strange feeling which I had before experienced, a feeling as if she were present. Motioning to Marjory to put out the light, I stole to the window. The heavy curtains, when I had passed through them, shut out the glimmer of the firelight. Marjory came and joined me, and we looked out together. There were drifting clouds, and thus, moments of light and shadow. In one of the former I saw a dark mass on the edge of the deep grass that crowns the rock just over the entrance of Witsennan Point. If it was a woman it was probably Gormala; and if it was Gormala she was probably watching me, for of course she could not know that Marjory was with me. I determined to find out if I could; so I told Marjory to slip out by the back door whilst I went to the point. We arranged to join at the upper village of old Whinnyfold.

Having placed my bicycle ready to start, and shut the door behind me softly, I stole over to the cliff. Lying just below the edge, but so that her head was at the top lay Gormala, asleep. At first I thought it was pretence, for I knew the wily nature of the old woman; but on examining closely I found her sleep was real. She looked worn and tired out, and I concluded that it was the second night of watching on end which had finished her. It was well she slept, for had she been awake she must have seen us. The place she had chosen commanded both paths away from the house left and right; only by stealing back over the hill and keeping the house all the time between us and herself could we have avoided her prying eyes. Even then, were there light enough, she might have seen us debouching on the roadway had we gone inland by Whinnyfold. I could not but be sorry for her; she looked so old and feeble, and yet with such purpose in her strong, stern face. I could afford to be pitiful now; my life was running on happy lines. I had won Marjory, and we had found the treasure!

I left her undisturbed; I would have put some rug or covering over her; but I was afraid lest I should awake her, and so make discovery of our plans. Besides it would be hard to account for my being awake myself and about at that hour of the night—or morning, I hardly knew which it was. Almost as hard as it would have been for Gormala to explain why she was in similar case.

When I joined Marjory, we took our way as quickly as possible to Crom; we were both anxious that she should get into the castle before daylight. It was with a certain dread, for the experiences of the night were not yet hardened in memory, that I saw Marjory descend into the cave when we rolled away the stone. She too was not free from misgiving; I knew it from the emphasis with which she impressed on me that I was not to fear for her. She was to wave a white handkerchief from the roof when she had got in safely.

Looking over the stone towards the castle whence must come her signal I waited with an anxiety which I could not conceal from myself. The grey dawn grew paler and paler as I looked, and the sky began to quicken. Here and there around me came every now and again the solitary pipe of an awakening bird. I could just see the top of the castle, looking bare and cold through the vista between the treetops. In a short time, almost shorter than I could have anticipated, I saw on the roof the flutter of a white handkerchief. My heart leaped; Marjory was safe. I waved my own handkerchief; she answered again, and there was no more sign. I came away satisfied, and wheeled back to Cruden with what speed I could. It was still very early morning, when I reached Whinnyfold. Not a soul was up as I passed on my way, and I crept in secretly by the back of the house.

When I looked carefully out of a window in front, I could see in the growing light of morning that Gormala still lay on the edge of the cliff, motionless and manifestly asleep.

I lay down for a while and dozed till the morning was sufficiently advanced. Then after a cold bath and a cup of hot tea, took my way to Crom, timing myself so as to arrive for an early breakfast.

Mrs. Jack met me, beaming. She was so hearty, and so manifestly glad to see me, that I bent over and kissed her. She was not a bit displeased;

she seemed a little touched by the act, and smiled at me. Then Marjory came in, looking radiant. She greeted me with a smile, and went over to and kissed Mrs. Jack affectionately. Then she kissed me too, and there was a glad look in her eyes which made my heart thrill.

After breakfast she sat in the window with Mrs. Jack, and I went to the fireplace to light a cigarette. I stood with my back to the fire and looked over at Marjory; it was always a joy to me when she was in my sight. Presently she said to Mrs. Jack:

"Weren't you frightened when I didn't come back the night before last?" The elderly lady smiled complacently as she answered:

"Not a bit, my dear!" Marjory was astonished into an exclamation:

"Why not?" The affectionate old woman looked at her gravely and tenderly:

"Because I knew you were with your husband; the safest place where a young woman can be. And oh! my dear, I was rejoiced that it was so; for I was beginning to be anxious, and almost unhappy about you. It didn't seem right or natural for two young people like you and your husband to be living, one in one place and one in another." As she spoke she took Marjory's hand in hers and stroked it lovingly. Marjory turned her head away from her, and, after one swift glance at me from under her eyelashes, from me also. Mrs. Jack went on in a grave, sweet way, lecturing the girl she loved and that she had mothered; not as a woman lectures a child but as an old woman advises her junior:

"For oh! Marjory, my dear one, when a woman takes a husband she gives up herself. It is right that she should; and it is better too, for us women. How can we look after our mankind, if we're thinking of ourselves all the time! And they want a lot of looking after too, let me tell you. They're only men after all—the dears! Your bringing-up, my child, has not made you need them. But you would well understand it, if when you was a child, you was out on the plains and among the mountains, like I was; if you didn't know when you saw your daddy, or your brother, or your husband go out in the morning whether you'd ever see him come back at night, or would see him brought back. And then, when the work was over, or the fight or whatever it might be, to see them come home all dirty and ragged and hungry, and may be sick or wounded—for the Indians made a lot of harm in my time with their good old bows and their bad new guns—where would we women and girls have been. Or what sort of women at all at all, if we didn't have things ready for them! My dear, as I suppose you know now, a man is a mighty good sort of a thing after all. He may be cross, or masterful, or ugly to deal with when he has got his shirt out; but after all he's a man, and that's what we love them for. I was beginning to wonder if you was a girl at all, when I see you let your husband go away from you day after day and you not either holdin' him back, or goin' off with him, way the girls did in my time. I tell you it would have been a queer kind of girl in Arizony that'd have let her man go like that, when once they had said the word together. Why, my dear, I lay awake half the night sayin' my prayers for the both of you, and blessin' God that He had sent you such a happiness as true love; when there might have been them that would have ben runnin' after your fortun' and gettin' on your weak side enough to throw dust in your eyes. And when in the grey of the dawn I looked into your room and found you hadn't come, why I just tip-toed back to my bed and went to sleep happy. And I was happy all day, knowin' you were happy too. And last night I just went to sleep at once and didn't bother my head about listenin' for your comin'; for well I knew you wouldn't be home then. Ah! my dear, you've done the right thing. At the least, your husband's wishes is as much as your own, seein' as how there's two of you. But a woman only learns her true happiness when she gives up all her own wishes, and thinks only for her husband. And, mind you, child, it isn't givin' up much after all—at least we didn't think so in my time—when she pleases her husband that she loves, by goin' off to share his home."

I listened full of deep emotion as the old lady spoke. I felt that every word she said was crystallised truth; and there was no questioning the deep, earnest, loving-kindness of her intent. I was half afraid to look at Marjory lest I should disconcert her; so I turned round quietly till I faced the fireplace, and leaning on the plinth of it stole a glance in the old oval mirror above. Marjory sat there with her hand in Mrs. Jack's. Her head was bent, and there was a flush on her neck and arms which told its own story. I felt that she was silently crying, or very near it; and a lump rose in my own throat. This was one of the crises in her life. It was so borne in upon me; and I knew its truth. We have all, as the Scotch say, to "dree our own weird," this was a battle with her own soul which Marjory must fight alone. The old woman's wise words sounded a trumpet note of duty. She was face to face with it, and must judge for herself. Even with all my love, I could not help her. I stood silent, scarcely daring to breathe lest I should disturb or distract her. I tried to efface myself, and for a few minutes did not even look in the mirror.

The old woman too, knew the value of silence, for she sat still; there was not even the rustle of her dress. At last I could hear Marjory's in-drawn breath, and looked in the mirror. Her attitude had not changed, except that she had raised her head; I could tell by its proud poise that she was her own woman again. She still kept her face away; and there was the veil of recent tears over her sweet voice as she spoke tenderly:

"Thank you, dear. I am so glad you have spoken to me so freely and so lovingly." I could see from the motion of the two hands and her own whitening knuckles that she was squeezing her companion's fingers. Then, after a few moments she rose quietly, and, still keeping her head averted, sailed quietly out of the room in her own graceful manner. I did not stir; I felt that I could please her best by keeping quiet.

But oh! how my heart went with her in her course.

XXXIX

An Unexpected Visitor

I chatted with Mrs. Jack for a few minutes with what nonchalance I could muster, for I wanted to cover up Marjory's retreat. I have not the faintest idea what we talked about; I only know that the dear old lady sat and beamed on me, with her lips pursed up in thought, and went on with her knitting. She agreed with everything I said, whatever it was. I longed to follow Marjory and comfort her. I could see that she was distressed, though I did not know the measure of it. I waited patiently, however, for I knew that she would either come to me, or send me word to join her when she wanted me.

She must have come back very quietly, almost tip-toe, for I had not heard a sound when I saw her in the doorway. She was beckoning to me, but in such a manner that Mrs. Jack could not see her. I was about to go quietly, but she held up a warning hand with five fingers outspread; from which I took it that I was to follow in five minutes.

I stole away quietly, priding myself on the fact that Mrs. Jack did not notice my departure; but on thinking the matter over later, I came to the conclusion that the quiet old lady knew a good deal more of what was going on round her than appeared on the surface. Her little homily to Marjory on a wife's duty has set me thinking many a time since.

I found Marjory, as I expected, in the Ladies' Room. She was looking out of the window when I came in. I took her in my arms for an instant, and she laid her head on my shoulder. Then she drew herself away, and pointed to a great chair close by for me to sit down. When I was seated she took a little stool, and placing it beside me, sat at my feet. From our position I had to look down at her, and she had to look up at me. Often and often since then have I recalled the picture she made, sitting there in her sweet graceful simplicity. Well may I remember it, for through many and many an aching hour has every incident of that day, however trivial, been burned into my brain. Marjory leant one elbow on the arm of my chair, and put the other hand in mine with a sweet confiding gesture which touched me to the heart. Since our peril of two nights before, she was very, very dear to me. All the selfishness seemed to have disappeared from my affection for her, and I was her true lover as purely as it is given to a man to be. She wanted to speak; I could see that it was an effort to do so, for her breast heaved a few times, as a diver breathes before making his downward leap. Then she mastered herself, and with infinite grace and tenderness spoke:

"I'm afraid I have been very selfish and inconsiderate. Oh! yes I have" for I was commencing a protest. "I know it now. Mrs. Jack was quite right. It never occurred to me what a brute I have been; and you so good to me, and so patient. Well, dear, that's all over now! I want to tell you, right here, that if you like I'll go away with you to-morrow—to-day if you wish; and we'll let every one know that we are married, and go and live together." She stopped, and we sat hand in hand with our fingers clasping. I remained quite still with a calm that amazed me, for my brain was in a whirl. But somehow there came to me, even as it had come to her, a sense of duty. How could I accept such a sweet sacrifice. The very gravity of her preparation for thought and speech showed me that she was loth to leave the course on which she had entered. That she loved me I had no doubt; was it not for me that she was willing to give it all up. And then my course of action rose clear before me. Instinctively I stood up as I spoke to her, and I felt that big stalwart man as I was, the pretty self-denying girl at my feet ruled me, for she was more to me than my own wishes, my own hopes, my own soul.

"Marjory, do you remember when you sat on the throne in the cave, and gave me the accolade?" She bowed her head in acquiescence; her eyes fell, and her face and ears grew rosy pink. "Well, when you dubbed me your knight, and I took the vow, I meant all I said! Your touch on my shoulder was more to me than if it had come from the Queen on her throne, with all the glory of a thousand years behind her. Oh, my dear, I was in earnest—in earnest then, as I am in earnest now. I was, and am, your true knight! You are my lady; to serve, and make her feet walk in easy ways! It is a terrible temptation to me to take what you have offered as done, and walk straightway into Paradise in our new life. But, my dear! my dear! I too can be selfish if I am tempted too far; and I must not think of my own wishes alone. Since I first saw your face I have dreamt a dream. That a time would come when you, with all the world to choose from, would come to me of your own free will. When you wouldn't want to look back with regret at anything, done or undone. I want you to be happy; to look forward only—unless the backward thought is of happiness. Now, if you give up your purpose and come to me with the feeling that you have only made a choice, the regret that you did not have the opportunity you longed for, may grow and grow, till—till it may become an unhappiness. Let me be sententious for a moment. 'Remember Lot's wife' was not merely the warning of a fact; it touched a great allegory. You and I are young; we are both happy; we have all the world before us, and numberless good things to thank God for. I want you to enjoy them to the full; and, my dear one, I will not stand in your way in anything which you may wish. Be free, Marjory, be quite free! The girl I want beside my hearth is one who would rather be there than anywhere else in the wide world. Isn't that worth wishing for; isn't it worth waiting for? It may be selfish in the highest plane of selfishness; I suppose it is. But anyhow, it is my dream; and I love you so truly and so steadfastly that I am not afraid to wait!"

As I spoke, Marjory looked at me lovingly, more and more. Then all at once she broke down, and began to sob and cry as if her heart would break. That swept away in a moment all my self-command; I took her in my arms and tried to comfort her. Kisses and sweet words fairly rained upon her. Presently she grew calm, and said as she gently disengaged herself:

"You don't know how well you argue. I'm nearer at this moment to giving up all my plans, than I ever thought I should be in my life. Wait a little longer, dear. Only a little; the time may be shorter than you think. But this you may take for your comfort now, and your remembrance later; that in all my life, whatever may come, I shall never forget your goodness to me, your generosity, your love, your sympathy—your—! But there, you are indeed my Knight; and I love you with all my heart and soul!" and she threw herself into my arms.

When I left Crom after lunch the weather seemed to have changed. There was a coldness in the air which emphasised the rustling of the dry leaves as they were swept by intermittent puffs of wind. Altogether there was a sense of some presage of gloom—or disaster—of discontent, I knew not what. I was loth to part with Marjory, but we both felt it was necessary I should go. I had not had my letters for three days; and besides there were a thousand things to be attended to about the house at Whinnyfold. Moreover, we began to think of the treasure, the portable part of which—the jewels—was left almost open in the dining room. I did not want to alarm Marjory by any dim fears of my own; I knew that, in any case, there might be a reaction from her present high spirits. The remembrance of the trials and anxieties of the past few days would come back to her in the silence of the night. She saw, however, with the new eyes of her wifely love, that I was anxious about something; justly inferring that it was about her, she said to me quietly:

"You need not be alarmed about me, darling. I promise you I shall not stir out of the house till you come. But you will come as early as you can to-morrow; won't you. Somehow, I don't like your leaving me now. I used not to mind it; but to-day it all seems different. We don't seem to be the same to each other, do we, since we felt that water creep up us in the dark. However, I shall be very good. I have a lot of work to do, and letters to write; and the time may not go so very slowly, or seem so very long, till I see my husband again."

Oh! it was sweet to look in her eyes, and see the love that shone from them; to hear the delicate cooing music of her voice. My heart seemed to fly back to her as I moved away; and every step I took, its strings seemed nearer and nearer to the breaking point. When I looked back at the turn of the winding avenue between the fir trees, the last I saw through my dimming eyes was the wave of her hand and the shining of her eyes blending into one mass of white light.

In my rooms at the hotel I found a lot of letters about business, and a few from friends. There was one however which made me think. It was in the writing of Adams, and was as follows, no place or date being given:

"The people at Crom had better be careful of their servants! There is a footman who often goes out after dark and returns just before morning. He may be in league with enemies. Anyhow, where he gets out and in, and how, others may do the same. *Verb. sap, suff. A.* "

We had been watched then, and by the Secret Service detectives. I was glad that Marjory had promised not to go out till I came. If "Mac's men" had seen her, others might also; and the eyes of the others might have been more penetrating, or their reasoning powers more keen. However, I thought it well to send her a word of warning. I copied Adams's letter into mine, with just a word or two of love added. I was amazed to find that altogether it ran to several pages! The gillie of the hotel took it over in a pony cart, with instructions to bring me back an answer to Whinnyfold. For safety I enclosed it in an envelope to Mrs. Jack. Then, when I had written a few notes and telegrams, I biked over to my house on the cliff.

It was a bleak afternoon and everything seemed grey, sky and sea alike; even the rocks, with their crowning of black seaweed swept with the foam of lapping waves. Inside the house nothing had of course been stirred; but it seemed so bleak without a fire and with the curtains wide, that I made up a fire of billets and drew the heavy curtains close. As I stood in the great bay window and looked out on the fretting sea, and listened to the soughing of the rising wind, a great melancholy seemed to steal over me, so that I became in a way lost in a mist of gloom. So far as I remember, my thoughts were back with the time when I had seen the procession of the dead coming up out of the sea from the Skares beyond, and of the fierce looking Spaniard who walked alone in their ranks and looked at me with living eyes. I must have been in a sort of day-dream and unconscious of all around me; for, though I had not noticed any one approaching, I was startled by a knocking at the door. The house was not quite finished; there were electric bells in position, but they had not yet been charged, and there was no knocker on the door. The knocking was that of bare knuckles on a panel. I thought of course that it was the gillie back from Crom, for I did not expect any one else; so I went at once and opened the door. I recoiled with pure wonder. There, looking grave and dignified, an incarnation of the word 'gentleman' stood Don Bernardino. His eyes, though now serene, and even kindly, were the eyes of the dead man from the sea. Behind him, a few yards off, stood Gormala MacNiel with an eager look on her face, half concealed by such a grin as made me feel as though I had been trapped, or in some way brought to book. The Spaniard at once spoke:

"Sir, your pardon! I wish much that I may speak with you in private, and soon. Forgive me if that I trouble you, but it is on a matter of such moment, to me at the least, that I have ventured an intrusion. I learned at the hotel that you had hither come; so with the guidance of this good lady, who did me much inform, I have found." As he spoke of Gormala, he half turned and made a gesture towards her. She had been watching our every movement with cat-like eagerness; but when she saw that we were speaking of her, a dark look swept her face, and she moved away scowling. The Spaniard went on:

"What I have to say is secret, and I would be alone with you. May it be that I enter your house; or will you come to mine? I do not mean my castle of Crom, but the house at Ellon which I have taken, until such time as the Senora Jack and that so fair patriot of hers shall wish to leave it." His manner was so gravely courteous and his bearing so noble, that I found it almost impossible to mistrust him, even when there flashed across my memory that dark red-eyed look of his at Crom, which recalled so vividly the dead Spaniard with the living eyes of hate in the procession of ghosts from the Skares. I felt that, in any case, it could not do any harm to hear what he had to say: 'Forewarned is forearmed' is a good apothegm in dealing with an enemy. I motioned him into the house; he bowed gravely and entered. As I shut the door behind us, I caught sight of Gormala with an eager look on her face stealing swiftly towards the house. She evidently wanted to be near enough to watch, and to hear if she could.

As I was opening the door of the drawing-room for Don Bernardino to enter, a sudden glimpse of its interior, seen in the dim light through the chinks of the shutters, changed my plans. This was the room improvised as a dressing room for Marjory, and the clothes which she had worn in the cave were scattered about the room, hung over the backs of chairs to dry. Her toilet matters also were on the table. Altogether I felt that to bring the stranger into the room would not only be an indelicacy towards my wife, but might in some way give a clue to our enemy to guess our secret. With a hasty excuse I closed the door and motioned my guest into the dining room across the hall. I asked him to be seated, and then went over to the window and pulled aside the curtains to give us light. I felt that somehow I was safer in the light, and that it might enable me to learn more than I could have done in the dim twilight of the curtained room.

When I turned round, the Spaniard was still standing, facing me. He appeared to be studiously keeping himself still; but I could see that under his long black lashes his eyes were roaming round the room. Unconsciously to myself, as I know now, my eyes followed his and took in the frightful untidiness of the place. The great hearth was piled with extinct ashes; the table was littered with unwashed cups and plates and dishes, for we had not cleared up anything after our night in the cave. Rugs and pillows were massed untidily on the floor, and the stale provisions on the table made themselves manifest in the close atmosphere of the room. I was moving over to throw up the window so as to let in a little fresh air, when I remembered that Gormala was probably outside with her ears strained close to the wall to hear anything that we might say. So, instead, I apologised for the disorder, saying that I had camped me there for some days whilst working at my book—the excuse I had given at the hotel for my spells of solitary life.

The Spaniard bowed low with grave courtesy, and implored that I would make no apology. If there were anything not perfect, and for himself he did not see it, such deficiencies were swept away and lost in the tide of honour with which I had overwhelmed him in the permission to enter my house; and much more to the same effect.

Then he came to the serious side of things and began to speak to the point.

XL

The Redemption of a Trust

S enor, you may wonder why I am here, and why I would speak with you alone and in secret. You have seen me only in a place, which though my own by birthright, was dominated by the presence of ladies, who alas! by their nationality and the stress of war were mine enemies. From you is not such. Our nations are at peace, and there is no personal reason why we should not be of the most friendly. I come to you, Senor, because it is borne to me that you are cavalier. You can be secret if you will, and you will recognise the claims of honour and duty, of the highest. The common people know it not; and for the dear ladies who have their own honour, our duties in such are not a part of their lives—nay! they are beyond and above the life as it is to us. I need not tell you of a secret duty of my family, for it is known to me that all of such is already with you. The secret of the Pope's treasure and of the duty of my House to guard and restore it has been in your mind. Oh yes, this I know" for he saw I was about to speak. "Have I not seen in your hands that portion of the book, so long lost!" Here he stopped and his eyes narrowed; some thought of danger, necessitating caution, had come to him. I, too, was silent; I wanted to think. Unless I had utterly misconceived him, he had made an extraordinary admission; one which had given him away completely. The only occasion on which I had seen him was when he had pointed out to us that the pages which I had found belonged to the book in the library. It is true that we had suggested to him that there was a cipher in the marking of the letters, but he had not acknowledged it. At the time he certainly did not convey the idea to us that he believed we had grasped the secret. How then did he know; or on what assumption did he venture to state that I knew his secret. Here was a difficult point to pass. If I were silent he would take all for granted; in such case I might not learn anything of his purpose. So I spoke:

"Your pardon, Sir, but you presume a knowledge on my part of some secret history of your family and of a treasure of the Pope; and then account for it that you have seen in my hand the book, a part of which was long lost. Am I to take it that because there is, or may be, a secret, any one who suspects that there is one must know it?" The steady eyes of the Spaniard closed, narrower and narrower still, till the pupils looked like those of a cat in the dark; a narrow slit with a cavern of fire within. For fully half a minute he continued to look at me steadily, and I own that I felt disconcerted. In this matter he had the advantage of me. I knew that what he said was true; I did know the secret of the buried treasure. He had some way of knowing the extent of my knowledge of the matter. He was, so far, all truth; I was prevaricating—and we both knew it! All at once he spoke; as though his mind were made up, and he would speak openly and frankly. The frankness of a Latin was a fell and strange affair:

"Why shall we beat about the bush. I know; you know; and we both know that the other knows. I have read what you have written of the secret which you have drawn from those marked pages of the law book."

As he spoke the whole detail of his visit to Crom rose before me. At that time he had only seen the printed pages of the cipher; he had not seen my transcript which had lain, face down, upon the table. We had turned it, on hearing some one coming in.

"Then you have been to the castle again!" I said suddenly. My object was to disconcert him, but it did not succeed. In his saturnine frankness had been a complete intention, which was now his protection against surprise.

"Yes!" he said slowly, and with a smile which showed his teeth, like the wolf's to Red Ridinghood.

"Strange, they did not tell me at Crom," I said as though to myself.

"They did not know!" he answered. "When next I visited my own house, it was at night, and by a way not known, save to myself." As he spoke, the canine teeth began to show. He knew that what he had to tell was wrong; and being determined to brazen it out, the cruelty which lay behind his strength became manifest at once. Somehow at that moment the racial instinct manifested itself. Spain was once the possession of the Moors, and the noblest of the old families had some black blood in them. In Spain, such is not, as in the West, a taint. The old diabolism whence sprung fantee and hoo-doo seemed to gleam out in the grim smile of incarnate, rebellious purpose. It was my cue to throw my antagonist off his guard; to attack the composite character in such way that one part would betray the other.

"Strange!" I said, as though to myself again. "To come in secret into a house occupied by another is amongst civilised people regarded as an offence!"

"The house is my own!" he retorted quickly, with a swarthy flush.

"Strange, again!" I said. "When Mrs. Jack rented the castle, there was no clause in her agreement of a right to the owner to enter by a secret way! On the contrary such rights as the owner reserved were exactly specified."

"A man has a right to enter his own house, when and how he will; and to protect the property which is being filched from him by strangers!" He said the last words with such manifest intention of offence that I stood on guard. Evidently he wanted to anger me, as I had angered him. I determined that thenceforward I should not let anything which he might say ruffle me. I replied with deliberate exasperation:

"The law provides remedies for any wrongs done. It does not, that I know of, allow a man to enter secretly into a house that he has let to another. There is an implied contract of peaceful possession, unless entry be specified in the agreement." He answered disdainfully:

"My agent had no right to let, without protecting such a right."

"Ah, but he did; and in law we are bound by the acts of our agents. '*Facit per alium*' is a maxim of law. And as to filching, let me tell you that all your property at Crom is intact. The pieces of paper that you claimed were left in the book; and the book has remained as you yourself placed it on the shelf. I have Mrs. Jack's word that it would be so." He was silent; so, as it was necessary that the facts as they existed should be spoken of between us, I went on:

"Am I to take it that you read the private papers on the table of the library during your nocturnal visit? By the way, I suppose it was nocturnal."

"It was."

"Then sir," I spoke sharply now, "who has done the filching? We—Miss Drake and I—by chance discovered those papers. As a matter of fact they were in an oaken chest which I bought at an auction in the streets of Peterhead. We suspected a cipher and worked at it till we laid bare the mystery. This is what we have done; we who were even ignorant of your name! Now, what have you done? You come as an admitted guest, by permission, into a house taken in all good faith by strangers. When there you recognised some papers which had been lost. We restored them to you. Honour demanded that you should have been open with us after this. Did you ask if we had discovered the secret of the trust? No! You went away openly; and came back like a thief in the night and filched our secret. Yes sir, you did!" He had raised his hand in indignant protest. "It was our secret then, not yours. Had you interpreted the secret cipher for yourself, you would have been within your rights; and I should have had nothing to say. We offered to let you take the book with you; but you refused. It is evident that you did not know the whole secret of the treasure. That you knew there was a treasure and a secret I admit; but the key of it, which we had won through toil, you stole from us!"

"Senor!" the voice was peremptory and full of all that was best and noblest in the man. "A de Escoban is not wont to hear such an allegation; and he who makes such shall in the end have his own death to answer for!" He stopped suddenly, and at his stopping I exulted secretly; though I wished to punish him for his insinuation that Marjory had filched from him, I had no desire to become entangled in a duel. I was determined to go on, however; for I would not, at any hazard, pass a slight upon my peerless wife. I think that his sudden pause meant thought; and thought meant a peaceful solution of things on my own lines. Nevertheless, I went on forcing the issue:

"I rejoice, sir, that you are not accustomed to hear such allegations; I trust that you are also not accustomed to deserve them!" By this time he was calm again, icily calm. It was wonderful with what rapidity, and how widely, the pendulum of his nature swung between pride and passion. All at once he smiled again, the same deadly, dreadful smile which he imagined to be the expression of frankness.

"I see I am punished! 'Twas I that first spoke of stealing. Senor, you have shown me that I was wrong. My pardon to that so good lady who is guest of my house; and also to that other patriotic one who so adorns it. Now let me say, since to defend myself is thrust upon me, that you, who have, with so much skill made clear the hidden mystery of that law book which I have only lately read, know best of all men how I am bound to do all things to protect my trust. I am bound, despite myself, even if it were not a duty gladly undertaken for the sake of the dead. It was not I who so undertook; but still I am bound even more than he who did. I stand between law and honour, between life and death, helpless. Senor, were you in my place, would you not, too, have acted as I did? Would you not do so, knowing that there was a secret which you could not even try to unravel, since long ago that in which it was hidden had been stolen or lost. Would you not do so, knowing, too, that some other—in all good faith and innocence let us say—had already made discovery which might mock your hopes and nullify the force of that long vigil, to which ten generations of men, giving up all else, had sacrificed themselves? Would not you, too, have come in secret and made what discovery you could. Discovery of your own, mark you! Would not also that lady so patriotic, to whom all things come after that devotion to her country, which so great she holds?"

Whilst he was speaking I had been thinking. The pretence of ignorance was all over to both of us; he knew our knowledge of the secret trust, and we knew that he knew. The only thing of which he was yet ignorant, was that we had discovered the treasure itself. There was nothing to be gained by disputing points of conjectural morals. Of course he was right; had either Marjory or myself considered ourselves bound by such a duty as lay so heavy on him we should have done the same. I bowed as I answered;

"Sir, you are right! Any man who held to such a duty would have done the same."

"Senor," he answered quickly, "I thank you with all my heart!" Poor fellow, at that moment I pitied him. The sudden flash of joy that leaped to his face showed by reaction in what a hell he must have of late been living. This momentary episode seemed to have wiped away all his bitterness; it was in quite a different way that he spoke again:

"And now, Senor, since your engaging frankness has made my heart so glad, may I ask further of your kindness. Believe me that it is not of my own will, but from an unbending sense of duty that I do and may have to do such things; my life till lately has been otherwise, oh! so much so! You have the feelings of honour yourself; like me you are also man of the world, and as such we can sacrifice all things save honour. Is there no way in which you can aid me to fulfill my trust; and let there be peace between us?" He looked at me anxiously; I said:

"I fear I hardly understand?" With manifest embarrassment he went on;

"You will forgive me if I err again; but this time I must make myself clear. It is manifest to me that in these days of science nothing can long remain hidden, when once a clue has been found. You already know so much that I am placed almost as though the treasure has already been found. Thereafter where am I; what am I? One who has failed in his trust. Who has allowed another to step in; and so dishonour him! A moment, Senor, and I am done," for he saw that I was about to speak. "It is not the treasure itself that I value, but the trust. If I could make it safe by the sacrifice of all my possessions I would gladly do so. Senor, you are still free. You have but to abandon your quest. It is not to you a duty; and therefore you sacrifice naught of honour should you abandon it. Here I pledge to you—and, oh Senor, I pray have patience that you take no affront that I do so—that in such case I shall give to you all that I have. Give it gladly! So, I may redeem the trust of my House; and go out into the wide world, though it may be as a beggar, yet free—free! Oh! pause, Senor, and think. I am rich in the world's goods. My ancestors were of vast wealth; even at that time when the great Bernardino did give his ship to his king. And for three centuries all have been prudent; and all their possessions have grown. There are vast lands of corn, great forests, many castles, whole ranges of mountains as yet untouched for their varied treasures which are vast. There are seaports and villages; and in all, the dwellers are happy and content. I am the last of my race. There is none to inherit; so I am free to pledge myself." He did not bow or bend; there was no persistence of request in his voice, or tone, or manner. In all there was no feeling of a bargain. It was an offer, based on the fulfillment of his own desires; given in such a lordly way that there could be no offence in it. He recognised so thoroughly the strength of my own position, that the base side of barter became obliterated; it was an exchange of goods between gentlemen. Such, at least, I recognised was his intellectual position; my own remained the same. How could I, or any man, take advantage of such an offer. After thinking a few seconds I said to him:

"Sir, you have honoured me by grouping us as men of honour. What would you do in my place?" His eye brightened, and his breath came more quickly as he replied:

"Were it my case, I should say: 'Senor, your duty is one of honour; mine is one of gain. There can be no comparisons. Fulfill your debt to your forefathers! Redeem the pledge that they have made in your name! Discover your treasure; and be free!'" There was infinite pride in his voice and manner; I think he really meant what he said. I went on with my questioning:

"And what about the taking of your estate as a reward of forbearance?"

He shrugged his shoulders: "For that," he said, "it matters not."

"Ah, for you to give you mean?" He nodded.

"But what for me to take? Would you do so in my place?" He was manifestly in a dilemma. I could see something of the working of his mind in his face. If he said he would himself take it, he would manifestly lower himself in his own eyes; and to such pride as his, his own self-respect was more than the respect of others, in proportion to his self-value. If he said he would not, then he might peril his chance of getting what he desired. The temptation was a cruel one; with all my heart I honoured him for his answer, given with the fullness of his mighty pride:

"Senor, I can die; I cannot stoop! But what avails my own idea? The answer is not for me! I have offered all I have. I will in addition pledge myself to hold my life at your service when this great trust is relieved. To this my honour is guardian; you need not fear it shall be redeemed! Now Senor, you have my answer! To redeem the trust of my sires I give all I have in the world, except my honour! The answer rests with you!"

XLI

Treasure Trove

There was no doubt that the Spaniard's devotion to his cause placed me in a considerable difficulty. I could not disguise from myself that he put forward a very strong claim for the consideration of one gentleman by another. It was only on hurriedly thinking the matter over that the weakness of his cause was apparent. Had the whole affair been a private or personal one; had the treasure belonged to his ancestors, I should have found it in my own heart a very difficult matter to gainsay him, and be subsequently at ease with myself. I remembered, however, that the matter was a public one. The treasure was collected by enemies of England for the purpose of destroying England's liberty, and so the liberty of the whole human race for which it made. It was sent in charge of a personal enemy of the country in a ship of war, one of many built for the purpose of invading and conquering England. In time of national stress, when the guns were actually thundering along our coast from the Thames to the Tyne, the treasure had been hidden so as to preserve it for future use in its destined way. Though centuries had passed, it was still held in mind; and the very men who had guarded it were, whilst professing to be Britons, secret enemies of the country, and devoted to her ultimate undoing. Beyond this again, there was another reason for not giving it up which appealed to me more strongly than the claim of my own natural duty, because it came to me through Marjory. Though Spain was at peace with my country, it was at war with hers; the treasure collected to harm England might—nay, would—be used to harm America. Spain was impoverished to the last degree. Her treasuries were empty, her unpaid soldiers clamourous for their arrears. Owing to want at home, there was in places something like anarchy; abroad there was such lack of all things, ships, men, stores, cannon, ammunition, that the evil of want came across the seas to the statesmen of the Quirinal with heart-breaking persistence. America, unprepared for war at first, was day by day becoming better equipped. The panic had abated which had set in on the seaboard towns from Maine to California, when each found itself at the mercy of a Spanish fleet sweeping the seas, no man knew where. Now if ever, money would be of value to impoverished

Spain. This great treasure, piled up by the Latin for the conquering of the Anglo-Saxon, and rescued from its burial of three centuries, would come in the nick of time to fulfill its racial mission; though that mission might be against a new branch of the ancient foe of Spain, whose roots only had been laid when the great Armada swept out in all its pride and glory on its conquering essay. I needed no angel to tell me what would be Marjory's answer, were such a proposition made to her. I could see in my mind's eye the uprearing of her tall figure in all its pride and beauty, the flashing of her eyes with that light of patriotic fire which I knew so well, the set of her mouth, the widening of her nostril, the wrinkling of her ivory forehead as the brows were raised in scorn—

"Sir," said I with what dignity I had, "the matter is not for you or me to decide. Not for us both! This is an affair of two nations, or rather of three: The Papacy, the Spaniard, the Briton. Nay, it touches another also, for the lady who shares the secret with me represents the country with which your nation is at war!" The Spaniard was manifestly baffled; the red, hellish light shone in his eyes again. His anger found expression in a sneer:

"Ah! so I suppose you do not propose to deal with the treasure, when found, as a private matter; but shall hand it over to your government to deal with!" The best answer to his scorn was complacency; so I said quietly:

"There again we are in a difficulty. You see, my dear fellow, no one exactly knows how we stand in this matter. The law of Treasure Trove, as we call it in this country, is in a most chaotic state. I have been looking it up since I undertook this quest; and I am rather surprised that in all the years that have elapsed since our practical law-making began, nothing has been done to put such matters on an exact basis. The law, such as it is, seems to rest on Royal Prerogative; but what the base of that prerogative is, no one seems exactly to know. And besides, in the various constitutional changes, and the customs of different dynasties, there are, or certainly there may be, barriers to the assertion of any Crown right—certainly to the fulfillment of such!" He seemed staggered. He had manifestly never regarded the matter as other than the recovery of property entrusted to him through his ancestors. I took advantage of his mental disturbance; and as I myself wanted time to think, so that I might fix on some course of action which would suit Marjory's wishes as well as my own, I began to tell him the impression left on my mind by such study of the subject of Treasure Trove as I had been able to achieve. I quoted now and again from notes made in my pocket book.

"The Scotch law is much the same as the English; and as we are in Scotland, we are of course governed by the former. The great point of difference, seen with the eyes of a finder, is that in Scotland the fraudulent concealment of Treasure Trove is not a criminal offence, as it is in England. Thus, from my point of view, I have nothing to fear as to results; for though by the General Police Act the finder is bound to report the find to the Chief Constable, the statute only applies to things found on roads or in public places. So far as this treasure is concerned, it may turn out that it can, in a sense, be no treasure trove at all."—

"According to Blackstone, treasure trove is where any money or coin, gold, silver, plate or bullion is found hidden *in* the earth or other private place, the owner thereof being unknown. If found *upon* the earth, or in the sea, it belongs, not to the Crown, but to the finder, if no owner appears. It is the hiding, not the abandoning, which gives the Crown the property."—

"Coin or bullion found at the bottom of a lake or in the bed of a river is not treasure trove. It is not hidden in the earth."—

"The right of the Crown is. . . limited to gold or silver, bullion or coin. It extends to nothing else.". . .

When I had got thus far the Spaniard interrupted me:

"But sir, in all these that you say, the rights of the owner seem to be recognised even in your law."

"Ah, but there comes in again a fresh difficulty; or rather a fresh series of difficulties, beginning with what is, in the eye of the law, the 'owner.' Let us for a moment take your case. You claim this treasure—if it can be found—as held by you for the original possessor. The original possessor was, I take it, the Pope, who sent it with the Armada, to be used for the conversion or subduing of England. We will take the purpose later, but in the meantime we are agreed that the original owner was Pope Sixtus V. Now, the Popedom is an office, and on the death of one incumbent his successor takes over all his rights and powers and privileges whatever they may be. Thus, the Pope of to-day stands in exactly the same position as did Pope Sixtus V, when he sent through King Philip, and in trust of Bernardino de Escoban the aforesaid treasure." I felt that the words 'aforesaid treasure' sounded very legal; it helped to consolidate even my own ideas as I went along. "So, too, you as the representative of your own family, are in the same position of original trustee as was your great ancestor of which this record takes cognisance." This too was convincingly legal in sound. "I do not think that British law would recognise your position, or that of your predecessors in the trust, in the same way as it would the continuation of the ownership, if any, on the part of the succession of the Popes. However, for the sake of the argument, let us take it they would be of equal force. If this be so, the claim of ownership and guardianship would be complete." As I paused, the Spaniard who had been listening to me with pent up breath, breathed more freely. With a graceful movement, which was almost a bow, he said:

"If so that you recognise the continued ownership, and if you speak as the exponent of the British law, wherein then is the difficulty of ownership at all; should it be that the treasure may be found?" Here was the real difficulty of both my own argument and Don Bernardino's. For my own part, I had not the faintest idea of what the law might be; but I could see easily enough that great issues might be raised for the British side against the Spanish. As I had to 'bluff' my opponent to a certain extent, I added the impressions of personal conviction to my manner as I answered:

"Have you considered what you, or rather your predecessors in title and trust, have done to forfeit any rights which you may have had?" He paled and was visibly staggered; it was evident that this view of the question had not entered his mind. The mere suggestion of the matter now opened up for him grave possibilities. His lips grew dry, and it was with a voice hoarser than hitherto that, after a pause, he said:

"Go on!"

"This treasure was sent, in time of war, by the enemies of England, for the purpose of her undoing—that is her undoing from the point of view of the established government of the time. It was in itself an act of war. The very documents that could, or can, prove the original ownership, would serve to prove the hostile intent of such owners in sending it. Remember, that it came in a warship, one of the great Armada built and brought together to attack this country. The owner of the treasure, the Pope, gave it in trust for the *cestui que trust*, the King of Spain to your ancestor Bernardino de Escoban, as hereditary trustee. Your ancestor himself had the battleship *San Cristobal* built at his own cost for the King's service in the war against England. You see, they were all—the individual as well as the nation—hostile to England; and the intention of evil towards that country, what British law calls 'malice prepense' or the '*mens rea*' was manifest in all!" The Spaniard watched me intently; I could see by the darkening of his swarthy face and the agonised contraction of his brows that the argument was striking home to his very heart. The man was so distressed that, enemy as I felt him to be, it was with a pang that I went on:

"It remains to be seen what view the British law would take of your action, or what is the same, that of your predecessor in the trust, in hiding the treasure in the domains of Britain. As a foreigner you would not have, I take it, a right in any case. And certainly, as a foreigner in arms against this country, you would have—could have—no right in either domestic or international law. The right was forfeit on landing from your warship in time of war on British shores!"

There was a long pause. Now that I came to piece out into an argument the scattered fragments of such legal matters as I had been able to learn, and my own ideas on the subject, the resulting argument was stronger than I had at first imagined. A whole host of collateral matters also cropped up. As I was expounding the law, as I saw it, the subject took me away with it:

"This question would then naturally arise: if the forfeiture of the rights of the original owner would confer a right upon the Crown of Britain, standing as it does in such a matter as the 'remainder man.' Also whether the forfeited treasure having been hidden, being what the law calls '*bona vacantia*,' can be acquired by the finder, subject to the law relating to the Royal prerogative. In both the above cases there would arise points of law. In either, for instance, the nature of the treasure might limit the Crown claim as over against an individual claiming rights as finder."

"How so?" asked Don Bernardino. He was recovering his *sang froid*, and manifestly was wishful to reassert himself.

"According to the statement of Don Bernardino, which would assuredly be adduced in evidence on either side, the treasure was, or is, of various classes; coined money, bullion, gems and jewel work. By one of the extracts which I have read you, the Crown prerogative only applies to precious metals or bullion. Gems or jewellery are therefore necessarily excluded; for it could not, I think, be claimed that such baubles were contraband of war."

"Again, the place of hiding may make a bar to Crown claim as treasure trove. According to the cipher narrative the place of hiding was a sea cave. This could not be either 'on' the ground, which would give title to the finder; or 'in' the ground which would give Crown claim. But beyond this again, there might arise the question as to whether the treasure should in any way come into the purview of the law at all. You will remember, in one of my excerpts Blackstone excepts the sea from the conditions of treasure trove. It might have to be fought out in the Law Courts, right up to the House of Lords which is our final Court of Appeal, whether the definition of 'sea' would include a cave into which the tide ran." Here I stopped; my argument was exhausted of present possibilities. The Spaniard's thought now found a voice:

"But still ownership might be proved. Our nations have been at peace ever since that unhappy time of the Invincible Armada. Nay more, have not the nations fought side by side in the Peninsula! Besides, at no time has there been war between England and the Pope, even when his priests were proscribed and hunted, and imprisoned when captured. The friendship of these countries would surely give a base for the favourable consideration of an international claim. Even if there may have been a constructive forfeiture, such was never actually exacted; England might, in her wisdom, yield the point to a friendly nation, when three hundred years had elapsed." Here another idea struck me.

"Of course" I said "such might be so. England is rich and need not enforce her right to a treasure, however acquired. But let me remind you that lawyers are very tenacious of points of law, and this would have to be decided by lawyers who are the servants of the state and the advisers of the governments. Such would, no doubt, be guided by existing principles of law, even if the specific case were not on all fours with precedents. I learn that in India, which is governed by laws made by Britons and consonant with the scheme of British law, there is actually an act in existence which governs Treasure Trove. By this, the magisterial decision can be held over to allow the making of a claim of previous ownership within a hundred years. So you see that by analogy your claim of three hundred years of peace would put you clean out of court." We both remained silent. Then the Spaniard, with a long sigh, rose up and said courteously:

"I thank you Senor, for the audience which you have given to me. As there is to be no *rapprochement* to us, what I can say may not avail. I must now take my own course. I am sad; for what that course may have to be, I know not. I would have given my fortune and my life to have acquitted me honourably of the trust imposed on me. But such happiness may not alas! be mine. Senor" this he said very sternly "I trust that you will always remember that I tried all ways that I know of, of peace and honour, to fulfill my duty. Should I have to take means other to discharge my duty, even to the point of life and death, you will understand that I have no alternative."

"Would you take life?" I said impulsively, half incredulous.

"I would not scruple regarding my own life; why should I, regarding that of another?" he said simply, then he went on:

"But oh! Senor, it is not the taking of life, my own or another's, which I dread. It is that I may have to walk in devious ways, where honour is not; have I not already tasted of its bitterness! Understand me that this duty of guardianship of the trust is not of my choosing. It was set to me and mine by other and greater powers than ourselves, by the Vicegerent of God Himself; and what is ordained by him I shall do in all ways that are demanded of me."

I was sorry for him, very sorry; but his words made a new fear. Hitherto I had been dealing with a gentleman, and there is much protection in this thought to any opponent. Now, however, he calmly announced that he would act without scruple. I was in future to dread, not fair fighting alone, but crooked ways and base acts. So I spoke out:

"Am I not then to look on you as a man of honour?" His face darkened dangerously; but all its haughty pride was obliterated by a look of despair and grief as he said sadly:

"Alas I know not. I am in the hands of God! He may deal mercifully with me, and allow me to pass to my grave not dishonoured; but for myself my path has been set in ways that may lead I know not whither."

Somehow his words made me feel like a cad. I didn't mind fighting a man fair; or indeed fighting him anyway, so long as we understood the matter from the first. But this was against the grain. The man had shown himself willing to give up everything he had, so as to fulfill his trust and be free; and for me now to have a part in forcing him into ways of dishonour seemed too bad. It didn't seem altogether fair to me either. I had always tried to act honourably and mercifully, so that to have my own hand forced to acquiesce in the downfall of another man was in its way hard lines on me too. Truly, the ways of wealth are full of thorns; and when war and politics and intrigue are joined in the chase for gold, there is much suffering for all who are so unhappy as to be drawn within the spell. I was weakening in my resolve regarding the treasure, and would, I am sure, in a moment of impulse have made some rash proffer to the Spaniard; when once more there came back to me the purpose of the treasure, and what Marjory might think if I allowed it to go back where it might be used against her country. Whatever I might do, there was no hope of compromise on the part of Don Bernardino. His one purpose, blind and set, was to fulfill the obligation set by his forefather and to restore the treasure to Spain, by whom it might or might not be restored to the Pope. The intensity of my thought had concentrated my interests to such an extent that I did not consciously notice what was going on around me. Only in a sort of dim way did I know that the Spaniard's eyes were roving round the room; seeking, in the blind agony of the despair which was upon his soul for a clue or opening somewhere.

All at once I became broad awake to the situation of things which had happened in those few seconds. He was gazing with eyes of amazement on the heap of metal caskets, dimmed with three centuries of sea water, which were piled on the side table amongst the scattered heaps of odds and ends of various kinds, made manifest by some trick of light. Then there came a light into his eyes as he raised his hand and pointed saying:

"So the treasure has been found!"

XLII

A Struggle

I think that at first sheer amazement had controlled the Spaniard's thoughts. But whatever the cause of the control was, it soon passed away; then the whole fiery nature of the man seemed to sweep from him like a torrent:

"And so all the learned arguments with which you have overwhelmed me, were but a cloak to cover your possession of the treasure which it was given to me and mine to guard. I might have guessed, that without the certainty of possession you would not have been so obdurate to my offer, given in all sincerity as it was. From other things, too, I might have known! That woman, so old, who watches you with eyes that see more than is to see, and who have reason of her own to mistrust you, she telled to me that nightly she has heard you dig in the rock as though you make grave. Take care it is not so! I am guardian of that treasure; and I am desperate! Already have I told you that all things are to me, all ways to fulfill the trust of my fathers. We are here alone! I am armed; and already my life is forfeit to this course. Yield yourself, then, to me!"

Like a flash of light he had drawn a dagger from his breast; and with an upward sweep of his hand held it poised, either to strike or throw. But already I had taken warning from his eyes. Ever since danger had threatened Marjory, I had carried my revolver with me; even at night it rested under my pillow. The practice which Marjory and I had often had, till she had taught me the old trick which her father had taught her of getting "the drop" on an adversary, stood me now in good stead. Whilst he had been drawing his dagger, I had already covered him; he finished the words of his command straight into the muzzle of my six-shooter. I said as quietly as I could, for it was with a mighty effort I kept approximately calm under stress of such a sudden attack:

"Drop that dagger! Quick; or I shall shoot it from your hands!" He recognised his helplessness in the matter. With a despairing sigh he opened his fingers; the dagger fell jingling to the floor. I went on:

"Now hold up your hands, well above your head! Move back to the wall!" He did so, and stood facing me with a disdainful smile. I stooped, and with my right hand picked up the dagger, still keeping him covered with my left. I put the weapon on the far side of the table, and approached him. He did not move, but I could see that he was sizing me up. This gave me no anxiety, for I knew my own strength; and I had also a shrewd idea that if he had any other arm about him he would not be calculating his chances for a physical struggle. Cautioning him that his life depended on his stillness, for I still held my revolver to his breast, I passed my hand lightly over him; he had manifestly no other weapon. The only sign of one was the sheath of his dagger; this I took from him. I placed the dagger in it and put it in my own pocket; then I drew a chair to the middle of the room and motioned him to sit down. He obeyed sullenly. Having by this time regained something of my serenity of mind, I spoke:

"Your pardon, Sir, for the indignity to which I have been obliged to submit you; but I am sure you will remember that it was not I who began the question of force. When you thought it right to draw arms upon me in my own house, you made it necessary that I should protect myself. Now, let me say something in answer to your charge against me. The finding of the treasure has nothing whatever to do with my theory of action; I should hold my present view just as strongly had we not made the discovery. Indeed, I may say that since we have had actual possession of the treasure, it seems not nearly so desirable as it had been. So far as I am concerned, I don't care a straw whether I have ultimate possession of it or not; but I am so fixed up that if I waive my rights— that is if I have any to waive—that I may aid in doing a repugnant thing to a very dear friend. That I shall not do. I shall oppose its doing by any means in my power!" The Spaniard saw a chance, and spoke:

"But if I undertake—" I cut him short:

"Sir, in this matter you are not in a position to undertake. By your own showing, you are simply bound to fulfill your trust and to restore the treasure to the King, who will restore it to the Pope; or to restore it to the Pope direct." He answered quickly:

"But I can stipulate—" again I interrupted him for this was a useless road to travel;

"How can you stipulate? You would, or might, be told to simply fulfill the duty that had been undertaken for you. Did you refuse, from whatever motive, no matter how justly founded, on ground of right or honour, you would not be holding to the simple terms of your trust. No! sir. This is no private affair to be settled by you or me, or by us both together. It belongs to politics! and international politics at that. The

Government of Spain is desperately in want of money. How do you know to what shift, or to what specious argument it will condescend in its straits. I have no doubt that, should anything be done contrary to your idea of fair play, you would be grievously pained; but that is not to the point. Your Government would not take thought for any wish of yours, any more than for aught of mine. Your King is a minor; his regent is a woman, and his councillors and governors are all men chosen to do what they can to save their country. Sir, but a few minutes ago you professed it your duty to take any step, even to crime and dishonour, to carry out your duty. Indeed, you drew a weapon upon me, a presumably unarmed man, in my own house in which you are a self-invited guest. Suppose some of the Government of Spain hold ideas of their duty, equally strong and equally unscrupulous; who then is to answer for what they do. Why, in such case, they would undertake anything, until they had got possession of the treasure; and would then act entirely upon what they would call their 'better judgment.'" His native pride awoke in an instant for he said hotly:

"I would have you know, Senor, and remember always when you talk with a Spaniard, that our statesmen are not criminals, but men of honour." I bowed instinctively as I answered him:

"Sir, I have no doubt whatever, and I speak in all sincerity, that you yourself are, under normal circumstances, a man of the highest honour. Your self-sacrificing offer has shewn me that; and I have added to that knowledge by seeing the pain you have suffered at even the thought of dishonour." Here he bowed low, and there was a look of gratitude in his eyes which touched me to the quick. "And yet even you have openly told me that all your belief in honour, all your life-long adherence to its behests, will not keep you from fulfilling a duty should these things clash. Nay more, you have already done things which I take it are at variance with your principles. How then can you, or I, believe that other men, of less lofty lineage and less delicate sense of honour, will forego an advantage for their country in distress, yielding to a theoretical point of right or wrong. No sir" I went on pitilessly, for I felt that it would be a kindness to him to shut absolutely this door of hope, "We must take no step which will place in the hands of others the guardianship of that treasure, of which you have hitherto conceived yourself trustee, and of which I now believe myself to be the owner." For fully several minutes we faced each other in silence. His face grew more and more fixed and stern; at last he stood up with such a look of resolution that instinctively my fingers tightened round the butt of my revolver. I thought that he might be about to throw himself upon me, and attempt even at such odds as were against him, a struggle for present mastery. Then, without moving from his place, he spoke:

"When I have done all I can to fulfill my trust in its completeness, and have failed, I shall ask the government of my country to make representation to her friend England of a friendly claim, so that we may get even a part of the treasure; and then I will devote myself to the avenging of my honour on those who have foiled me in my duty!" This was a sort of speech which braced me up again. It was a promise of war, man to man, and I could understand it better than the subtleties which now enmeshed us. I put my pistol back in my pocket, and bowed to my opponent as I answered:

"And when that time comes, Sir, you will find me at your service; how you will; where you will; and when you will. In the meantime, when first you place the matter on the international plane, I shall take care that the American government, in which dear friends of mine are interested, shall make friendly demand of her friend, England, that she shall take no step with regard to this particular treasure—if indeed it be then in her possession—which may be used to the detriment of the trans-Atlantic power. Thus you see, sir, that time must in any case elapse before a final settlement. Nothing can be done till the close of the present war, when I take it that immediate need of the sinews of war shall have ceased to exist. Be very careful, then, how you take any steps to bring upon the scene other powers than ourselves; powers vastly more strong, and vastly less scrupulous—perhaps." He answered nothing, but looked at me a long time in silent cold disdain. Then he said quietly:

"Have I your permission, Senor, to depart?" I bowed, and brought him to the door. When outside he turned, and, lifting his hat high in an old-fashioned, stately way, bowed. He passed up the laneway towards Whinnyfold, without once glancing back.

As I stood looking at him, I saw in the dusk Gormala's head now and again showing above the low green bank which guarded the edge of the cliff. She was bent double, and was in secret following the Spaniard.

I went back to the house to think over matters. Altogether, we were getting so complicated that there did not seem any straight road to take. In the back of my mind I had a firm idea that the best thing I could do would be to hand over the treasure to the custody of the police; inform the Sheriff; and get my solicitor to enter a formal claim of ownership, wherever the claim should be made. Then I should get Marjory to come upon our honeymoon. I could see that her mind was almost, if not quite, made up to accept this step; and for a while I lost myself in a day dream.

I came back to the reality of things by dimly and gradually realising that it had grown dark. So I made preparation for the night, bearing in mind that I had a vast treasure in my possession, and that a desperate man who claimed to represent its ownership was aware that I had it in the house. It was not till I had seen to the fastenings of every window and door, that I began to prepare a meal.

By this time I was exceedingly hungry; when I had eaten I seated myself before a rousing fire of pine logs, lit my pipe, and began to think. Without, the wind was rising. I could hear it whistle along the roof, and now and again it roared and boomed down the chimney; the leaping fire seemed to answer its call. I could not think definitely; my thoughts kept whirling in a circle from the Spaniard to the treasure, from the treasure to Gormala, from Gormala to Marjory, and from Marjory back to the Spaniard again. Every time the cycle became complete and my thoughts came back to Marjory, my rapture as I thought of her and of our future, became clouded by a vague uneasiness. It was out of this that the thought of Don Bernardino came to commence the next round of thought. In all my mental wanderings he became a dominant character; his pride, his sense of duty which subordinated even honour, his desperation, his grief, all seemed to be with me and around me. Now and again I trembled, when I thought that such self-sacrificing forces might be turned against Marjory.

Little by little, despite all my anxiety, stole over me the disposition of sleep. I was indeed almost worn out. The events of the past few days had crowded together so quickly that I had had no time for pause. Even the long sleep which had crowned the vigil in the water cave had not enabled me to lay in, so to speak, a provision of sleep; it had been the payment of a debt to nature rather than the putting by of capital. I had the consoling thought that Marjory had promised me she would not leave Crom Castle till I came. Safe in this thought I rolled myself in rugs—choosing those that she had used—and fell asleep.

I think that even in sleep I did not lose the sense of my surroundings, for in dreams my thoughts ran in their waking channel. Here again, all the disturbing elements of my life of late became jumbled together; and a sort of anxiety regarding something unknown seemed to brood over me. So far as I remember, I slept fitfully; waking often in a sort of agony of indefinite apprehension. A couple of times I made up the fire which was falling low, for there was a sort of companionship in it. Without, the wind howled more loudly, and each time as I sank back to rest I pulled the rugs more closely around me.

Once, I started broad awake. I thought I heard a cry, and naturally, in my present frame of mind, my thoughts flew to Marjory in some danger; she was calling me. Whatever the cause was, it reached my brain through a thick veil of sleep; my body answered, and before I had time to think of why or wherefore, I was standing on the floor broad awake, alert and panting. Again there came a sharp cry outside, which threw me in an instant into a cold sweat. Marjory was in danger and was calling me! Instinctively I ran to the window, and pulling open the shutters, threw up the sash. All was dark outside, with just that cold line on the far Eastern horizon which told of coming dawn. The wind had risen high, and swept past me into the room, rustling papers and making the flames dance. Every now and again a bird swept by me on the wings of the wind, screaming as it flew; for the house was so close to the sea that the birds took no note of it as they would ordinarily do of a human habitation. One of them came so close that its scream seemed to sound loudly in my ears; it was doubtless just such a cry as this which had torn me from my sleep. For a while I hesitated whether I should go right away to Crom; but second thoughts prevailed. I could not get into the house at such an hour, without creating alarm and causing comment. So I went back to the chimney corner, and, piling on fresh logs and snuggling into my nest of rugs, soon found sleep again descending on me. The serenity of thought which comes with the day was using its force. . .

This time I woke more slowly. The knocking was continuous and imperative; but it was not a terrifying sound. We are all more or less used to such sounds. I listened; and gradually consciousness of my surroundings came back to me. The knocking was certainly persistent. . . I put on my shoes and went to the door.

Outside was Mrs. Jack, looking troubled and hot in spite of the cold of the wind which seemed to sing around the house. As I opened the door, she slipped past me and closed it behind her. Her first words made my heart sink, and my blood run cold with vague terror:

"Is Marjory here?"

XLIII

The Honour of a Spaniard

M rs. Jack saw the answer in my eyes before speech came, and staggered back against the wall.

"No," I said "Why do you ask?"

"She is not here! Then there is something wrong; she was not in her room this morning!"

This morning! The words set my thoughts working. I looked at my watch; it was past ten o'clock. In a dazed kind of way I heard Mrs. Jack go on.

"I did not say a word to any of the servants at first, for I didn't want to set them talking. I went all over the house myself. Her bed had not been slept in; I pulled the clothes off it and threw them on again roughly so that the maid might not suspect. Then I asked quietly if any of the maids had seen her; but none had. So I said as quietly as I could that she must have gone out for an early walk; and I took my breakfast. Then I had the cart got ready, and drove over here myself. What can it be? She told me last night that she was not going out until you came; and she is always so exact when she says a thing, that there must be something wrong. Come back with me at once! I am so anxious that I don't know what to do."

Two minutes sufficed for my toilet; then shutting the door behind us, we got into the cart and drove to Crom. At the first and at the last we went quietly, so as not to arouse attention by our speed; but in the middle space we flew. During the journey Mrs. Jack had told me that last night she had gone to bed as usual, leaving in the drawing room Marjory, who had told her that she was going presently into the library to write as she had a lot of letters to get through, and that no one was to wait up for her. This was her usual habit when she sat late; it therefore excited no extra attention. Mrs. Jack who was an early riser, had been dressed for an hour before she went to Marjory's room. In the course of her enquiries amongst the servants, one of them, whose business it was to open the hall door, told her that she had found it locked and chained as usual.

Within the house at Crom we found all quiet. I went at once into the library, as that was presumably the last place where Marjory had been. As we went, I asked Mrs. Jack if any letters had been left out to post. She said no! that the usual habit was to put such in the box on the hall table, but she had herself, looked, when she came down to put in a letter for America. I went over at once to the table near the fire where Marjory usually sat at night. There were plenty of writing materials and blank paper and envelopes; but not a sign of a letter or anything written. I looked all round the room but could see nothing to attract my attention. Once more I asked Mrs. Jack what Marjory had said to her about her intention of not leaving the castle till I had come. With some hesitation at first, as though she were fearful of breaking confidence, but afterwards more freely as if glad to be able to speak, she told me all:

"The dear child took to heart what I said yesterday about her living with her husband. After you had gone she came to me and laid her head on my breast, as she used to do as a little child, and began to cry; and told me that I had been very good to her. The darling! And that her mind was made up. She realised now her duty to her husband; and that as he wished her to stay in the house, nothing in the world would induce her to leave it till he came. That was the first act of her new duty! And, oh my dear! that is why I was so concerned when I found that after all she was not in the house. I don't understand it; there must be something on foot that I don't know; and I am full of fear!" Here the old lady quite broke down. I felt that any self control now was precious. It would not do to leave Mrs. Jack in ignorance of the danger, so I told her in as few words as I could of the blackmailing going on and of the watch set by the United States Secret Service. At first she was overwhelmed; but her early apprenticeship to dangers of all kinds stood her in good stead. Very soon her agitation took practical shape. I told her I was off to seek for help, and that she must keep the house till I returned. I would have tried the secret tunnel, but from what Mrs. Jack had said I was convinced that Marjory had never left the house of her own accord. If she had been captured she was doubtless far away by this time. It was possible that the blackmailers had found the secret passage into the Castle by which Don Bernardino had come. Here the thought came to me in full force; that was how they had discovered it. They had seen and watched the Don! . . . I felt that another debt for our day of reckoning had been piled up against him.

I got in the cart again and went to Cruden as hard as the mare could go. As I went, I formed my plans, and had my telegrams made up in my mind ready to write them out at once. For a while I doubted whether I should go to another telegraph office, lest the Cruden people might come to know too much. But there was no need of concealment now. I was not afraid of any one knowing, though I determined to be discreet and secret if possible. The circuit was occupied, so I found the use of the priority telegraph forms Adams had sent me. There was not a moment lost; one was being despatched whilst I was writing the next. To Adams I said:

"They have succeeded: Wire men see me at Crom right away. Come if you can. Want all help can get. Time vital. . ."

To Cathcart I wired at his house in Invernesshire:

"Come to me without moment's delay. Vital. Want every kind of help." I knew he would understand, and would come armed.

As it would be some little time before anything could be done, I determined to find Don Bernardino if possible; and induce him to show me the secret exit. Without knowledge of this we would be powerless; with it we might find some clue. I did not make up my mind as to what I would do if he refused; but to myself the instinctive grinding of my teeth, and clenching of my fingers, seemed to answer my question. Of one thing I was glad, he was a gentleman. In such a matter as that in which I was engaged, there were possibilities, if even there were not definite hope.

I drove to Ellon; and from the agent there got his address. I soon found it; an old-fashioned house near the town, in a tiny park surrounded with great trees. I left the cart on the road, with the mare tethered to the gate post, there being no lodgekeeper or no lodge. Before I rang the hall-door bell I saw that my revolver was ready to my hand. The instant the door was opened I stepped in, and said to the old woman who opened it:

"Mr. Barnard is in the study I suppose? I have pressing business with him!" She was so taken aback by the suddenness of my entry and speech that she pointed to a door saying: "He is in there."

As I entered the room, closing the door behind me, the Don, who had been seated in a large chair with his back to the door turned unconcernedly. He had evidently not expected any disturbing visitor. The instant he saw me, however, he leaped to his feet, all his hostility awake. As he scanned my face his concern grew; and he glanced around, as though seeking for some weapon. I put my hand on my revolver, and said as quietly as I could, remembering his own precision of manner:

"Forgive my intrusion, Sir; but I have urgent need of speech with you." I suppose there was something in my tone which bore home to his brain the idea that I had changed in some way since we had met. Do what I would, I could not conceal the anxiety of my voice. After a pause he said:

"Regarding the treasure?"

"No!" said I: "Since last night I have not even given it a thought." A strange, new look came over his face, a look in which hope and concern seemed to have equal parts. He paused again; I could see he was thinking. Mechanically I tapped my foot on the floor with impatience; the golden moments were flying by. He realised my gravity of purpose, and, manifestly turning his attention to me, said:

"Speak on Senor!" By this time I had well in my mind what I intended to say. It was not my purpose to further antagonise the Spaniard; at the outset at any rate. Later on, that might be necessary; but I should exhaust other means first.

"I have come, Sir, to ask your aid, the help of a gentleman; and I feel at a loss how to ask it." Through the high-bred courtesy of the Spaniard's manner came a note of bitterness, as he answered:

"Alas! Senor, I know the feeling. Have not I myself asked on such a plea; and stooped in vain!" I had nothing to say in reply to this, so went on:

"Sir, I am aware that you can make much sacrifice: I ask, not for myself, but for a lady in peril!" He answered quickly:

"A lady! in peril! Say on Senor!" There was such hope and purpose in his quick tone that my heart instinctively leaped as I went on:

"In peril, sir; of life; of honour. To you I appeal to lay aside your feelings of hate towards me, however just they may be; and come like a true gentleman to her aid. I am emboldened to ask this because it was, I think, by your act that the peril—the immediate peril, has come to her." He flushed at once:

"Through me! Peril to a lady's honour through me! Have a care, sir! Have a care!" With a rush I went on:

"By your going into the castle through a secret passage, other enemies of the lady, low, base and unscrupulous who have been plotting to carry her off for ransom, have doubtless made an entry otherwise impossible to them. Now we must find a clue, and at once. Tell me, I implore you, of the secret way; that thus we may at once begin our search." For a few seconds he looked me through and through; I think he suspected some plot or trap, for he said slowly:

"And the treasure; can you leave it?" I answered hotly:

"The treasure! I have not even thought of it since the news came of Marjory's disappearance!" Here I took it that he was beginning his unscrupulous purpose, and was playing my loss against his own; and a thought came to me that had not even crossed my mind before—had he been the abductor for the purpose of just such a bargain? I took from my pocket the key of the house in Whinnyfold and held it out to him. "Here Sir" I said "is the key of my house. Take it with all it contains, and all it leads to! The treasure is as you left it last night; only help me in my need."

He waved my hand aside with an impatient gesture as he said simply:

"I do not bargain with a woman's honour. Such comes before all the treasures of Popes or Kings; before the oath and duty of a de Escoban. Come! Senor, there is no time to lose. Let us settle this affair first; later we can arrange matters that rest between thee and me!"

"Your hand, Sir" was all I could say. "In such trouble as mine, there is no help like that of a gentleman. But will you not honour me by keeping the key? This other is a trust which you have won by honour; as your great ancestor won his glorious duty long ago." He did not hesitate; all he said as he took the key was:

"It is a part of my duty which I must not forego."

As we left the house he looked like a new man—a man born again; there was such joyous gladness in his face and voice and movements that I wondered. I could not help saying when we had got into the cart and were on our way:

"You seem happy, Sir. I would that I could feel the same."

"Ah, Senor, I am happy beyond belief. I am happy as one raised from Hell to Heaven. For now my honour is no more perilled. God has been good to me to show a way, even to death, without dishonour."

As we flew along to Crom I told him what I knew of the secret passage between the chapel and the monument. He wondered at my having discovered the secret; but when I told him of how the blackmailing gang had used the way to evade the Secret Service men, he suddenly cried out:

"There was but one who ever knew the secret of that passage; my kinsman, with whom I stayed in Crom when young, told me of him. He tried much to find the entrance to the Castle, and finally under threat he went away to America. He was a base-born and a thief. It must be he who has come back after these years and has told of the secret way. Alas! they must have watched me when I went, all unsuspicious; and so discovered the other secret." Then he tried to explain where the entrance was. It was not in the chamber where we had expected it would be, but in a narrow corner of the stair, the whole corner being one stone and forming the entrance.

When we arrived at Crom we found that the Secret Service men were waiting for me, having been instructed from London. There were also telegrams from Adams and Cathcart saying that they were on the way to join me. Adams wired from Aberdeen, and Cathcart from Kingussie. Mrs. Jack was with the detectives and had taken them through the rooms which Marjory had used. They had had up the servants one by one and examined them as to what they knew. The chief man had insisted on this; he said matters were now too serious to play the fool any longer. The servants were not told anything, even that Marjory was missing; but of course they had their suspicions. A peremptory order was given that no one should leave the house without permission. The chief confided to me that Mrs. Jack had quite broken down when she was telling him that Marjory knew all along about the blackmailers and had never told her. "But she's all right now, Sir," he concluded. "That old lady is just full of sand; and I tell you her head is level. She's been thinking of everything which could possibly be of use to us. I guess I have heard more of this racket within the last half hour than I have done in the last two weeks."

By the instructions of Don Bernardino we went into the library. I asked Mrs. Jack to send for lamps and candles, and these were brought shortly. In the meantime I asked that one of the detectives should be sent into the old chapel and another to the monument on the hill. Both were warned to have their guns ready, and to allow no one to pass at any hazard. To each before going I explained the secret mode of entry.

The Don went over to one of the book-cases—the very section containing the shelf in which I had replaced the old law book. Taking out that particular volume, he put his hand in and pressed a spring. There was a faint click. He replaced the book and pressed against the bookcase with slow level pressure. Very slowly it seemed to give way before him; and then turning on a hinge at one side, left an open cavity through which a man could easily pass. I was about to rush in, and was quite ready, with a lamp in one hand and a revolver in the other, when the chief of the detectives laid a restraining hand on my arm as he said:

"Wait a moment. If you go too fast you may obliterate some sign which would give us a clue!" The wisdom of his speech was not to be gainsaid. Instinctively I fell back; two of the trained observers drew close to the doorway, and holding their lamp in such wise as to throw light all round the opening, began an exact scrutiny. One of them knelt down and examined the flooring; the other confined his attention to roof and walls. After a silence, lasting perhaps a minute, the man kneeling stood up and said:

"Not a doubt about it! There has been a violent struggle here at the doorway!"

XLIV

The Voice in the Dust

One of the men produced his note book and began taking down in shorthand the rapid utterances of the chief, repeating it so as to check the accuracy as he went on:

"Easy to see the marks; the floor is deep in dust, and the walls are thick with it. On floor, mark of several feet—confused in struggle, may articulate separately later on—one woman's—also trailing of long skirt. On walls marks of hands, fingers outspread, as if trying to grasp. Some of the long marks down the wall others across." The speaker here raised his lamp and held it in the opening as far as his arm would go; then he went on:

"Steps wind downwards to right. Struggle seems to have stopped. Footmarks more clear.". . . Then the chief turned to us:

"I think gentlemen, we may follow in now. The footmarks may be discriminated and identified later. We must chance destroying them, or we cannot pass in this narrow passage." Here I spoke; a thought had been surging up in my brain ever since the detective had pointed out the finger marks on the wall "down and across":

"Stop a moment please! Let me see the marks on the wall before any one enters; the passage is narrow and they may be rubbed off." A glance was enough, just time enough to formulate which was the symbol of "a" and which of "b." The perpendicular strokes were "a" and the horizontal "b." Marjory had kept her head, even at this trying time, and was leaving a message for me as she was forced along. I understood why the struggle had ceased. Seized and forced through the narrow doorway, she had at first struggled hard. Then, when she realised that she could leave a clue behind her, she had evidently agreed to go quietly; for so she might have her hands free. It would be a hard job to carry or force along an unwilling captive through that narrow uneven passage; doubtless the captors were as willing as she was that she should go quietly. I said to the detectives:

"These marks on the wall are in a cipher which I can read. Give me the best lamp we have, and let me go first."

So, in an orderly procession, leaving two men in the library with Mrs. Jack to guard the entrance, we passed into the secret passage. As I read off the words written on the wall, the man with the note-book took them down, his companion holding a candle so as to enable him to do so. How my heart beat as I read my dear girl's message, marked on the wall on the inner side whichever way the curves ran. Obviously it would create less attention by guiding herself in this wise as she passed. She had kept her hand well down so that her signs should not be confused with the marks made by the men who, guiding themselves likewise, had held their hands at a natural height. Her sign marks ran continuously, even after we had passed into the passage between the chapel and the monument; the writing ran as follows:

"Four men came in—two waiting in passage through bookcase—late—striking one—struggled—then quiet—hands free—same voice we heard in Chapel. Feathers thin voice, small man, dark—all masked—Whisky Tommy hoarse voice, big man, sandy, large hands—Dago, deep voice, swarthy, little finger missing left hand—Max, silent, nods for speech, think dumb—two others on ahead too far see, hear."

In a pause I heard the chief detective murmur:

"That girl's a peach. We'll get her yet!" The spot at which we were pausing was where the way to the reservoir branched off. Here Marjory probably stood with her back to the wall and used her hands behind her back, for the strokes were smaller and more uneven. There were faults which put me out and I could only read a few words—"whispering"—"only word can hear 'manse.'" There was evidently some conversation going on between her captors, and she was making use of her opportunities. Then we went on and found the signs renewed. It cut me to the heart when I saw a smear of blood on one of the marks; the rough uncertain movement and the sharp edges of the rock had told on her delicate skin. But later on, the blood marks were continued, and I could not but think that she had cut her fingers on purpose to make a more apparent clue. When I mentioned my surmise to the detective, his instinct having been trained in such matters, showed a keener insight than my own:

"More likely she is preparing to leave a mark which we can see when they get her out of the tunnel. They may not suspect intention if her fingers are bleeding already!" The words following the stop where I had read "manse" were:

"Boat ready—Seagull—Coffin—Hearse—bury isl—" Here the next mark instead of being horizontal took a sudden angle down, and the blood was roughly rubbed off. It was as though her hand had been struck in the act of making the mark. Her captors had suspected her. There were no more marks on the wall. I could not imagine, however, that Marjory would be entirely baffled. She had infinite resource, and would doubtless find some other means of leaving a clue. Telling the others therefore to keep back I threw the rays of the lamp over roof and walls and floor as we proceeded.

It was a strange scene. The candles and lamp showing up but patches of light in the inky black darkness; the moving figures projected against the lights as I looked back; the silence broken by the shuffling tread of stumbling feet on the rock floor; the eager intense faces, when a change in the light flashed them into view. It all moved me at moments, for there was a gleam of hope in its earnestness.

I tried to put myself in Marjory's position. If her hands were useless, as they would be if she could not use them without suspicion—even were they not tied now as was probable—her next effort would be with her feet; I therefore looked out carefully for any sign made this way. Presently I came across a mark which I suspected. It was only a few steps beyond the last mark on the wall. It was a sort of drag of the foot, where there was any slight accumulation of dust, or rubbish, or sand. There were more such traces ahead. So motioning to the others to keep back, I followed them up, taking care not to disturb any of them. They were but the rough marks made during a stumbling progress; and for a time I was baffled; though I could distinguish the traces of Marjory's little feet amongst the great ones. Then I went back and looked at them afresh from the beginning, and a light burst upon me. They were made with the right or left foot as required; thus she could reproduce the bi-literal symbol. Interpretation was now easy enough, and hence on, to the exit from the tunnel, I could tell almost every word written. There being only a few cases where the sign was not sufficiently marked for me to read it.

"Suspicious. Hands tied—gagged—find Seagull—find Manse."

It was sadly slow work, and my heart at times sank within me at the exasperating delay in our progress. However, it was progress after all; and that sustained us. All along, as we worked our way towards the monument, I had been thinking of the word "manse;" and now its repetition showed its importance. It would be necessary that the abductors have some place in which to conceal their captive, before they should be able to get her out of the country. That this latter would be a necessary step towards their object was manifest; but the word *Seagull* settled it.

When we got to the entrance of the tunnel we examined every inch of the way; this was the wish of the detective rather than my own. Marjory would, it seemed to me, go quietly through the entrance. She would know that she was being watched here with extra carefulness; and would reserve herself for a less suspicious opportunity. She would also know that if I were on her track at all, I would be able to follow through the secret entrance.

Outside, on the ground beside the monument, were no unusual signs of passage. The patch of bare earth and gravel, which we had before noticed, left no trace of footsteps. Those who had used it had evidently taken care that there should be no sign. We went slowly along the route, which, by my former experiments with the thread, I had found was habitually used. Presently one of the Americans asked me to stop, as he had seen a trace of feet. For my life I could distinguish nothing in the seemingly undisturbed mass of pine needles. But the man, who in his youth had been in Indian country, had learned something of tracking; he could interpret signs unseen to others with less highly developed instincts. He went down on his knees and examined the ground, inch by inch, using a microscope. For some ten yards he crawled along on hands and knees engaged in this way. Then he stood up and said:

"There's no error about it now. There are six men and a woman. They have been carrying her, and have let her down here!" We did not challenge his report, or even ask how he had arrived at it; we were all well content to accept it.

We then moved on in the manifest direction in which the ground trended; we were working towards the high road which ran past the gates of Crom. I asked the others to let me go first now, for I knew this would be Marjory's chance to continue her warning. Surely enough, I saw presently a slight disturbance in the pine needles, and then another and another. I spelled out the word "Manse" and again "Manse" and later on "try all Manses near." Then the sign writing ceased; we had come out of the wood on to a grass field which ran down to the high road. Here, outside a gap at the bottom of the field, were the marks in the dust of several feet, the treading of horses, and the ruts of wheels. A little further on, the wheel marks—some four-wheeled vehicle—were heavy; and from the backward propulsion of the dust and gravel in the hoof-tracks we could easily see that the horses were galloping.

We stopped and held a council of war. It was, of course understood by us all that some one should follow on the track of the carriage, and try to reach the quarry this way. For my own part, I felt that to depend on a wheel mark, in such a country of cross roads, was only the off chance. In any case, this stern chase must be a long one; whereas time was vital, every moment being precious. I determined to try to follow out Marjory's clue. "Try every Manse near." To do this we should get to some centre where we could obtain a list of all the churches in the neighbourhood. Ellon was naturally the place, as it was in the centre of the district. They all acquiesced in my view; so we hurried back to Crom, leaving two men, the tracker and another, to follow the fugitives. Hitherto Don Bernardino had hardly said a word. He was alert, and the eager light of his eye was helpful; but after he had shown us the secret way, and found that already I knew the outer passage as well as he did, or better, he had contented himself with watchfulness. Now he suggested:

"There is also the boat! May it not be well that some one should follow up that side of the matter? Thus we shall be doubly armed."

His advice commended itself to the chief of the detectives; though I could see that he took it suspiciously from the Spaniard. It was with manifest purpose of caution that he answered:

"Quite right! But that we shall see to ourselves; when Mr. Adams comes he will work that racket!" The Spaniard bowed, and the American returned the courtesy with a stiff back. Even in such a time of stress, racial matters were not to be altogether forgotten.

In the hall at Crom, we found, when we came back through the old chapel, Sam Adams. He had arrived just after we had set out on our search, but was afraid to follow over-ground lest he should miss us; wisely he did not attempt the underground way as he had no proper light. His coming had been a great comfort to Mrs. Jack, who, always glad to see a countryman of her own, now almost clung to him. He had brought with him two young men, the very sight of whom made my heart warmer. One of them he introduced as "Lootenant Jackson of West Point" and the other as "Lootenant Montgomery of Annapolis." "These boys are all right!" he added, laying a hand affectionately on the shoulder of each.

"I am sure they are! Gentlemen, I thank you with all my heart for coming!" I said as I wrung their hands. They were both fine specimens of the two war Academies of the United States. Clean-built from top to toe; bright-eyed, resolute and alert; the very type of highly bred and trained gentlemen. The young soldier Jackson answered me:

"I was too delighted to come, when Adams was good enough to get leave for me."

"Me too!" echoed the sailor "When I heard that Miss Drake was in trouble, and I was told I might come, I think I danced. Why, Sir, if you want them, we've only to pass the word, and we can get you a man of war's crew—if every man of them has to desert!"

Whilst we were speaking there was a sound of rapid wheels, and a carriage from Ellon drew up at the door. Out jumped Cathcart, followed by a tall, resolute looking young man who moved with the freedom of an athlete.

"Am I in time?" was Cathcart's greeting as he rushed towards me. I told him exactly how we stood. "Thank God!" he said fervently "we may be in time yet." Then he introduced his friend MacRae of Strathspiel. This was the host with whom he had been staying; and who had volunteered to come, on hearing of his summons:

"You may trust Donald!" was his simple evidence of the worth of his friend.

This addition to our forces gave us great hope. We had now a sufficiency of intelligent, resolute men to follow up several clues at once; and in a brief council we marked out the various duties of each. Cathcart was to go to Ellon and get a list of all the manses in the region of Buchan, and try to find out if any of them had been let to strangers. We took it for granted that none of the clergy of the place were themselves concerned in the plot. MacRae was to go with Cathcart and to get all the saddle horses he could without attracting public attention, and bring them, or have them brought, to Crom as soon as possible. Secrecy of movement was insisted on with almost agonised fervour by Adams and the Secret Service men. "You don't know these wretches," said the chief of the latter "They are the most remorseless and cruel villains in the world; and if they are driven to bay will do anything however cruel or base. They are well plucked too, and don't know what fear means. They will take any chances, and do anything to get their way and protect themselves. If we don't go right in this matter, we may regret it to the last of our days."

The silence in the room was only broken by the grinding of teeth, and by Mrs. Jack's suppressed sobs.

Adams was to go to Aberdeen as a working centre, and was to look after the nautical side of the adventure; he was to have Montgomery in this work with him. Before he left Crom, he wrote some cipher telegrams to the Embassy. He explained to me that one of his suggestions was that an American war-ship which was cruising in the North Sea should, if possible, be allowed to lie off the coast of Aberdeen ready for any emergency. When Montgomery heard it, he asked that if possible a message should be sent from him to the first officer of the *Keystone*: "Tell the men privately that they are helping Marjory Drake!—There will be a thousand pair of eyes on the watch then!" he added by way of explanation.

I was to wait with the detectives till we should get word from any of our sources as to what could be done.

For there were several possibilities. The trackers might mark down the locality where the prisoner was hidden. Cathcart might, before this, come with the list of manses and their occupants. Adams or Montgomery might get wind of the *Seagull*; for Montgomery had already orders to go to Petershead and Fraserburgh, where the smacks for the summer fishing were gathered.

Don Bernardino remained with me at Crom.

XLV

DANGER

The time of waiting was inconceivably long and dreary. When Marjory and I had been waiting for death in the water-cave, we thought that nothing could be so protracted; but now I knew better. Then, we had been together, and whatever came, even death itself, would be shared by us. But now I was alone; and Marjory away, and in danger. In what danger I knew not, I could only imagine; and at every new thought of fear and horror I ground my teeth afresh and longed for action. Fortunately there was something to do. The detectives wanted to know all I could tell them. At the first, the chief had asked that Mrs. Jack would get all the servants of the house together so that he might see them. She had so arranged matters that they would be together in the servants' hall, and he went down to inspect. He did not stay long; but came back to me at once with an important look on his face. He closed the door and coming close to me said:

"I knew there was something wrong below stairs! That footman has skipped!" For a few seconds I did not realise what he meant, and asked him to explain.

"That footman that went out gallavantin' at nights. He's in it, sure. Why isn't he in the hall where the others are? Just you ask the old lady about him. It'll be less suspicious than me doing it." Then it dawned on me what he meant.

"There is no footman in the house!" I said.

"That's so, Mister. That's just what I'm tellin'! Where is he?"

"There is none; they don't have any male servants in the house. The only men are in the stables in the village."

"Then that makes it worse still. There is a man who I've seen myself steal out of the house after dark, or in the dusk; and sneak back again out of the wood in the grey of the dawn. Why, I've reported it to Mr. Adams. Didn't he warn you about it; he said he would."

"He did that."

"And didn't you take his tip?"

"No!" here from the annoyed expression of his face I took warning.

It would never do to chagrin the man and set him against me by any suspicion of ridicule. So I went on:

"The fact is, my friend, that this was a disguise. It was Mar—Miss Drake who used it!" He was veritably surprised; his amazement was manifest in his words:

"Miss Drake! And did she put on the John Thomas livery? In the name of thunder, why?"

"To escape you!"

"To escape me! Wall, I'm damned! That elegant young lady to put on livery; and to escape me!"

"Yes; you and the others. She knew you were watching her! Of course she was grateful for it!" I added, for his face fell "but she couldn't bear it all the same. You know what girls are," I went on apologetically, "They don't like to be cornered or forced to do anything. She knew you were all clever fellows at your work and didn't take any chances." I was trying to conciliate him; but I need not have feared. He was of the right sort. He broke into a laugh, slapping his thigh loudly with his open hand as he said heartily:

"Well, that girl's a daisy! she's a peach; she's "It"! To think of her walking out under our noses, and us not having an idea that it might be her, just because we didn't think she'd condescend to put on the breeches—and the footman's at that. Well, it's a pity we didn't get on to her curves; for it might have been different! Never mind! We'll take her out of her trouble before long; and Mr. Whisky Tommy and his push will have to look out for their skins!"

This little episode passed some of the time; but the reaction to the dreary waiting was worse than ever. As I began again an endless chain of surmises and misgivings, it occurred to me that Don Bernardino might be made of some use. The blackmailers had evidently watched him; it might be that they would watch him again. If so, he could be the means of a trap being laid. I turned the matter over in my mind, but at present could see no way to realise the idea. It gave me another thought, however. The Don had been very noble in his attitude to me; and I might repay some of his goodness. Although he was so quiet and silent, I knew well that he must be full of his own anxiety regarding the treasure, now exposed as it might be to other eyes than his own. I could ask him to go to see after it. With some diffidence I broached the matter to him, for I did not want in any way to wound him. Since I had determined to relinquish the treasure if necessary, I was loth to make the doing so seem like an ungracious act. At first he almost took offence, reminding me with overt haughtiness that he had already assured me that all the treasures of Spain or of the Popedom were secondary to a woman's honour. I liked him all the better for his attitude; and tried to persuade him that it was his duty to guard this trust, as otherwise it might fall into bad hands. Then a brilliant idea struck me, one which at once met the case and made the possibility of a trap. I told him that as the blackmailers had watched him once they might have done so again, and have even followed him to my house. As I was speaking, the thought struck me of how well Providence arranges all for the best. If Don Bernardino had not taken from the library the typescript of the secret writing, it might have fallen into the hands of the gang. When I mentioned the idea to him he said in surprise:

"But I did not take the papers! I read them on the table; but did not think of moving them. Why, had I done so, I should have at once made suspicion; and it was my purpose to keep the secret if I could." An idea struck me and I ran over to the table to look where the papers usually were.

There was not a sign of them about. Somebody had secured them; it could hardly have been Marjory who lacked any possible motive for doing so. The Spaniard, eagerly following my face, saw the amazement which I felt; he cried out:

"Then they have taken them. The treasure may yet prove a lure through which we may catch them. If it be that they have followed me to your house, and if they have any suspicions that came to me on reading that paper, then they will surely make some attempt." If anything were to be tried on this line, there was no time to lose. I had to carry out the matter privately; for on mentioning to Don Bernardino that I should ask one of the detectives to go with him, he at once drew back.

"No!" he said, "I have no right to imperil further this trust. The discovery was yours, and you knew of the hiding place before I did; but I could not with my consent allow any other person to know the secret. Moreover, these men are enemies of my country; and it is not well that they should know, lest they should use their knowledge for their country's aid. You and I, Senor, are *caballero*. To us there is, somewhere, a high rule of honour; but to these people there is only law!"

"Well," I said, "if you are going, you had better lose no time. These people have had nearly six hours already; I left the house with Mrs. Jack a little after ten. But you had better go carefully. The men are desperate; and if they find you alone, you may have a bad time."

For answer he pulled a revolver from his pocket. "Since yesterday," he said, "I go armed, till these unhappy businesses are all over!"

I then told him of the entrance to the caves, and gave him the key of the cellar. "Be sure you have light." I cautioned him "Plenty of light and matches. It will be towards low water when you get there. The rope which we used as a clue is still in its place; we did not take it away." I could see that this thought was a new source of anxiety to him; if the gang were before him it would have served to lead them to the treasure itself. As he was going, I bade him remember that if there was any sign of the men about, he was to return at once or send us word, so that we could come and catch them like rats in a trap. In any case he was to send us word, so that we might have knowledge of his movements, and inferentially of those of our enemies. In such a struggle as ours, knowledge was everything.

Not long after he had gone, Cathcart and MacRae arrived on horseback. They said there were three other saddle horses coming after them. Cathcart had a list of all the churches, and the manses of all the clergy of all shades of doctrine, in Buchan; and a pretty formidable list it made. He had also a map of Aberdeen County, and a list of such houses as had been let for the summer or at any period during it. Such was of course only an agent's list, and would not contain every letting privately.

We set to work at once with the map and the lists; and soon marked the names which were likely to be of any use to us, those which had at any time lately been let to strangers. Then Cathcart and Gordon and all the detectives, except the chief, went off on horseback with a list of places to visit. They were all to return to report as soon as possible. The chief kept tab of the places to be visited by each. When the rest had gone, I asked him if he knew where any of those supposed to be of the gang lived in the neighbourhood. He said he felt awkward in answering the question, and he certainly looked it. "The fact is," he said sheepishly, "since that young lady kicked those names on the dirt, and so into my thick head, I know pretty well who they are. Had I known before, I could easily have got those who could identify them; for I never saw them myself. I take it that 'Feathers' is none other than Featherstone who was with Whisky Tommy—which was Tom Mason—in the A. T. Stewart ransom case. If those two are in it, most likely the one they called the 'Dago' is a half-bred Spaniard that comes from somewheres over here. That Max that she named, if he's the same man, is a Dutchman; he's about the worst of the bunch. Then for this game there's likely to be two Chicago bums from the Levee, way-down politicians and heelers. It's possible that there are two more; a man from Frisco that they call Sailor Ben—what they call a cosmopolite for he doesn't come from nowhere in particular; and a buck nigger from Noo Orleans. A real bad 'un he is; of all the. . . But I hope he isn't in the gang. If he is, we haven't no time to lose."

His words made my blood run cold. Was this the crowd, within whose danger I had consented that Marjory should stand. The worst kind of scoundrels from all over the earth. Oh! what it was to be powerless, and to know that she was in their hands. It took me all my strength of purpose not to weep, out of very despair. I think the detective must have wished to cheer me a little, for he went on:

"Of course it's not their game to do her any harm, or let harm come to her. She's worth too many millions, alive and unharmed, for them to spoil their market by any foolishness. It's here that I trust Whisky Tommy to keep the rest straight. I suppose you know, Sir, that criminals always work in the same way every time. We know that when the Judge wouldn't pay up for old A. T., Featherstone threatened to burn up the stiff; but Whisky Tommy knew better than to kill the golden goose like that. Why he went and stole it from Featherstone and hid it somewhere about Trenton till the old lady coughed up about twenty-five thousand. Tommy's head's level; and if that black devil isn't in the squeeze, he'll keep them up to the collar every time."

"Who is the negro?" I asked, for I wanted to know the worst. "What has he done?"

"What hasn't he done that's vile, is what I'd like to know. They're a hard crowd in the darkey side of Noo Orleans; and a man doesn't get a bad name there easily, I tell you. There are dens there that'd make God Almighty blush, or the Devil either; a darkey that is bred in them and gets to the top of the push, doesn't stick at no trifles!

"But you be easy in your mind as yet, Sir; at present there's naught to fear. But if once they get safe away, they will try to put the screw on. God knows then what may happen. In the meantime, the only fear is lest, if they're in a tight place, they may kill her!"

My heart turned to ice at his words. What horrible possibilities were there, when death for my darling was the "only" fear. It was in a faint enough voice I asked him:

"Would they really kill her?"

"Of course they would; if it was their best course. But don't you be downhearted, Sir. There's not much fear of killing—as yet at all events. These men are out for dough; and for a good heap of it, too. They're not going to throw away a chance till the game's up. If we get on to their curves quick, they'll have to think of their own skins. It's only when all's up that they'll act; when they themselves must croak if she doesn't!"

Oh! if I had known! If I had had any suspicion of the dangerous nature of the game we were playing—that I had consented that Marjory should play—I'd have cut my tongue out before I'd have agreed. I might have known that a great nation like the United States would not have concerned itself as to any danger to an individual, unless there had been good cause. Oh fool! fool! that I had been!

If I had been able to do anything, it might not have been so bad. It was necessary, however, that I should be at the very heart and centre of action; for I alone knew the different ramifications of things, and there was always something cropping up of which I had better knowledge than the others. And so I had to wait in what patience I could pray for. Patience and coolness of head were what were demanded of me for the present. Later on, the time might come when there would be action; and I never doubted that when that time did come it would not find me wanting—even in the issues of life and death.

XLVI

Ardiffery Manse

In the dreary time of waiting I talked with the detective chief. Everything which he told me seemed to torture me; but there was a weird fascination in his experience as it bore on our own matter. I was face to face, for the first time in my life, with that callousness which is the outcome of the hard side of the wicked world. Criminal-hunters, as well as criminals, achieve it; so I suppose do all whose fortunes bring them against the sterner sides of life. Now and again it amazed me to hear this man, unmistakably a good fellow and an upright one, weighing up crime and criminals in a matter-of-fact way, without malice, without anger, without vindictiveness. He did seem to exercise in his habitual thought of his *clientele* that constructive condemnation which sways the rest of us in matters of moral judgment. The whole of his work, and attitude, and purpose, seemed to be only integral parts of a game which was being played. At that time I thought light of this, and consequently of him; but looking back, with judgment in better perspective, I am able to realise the value of just such things. There was certainly more chance of cooler thought and better judgment under these conditions, than when the ordinary passions and motives of human life held sway. This man did not seem to be chagrined, or put out personally in any way, by the failure of his task, or to have any rancour, from this cause, in his heart for those to whom the failure was due. On the contrary, he, like a good sportsman, valued his opponent more on account of the cleverness which had baffled him. I imagined that at first he would have been angry when he learned how all the time in which he and his companions had been watching Crom Castle, and were exulting in the security which their presence caused, their enemies had been coming and going as they wished by a safe way, unknown; and had themselves been the watchers. But there was nothing of the kind; I really believe that, leaving out of course the possibly terrible consequences of his failure, he enjoyed the defeat which had come to him. In his own way he put it cleverly:

"Those ducks knew their work well. I tell you this, in spite of the softies we have been, it isn't easy to play any of us for a sucker. Just fancy! the lot of us on sentry-go day and night round the castle, for, mind you, we never neglected the job for one half hour; and all the time, three lots of people—this push, you and the girl, and this Dago lord of yours—all going and coming like rabbits in a warren. What puzzles me is how you and Miss Drake managed to escape the observation of Whisky Tommy's lot, even if you went through us!"

It had been after five o'clock when the party set out to visit the manses; at six o'clock the reports began to come in. The first was a message scribbled on a leaf torn from a note book, and sent in one of the envelopes taken for the purpose.

"All right at Auquharney." From this on, messengers kept arriving, some on foot, some on horseback, some in carts: but each bearing a similar message, though couched in different terms. They came from Auchlenchries, Heila, Mulonachie, Ardendraught, Inverquohomery, Skelmuir, and Auchorachan. At nine o'clock the first of the searchers returned. This was Donald MacRae; knowing the country he had been able to get about quicker than any of the others who had to keep to the main roads. His report was altogether satisfactory; he had been to six places, and in each of them there was no ground for even suspicion.

It was nearly three hours before the rest were in, but all with the same story; in none of the manses let to visitors through an agent, and in none if occupied by their incumbents, could the fugitives have hidden. The last to come in were the two trackers, disappointed and weary. They had lost the track several times; but had found it again on some cross road. They had finally lost it in a dusty road near Ardiffery and had only given up when the light had altogether gone. They themselves thought their loss was final, for they could not take up the track within a quarter of a mile of either side of the spot where they had lost it.

It was now too late to do anything more for this night; so, after a meal, all the men, except one who remained on watch, went to sleep for a few hours. We must start again before dawn. For myself I could not rest; I should have gone mad, I think, if I had to remain the night without doing something. So I determined to wheel over to Whinnyfold and see how Don Bernardino had progressed. I was anxious, as I had not heard from him.

At Whinnyfold all was still, and there was no sign of light in the house. I had brought with me the duplicate key which I had given to Marjory, and which Mrs. Jack found for me on her dressing table; but when I inserted it, it would not turn. It was a Yale lock; and it was not likely that it should have got out of order without the use of some force or clumsiness. I put it down in the first instance to the inexperience of the Don in such mechanism. Anyhow, there was nothing to be done as to entry by that way, so I went round to the back to see if I could make an entry there. It was all safe, however; I had taken care to fasten every door and window on the previous night. As the front door was closed to me, it was only by force that I could effect entrance to my own house. I knocked softly at the door, and then louder; I thought perhaps, for some reason to be explained, the Don had remained in the house and might now be asleep. There was no sound, however, and I began to have grave doubts in my own mind as to whether something serious might have happened. If so, there was no time to lose. Anything having gone wrong meant that the blackmailers had been there. If I had to break open the door I might as well do it myself; for if I should get help from the village, discussion and gossip would at once begin, if only from the fact that I could not wait till morning.

I got a scaffold pole from the yard where some of the builder's material still remained, and managed by raising it on my shoulder and making a quick run forward to strike the door with it just over the lock. The blow was most efficacious; the door flew open so quickly that the handle broke against the wall of the passage. For a few seconds I paused, looking carefully round to see if the sound had brought any one to the spot; but all was still. Then carefully, and with my revolver ready in my right hand and the lamp of my bicycle in my left, I entered the house.

A glance into each of the two sitting-rooms of the ground floor showed me that there was no one there; so I closed the hall-door again, and propped it shut with the scaffold pole. Quickly I ran over the house from top to bottom, looking into every room and space where anyone could hide. The cellar door was locked. It was odd indeed; there was not a sign of Don Bernardino anywhere. With a sudden suspicion I turned into the dining-room and looked on the table, where the several caskets which we had taken from the cave had lain.

There was not a sign of them! Some one had carried them off.

For a while I thought it must have been Don Bernardino. There came back to me very vividly the conversation which we had had in that very room only a day before; I seemed to see the red light of his eyes blaze again, as when he had told me that he would not stop at anything to gain possession of the treasure. It must have been, that when he found himself in possession, the desire overcame him to take away the treasure to where he could himself control it.

But this belief was only momentary. Hard upon its heels came the remembrance of his noble attitude when I had come to ask his help for a woman in distress—I who had refused his own appeal to my chivalry only a few hours before. No! I would not believe that he could act so now. In strength of my belief I spoke aloud: "No! I will not believe it!"

Was it an echo to my words? or was it some mysterious sound from the sea beneath? Sound there certainly was, a hollow, feeble sound that seemed to come from anywhere, or nowhere. I could not locate it at all. There was but one part of the house unsearched, so I got a great piece of wood and broke open the door of the cellar. There was no one in it, but the square hole in the centre of it seemed like a mystery itself. I listened a moment; and the hollow sound came again, this time through the hole.

There was some one in the cave below, and the sound was a groan.

I lit a torch and leaning over the hole looked down. The floor below was covered with water, but it was only a few inches deep and out of it came the face of the Spaniard, looking strangely white despite its natural swarthiness. I called to him. He evidently heard me, for he tried to answer; but I could distinguish nothing, I could only hear a groan of agony. I rigged up the windlass, and taking with me a spare piece of rope lowered myself into the cave. I found Don Bernardino just conscious; he was unable, seemingly, to either understand my questions or to make articulate reply. I tied the spare rope round him, there being no time or opportunity to examine him as he lay in the water, and taking the spare end with me pulled myself up again. Then, putting the rope to which he was attached on the windlass, I easily drew him up to the cellar.

A short time sufficed to give him some brandy, and to undress him and wrap him in rugs. He shivered at first, but the warmth soon began to affect him. He got drowsy, and seemed all at once to drop asleep. I lit a fire and made some tea and got provisions ready. In less than half an hour he awoke, refreshed and quite coherent. Then he told me all that had passed. He had opened the door without trouble, and had looked into the dining-room where he found the caskets still on the table. He did not think of searching the house. He got a light and went into the cellar, leaving the door open, and set about examining the winch, so as to know the mechanism sufficiently well as to be able to raise and lower himself. Whilst stooping over the hole, he got a violent blow on the back of the head which deprived him of his senses. When he became conscious again there were four men in the cellar, all masked. He himself was tied up with ropes and gagged. The men lowered each other till only one remained on guard. He heard them calling to each other. After a long wait they had come back, all of them carrying heavy burdens which they began to haul up by the windlass. He said that it creaked loudly with the weight as they worked it. He had the unutterable chagrin of seeing them pack up in sacks and bags, extemporised from the material in the house, the bullion of the treasure which his ancestor had undertaken to guard, and to which he had committed his descendants until the trust should have been fulfilled. When all was ready for departure—which was not for many hours, and when two of the men had returned with a cart of some sort, whose wheels he heard rumbling—they consulted as to what they should do with him. There was no disguise made of their intent; all was spoken in his hearing with the most brutal frankness. One man, whom he described as with grey lips of terrific thickness, and whose hands were black, was for knifing him at once or cutting his throat, and announced his own readiness to do the job. He was overruled, however, by another, presumably the leader of the gang, who said there was no use taking extra risks. "Let us put him into the cave," he said. "He may break his neck; but anyhow it does not matter for the tide is rising fast and if anyone should come they will find that he met his death by an accident."

This suggestion was carried out; he was, after the ropes and gag were removed with the utmost care but with the utmost brutality, lowered into the cave. He remembered no more till the deadly silence around him was broken by the sound, seemingly far away, of a heavy blow on wood which reverberated.

I examined him all over carefully, but could find no definite harm done to him. This knowledge in itself cheered him up, and his strength and nerve began to come back; with his strength came determination. He could, however, tell me nothing of the men who had attacked him. He said he would know their voices again, but, what with their masks and his cramped position, he could not see enough to distinguish anything.

Whilst he was recovering himself I looked carefully round the room and house. From the marks at one of the windows at the back I gathered that this was the means by which they had gained admission. They were expert housebreakers; and as I gathered from the detective that Whisky Tommy was a bank burglar—most scientific and difficult of all criminal trades, except perhaps, banknote forgery—I was not surprised that they had been able to gain admittance. None of the jewels which Marjory and I had taken from the cave were left behind. The robbers had evidently made accurate search; even the rubies, which I had left in the pocket of the shooting-coat which I had worn in the cave, had disappeared.

One thing I gathered from their visit; they evidently felt secure as to themselves. They dared not risk so long delay had not their preparations been complete; and they must have been satisfied as to the mechanism of their escape since they could burden themselves with such weight of treasure. Moreover, their hiding place, wherever it was, could not be far off. There were engaged in this job four men; besides, there were probably watchers. Marjory had only recorded in her cipher six engaged in her abduction, when presumably their full strength would have been needed in case of unexpected difficulties or obstacles. The Secret Service chief presumed at least eight. I determined, therefore, that I would get back to Crom as soon as possible, and, with the aid of this new light, consult as to what was best to be done. I wanted to take Don Bernardino with me, or to try to get a trap to take him on; but he said he would be better remaining where he was. "I can be of no use to any one till I get over this shock," he said. "The rest here, if I remain longer, will do me good; and in the morning I may be able to help." I asked him if he was not afraid to be left alone in his present helpless condition: His reply showed great common sense:

"The only people whom I have to fear are the last who will come to this place!"

I made him as comfortable as I could, and fixed the catch of the door so that the lock would snap behind me. Then I got on my bicycle and rode to Crom as quickly as I could. As it was now nearly early morning the men were getting ready for their day's work. Cathcart and I discussed the new development with the detective chief. I did not tell him of the treasure. It was gone; and all I could do was to spare the Spaniard's feelings. It was enough that they knew of the attack on Don Bernardino, and that they had taken from my house whatever was of value in it. As I went over the practical side of the work before us, I had an idea. It was evident that these men had some secret hiding place not far away; why should it not be an empty house? I made the suggestion to my two companions, who agreed with me that we should at once make search for such a place. Accordingly we arranged that one man of the force should go into Ellon, as soon as it was possible to find any one up, and another into Aberdeen to try to find out from various agents what houses in the district were at present unoccupied. In the meantime I looked over the list of Manses and found that there were two which were open for letting, but had not yet been occupied, Aucheries and Ardiffery. We determined to visit the latter first, as it was nearer, amid a network of cross roads on the high road to Fraserburgh. When we were arranging plans of movement, the two trackers who wanted to resume their work said that we might put them down on our way, as the spot they aimed for lay in the same direction. We left two men behind; the rest of us kept together.

As we drove along in the brake, the trackers showed us how they had followed the carriage. It brought an agonising hope to me to think that we were actually travelling on the same road as Marjory had gone. I had a secret conviction that we were going right. Something within me told me so. I had in former days—days that now seemed so long ago—when I realised that I had the Second Sight, come to have such confidence in my own intuition that now something of the same feeling came back to me as a reality. Oh! how I longed that the mysterious gift might now be used on behalf of her I loved. What would I not have given for one such glimpse of her in her present situation, as I had before seen of Lauchlane Macleod, or of the spirits of the Dead from the Skares. But it is of the essence of such supernatural power that it will not work to command, to present need, to the voice of suffering or of prayer; but only in such mysterious way and time as none can predicate. Whilst I thought thus, and hoped thus, and prayed with all the intensity of my poor breaking heart, I seemed to feel in me something of the mood in which the previous visions had come. I became lost to all surroundings; and it was with surprise that I became conscious that the carriage had stopped and that the trackers were getting off. We arranged with them that after our visit to the Manse at Ardiffery we should return for them, or to see how they had got on with their task. They were not hopeful of following a two-day-old trail of a carriage on these dusty roads.

The cross road to Ardiffery branched off to our left, and then to the left again; so that when we came near the place, we were still within easy distance, as the crow flies, from where we had left our men.

The Manse at Ardiffery is a lonely spot, close to the church, but quite away from the little clachan. The church stands in its own graveyard, in a hollow surrounded with a wall of considerable dimensions. The garden and policies of the house seem as though carved out of the woodland growth. There is a narrow iron gate, sheer in the roadway, and a straight path up to the front of the house; one arm branches to the right in a curved lane-way through fir trees leading to the stable and farm offices at the back of the house. At the gateway was a board with a printed notice that the house, with grounds, gardens and policies, was to be let until Christmas. The key could be had from, and details supplied by, Mrs. MacFie, merchant at the Ardiffery cross roads. The whole place had a deserted air; weeds were growing everywhere, and, even from the roadway, one could see that the windows were fouled from disuse.

As we drew near, the odd feeling of satisfaction—I can hardly describe it more fully—seemed to grow in me. I was not exultant, I was scarcely hopeful; but somehow the veil seemed to be lifting from my soul. We left the brake on the road, and went up the little avenue to the front of the house. For form's sake we knocked, though we knew well that if those we sought should be within there would be little chance of their responding to our call. We left one man at the door, in case by any chance any one should come; the rest of us took the other way round to the back of the house. We had got about half way along it, where there was an opening into the fields, when the detective chief who was in front of us held up his hand to stop. I saw at a glance what had struck him.

Whilst the rest of the rough roadway was unkempt and weed-grown, the gravel from this on, to the back of the house, had been lately raked.

"Why?"

The only answer to the unspoken query of each of us was that Marjory had made some marks, intentionally or unintentionally—or some one had; and the gang had tried to efface them.

Fools! their very effort to obliterate their trace was a help to us.

XLVII

The Dumb Can Speak

The Secret Service men spread round the house, moving off silently right and left, in accordance with the nods of their chief in answer to their looks of query. As they moved, keeping instinctively in shelter from any possible view from the house so far as the ground afforded opportunity, I could see that each felt that his gun was in its place. They all knew the gang they had to deal with, and they were not going to take any chances. MacRae said to me:

"I'll go and get the key! I know this country better than any of you; I can run over to the cross roads in a few minutes and it will be less marked than driving there." As he went out at the gate he told the driver to pull down the road, till the curve shut him out of sight. Whilst he was gone, the men surrounded the house, keeping guard at such points that nothing coming from it could escape our notice. The chief tried the back door but it was shut; from its rigidity it was manifestly bolted top and bottom.

In less than a quarter of an hour MacRae returned and told us that Mrs. MacFie was coming with the key as quickly as she could. He offered to take it, telling her who he was; but she said she would come herself and make her service, as it would not be respectful to him and the other gentlemen to let them go alone. In a few minutes she was with us; the chief detective, Cathcart, and I stayed with MacRae, the rest of the men remaining on watch and hidden. There was a little difficulty with the lock, but we shortly got in, Mrs. MacFie leading the way. Whilst she was opening the shutters of the back room, which was evidently the Minister's study, Cathcart and the chief left the room, and made a hurried, though thorough, search of the house. They came back before the old lady was well through her task, and shook their heads.

When the light was let in, the room presented a scene of considerable disorder. It was evident that it had been lately inhabited, for there were scattered about, a good many things which did not belong to it. These included a washing jug, and a bowl full of dirty water; a rug and pillows on the sofa; and a soiled cup and plate on the table. On the mantlepiece was a guttered out candle. When the old woman saw the state of the room, she lifted her hands in horrified amazement as she spoke:

"Keep's 'a! The tramps must ha' been here. In the Meenester's own study, too! An' turnin' the whole place topsal-teerie. Even his bukes all jumm'lt up thegither. Ma certes! but won't he be upset by yon!"

Whilst she had been speaking, my eyes had been taking in everything. All along one side of the room was a bookcase, rough shelves graduated up in height to suit the various sizes of books. There were in the room more than enough books to fill them; but still some of the shelves towards the right hand end were vacant and a great quantity of books lay on the floor. These were not tumbled about as if thrown down recklessly, but were laid upon the floor in even rows. It looked as if they had been taken down in masses and laid out in the same order as though ready to put back. But the books on the shelves! It was no wonder that the old woman, who did not understand the full meaning, was shocked; for never was seen such seeming disorder in any library. Seldom did a volume of a series seem to be alongside its fellow; even when several were grouped together, the rest of the selection would be missing, or seen in another part of the shelf. Some of the volumes were upside down; others had the fronts turned out instead of the back. Altogether there was such disorder as I had never seen. And yet! . . .

And yet the whole was planned by a clever and resolute woman, fighting for her life—her honour. Marjory, evidently deprived of any means of writing—there was neither pen nor ink nor pencil in the room—and probably forbidden under hideous threats to leave any message, had yet under the very eyes of her captors left a veritable writing on the wall, full and open for all to read, did they but know how. The arrangement of the books was but another variant of our biliteral cipher. Books as they should be, represented A; all others B. I signed to the man with the notebook, who took down the words wrought in the cipher as I read them off. Oh, how my heart beat with fear and love and pride as I realised in the message of my dear girl the inner purpose of her words:

"To-morrow off north east of Banff *Seagull* to meet whaler *Wilhelmina*. To be Shanghaied—whatever that means. Frightful threats to give me to the negro if any trouble, or letters to friends. Don't fear, dear, shall die first. Have sure means. God with us. Remember the cave. Just heard Gardent—" Here the message ended. The shelf was empty; and the heap of books, from which she had selected so many items, remained as they had been placed ready to her hand. She had been coerced; or else she feared interruption in her task, and did not want to cause suspicion.

Coerced! I felt as though choking!

There was nothing further to be gained here; so we told the old lady that we should write regarding the rental if we decided to take the house. When we went back to our wagonette, we picked up our two trackers—there was no use for them now—and went back to Crom as fast as the horses could gallop. It was necessary that we should arrange from headquarters our future plans; such maps and papers as we had were at Crom, where also any telegrams might await us. In the carriage I asked the detective chief what was meant by 'Shanghaied' for it was evidently a criminal class word.

"Don't you know the word," he said surprised. "Why I thought every one knew that. It isn't altogether a criminal class word, for it belongs partly to a class that call themselves traders. The whalers and others do it when they find it hard to get men; as a rule men nowadays don't like shipping on long whaling voyages. They get such men delivered on board by the crimps, drunk or, more generally, hocussed. Then when they get near a port they make them drunk again, which isn't much of a job after all, and they don't make no kick; or if things are serious they hocus them a bit again. So they keep them one way or another out of sight for months or perhaps years. Sometimes, when those that are not too particular want to get rid of an inconvenient relative—or mayhap a witness, or a creditor, or an inconvenient husband—they just square some crimp. When he gets his hooks on the proper party, there ain't no more jamboree for him, except between the bulwarks, till the time is up, or the money spent, or whatever he is put away for is fixed as they want it."

This was a new and enlightening horror to me. It opened up fresh possibilities of distress for both Marjory and myself. As I thought of this, I could not but be grateful to Montgomery for his message to the man-of-war's men. If once they succeeded in getting Marjory on board the *Seagull* we should, in the blindness of our ignorance as to her whereabouts, be powerless to help her. The last word of her message through the books might be a clue. It was some place, and was east of Banff. I got the big map out at once and began to search. Surely enough, there it was. Some seven or eight miles east of Banff was a little port in a land-locked bay called Gardentown. At once I sent off a wire to Adams at Aberdeen, and another to Montgomery to Peterhead on chance that it might reach him even before that which Adams, whom he kept posted as to his every movement, would be sure to send to him! It was above all things necessary that we should locate first the *Seagull* and then the *Wilhelmina*. If we could get hold of either vessel we might frustrate the plans of the miscreants. I asked Adams to have the touching of the *Wilhelmina* at any port telegraphed to him at once from Lloyds.

He was quite awake at his end of the wire; I got back an answer in an incredibly short time:

"*Wilhelmina* left Lerwick for Arctic seas yesterday."

Very shortly afterwards another telegram came from him:

"Montgomery reports *Seagull* fishing this summer at Fraserburgh. Went out with fleet two days ago." Almost immediately after this came a third telegram from him:

"*Keystone* notified. Am coming to join you."

After a consultation we agreed that it was better that some of us should wait at Crom for the arrival of Adams, who had manifestly some additional knowledge. In the meantime we despatched two of the Secret Service men up to the north of Buchan. One was to go to Fraserburgh, and the other to Banff. Both were to follow the cliffs or the shore to Gardentown. On their way they would get a personal survey of the coast and might pick up some information. MacRae went off himself to send a telegram ordering his yacht, which was at Inverness, to be taken to Peterhead, where he would join her. "It may be handy to have her at the mouth of the Firth," he said. "She's a clipper, and if we should want to overhaul the *Seagull* or the *Wilhelmina*, she can easily do it."

It was a long, long wait till Adams arrived. I did not think that a man could endure such misery as I suffered, and live. Every minute, every second, was filled with some vague terror. *Omne ignotum pro mirifico.* When Fear and Fancy join hands, there is surely woe and pain to some poor human soul.

When Adams at last arrived he had much to tell; but it was the amplification of what we had heard, rather than fresh news. The U. S. cruiser *Keystone* had been reached from Hamburgh, and was now on her way to a point outside the three-mile limit off Peterhead; and a private watch had been set on every port and harbour between Wick and Aberdeen. The American Embassy was doing its work quietly as befits such an arm of the State; but its eyes and ears were open, and I had no doubts its pockets, too. Its hand was open now; but it would close, did there be need.

When Adams learned our purpose he became elated. He came over to me and laid his hand tenderly on my shoulder as he said:

"I know how it is with you, old fellow; a man don't want more than two eyes for that. But there's a many men would give all they have to stand in your shoes, for all you suffer. Cheer up! At the worst now it's her death! For myself I feared at first there might be worse; but it's plain to me that Miss Drake is up to everything and ready for everything. My! but she's a noble girl! If anything goes wrong with her there's going to be some scrapping round before the thing's evened up!" He then went on to tell me that Montgomery would be joined at Peterhead by two other naval fellows who were qualified in all ways to do whatever might be required. "Those boys won't stop at much, I can tell you," he said. "They're full of sand, the lot; and I guess that when this thing is over, it won't harm them at Washington to know that they've done men's work of one kind or another."

It was comfort to me to hear him talk. Sam Adams knew what he meant, when he wanted to help a friend; thinking it all over I don't see what better he could have said to me—things being as they were. He went back to Aberdeen to look out for news or instructions, but was to join us later at Banff.

We left two men at Crom; one to be always on the spot, and the other to be free to move about and send telegrams, etc. Then the rest of us drove over to Fyvie and caught the train to Macduff.

When we arrived we sent one man in the hotel in Banff in case we should want to communicate, and the rest of us drove over in a carriage to Gardentown. It is a lovely coast, this between Banff and Gardentown, but we should have preferred it to be less picturesque and more easy to watch.

When our man met us, which he did with exceeding caution, he at once began:

"They've got off, some of them; but I think the rest of the gang's ashore still. That's why I'm so particular; they may be watchin' us now for all I can tell." Then he proceeded to give us all the information he had gleaned.

"The *Seagull* was here until yesterday when she went out into the Firth to run down to Fifeshire, as the fish were reported going south. She had more than her complement of men, and her skipper volunteered the information that two of them were friends whom they were taking to join their own boat which was waiting for them at Burnt Island. From all accounts I gather," he went on, "that they wasn't anything extra high-toned. Most of them were drunk or getting a jag on them; and it took the two sober ones and the Skipper to keep them in order. The Skipper was mighty angry; he seemed somehow ashamed of them, and hurried out of port as quick as he could when he made his mind up. They say he swore at them frightful; though that was not to be wondered at when he himself had to help bring the nets on board. One of the men on the quay told me that he said if that was the effect on his men of waiting round for weeks doing nothing, he would see that another time their double-dashed noses were kept to the grindstone. I've been thinking since I heard of the trouble they had in carrying on the nets, that there was something under them that they meant to hide. The men here tell me that the hand-barrow they carried would have been a job for six men, not three, for it was piled shoulder high with nets. That's why the skipper was so wrathy with them. They say he's a sort of giant, a Dutchman with an evil, cunning face; and that all the time he was carrying the back handles he never stopped swearing at the two in front, though they was nigh speechless with the effort of carrying, and their faces as red as blazes. If I'm right we've missed them this time. They've got the girl on the fishing boat; and they're off for the whaler. She's the one we'll have to find next!"

As he spoke my heart kept sinking deeper and deeper down. My poor girl, if alive, was in the hands of her enemies. In all the thoughts which filled me with anguish unspeakable there was but one gleam of consolation—the negro was not on board, too. I had come to think of this miscreant as in some way the active principle of whatever evil might be.

Here, we were again at a fault in our pursuit. We must wait for the reports of Montgomery who was making local inquiries. We had wired him to join us, or send us word to Gardentown; and he had replied that he was on the way.

XLVIII

Dunbuy Haven

We had to-day been so hot in the immediate pursuit of Marjory that we had hardly been able to think of the other branches of our work; but all at once, the turn of the wheel brought up as the most important matter before us what had been up to now only a collateral. Hitherto the *Seagull* had been our objective; but now it must be the *Wilhelmina*. Adams had been in charge of the general investigation as to these boats, whilst Montgomery had been attending to local matters. It was to the former, therefore, rather than the latter, that we had to look for enlightenment. Montgomery and MacRae were the first to arrive, coming on horseback from Fraserburgh, the former with all the elan and abandonment of a sailor ashore. He was frightfully chagrined when he heard that the *Seagull* had got safely away. "Just like my luck!" he said, "I might have got her in time if I had known enough; but I never even heard of Gardentown till your wire came to me. It isn't on the map." He was still full of lamentings, though I could tell from the way he was all nerved and braced up that we should hear of him when the time for action came. When we arrived at the station at Macduff to meet Adams, we hurried him at once into the carriage which we had waiting; he gave us his news as we hurried off to Gardentown. We felt that it might be a mistake our going there, for we should be out of the way of everything; but we had made arrangements for news to be sent there, and it was necessary we should go there before holding our council of war. Adams told us that the whaler *Wilhelmina* had been reported at Lerwick two days ago, but that she had suddenly left on receipt of a telegram, hurrying in the last of her stores at such a rate that some of them had been actually left behind. He had not been able to gain any specific information by wire. The Master of the ship had said to the Harbour Master that he was going to Nova Zembla; but nothing more definite could be obtained.

When we got together in the hotel at Gardentown we were surprised by another arrival; none other than Don Bernardino, who had come by the same train as Adams, but had had to wait to get a carriage. We had got away so quickly that none of us had seen him.

Things were now at such a stage that it would not do to have any concealment whatever; and so after a moment in private with the Don, I told my companions of the attack on the Spaniard in my house, and of the carrying off the great treasure. I did not give any details of the treasure or its purpose; nor did I even mention the trust. This was now the Don's secret, and there was no need to mention it. We all agreed that if we should have any chance at all of finding Marjory, it would be by finding and following the members of the gang left on shore. Sam Adams who was, next to the Secret Service men, the coolest-headed of our party, summed up the situation.

"Those fellows haven't got off yet. It is evident that they only came to look for the treasure after Miss Drake had been shipped off from Gardentown. And I'm pretty sure that they are waiting somewhere round the coast for the *Wilhelmina* to pick them up; or for them to get aboard her somehow. They've got a cartload of stuff at the very least to get away; and you may bet your sweet life that they don't mean to leave it to chance. Moreover, you can't lay your hand at any minute on a whaler ready for shanghaieing any one. This one has been fixed up on purpose, and was waiting up at Lerwick for a long time ready to go when told. I think myself that it's more than likely she has orders to take them off herself, for a fishing smack like the *Seagull* that has to be in and out of these ports all the time, doesn't want to multiply the chances of her discovery. Now that she has done a criminal thing and is pretty sure that it can't be proved against her, she'll take her share of the swag, or whatever was promised her, and clear out. If the *Wilhelmina* has to get off the gang it'll have to be somewhere off this coast. They are nearly all strangers to start with, and wouldn't know where else to go. If they go south they get at once into more thickly peopled shores, where the chances of getting off in secret would be less. They daren't go anywhere along the shore of the Firth, for their ship might be cut off at the mouth, and they might be taken within the three-mile limit and searched. Beyond the Firth they can know nothing. Therefore, we have got to hunt them along this shore; and from the lie of the land I should say that they will try to get off somewhere between Old Slains and Peterhead. And I'll say further that, in-as-much-as the shore dips in between Whinnyfold and Girdleness outside Aberdeen, the ship will prefer to keep up the north side, so that she can beat out to sea at once, when she has got her cargo aboard."

"Sam is about right!" broke in Montgomery "I have been all along the coast since we met, surveying the ground for just this purpose. I tried to put myself in the place of that crowd, and to find a place just such as they would wish. They could get out at Peterhead or at Boddam, and so I have set a watch at these places. Some of our sailors who were sent up to me from London are there now, and I'll stake my word that if the *Wilhelmina* tries to come in to either of these places she won't get out again with Marjory Drake on board. But it's not their game to come near a port. They've got to lie off shore, somewhere agreed on, and take off their friends in a boat. There are dozens of places between Cruden and Peterhead where a boat could lie hidden, and slip out safely enough. When they got aboard they could hoist in the boat or scuttle her; and then, up sails and off before any one was the wiser. What I propose, therefore, is this, for I take it I'm the naval expert here such as it is. We must set a watch along this bit of coast, so as to be ready to jump on them when they start out. We can get the *Keystone* to lie off Buchan; and we can signal her when we get sign of our lot. She'll be well on the outside, and these scallywags don't know that she'll be there to watch them. When the time comes, she'll crowd them into shore; and we'll be ready for them there. If she can hunt the *Wilhelmina* into the Firth it will be easy enough to get her. "Fighting Dick" Morgan isn't a man to stand on ceremony; and you can bet your bottom dollar that if he gets a sight of the Dutchman he'll pretty well see that she hasn't any citizen of the United States aboard against her will. Dick wouldn't mind the people in Washington much, and he'd take on the Dutch to-morrow as well as the Spaniards. Now, if in addition this gentleman's yacht is to the fore, with any one of us here aboard to take responsibility, I guess we can overhaul the whaler without losing time."

"I'll be aboard!" said Donald MacRae quietly. "The *Sporran* is due at Peterhead this afternoon. Just you fit me up with signals so that we'll know what to do when we get word; and I'll see to the rest. My men are of my own clan, and I'll answer for them. They'll not hang back in anything, when I'm in the front of them."

I wrung the hands of the two young fellows. East and West, it was all the same! The old fighting gallantry was in their hearts; and with the instinct of born Captains they were ready to accept all responsibility. All they asked was that their men should follow them.

They immediately sat down to arrange their signals. Montgomery was of course trained in this work, and easily fixed up a simple scheme by which certain orders could be given by either flags, or lights, or rockets. There was not need for much complication; it was understood that when the *Wilhelmina* should be sighted she should be boarded at once, wherever or however she might be. We were, one and all of us, prepared to set at defiance every law—international, maritime, national or local. Under the circumstances we felt that, given we could once get on track with our enemy, we held a great power in our hands.

Before long, MacRae was off to Peterhead to join his yacht, which would at once start on a sort of sentry-go up and down the coast. The rest of us set about arranging to spread ourselves along the shore between Cruden and Peterhead. We did not arrange watches, for time was now precious to all, on both sides of the encounter. If an attempt was to be made to take off the treasure, it would in all probability be made before morning; every hour that passed multiplied the difficulties and dangers of the blackmailers. The weather was becoming misty, which was a source of inconvenience to us all. Thick patches of white fog began to drift in from the north east, and there was ominous promise in the rising wind of there being danger on sea and shore before many hours had passed. We each took provision with us for the night, and a sufficiency of rockets and white and red lights for our signalling work, in case there might be need of such.

In disposing of our forces, we had not of course a sufficiency of men to form a regular cordon; but we so arranged ourselves that there was no point at which a boat could land which was not in view of some of us. I was terribly anxious, for as the evening came on, the patches of white mist came driving in more quickly, and getting thicker and more dense. Between them the sea was clear, and there was no difficulty in keeping accurate observation; but as each fog belt came down on the rising wind our hearts fell. It would come on like a white cloud, which would seem to strike the land and then close in on every side, as though wrapping the shore in a winding sheet. My own section for watching was between Slains Castle and Dunbuy, as wild and rocky a bit of coast as any one could wish to see. Behind Slains runs in a long narrow inlet with beetling cliffs, sheer on either side, and at its entrance a wild turmoil of rocks are hurled together in titanic confusion. From this point northward, the cliffs are sheer, to where the inlet of Dunbuy has its entrance guarded by the great rock, with its myriad of screaming wildfowl and the white crags marking their habitation. Midway between those parts of my sentry-go is a spot which I could not but think would be eminently suited for their purpose, and on this for some time I centred my attention. It is a place where in old days the smugglers managed to get in many a cargo safe, almost within earshot of the coastguards. The *modus operandi* was simple. On a dark night when it was known that the coastguards were, intentionally or by chance, elsewhere, a train of carts would gather quickly along the soft grass tracks, or through the headlands of the fields. A crane was easily improvised of two crossed poles, with a longer one to rest on them; one end held inland, could be pushed forward or drawn back, so as to make the other end hang over the water or fall back over the inner edge of the cliff. A pulley at the end of this pole, and a long rope with its shore end attached to the harness of a strong horse completed the equipment. Then, when the smugglers had come under the cliff, the rope was lowered and the load attached; the waiting horse was galloped inland, and in a few seconds the cluster of barrels or cases was swung up on the cliff and distributed amongst the waiting carts.

It would be an easy matter to invert the process. If all were ready— and I knew that the gang were too expert to have any failing in that respect—a few minutes would suffice to place the whole of the treasure in a waiting boat. The men, all save one, could be lowered the same way, and the last man could be let down by the rope held from below. I knew that the blackmailers had possession of at least one cart; in any case, to men so desperate and reckless to get temporary possession of a few carts in a farming country like this would be no difficult task. So I determined to watch this spot with extra care. It was pretty bare at top; but there was a low wall of stone and clay, one of those rough fences which are so often seen round cliff fields. I squatted down behind a corner of this wall, from which I could see almost the whole stretch of my division. No boat could get into Dunbuy or Lang Haven, or close to the Castle rocks without my seeing it; the cliff from there up to where I was was sheer, and I could see well into the southern passage of the Haven inside Dunbuy Rock. Sometimes when the blanket of fog spread over the sea, I could hear the trumpeting of some steamer far out; and when the fog would lift, I would see her funnels spouting black smoke in her efforts to clear so dangerous a coast. Sometimes a fishing boat on its way up or down would run in shore, close hauled; or a big sailing vessel would move onward with that imperceptible slowness which marks the progress of a ship far out at sea. When any fishing boat came along, my heart beat as I scanned her with the field glass which I had brought with me. I was always hoping that the *Seagull* would appear, though why I know not, for there was now little chance indeed that Marjory would be on board her.

After a spell of waiting, which seemed endless and unendurable, in one of the spells of mist I thought I saw on the cliff a woman, taking shelter of every obstacle, as does one who is watching another. At that moment the mist was thick; but when it began to thin, and to stream away before the wind in trails like smoke, I saw that it was Gormala. Somehow the sight of her made my heart beat wildly. She had been a factor of so many strange incidents in my life of late years—incidents which seemed to have some connection or fatal sequence—that her presence seemed to foretell something fresh, and to have some kind of special significance. I crouched still lower behind the corner of the wall, and watched with enhanced eagerness. A very short study of her movements showed me that she was not watching any specific individual. She was searching for some one, or some thing; and was in terror of being seen, rather than of missing the object of her search. She would peer carefully over the edge of the cliff, lying down on her face to do so, and putting her head forward with the most elaborate care. Then, when she had satisfied herself that what she sought was not within sight, she would pass on a little further and begin her survey over again. Her attitude during the prevalence of a mist was so instructive, that I found myself unconsciously imitating her. She would remain as still as if turned to stone, with one ear to windward, listening with sharp, preternatural intentness. I wondered at first that I could not hear the things that she manifestly did, for the expression of her face was full of changes. When, however, I remembered that she was born and reared amongst the islands, and with fisher folk and sea folk of all kinds whose weather instincts are keener than is given to the inland born, her power was no longer a mystery. How I longed at that moment to have something of her skill! And then came the thought that she had long ago offered to place that very power at my disposal; and that I might still gain her help. Every instant, as past things crowded back to my memory, did that help seem more desirable. Was it not her whom I had seen watching Don Bernardino when he left my house; mayhap she had guided him to it. Or might it not have been Gormala who had brought the blackmailers to my door. If she had no knowledge of them, what was she doing here now? Why had she sought this place of all places; why at this time of all times? What or whom was she seeking amongst the cliffs?

I determined not to lose sight of her at present, no matter what might happen; later, when I had come at her purpose, either by guessing or by observation, I could try to gain her services. Though she had been enraged with me, I was still to her a Seer; and she believed—must believe from what had passed—that I could read for her the Mystery of the Sea.

As she worked along the cliff above Dunbuy Haven, where the rock overhung the water, she seemed to increase both her interest and her caution. I followed round the rude wall which ran parallel to the cliff, so that I might be as near to her as possible.

Dunbuy Haven is a deep cleft in the granite rock in the shape of a Y, the arms of which run seawards and are formed by the mother cliff on either hand and the lofty crags of the island of Dunbuy. In both these arms there is deep water; but when there is a sea on, or when the wind blows strong, they are supremely dangerous. Even the scour of the tide running up or down makes a current difficult to stem. In fair weather, however, it is fairly good for boating; though the swell outside may be trying to those who are poor sailors. I had often tossed on that swell when I had been out with the salmon fishers, when they had been drawing their deep floating nets.

Presently I saw Gormala bend, and then disappear out of sight. She had passed over the edge of the cliff. I went cautiously after her, and throwing myself on my face so that she could not see me, peered over.

There was a sort of sheep track along the face of the cliff, leading downward in a zigzag. It was so steep, and showed so little foothold, that even in the state of super-excitement in which I then was, it made me dizzy to look at it. But the old woman, trained on the crags of the western islands, passed along it as though it were the broad walk of a terraced garden.

XLIX

GORMALA'S LAST HELP

After Gormala had disappeared down the zigzag under the rock, where I could no longer see her movements, I waited for her return. At the end of the Haven, where the little beach runs up to the edge of the cliff, there is a steep path. Even this is so steep that it is impracticable to ordinary persons; only fisher folk, dalesmen and hunters can use such ways. For myself I dare not leave my post; from the end of the Haven I could not see any part at all of the coast I had come to watch, except the narrow spot between great cliffs where the channels ran right and left of the Rock of Dunbuy. So I crept back to my hiding place behind the angle of the wall, from which I could watch the entrance to the track down which she had passed.

Time wore away slowly, slowly; and the mist kept coming in more frequent belts, heavier and more dank. After the sunset the fog seemed to come more heavily still, so that the promise of the night was darkness invincible. In Aberdeen, however, the twilight is long, and under ordinary conditions it is easy to see for hours after sunset. All at once, after the passing of a belt of mist, I was startled by a voice behind me:

"And for what is it ye watch, the nicht? Is it the Mystery o' the Sea that holds ye to the dyke; or maybe it is the treasure that ye seek!" Gormala had evidently come up the path at the end of the Haven. For a while I did not say a word, but thought the matter over. Now, if ever, was there need to use my wits, and I could best deal with Gormala if I should know something of her own wishes beforehand; so I tried to master her purpose and her difficulties. Firstly, she must have been in search of some hiding place herself, or she would not have come behind the wall; I was quite sure that she had not known of my presence before she went down the sheep track. If she wanted cover, what then was it she was watching? She had been down to the beach of the Haven, and so must have known whether or no it was bare of interest. As she was choosing a corner whence she could watch the track, it was at least likely that she expected some one to go up or down by it. If she were looking for some one to go down, she would surely rather watch its approaches than the place itself. It was, therefore, for some one to come up for whom she wished to watch. As, instead of hurrying away or hiding herself from me when she had seen me without my seeing her, she had deliberately engaged with me in conversation, it was evident that she did not expect whomever she watched for to come up at once. In fine I concluded, she intended to watch for some one who *might* come; with this knowledge I drew a bow at a venture:

"So your friend isn't coming up yet? Why didn't you fix matters when you were down below?" For an instant she was betrayed into showing astonishment; the surprise was in both her expression and in the tones of her voice as she replied:

"How kent ye that I was doon the Haven?" Then she saw her mistake and went on with a scowl:

"Verra clever ye are wi' yer guesses; and a daft aud wife am I to no ken ye better? Why did—"

"Did you find him down below?" even whilst I was speaking the conviction came to me—I scarcely know how, but it was there as though deep-rooted in my brain all my life—that our enemies were down below, or that they had some hiding place there. Gormala must have seen the change in my face, for she exclaimed with jubilation:

"It would hae been better for ye that ye had taken my sairvice. The een that watched others micht hae been watchin' to yer will. But it's a' ower the noo. What secret there was is yours nae mair; an' it may be waur for ye that ye flouted me in the days gone." As she spoke, the bitterness of her manner was beyond belief; the past rushed back on me so fiercely that I groaned. Then came again, but with oh! what pain, the thought of my dear one in the hands of her enemies.

Let no man question the working of the Almighty's hand. In that moment of the ecstasy of pain, something had spoken to the heart of the old woman beside me; for when I came back to myself they were different eyes which looked into mine. They were soft and full of pity. All the motherhood which ever had been, or might have been, in that lonely soul was full awake. It was with a tender voice that she questioned me:

"Ye are muckle sad laddie. Do I no ken a look like that when I speer it, and know that the Fates are to their wark. What maks ye greet laddie; what maks ye greet?" for by this time the revulsion of tenderness had been too much for me and I was openly weeping. "Is it that the lassie is gone frae ye? Weel I ken that nane but a lassie can mak a strong man greet." I felt that the woman's heart was open to me; and spoke with all the passion of my soul:

"Oh, Gormala help me! Perhaps you can, and it may not be too late. She is stolen away and is in the hands of her enemies; wicked and desperate men who have her prisoner on a ship somewhere out at sea. Her life, her honour are at stake. Help me if you can; and I will bless you till the last hour of my life!" The old woman's face actually blazed as I spoke. She seemed to tower up in the full of her gaunt height to the stature of her woman's pride, as with blazing eyes she answered me:

"What! a woman, a lassie, in the hands o' wicked men! Aye an' sic a bonnie, gran' lassie as yon, though she did flout me in the pride of her youth and strength. Laddie, I'm wi' ye in all ye can dae! Wi' a' the strength o' my hairt an' the breath o' my body; for life or for death! Ne'er mind the past; bad or good for me it is ower; and frae this oot I'm to your wark. Tell me what I can dae, an' the grass'll no grow under my feet. A bonnie bit lassie in the power o' wicked men! I may hae been ower eager to win yer secret; but I'm no that bad to let aught sic come between me and the duty to what is pure and good!" She seemed grand and noble in her self-surrender; such a figure as the poets of the old sagas may have seen in their dreams, when the type of noble old womanhood was in their hearts; in the times when the northern nations were dawning. I was quite overcome; I could not speak. I took her hand and kissed it. This seemed to touch her to the quick; with a queer little cry she gasped out:

"Oh, laddie, laddie!" and said no more. Then I told her of how Marjory had been carried off by the blackmail gang; I felt that she was entitled to this confidence. When I had spoken, she beat with her shut hand on the top of the wall and said in a smothered way:

"Och! if I had but kent; if I had but kent! To think that I might hae been watchin' them instead o' speerin' round yon hoose o' yours, watchin' to wring yer secret frae ye, an' aidin' yer enemies in their wark. First the outland man wi' the dark hair; an' then them along wi' the black man wi' the evil face that sought ye the nicht gone. Wae is me! Wae is me! that I ha' done harm to a' in the frenzy o' my lust, and greed, and curiosity!" She took on so badly that I tried to comfort her. I succeeded to a measure, when I had pointed out that the carrying off of Marjory was altogether a different matter from what had gone on in my house. Suddenly she stopped rocking herself to and fro; holding up one long gaunt arm as I had seen her do several times before, she said:

"But what matters it after a'! We're in the hands o' Fate! An' there are Voices that speak an' Een that see. What is ordered of old will be done for true; no matter how we may try to work our own will. 'Tis little use to kick against the pricks."

Then all at once she became brisk and alert. In a most practical tone of voice she said:

"Noo tell me what I can dae! Weel I ken, that ye hae a plan o' yer ain; an' that you and ithers are warkin' to an end that ye hae set. Ye hae one ither wi' ye the nicht; for gude or ill." She paused, and I asked her:

"Why did you go down the sheep path to the Haven. For what or for whom were you looking?"

"I was lookin' for the treasure that I suspect was ta'en frae your hoose; an' for them that took it! 'Twas I that guided them, after the dark man had gone; and watched whiles they were within. Then they sent me on a lang errand away to Ellon; and when I got back there was nane there. I speered close, and saw the marks o' a cairt heavy loaden. It was lost on the high road; an' since then, nicht an' day hae I sought for any trace; but all in vain. But I'm thinkin' that it's nigh to here they've hid it; I went down the yowes' roadie, an' alang the rock, an' up the bit beach; but never a sign did I see. There's a many corners aboot the crags here, where a muckle treasure might lie hid, an' nane the wiser save them that pit it there!" Whilst she was talking I was scribbling a line in my pocket-book; I tore out the page and handed it to her:

"If you would help me take that letter for I must not leave here. Give it to the dark gentleman whom you know by sight. He is somewhere on the rocks beyond the Castle." My message was to tell Don Bernardino that I believed the treasure was hidden somewhere near me, and that the bearer of the note would guide him if he thought wise to join me.

Then I waited, waited. The night grew darker and darker; and the fog belts came so thick and so heavy that they almost became one endless mass. Only now and again could I get a glimpse of the sea outside the great rock. Once, far off out at sea but floating in on the wind, I heard eight bells sound from a ship. My heart beat at the thought; for if the *Keystone* were close at hand it might be well for us later on. Then there was silence, long and continuous. A silence which was of the night alone; every now and again when some sound of life from near or far came to break its monotony the reaction became so marked that silence seemed to be a positive quality.

All at once I became conscious that Gormala was somewhere near me. I could not see her, I could not hear her; but it was no surprise to me when through the darkness I saw her coming close to me, followed by Don Bernardino. They both looked colossal through the mist.

As quickly as I could, I told the Don of my suspicions; and asked his advice. He agreed with me as to the probabilities of the attempt to escape, and announced his willingness to go down the path to Dunbuy Haven and explore it thoroughly so far as was possible. Accordingly, with Gormala to guide him, he went to the end of the Haven and descended the steep moraine—it was a declension rather than a path. For myself I was not sanguine as to a search. The night was now well on us, and even had the weather been clear it would have been a difficult task to make search in such a place, where the high cliffs all around shut out the possibilities of side light. Moreover, along the Haven, as with other such openings on this iron-bound coast, there were patches of outlying rock under the cliffs. Occasionally these were continuous, so that at the proper state of the tide a fairly good climber could easily make way along them. Here, however, there was no such continuity; the rocks rising from the sea close under the cliffs were in patches; without a boat it would be useless to attempt a complete exploration. I waited, however, calmly; I was gaining patience now out of my pain. A good while elapsed before the Don returned, still accompanied by Gormala. He told me that only the beach had been possible for examination; but as far as he could see out by either channel, there was no sign of anyone hiding, or any bulk which could be such as we sought.

He considered it might be advisable if he went to warn the rest of our party of our belief as to the place appointed, and so took his way up north. Gormala remained with me so as to be ready to take any message if occasion required. She looked tired, so tired and weary that I made her lie down behind the rough wall. For myself sleep was an impossibility; I could not have slept had my life or sanity depended on it. To soothe, her and put her mind at rest, I told her what she had always wanted to know; what I had seen that night at Whinnyfold when the Dead came up from the sea. That quieted her, and she soon slept. So I waited and waited, and the time crept slowly away.

All at once Gormala sat up beside me, broad awake and with all her instincts at her keenest. "Whish!" she said, raising a warning hand. At this moment the fog belt was upon us, and on the wind, now risen high, the white wreaths swept by like ghosts. She held her ear as before towards seaward and listened intently. This time there could be no mistake; from far off through the dampness of the fog came the sound of a passing ship. I ran out from behind the wall and threw myself face down at the top of the cliff. I was just at the angle of the opening of the Haven and I could see if a boat entered by either channel. Gormala came beside me and peered over; then she whispered:

"I shall gang doon the yowes' roadie; it brings me to the Haven's mooth, and frae thence I can warn ye if there be aught!" Before I replied she had flitted away, and I saw her pass over the edge of the cliff and proceed on her perilous way. I leaned over the edge of the cliff listening. Down below I heard now and again the sound of a falling pebble, dislodged from the path, but I could see nothing whatever. Below me the black water showed now and again in the lifting of the fog.

The track outwards leads down to the sea at the southern corner of the opening of the Haven; so I moved on here to see if I could get any glimpse of Gormala. The fog was now on in a dense mass, and I could see nothing a couple of feet from me. I heard, however, a sort of scramble; the rush and roll of stones tumbling, and the hollow reverberating plash as they struck the water. My heart jumped, for I feared that some accident might have happened to Gormala. I listened intently; but heard no sound. I did not stay, however, for I knew that the whole effort of the woman, engaged on such a task, would be to avoid betraying herself. I was right in my surmise, for after a few minutes of waiting I heard a very faint groan. It was low and suppressed, but there was no mistaking it as it came up to me through the driving mist. It was evident that Gormala was in some way in peril, and common humanity demanded that I should go down to help her if I could. It was no use my attempting the sheep track; if she had failed on it there would not be much chance of my succeeding. Besides, there had been a manifest slip or landslide; and more than probably the path, or some necessary portion of it, had been carried away. It would have been madness to attempt it, so I went to the southern side of the cliff where the rock was broken, and where there was a sort of rugged path down to the sea. There was also an advantage about this way; I could see straight out to sea to the south of Dunbuy Rock. Thus I need not lose sight of any shore-coming boat; which might happen were I on the other path which opened only in the Haven.

It was a hard task, and by daylight I might have found it even more difficult. In parts it actually overhung the water, with an effect of dizziness which was in itself dangerous. However, I persevered; and presently got down on the cluster of rocks overhung by the cliff. Here, at the very corner of the opening to the Haven, under the spot where the sheep track led down, I found Gormala almost unconscious. She revived a little when I lifted her and put my flask to her lips. For a few seconds she leaned gasping against my breast with her poor, thin, grey hair straggling across it. Then, with a great effort, she moaned out feebly, but of intention keeping her voice low lest even in that lone spot amid the darkness of the night and the mist there might be listeners:

"I'm done this time, laddie; the rocks have broke me when the roadie gav way. Listen tae me, I'm aboot to dee; a' the Secrets and the Mysteries 'll be mine soon. When the end is comin' haud baith my hands in ane o' yours, an' keep the ither ower my een. Then, when I'm passin' ye shall see what my dead eyes see; and hear wi' the power o' my dead ears. Mayhap too, laddie, ye may ken the secrets and the wishes o' my hairt. Dinna lose yer chance, laddie! God be wi' ye an' the bonny lass. Tell her, an' ye will, that I forgie her floutin' me; an' that I bade the gude God keep her frae all harm, and send peace and happiness to ye both—till the end. God forgie me all my sins!"

As she was speaking her life seemed slowly ebbing away. I could feel it, and I knew it in many ways. As I took her hand in mine, a glad smile was on her face, together with a look of eager curiosity. This was the last thing I saw in the dim light, as my hand covered her filming eyes.

And then a strange and terrible thing began to happen.

L

The Eyes of the Dead

As I knelt with the dead woman's hands in one of mine and the other over her eyes, I seemed to be floating high up in the air; and with amazing vision to see all round for a great distance. The fog still hung thick over the water. Around, the vast of the air and the depths of the sea were as open as though sunshine was on them and I was merely looking through bright water. In the general panorama of things, so far as the eye could range, all lay open. The ships on the sea, and the floor under it; the iron-bound coast, and the far-lying uplands were all as though marked on a picture chart. Far away on the horizon were several craft, small and large. A few miles out was a ship of war; and to the north of her but much closer in shore lay a graceful yacht, slowly moving with the tide and under shortened sail. The war ship was all alert; on every top, and wherever there was a chance of seeing anything, was the head of a man on the look-out. The search-light was on, and sea and sky were lit alternately with its revolving rays. But that which drew my eyes, as the magnet draws the iron, was a clumsily rigged ship close in shore, seemingly only a few hundred yards beyond the Dunbuy Rock. She was a whaler I knew, for on her deck were the great boats for use in rough seas, and the furnace where the blubber was melted. With unconscious movement, as though my soul were winged as a bird, I hung poised over this vessel. It was strange indeed, but she seemed all as though composed of crystal; I could see through her, and down into the deep below her where her shadow lay, till my eyes rested on the patches of bare sand or the masses of giant seaweed which swayed with the tide above the rocks on which it grew. In and out amongst the seaweed the fishes darted, and the flower-like limpets moved ceaselessly outside their shells on the rocks. I could even see the streaks on the water which wind and current invariably leave on their course. Within the ship, all was clear as though I were looking into a child's toy-house; but a toy-house wrought of glass. Every nook and cranny was laid bare; and the details, even when they did not interest me, sank into my mind. I could evermore, by closing my eyes, have seen again anything on which in those moments of spiritual vision the eyes of my soul had rested.

All the time there was to me a dual consciousness. Whatever I saw before me was all plain and real; and yet I never lost for a moment the sense of my own identity. I knew I was on shore amid the rocks under the cliff, and that Gormala's dead body was beside me as I knelt. But there was some divine guiding principle which directed my thought—it must have been my thought, for my eyes followed as my wishes led, as though my whole being went too. They were guided from the very bow of the ship along the deck, and down the after hatchway. I went down, step by step, making accurate and careful scrutiny of all things around me. I passed into the narrow cabin, which seemed even to me to smell evilly. The rank yellow light from the crude oil lamp with thick smoky wick made the gloom seem a reality, and the shadows as monstrous. From this I passed aft into a tiny cabin, where on a bunk lay Marjory asleep. She looked pale and wan; it made my heart sick to see the great black circles round her eyes. But there was resolution in her mouth and nostrils; resolution fixed and untameable. Knowing her as I did, and with her message "I can die" burned into my heart, it did not need any guessing to know what was in the hand clenched inside the breast of her dress. The cabin door was locked; on the outside was a rough bolt, newly placed; the key was not in the lock. I would have lingered, for the lightning-like glimpse made me hungry for more; but the same compelling force moved me on. In the next cabin lay a man, also asleep. He was large of frame, with a rugged red beard streaked with grey; what hair remained on his head, which was all scarred with cicatrices, was a dull red turning white. On a rack above him, under the chronometer—which marked Greenwich time as 2.15,—ready to his hand, were two great seven shooters; from his pocket peeped the hilt of a bowie knife. It was indeed strange to me that I could look without passion or vindictiveness on such a person so disposed. I suppose it was the impersonal spirit within me which was at the moment receptive, and that all human passion, being ultimately of the flesh, was latent. At the time, though I was conscious of it, it did not strike me as strange; no more strange than that I could see far and near at the same glance, and take in great space and an impossible wilderness of detail. No more strange, than that all things were for me resolved into their elements; that fog ceased to deaden or darkness to hide; that timber and iron, deck and panel and partition, beam and door and bulkhead were as transparent as glass. In my mind was a vague intention of making examination of every detail which could bear on the danger of Marjory.

But even whilst such an idea was in its incipient stage, so swift is the mechanism of thought, my eyes beheld, as though it were through the sides of the ship, a boat pass out from a watercave in the cliffs behind the Rock of Dunbuy. In it I saw, with the same seeing eye which gave me power in aught else, seven men some of whom I knew at a glance to be those whom Marjory had described in the tunnel. All but one I surveyed calmly, and weighed up as it were with complacency; but this one was a huge coal-black negro, hideous, and of repulsive aspect. A glimpse of him made my blood run cold, and filled my mind at once with hate and fear. As I looked, the boat came towards the ship with inconceivable rapidity. It was not that she moved fast through the water, for her progress was in reality slow and laboured. The wind and the sea had risen; half a gale was blowing and the seas were running so high that the ship rose and fell, pitched and rolled and tossed about like a toy. It was, that time, like distance, was in my mind obliterated. Truly, I was looking with spirit eyes, and under all spiritual conditions.

The boat drew close to the whaler on the port side, and I saw, as if from the former, the faces of several men who at the sound of oars came rushing from the other side of the ship and leaned over the bulwarks. It was evident that they had expected arrival from the starboard. With some difficulty the boat got close, for the sea was running wilder every moment; and one by one the men began to climb the ladder and disappear over the bulwark. With the extraordinary action of sight and mind and memory which was to me at present, I followed each and all of them at the same time. They hurriedly rigged up a whip and began to raise from the boat parcels of great weight. In the doing of this one of them, the negro, was officious and was always trying to examine each parcel as it came on board; but he was ever and always repulsed. The others would not allow him to touch anything; at each rebuff he retired scowling. All this must, under ordinary conditions, have taken much time, but to my spirit-ruled eyes it all passed with wondrous rapidity. . .

I became conscious that things around me were growing less clear. The fog seemed to be stealing over the sea, as I had seen it earlier in the evening, and to wrap up details from my sight. The great expanse of the sea and the ships upon it, and all the wonders of the deep became lost in the growing darkness. I found, quicker and quicker, my thoughts like my eyes, centred on the deck of the ship. At a moment, when all others were engaged and did not notice him, I saw the great negro, his face over-much distorted with an evil smile, steal towards the after hatchway and disappear. With the growing of the fog and the dark, I was losing the power to see through things opaque and material; and it came to me as an actual shock that the negro passed beyond my vision. With his going, the fear in my heart grew and grew; till, in my frantic human passion, all that was ethereal around me faded and went out like a dying flame. . .

The anguish of my soul, in my fear for my beloved, tore my true spirit out of its phantom existence back to stern working life. . .

I found myself, chilled and sick at heart, kneeling by the marble-cold, stiffening body of Gormala, on the lone rock under the cliff. The rising wind whistled by me in the crannies above, and the rising sea in angry rushes leaped at us by the black shining rocks. All was so dark around me that my eyes, accustomed to the power given in my vision of making their own light, could not pierce the fog and the gloom. I tried to look at my watch, but could only see the dial dimly; I could not distinguish the figures on it and I feared to light a match lest such might betray my presence. Fortunately my watch could strike the hours and minutes, and I found it was now half past one o'clock. I still, therefore, had three-quarters of an hour, for I remembered the lesson of the whaler's chronometer. I knew there would be no time nor opportunity to bring Gormala's body to the top of the cliff—at present; so I carried her up to the highest point of the underlying rock, which was well above high water mark.

Reverently and with blessing I closed her dead eyes, which still looked up at the sky with a sort of ghostly curiosity. Then I clambered up the steep pathway and made my way as quickly as I could round to the other side of the Haven, to try if I could discover any trace of the blackmailers, or any indication of the water-cave in which their boat was hidden. The cliffs here are wofully steep, and hang far over the sea; so that there is no possibility of lying on the cliff edge and peering over. Round here also the stark steepness forbids the existence of even the tiniest track; a hare could not find its way along these beetling cliffs. The only way of making search of this channel would be to follow round in a boat. The nearest point to procure one would be at the little harbour beside the Bullers O'Buchan, and for this there was not time. I was in dire doubt as to what was best to do; and I longed with a sickening force for the presence of Montgomery or some of our party who would know how to deal with such a situation. I was not anxious for the present moment; but I wanted to take all precautions against the time which was coming. Well I knew that the vision I had seen with the eyes of the dead Gormala was no mere phantasm of the mind; that it was no promise of what might be, but a grim picture of what would be. There was never a doubt in my mind as to its accuracy. Oh! if I could have seen more of what was to happen; if I could have lingered but a few instants longer! For with the speed at which things had passed before my inner eye in that strange time, every second might have meant the joy or sorrow of a lifetime. How I groaned with regret, and cursed my own precipitancy, that I could not wait and learn through the medium of the dead woman's spiritual eyes the truths that were to be borne in mind!

But it was of no use to fret; action of some sort would be necessary if Marjory was to be saved. In one way I might help. Even alone I might save her, if I could get out to the whaler unknown to her crew. I knew I could manage this, for anyhow I could swim; for a weapon which the water could not render useless I had the dagger I had taken from Don Bernardino. Should other weapons be necessary I might be able to lay hands on them in the cabin next Marjory's, where the red-bearded man lay asleep. I did not know whether it would be better to go in search of some of my comrades, or to wait the arrival of the Don, who was to be back within an hour of the time of leaving. I was still trying to make up my mind when the difficulty was settled for me by the arrival of the Spaniard, accompanied by one of the young American naval officers.

When I told them of my vision I could see, even in the darkness which prevailed, that neither of them was content to accept its accuracy in blind faith. I was at first impatient; but this wore away when I remembered that neither of them had any knowledge of my experiences in the way of Second Sight, or indeed of the phenomenon at all. Neither in Spain nor America does such a belief prevail; and I have no doubt that to both of them came the idea that worry and anxiety had turned my brain. Even when I told them how I meant to back my belief by swimming out beyond the Dunbuy Rock in time to reach the ship before the boat would arrive, they were not convinced. The method of reception of the idea by each was, however, characteristic of his race and nation. To the high-bred Spaniard, whose life had been ruled by laws of honour and of individual responsibility, no act done in the cause of chivalry could be other than worthy; he did not question the sanity of the keeping of such a purpose. The practical American, however, though equally willing to make self-sacrifice, and to dare all things in the course of honour and duty, looked at my intention with regard to its result; was I taking the step which would have the best result with regard to the girl whom we were all trying to save. Whilst the Spaniard raised his hat and said:

"May God watch over your gallant enterprise, Senor; and hold your life, and that of her whom you love, in the hollow of His hand!" The American said:

"Honest injun! old chap, is that the best you can do? If it's only a man and a life you want, count me in every time. I'm a swimmer, too; and I'm a youngster that don't count. So far as that goes, I'm on. But you've got to find the ship, you know! If she was there now, I should say 'risk it'; and I'd come with you if you liked. But there's the whole North Sea out there, with room for a hundred million of whalers without their jostling. No, no! Come, I say, let us find another way round; where we can help the girl all together!" He was a good young fellow, as well as a fine one, and it was evident he meant well. But there was no use arguing; my mind was made up, and, after assuring him that I was in earnest, I told him that I was taking a couple of rockets with me which I would try to keep dry so that should occasion serve I would make manifest the whereabouts of the whaler. He already knew what to do with regard to signalling from shore, in case the boats of the whaler should be seen.

When we had made what preparations we could for the work each of us had in hand, the time came for my starting on my perilous enterprise. As my purpose became more definite, my companions, who I think doubted in their hearts its sincerity, became somewhat more demonstrative. It was one thing to have a vague intention of setting out on a wild journey of the kind, and even here common sense rebelled. But on the edge of the high cliff, in the dark, amid the fog which came boiling up from below as the wind puffs drove it on shore; when below our feet the rising waves broke against the rocks with an ominous sound, made into a roar by the broken fastnesses of the cliffs, the whole thing must have seemed as an act of madness. When through a break in the fog-belt we could catch a glimpse of the dark water leaping far below into furious, scattering lines of foam, to dare the terrors of such a sea at such a time was like going deliberately to certain death. My own heart quailed at moments; when I saw through the fog wreaths the narrow track, down which I must again descend to where Gormala's body lay, fading into a horrid gloom; or when the sound of breaking water drove up, muffled by the dark mist. My faith in the vision was strong, however, and by keeping my mind fixed on it I could shut out present terrors.

I shook hands with my two friends, and, taking courage from the strong grip of their hands, set myself resolutely to my journey down the cliff. The last words the young navy man said to me were:

"Remember, if you do reach the whaler, that a gleam of light of any kind will give us a hint of where you are. Once the men of the *Keystone* see it, they'll do the rest at sea; as we shall on land. Give us such a light when the time comes—if you have to fire the ship to get it!"

At the foot of the cliff path the prospect was almost terrifying. The rocks were so washed with the churning water, as the waves leaped at them, that now and again only black tops could be seen rising out of the waste of white water; and a moment after, as the wave fell back, there would be a great mass of jagged rocks, all stark and grim, blacker than their own blackness, with the water streaming down them, and great rifts yawning between. Outside, the sea was a grim terror, a wildness of rising waves and lines of foam, all shrouded in fog and gloom. Through all came a myriad of disconcerting sounds, vague and fearsome, from where the waves clashed or beat into the sounding caverns of Dunbuy. Nothing but the faith which I had in the vision of Marjory, which came to me with the dead eyes of the western Seer, could have carried me out into that dreadful gloom. All its possibilities of horror and danger woke to me at once, and for a moment appalled me.

But Faith is a conquering power; even the habit of believing, in which I had been taught, stood to me in this wild hour. No sceptic, no doubter, could have gone forth as I did into that unknown of gloom and fear.

I waited till a great wave was swept in close under my bare feet. Then, with a silent prayer, and an emboldening thought: 'For Marjory!' I leaped into the coming water.

LI

In the Sea Fog

For a few minutes I was engaged in a wild struggle to get away from the rocks, and not to be forced back by the shoreward rush and sweep of the waves. I was buffeted by them, and half-choked by the boiling foam; but I kept blindly and desperately to my task, and presently knew that I had only to deal with the current and the natural rise and fall of the rollers. Down on the water the air was full of noises, so that it was hard to distinguish any individual sound; but the fog lay less dense on the surface than above it, so that I could see a little better around me.

On the sea there is always more or less light; even in this time of midnight gloom, with moon and stars hidden by the fog, and with none of that phosphorescence which at times makes a luminous glow of its own over the water, I could see things at an unexpected distance. More than all, was I surprised as well as cheered to find that I could distinguish the features of the land from the sea, better than I could from land discern anything at sea. When I looked back, the shore rose, a dark uneven line, unbroken save where the Haven of Dunbuy running inland made an angle against the sky. But beside me, the great Rock of Dunbuy rose gigantic and black; it was like a mountain towering over me. The tide was running down so that when I had got out of the current running inland behind the rock I was in comparatively calm water. There was no downward current, but only a slow backwater, which insensibly took me closer to the Rock. Keeping in this shelter, I swam on and out; I saved myself as much as I could, for I knew of the terrible demand on my strength which lay before me. It must have been about ten minutes, though it seemed infinitely longer, when I began to emerge from the shelter of the Rock and to find again the force of the outer current. The waves were wilder here too; not so wild as just in shore before they broke, but they were considerably larger in their rise and fall. As I swam on, I looked back now and then, and saw Dunbuy behind me towering upward, though not so monstrously as when I had been under its lee. The current was beginning already to bear me downwards; so I changed my course, and got back to the sheltered water again. Thus I crept round under the lee of the Rock, till all at once I found myself in the angry race, where the current beat on and off the cliff. It took me all my strength and care to swim through this; when the force of the current began to slacken, as I emerged from the race, I found myself panting and breathless with the exertion.

But when I looked around me from this point, where the east opened to me, there was something which restored all my courage and hope, though it did not still the beating of my heart.

Close by, seemingly only a couple of hundred yards off to the north east, lay a ship whose masts and spars stood out against the sky. I could see her clearly, before a coming belt of fog bore down on her.

The apprehension lest I should miss her in the fog chilled me more than the sea water in which I was immersed; for all possibilities of evil became fears to me, now that the realisation of my vision was clear. I was glad of the darkness; it was a guarantee against discovery. I swam on quietly, and was rejoiced to find as I drew close that I was on the port side of the ship; well I remembered how in my vision the boat approached to port, to the surprise of the men who were looking out for it on the other side. I found the rope ladder easily enough, and did not have much difficulty in getting a foothold on it. Ascending cautiously, and watching every inch of the way, I climbed the bulwark and hid behind a water barrel close to the mast. From this security I looked out, and saw the backs of several men ranged along the starboard bulwark. They were intent on their watching, and unsuspicious of my proximity; so I stole out and glided as silently as I could into the cabin's entrance. It was not new to me; I had a sense of complete security as to my knowledge. The eyes of Gormala's soul were keen!

In the cabin I recognised at once the smoky lamp and the rude preparations for food. Thus emboldened, I came to the door, behind which I knew Marjory lay. It was locked and bolted, and the key was gone. I slid back the bolt, but the lock baffled me. I was afraid to make the slightest noise, lest I should court discovery; so I passed on to the next cabin where was her jailer. He lay just as, in the vision, I had seen him; the chronometer was above him and the two heavy revolvers hung underneath it. I slipped in quietly—there were not shoes to remove—and reaching over so that the water would not drip from my wet underclothing on his face, unhooked the two weapons. I belted them round my waist with the strap on which they hung. Then I looked round for the key, but could see no sign of it. There was no time to lose, and it was neither time nor place to stand on ceremony; so I took the man by the throat with my left hand, the dagger being in my right, and held with such a grip that the blood seemed to leap into his face in a second. He could utter no sound, but instinctively his hand went back and up to where the revolvers had hung. I whispered in a low tone:

"It's no use. Give me the key. I don't value your life a pin!" He was well plucked, and he was manifestly used to tight places. He did not attempt to speak or parley; but whilst I had been whispering, his right hand had got hold of a knife. It was a bowie, and he was dexterous with it. With some kind of sharp wrench he threw it open; there was a click as the back-spring worked. If I had not had my dagger ready it would have been a bad time for me. But I was prepared; whilst he was making the movement to strike at me, I struck. The keen point of the Spanish dagger went right through the upturned wrist, and pinned his hand down to the wooden edge of the bunk. Whilst, however, he had been trying to strike with his right hand, his left had clutched my left wrist. He tried now to loose my grasp from his throat, whilst bending his chin down he made a furious effort to tear at my hand with his teeth. Never in my life did I more need my strength and weight. The man was manifestly a fighter, trained in many a wild 'rough-and-tumble', and his nerves were like iron. I feared to let go the hilt of the dagger, lest in his violent struggling he should tear his wrist away and so free his hand. Having, however, got my right knee raised, I pressed down with it his arm on the edge of the bunk and so freed my right hand. He continued to struggle ferociously. I knew well it was life and death, not only for me, but for Marjory.

It was his life or mine; and he had to pay the penalty of his crime.

So intent was I on the struggle that I had not heard the approach of the boat with his comrades. It was only when I stood panting, with the limp throat between my fingers which were white at the knuckles with the strain, that the sound of voices and the tramp of feet on deck reached my intelligence. Then indeed I knew there was no time to lose. I searched the dead man's pockets and found a key, which I tried in the lock of Marjory's cabin. When I opened the door she started up; the hand in her bosom was whipped out with a flash, and in an instant a long steel bonnet pin was ready to drive into her breast. My agonised whisper:

"Marjory, it is I!" only reached her mind in time to hold her hand. She did not speak; but never can I forget the look of joy that illumined her poor, pale face. I put my finger on my lip, and held out my hand to her. She rose, with the obedience of a child, and came with me. I was just going out into the cabin, when I heard the creak of a heavy footstep on the companion way. So I motioned her back, and, drawing the dagger from my belt, stood ready. I knew who it was that was coming; yet I dared not use the pistols, save as a last resource.

I stood behind the door. The negro did not expect anyone, or any obstacle; he came on unthinkingly, save for whatever purpose of evil was in his mind. He was armed, as were all the members of the blackmail gang. In a belt across his shoulder, slung Kentucky fashion, were two great seven shooters; and across his waist behind was a great bowie knife, with handle ready to grasp. Moreover, nigger-like, the handle of a razor rose out of the breast pocket of his dark flannel shirt. He did not, however, manifestly purpose using his weapons—at present at any rate; there was not any sign of danger or opposition in front of him. His comrades were busy at present in embarking the treasure, and would be for many an hour to come, in helping to work the ship clear into safety. Every minute now the wind was rising, and the waves swelling to such proportions that the anchored ship rocked like a bell-buoy in a storm. In the cabin I had to hold on, or I should have been shot from my place into view. But the huge negro cared for none of these things. He was callous to everything, and there was such a wicked, devilish purpose in his look that my heart hardened grimly in the antagonism of man to man. Nay more, it was not a man that I loathed; I would have killed this beast with less compunction than I would kill a rat or a snake. Never in my life did I behold such a wicked face. In feature and expression there was every trace and potentiality of evil; and these superimposed on a racial brutality which made my gorge rise. Well indeed did I understand now the one terror which had in all her troubles come to Marjory, and how these wretches had used it to mould her to their ends. I knew now why, sleeping or waking, she held that steel spike against her heart. If—

The thought was too much for me. Even now, though I was beside her, she was beset by her enemies. We were both still practically prisoners on a hostile ship, and even now this demon was intent on unspeakable wrong. I did not pause; I did not shrink from the terrible task before me. With a bound I was upon him, and I had struck at his heart; struck so truly and so terrible a blow, that the hilt of the dagger struck his ribs with a thud like the blow of a cudgel. The blood seemed to leap out at me, even as the blow fell. With spasmodic reaction he tumbled forwards; fell without a sound, and so quickly that had not I, fearing lest the noise of his falling might betray me, caught him, he would have dropped like a stricken bullock.

Never before did I understand the pleasure of killing a man. Since then, it makes me shudder when I think of how so potent a passion, or so keen a pleasure, can rest latent in the heart of a righteous man. It may have been that between the man and myself was all the antagonism that came from race, and fear, and wrongdoing; but the act of his killing was to me a joy unspeakable. It will rest with me as a wild pleasure till I die.

I took all the arms he had about him, two revolvers and a knife; they would give me fourteen more shots were I hard pressed. In any case they were safer, so far as Marjory and I were concerned, in my hands than in those of our enemies. I dragged the body of the negro into the cabin with the other dead man; then I closed the door on them, and when Marjory joined me, I locked the door of her cabin and took away the key. In case of suspicion this might give us a few minutes of extra time.

Marjory came with me up on deck; and as she caught sight of the open sea there was an unspeakable gladness on her face. We seized a favourable opportunity, when no one was looking, for all on deck were busy hauling up the treasure; and slipped behind the cask fastened to the mast. There we breathed freely. We both felt that should the worst come to the worst we could get away before any one could touch us. One rush to the bulwarks and over. They would never attempt to follow us, and there was a chance of a swim to shore. I gave Marjory a belt with two revolvers. As she strapped it on she felt safer; I knew it by the way she drew herself up, and threw back her shoulders.

When the last of the bags which held the treasure came on board, the men who had come with it closed in a ring around the mass as it lay on deck. They were all armed; I could see that they did not trust the sailors, for each moment some one's hand would go back to his gun. We heard one of them ask as he looked round: "What has become of that damned nigger? He must take his share of work!" Marjory was very brave and very still; I could see that her nerve was coming back to her. After a little whispered conversation, the newcomers began to carry the bags down to the cabin; it was slow work, for two always stood guard above, and two remained down below evidently on similar duty. Discovery of the dead man must come soon, so Marjory and I stole behind the foremast which was well away from every one. She was first, and as she began to pass behind she recoiled; she got the drop on some one in front of her. There was a smothered 'h-s-s-sh' and she lowered her weapon. Turning to me she said in a faint whisper:

"It is the Spaniard; what is he doing here?" I whispered back:

"Be good to him. He is a noble fellow, and has behaved like a knight of old!" I pressed forward and took his hand. "How did you get here?" I asked. His answer was given in so faint a voice that I could see that he was spent and tired, if not injured:

"I swam, too. When I saw their boat pull out of the northern channel, I managed to scramble down part of the cliff, and then jumped. Fortunately I was not injured. It was a long, weary swim, and I thought I should never be able to get through; but at last the current took me and carried me to the ship. She was anchored with a hawser, not a cable. I managed to climb up it; and when I was on board I cut it nearly through."

Even as he spoke there was a queer lurch of the ship which lay stern forward, and a smothered exclamation from all the seamen.

The hawser had parted and we were drifting before wind and tide. Then it was that I felt we should give warning to the yacht and the battleship. I knew that they were not far off; had I not seen them in my vision, which had now been proven. Then it was also that the words of the young American came back to me: "Give us a light, if you have to fire the ship to get it."

All this time, from the moment when I had set foot on the whaler's deck till this instant, events had moved with inconceivable rapidity. There had been one silent, breathless rush; during which two lives had been taken and Marjory set free. Only a few minutes had elapsed in all; and when I looked around under the altered conditions, things seemed to be almost where they had been. It was like the picture in one's mind made by a lightning flash; when the period of reception is less than the time of the smallest action, and movement is lost in time. The fog belt was thinning out, and there was in the night air a faint suggestion that one might see, if there were anything to be seen.

The great Rock of Dunbuy towered up; I could just distinguish so much on the land side. Whilst I was looking, there came a sudden light and then a whirr; high overhead through the sea fog we could see faintly the fiery trail of a rocket.

Instantly out at sea was an answer; a great ray of light shot upwards, and we could see its reflection in the sky. None of us said anything; but instinctively Marjory and I clasped hands. Then the light ray seemed to fall downward to the sea. But as it came down, the fog seemed to grow thicker and thicker till the light was lost in its density. There was stir of all on our ship. No loud word was spoken, but whispered directions, given with smothered curses, flew. Each man of the crew seemed to run to his post, and with a screeching and straining the sails rose. The vessel began to slip through the water with added speed. Now, if ever, was our time to warn our friends. The little rockets which I had brought had been sodden with water and were useless, and besides we had no way of getting a light. The only way of warning was by sound, and the only sound to carry was a pistol shot. For an instant I hesitated, for a shot meant a life if we should be pushed to it. But it must be done; so signing to the others I ran aft and when close to the mast fired my revolver. Instantly around me was a chorus of curses. I bent double and ran back, seeing through the darkness vague forms rush to where I had been. The fog was closing thicker around us; it seemed to boil over the bulwarks as we passed along. We had either passed into another belt of fog, or one was closing down upon us with the wind. The sound of the pistol shot had evidently reached the war ship. She was far off us, and the sounds came faintly over the waste of stormy sea; but there was no mistaking the cheer followed by commands. These sounded faint and hoarsely; a few words were spoken with a trumpet, and then came the shrill whistle of the boatswain's pipe.

On our own deck was rushing to and fro, and frenzied labour everywhere. The first object was to get away from the searchlight; they would seek presently, no doubt, for who had fired the betraying shot. If I could have known what to do, so as to stay our progress, there would have been other shots; for now that we were moving through the water, every second might take us further from the shore and place us deeper in the toils of our foes.

LII

The Skares

I whispered to Marjory and Don Bernardino:

"If they once get away we are lost! We must stop them at all hazards!" The Spaniard nodded and Marjory squeezed my hands; there was no need of speech. Then I fixed the order of battle. I was to fire first, then the Spaniard, then Marjory, each saving his fire till we knew whether another shot was required. This precaution was necessary, as we had no reserve ammunition. We took it for granted that the chambers of the revolvers were full; my one shot had been satisfactory in this respect. When the sails were set and we began rushing through the water I saw that even at the risk of betraying ourselves to our enemies we must give warning again, and so fired. There was an answering cheer from the *Keystone* through the fog; and then a sudden rush forward of those on our own deck. When they were close to us, the seamen hung back; but the men of the gang kept on firing as they came. Fortunately we were in a line behind cover, for I could hear the 'ping' and the tearing wood as the bullets struck the mast. I fired a shot just to show that we were armed; and heard a sharp cry. Then they fell back. In a moment or two they also had formed their plan of battle. These were men used to such encounters; and as they knew that at such times a quick rush may mean everything, they did not let the grass grow under their feet. I could see one of the seamen remonstrating with them, and hear the quick, angry tones of his voice, though I could not distinguish the words.

He pointed out into the fog, where now there was distinctly a luminous patch of light: the searchlight was moving towards us. The *Keystone* was coming down on us.

The blackmailer shook off the seaman and, then gave some directions to his comrades; they spread out right and left of us, and tried to find some kind of cover. I lifted Marjory and put her standing on the barrel fastened behind the mast, for I thought that as the flash of my pistol had come from the deck they would not expect any one to be raised so high. Don Bernardino and I curled down on the deck, and our opponents began to fire. In the thickening fog, and with the motion of the ship which threw us all about like ninepins, their aim was vague; fortunately no one was hit. When I thought I had a chance I fired, but there was no response; the Don got a shot and Marjory another, but there was no sound, save that of the bullets striking on wood or iron. Then Marjory, whose traditional instinct was coming into play, fired twice in rapid succession; there was a quick exclamation and then a flood of horrible profanity, the man was only winged. Again and again they fired, and I heard a groan behind me from the Don.

"What's that?" I whispered, not daring to stop or even to look back:

"My arm! Take my pistol, I cannot shoot with my left hand." I put my hand back, and he placed the revolver in it. I saw a dark form rush across the deck and fired—and missed. I tried another shot; but the weapon only answered with a click; the chambers were exhausted. So I used the other revolver. And so for a few minutes a furious fight went on. Marjory seldom fired, she was holding herself in reserve; but before I knew what was happening my second revolver was empty. Our antagonists were no chickens at their work; there was little to teach any of them in such a method of contest as this. Some one had evidently been counting the shots, for he suddenly called out:

"Not yet boys! They've at least three shots still!" With a sudden simultaneous rush they ran back into shelter.

During this time we had been tearing through the water at our full speed. But behind us on the port quarter was the sound of a great ship steaming on. The roar of the furnaces could be heard in the trumpeting of the funnels. The boatswain's whistles were piping, and there were voices of command cutting hoarsely through the fog. The searchlight too was at work; we could see its rays high up on the mist, though they did not at the moment penetrate sufficiently to expose us to the lookout of the *Keystone*. Closer on our starboard quarter was another sound which came on the trailing wind, the rush of a small vessel running fast. We could hear down the wind the sharp 'slap slap' of the waves on the bows, and the roaring of the wind among the cordage. This must be the *Sporran* following us close with grim disregard of danger. The commander of the whaler, recognising the possibility of discovery, put his helm hard to starboard. I could myself not see through the darkness; but the seaman did and took his chance of grounding in Cruden Bay. When we had run in a little way the helm was jammed hard down again, and we ran on the other tack; for the moment we were lost to both the war ship and the yacht. Marjory looked at me appealingly and I nodded; the situation was not one to be risked. She fired another shot from her pistol. There was an immediate reply from far out on our port side in the shape of more directions spoken with the trumpet and answering piping from the boatswains. Several shots were fired towards us by the gang; they were manifestly on chance, for they went wildly wide of us. Then we could hear an angry remonstrance from the whaler captain, and a threat that if there were any more firing, he would down with his sails and take chance of being captured. One of the gang answered him:

"That packet can't capture you within the three-mile limit; it's a cruiser of Uncle Sam's and they won't risk having to lie up in harbour here till the war is over." To which the other surlily replied:

"I wouldn't put money on it. Anyhow someone will! You keep quiet if you can. There's enough against us already if we should be caught!" The reply of the blackmailer was at least practical. I could not see what he did, but I took it that he put his pistol to the captain's head as he said with a frightful oath:

"You'll go on as you arranged with me; or I'll blow your brains out where you stand. There's quite enough against any of us, you included; so your one chance anyhow is to get out of this hole. See?" The captain accepted the position and gave his orders with a quiet delivery, to the effect that we ran first shorewards and then to starboard again till we were running back on our tracks like a hare.

Suddenly, however, this course was brought to an end by our almost running into a small vessel which as we passed I could see by its trim appearance was a yacht. We were so close for a few seconds, whilst we ran across her stern, that I shouted out:

"All right, MacRae. All safe as yet. She's trying to run out to sea. Try to tell the *Keystone*." The answer was a cheer from all aboard.

As our ship swept into the fog, several of our enemies ran at us. I handed Don Bernardino his own dagger and took the bowie knife myself. Then we stood ready in case our foes should get to close quarters. They got nearly up to us, firing as they came; but we were just then sheltering behind the mast and no injury was done. They hesitated to come on, not seeing us; and we waited. As we stood with beating hearts the ship began to come to starboard again. We must have been sheltered in some way, for we did not seem to feel either wind or tide so much as before. Suddenly one of the seamen said:

"Whist! I hear breakers!" The rest paused and listened, and the captain called out:

her shoulders and sank back. The habit of personal decorum had conquered fear. She closed her eyes for a moment or two to remember, and when she opened them was in full possession of all her faculties and her memory.

"It was no dream! It is all, all real! And I owe my life to you, darling, once again!" I kissed her, and she sank back with a sigh of happiness. A moment later, however, she started up, crying out to me:

"But the others, where are they? Quick! quick! let us go to help them if we can!" She looked wildly round. I understood her wishes, and hurrying into the other room brought her an armful of her clothes.

In a few minutes she joined me; and hand in hand we went out on the edge of the cliff. As we went, I told her of what had happened since she became unconscious in the water.

The wind was now blowing fiercely, almost a gale. The sea had risen, till great waves driving amongst the rocks had thrashed the whole region of the Skares into a wild field of foam. Below us, the waves dashing over the sunken rocks broke on the shore with a loud roaring, and washed high above the place where we had lain. The fog had lifted, and objects could be seen even at a distance. Far out, some miles away, lay a great ship; and by the outermost of the Skares a little to the north of the great rock and where the sunken reef lies, rose part of a broken mast. But there was nothing else to be seen, except away to south a yacht tossing about under double-reefed sails. Sea and sky were of a leaden grey, and the heavy clouds that drifted before the gale came so low as to make us think that they were the fog belts risen from the sea.

Marjory would not be contented till we had roused the whole village of Whinnyfold, and with them had gone all round the cliffs and looked into every little opening to see if there were trace or sign of any of those who had been wrecked with us. But it was all in vain.

We sent a mounted messenger off to Crom with a note, for we knew in what terrible anxiety Mrs. Jack must be. In an incredibly short time the good lady was with us; and was rocking Marjory in her arms, crying and laughing over her wildly. By and bye she got round the carriage from the village and said to us:

"And now my dears, I suppose we had better get back to Crom, where you can rest yourselves after this terrible time." Marjory came over to me, and holding my arm looked at her old nurse lovingly as she said with deep earnestness:

"You had better go back, dear, and get things ready for us. As for me, I shall never willingly leave my husband's side again!"

THE STORM CONTINUED FOR A whole day, growing rougher and wilder with each hour. For another day it grew less and less, till finally the wind had died away and only the rough waves spoke of what had been. Then the sea began to give up its dead. Some seamen presumably those of the *Wilhelmina* were found along the coast between Whinnyfold and Old Slains, and the bodies of two of the blackmailers, terribly mangled, were washed ashore at Cruden Bay. The rest of the sailors and of the desperadoes were never found. Whether they escaped by some miracle, or were swallowed in the sea, will probably never be known.

Strangest of all was the finding of Don Bernardino. The body of the gallant Spanish gentleman was found washed up on shore behind the Lord Nelson rock, just opposite where had been the opening to the cave in which his noble ancestor had hidden the Pope's treasure. It was as though the sea itself had respected his devotion, and had laid him by the place of his Trust. Marjory and I saw his body brought home to Spain when the war was over, and laid amongst the tombs of his ancestors. We petitioned the Crown; and though no actual leave was given, no objection was made to our removing the golden figure of San Cristobal which Benvenuto had wrought for the Pope. It now stands over the Spaniard's tomb in the church of San Cristobal in far Castile.

Appendices

one infolded. In the later and fuller period he speaks also of the one necessary condition "that the infoulding writing shall contain *at least five times as many letters* as the writing infoulded"—

Even in the example which he gives "Do not go till I come," there is a superfluous letter,—the final "e;" as though he wished to mislead the reader by inference as well as by direct statement.

Is it possible that he stopped short in his completion of this marvellous cipher? Can we believe that he who openly spoke from the first of symbols "*quintuple at most*," was content to use so large a number of infolding letters when he could possibly do with less? Why, the last condition of excellence in a cipher which he himself laid down, namely, that it should "bee without suspicion," would be endangered by a larger number than was actually necessary. It is by repetition of symbols that the discovery of secret writing is made; and in a cipher where, manifestly, the eye or the ear or the touch or the taste must be guided by such, and so marked and prolonged, symbols, the chances of discovery are enormously increased. Doubtless, then, he did not rest in his investigation and invention until he had brought his cipher to its least dimensions; and it was for some other reason or purpose that he thus tried to divert the mind of the student from his earlier suggestion. It will probably be proved hereafter that more than one variant and reduction to lower dimensions of his biliteral cipher was used between himself and his friends. When the secrets of that "Scrivenry" which, according to Mr. W. G. Thorpe in his interesting volume, "The Hidden Lives of Shakespeare and Bacon," Bacon kept at work in Twickenham Park, are made known, we shall doubtless know more on the subject. Of one point, however, we may rest assured, that Bacon did not go back in his pursuance of an interesting study; and the change from "Quintuple at most" of the infolding writing of 1605, to "Quintuple at least," of 1623, was meant for some purpose of misleading or obscuration, rather than as a limitation of his original setting forth of the powers and possibilities of his great invention. It will some day be an interesting theme of speculation and study what use of his biliteral cipher had been made between 1605 and 1623; and what it was that he wished to conceal.

That the original cipher, as given, can be so reduced is manifest. Of the Quintuple biliteral there are thirty-two combinations. As in the Elizabethan alphabet, as Bacon himself points out, there were but twenty-four letters, certain possibilities of reduction at once unfold themselves, since at the very outset one entire fourth of the symbols are unused.

Appendix B

On The Reduction of the Number of Symbols in Bacon's Biliteral Cipher

When I examined the scripts together, both that of the numbers and those of the dots, I found distinct repetitions of groups of symbols; but no combinations sufficiently recurrent to allow me to deal with them as entities. In the number cipher the class of repetitions seemed more marked. This may have been, however, that as the symbols were simpler and of a kind with which I was more familiar, the traces or surmises were easier to follow. It gave me hope to find that there was something in common between the two methods. It might be, indeed, that both writings were but variants of the same system. Unconsciously I gave my attention to the simpler form—the numbers—and for a long weary time went over them forward, backward, up and down, adding, subtracting, multiplying, dividing; but without any favorable result. The only encouragement which I got was that I got additions of eight and nine, each of these many times repeated. Try how I would, however, I could not scheme out of them any coherent result.

When in desperation I returned to the dotted papers I found that this method was still more exasperating, for on a close study of them I could not fail to see that there was a cipher manifest; though what it was, or how it could be read, seemed impossible to me. Most of the letters had marks in or about them; indeed there were very few which had not. Examining more closely still I found that the dots were disposed in three different ways: (a) in the body of the letter itself: (b) above the letter: (c) below it. There was never more than one mark in the body of the letter; but those above or below were sometimes single and sometimes double. Some letters had only the dot in the body; and others, whether marked on the body or not, had no dots either above or below. Thus there was every form and circumstance of marking within these three categories. The only thing which my instinct seemed to impress upon me continually was that very few of the letters had marks both above and below. In such cases two were above and one below, or *vice versa*; but in no case were there marks in the body and above and below also. At last I came to the conclusion that I had better, for the time, abandon attempting to decipher; and try to construct a cipher on the lines of Bacon's Biliteral—one which would ultimately accord in some way with the external conditions of either, or both, of those before me.

But Bacon's Biliteral as set forth in the *Novum Organum* had five symbols in every case. As there were here no repetitions of five, I set myself to the task of reducing Bacon's system to a lower number of symbols—a task which in my original memorandum I had held capable of accomplishment.

For hours I tried various means of reduction, each time getting a little nearer to the ultimate simplicity; till at last I felt that I had mastered the principle.

Take the Baconian biliteral cipher as he himself gives it and knock out repetitions of four or five aaaaa: aaaab: abbbb: baaaa: bbbba: and bbbbb. This would leave a complete alphabet with two extra symbols for use as stops, repeats, capitals, etc. This method of deletion, however, would not allow of the reduction of the number of symbols used; there would still be required five for each letter to be infolded. We have therefore to try another process of reduction, that affecting the variety of symbols without reference to the number of times, up to five, which each one is repeated.

Take therefore the Baconian Biliteral and place opposite to each item the number of symbols required. The first, (aaaaa) requires but one symbol "a," the second, (aaaab) two, "a" and "b;" the third (aaaba) three, "a" "b" and "a;" and so on. We shall thus find that the 11th (ababa) and the 22nd (babab) require five each, and that the 6th, 10th, 12th, 14th, 19th, 21st, 23rd and 27th require four each. If, therefore, we delete all these biliteral combinations which require four or five symbols each— ten in all—we have still left twenty-two combinations, necessitating at most not more than two changes of symbol in addition to the initial letter of each, requiring up to five quantities of the same symbol. Fit these to the alphabet; and the scheme of cipher is complete.

If, therefore, we can devise any means of expressing, in conjunction with each symbol, a certain number of repeats up to five; and if we can, for practical purposes, reduce our alphabet to twenty-two letters, we can at once reduce the biliteral cipher to three instead of five symbols.

The latter is easy enough, for certain letters are so infrequently used that they may well be grouped in twos. Take "X" and "Z" for instance.

In modern printing in English where the letter "e" is employed seventy times, "x" is only used three times, and "z" twice. Again, "k" is only used six times, and "q" only three times. Therefore we may very well group together "k" and "q," and "x" and "z." The lessening of the Elizabethan alphabet thus effected would leave but twenty-two letters, the same number as the combinations of the biliteral remaining after the elision. And further, as "W" is but "V" repeated, we could keep a special symbol to represent the repetition of this or any other letter, whether the same be in the body of a word, or if it be the last of one word and the first of that which follows. Thus we give a greater elasticity to the cipher and so minimise the chance of discovery.

As to the expression of numerical values applied to each of the symbols "a" and "b" of the biliteral cipher as above modified, such is simplicity itself in a number cipher. As there are two symbols to be represented and five values to each—four in addition to the initial—take the numerals, one to ten—which latter, of course, could be represented by 0. Let the odd numbers according to their values stand for "a":

$$a=1$$
$$aa=3$$
$$aaa=5$$
$$aaaa=7$$
$$aaaaa=9$$

and the even numbers according to their values stand for "b":

$$b=2$$
$$bb=4$$
$$bbb=6$$
$$bbbb=8$$
$$bbbbb=0$$

and then? Eureka! We have a Biliteral Cipher in which each letter is represented by one, two, or three, numbers; and so the five symbols of the Baconian Biliteral is reduced to three at maximum.

Variants of this scheme can of course, with a little ingenuity, be easily reconstructed.

Appendix C

The Resolving of Bacon's Biliteral Reduced to Three Symbols in a Number Cipher

P lace in their relative order as appearing in the original arrangement the selected symbols of the Biliteral:

a a a a a

a a a a b

&c

Then place opposite each the number arrived at by the application of odd and even figures to represent the numerical values of the symbols "a" and "b."

Thus aaaaa will be as shown 9

aaaab will be as shown 72

aaaba will be as shown 521

and so on. Then put in sequence of numerical value. We shall then have: 0. 9. 18. 27. 36. 45. 54. 63. 72. 81. 125. 143. 161. 216. 234. 252. 323. 341. 414. 432. 521. 612. An analysis shows that of these there are two of one figure; eight of two figures; and twelve of three figures. Now as regards the latter series—the symbols composed of three figures—we will find that if we add together the component figures of each of those which begins and ends with an even number they will tot up to nine; but that the total of each of those commencing and ending with an odd number only total up to eight. There are no two of these symbols which clash with one another so as to cause confusion.

To fit the alphabet to this cipher the simplest plan is to reserve one symbol (the first—"0") to represent the repetition of a foregoing letter. This would not only enlarge possibilities of writing, but would help to baffle inquiry. There is a distinct purpose in choosing "0" as the symbol of repetition for it can best be spared; it would invite curiosity to begin a number cipher with "0," were it in use in any combination of figures representing a letter.

Keep all the other numbers and combinations of numbers for purely alphabetical use. Then take the next five—9 to 45 to represent the vowels. The rest of the alphabet can follow in regular sequence, using up of the triple combinations, first those beginning and ending with even numbers and which tot up to nine, and when these have been exhausted, the others, those beginning and ending with odd numbers and which tot up to eight, in their own sequence.

If this plan be adopted, any letter of a word can be translated into numbers which are easily distinguishable, and whose sequence can be seemingly altered, so as to baffle inquisitive eyes, by the addition of any other numbers placed anywhere throughout the cipher. All of these added numbers can easily be discovered and eliminated by the scribe who undertakes the work of decipheration, by means of the additions of odd or even numbers, or by reference to his key. The whole cipher is so rationally exact that any one who knows the principle can make a key in a few minutes.

As I had gone on with my work I was much cheered by certain resemblances or coincidences which presented themselves, linking my new construction with the existing cipher. When I hit upon the values of additions of eight and nine as the component elements of some of the symbols, I felt sure that I was now on the right track. At the completion of my work I was exultant for I felt satisfied in believing that the game was now in my own hands.

Appendix D

On the Application of the Number Cipher to the Dotted Printing

The problem which I now put before myself was to make dots in a printed book in which I could repeat accurately and simply the setting forth of the biliteral cipher. I had, of course, a clue or guiding principle in the combinations of numbers with the symbols of "a" and "b" as representing the Alphabetical symbols. Thus it was easy to arrange that "a" should be represented by a letter untouched and "b" by one with a mark. This mark might be made at any point of the letter. Here I referred to the cipher itself and found that though some letters were marked with a dot in the centre or body of the letter, those both above and below wherever they occurred showed some kind of organised use. "Why not," said I to myself, "use the body for the difference between "a" and "b;" and the top and bottom for numbers?"

No sooner said than done. I began at once to devise various ways of representing numbers by marks or dots at top and bottom. Finally I fixed, as being the most simple, on the following:

Only four numbers—2, 3, 4, 5—are required to make the number of times each letter of the symbol is repeated, there being in the original Baconian cipher, after the elimination of the ten variations already made, only three changes of symbol to represent any letter. Marks at the top might therefore represent the even numbers "2" and "4"—one mark standing for "two" and two marks for "four"; marks at the bottom would represent the odd numbers "3" and "5"—one mark standing for "three" and two marks for "five."

Thus "a a a a a" would be represented by "a̤" aor any other letter with two dots below: "a a a a b" by ä b, or any other letters similarly treated. As any letter left plain would represent "a" and any letter dotted in the body would represent "b" the cipher is complete for application to any printed or written matter. As in the number cipher, the repetition of a letter could be represented by a symbol which in this variant would be the same as the symbol for ten or "0." It would be any letter with one dot in the body and two under it, thus—ṭ̈.

For the purpose of adding to the difficulty of discovery, where two marks were given either above or below the letter, the body mark (representing the letter as "b" in the Biliteral) might be placed at the opposite end. This would create no confusion in the mind of an advised decipherer, but would puzzle the curious.

On the above basis I completed my key and set to my work of deciphering with a jubilant heart; for I felt that so soon as I should have adjusted any variations between the systems of the old writer and my own, work only was required to ultimately master the secret.

The following tables will illustrate the making and working—both in ciphering and de-ciphering—of the amended Biliteral Cipher of Francis Bacon:

Cipher for Numbers and Dots

P (Plain) means letter left untouched
D (Dot) means letter with dot in body
One Dot—(.) at Top (t)—2
One Dot—(.) at Bottom (b)—3
Two Dots—(..) at Top (t)—4
Two Dots—(..) at Bottom (b)—5

NUMBER CIPHER

BACON CIPHER	No. of Symbols Required	No. Values of Symbols reported	Alphabet to be arranged in order	DOT CIPHER
A— 1—a a a a a	—1—	9	—A	—P..b
B— 2—a a a a b	—2—	7.2	—D	—P..t—D
C— 3—a a a b a	—3—	5.2.1	—Y	—P .b—D—P
D— 4—a a a b b	—2—	5.4	—B	—P .b—D.t
E— 5—a a b a a	—3—	3.2.3	—T	—P .t—D—P.t
F— 6—a a b a b	—4—	3.2.1.2		
G— 7—a a b b a	—3—	3.4.1	—X.Z.	—P .t—D.t—P
H— 8—a a b b b	—2—	3.6	—O	—P .t—D.b
I— 9—a b a a a	—3—	1.2.5	—P	—P—D—P.b
K—10—a b a a b	—4—	1.3.3.2		

L—11—a b a b a	—5—	1.2.1.2.1		
M—12—a b a b b	—4—	1.2.1.4		
N—13—a b b a a	—3—	1.4.3	—R	—P—D .t—P.t
O—14—a b b a b	—4—	1.4.1.2		
P—15—a b b b a	—3—	1.6.1	—S	—P—D .b—P
Q—16—a b b b b	—2—	1.8	—E	—P—D..t
R—17—b a a a a	—2—	2.7	—I	—D—P..t
S—18—b a a a b	—3—	2.5.2	—K.Q.	—D—P .b—D
T—19—b a a b a	—4—	2.3.2.1		
V—20—b a a b b	—3—	2.3.4	—H	—D—P .t—D.t
W—21—b a b a a	—4—	2.1.2.3		
X—22—b a b a b	—5—	2.1.2.1.2		
Y—23—b a b b a	—4—	2.1.4.1		
Z—24—b a b b b	—3—	2.1.6	—G	—D—P—D.b
25—b b a a a	—2—	4.5	—U.V.	—D.t—P.b
26—b b a a b	—3—	4.3.2	—M	—D.t—P.t—D
27—b b a b a	—4—	4.1.2.1		
28—b b a b b	—3—	4.1.4	—L	—D .t—P—D.t
29—b b b a a	—2—	6.3	—C	—D .b—P.t
30—b b b a b	—3—	6.1.2	—N	—D .b—P—D
31—b b b b a	—2—	8.1	—F	—D..t—P
32—b b b b b	—1—	9	—Repeat	—D..b

NOTE.—When there are to be two dots at either top or bottom of a letter, the dot usually put in the body of a letter which is to indicate "b" can be placed at the opposite end of the letter to the double dotting. This will help to baffle investigation without puzzling the skilled interpreter.

Key to Number Cipher

Divide off into additions of nine or eight. Thus if extraneous figures have been inserted, they can be detected and deleted.

Cipher	De-Cipher
A = 9	O = Repeat Letter
B = 54	125 = P
C = 63	143 = R
D = 72	161 = S
E = 18	18 = E
F = 81	216 = G
G = 216	234 = H
H = 234	252 = K or Q
I = 27	27 = I
K.Q = 252	323 = T
L = 414	341 = X or Z
M = 432	36 = O
N = 612	414 = L
O = 36	432 = M
P = 125	45 = U or V
R = 143	521 = Y
S = 161	54 = B
T = 323	612 = N
U.V = 45	63 = C
X.Z = 341	72 = D
Y = 521	81 = F
Repeat = O	9 = A

Finger Cipher

Values the same as Number Cipher.

The RIGHT hand, beginning at the thumb, represent the ODD numbers,

The LEFT hand, beginning at the thumb, represent the EVEN numbers.

P—Letter left plain.
D—Dot in centre or where are two dots t or b in other end (b or t).
.—Dot.
t—top of letter.
b—bottom of letter.

Cipher	De-Cipher
A = P .. b	P —— D ——P . b = P
B = P . b — D . t	P —— D . t — P . t = R
C = D . b — P . t	P —— D .. t ——— = E
D = P .. t — D	P —— D . b — P —— = S
E = P — D .. t	P . t — D ——— P . t = T
F = D .. t—P	P . t —D . t — P —— = X or Z
G = D — P — D . b	P . t — D . b ——— = O
H = D — P . t — D . t	P .. t— D——————— = D
I = D — P .. t	P . b — D——————P = Y
K.Q = D — P . b — D	P . b — D . t——— = B
L = D . t — P — D . t	P .. b ——————— = A
M = D . t — P . t — D	D ——— P ——— D . b = G
N = D . b — P — D	D ——— P . t — D . t = H
O = P . t — D . b	D ——— P .. t ——— = I
P = P — D — P . b	D ——— P . b — D — = K or Q
R = P — D . t — P . t	D . t — P ——— D . t = L
S = P — D . b — P	D . t — P . t — D — = M
T = P . t — D — P . t	D . t — P . b——— = U or V
U.V = D . t — P . b	D .. t — P——————— = F
X.Z = P . t — D . t — P	D . b — P—— D —— = N
Y = P . b — D — P	D . b — P . t——— = C
Repeat = D .. b (W = U repeated)	D .. b——— = Repeat (W)

Memoranda

Begin fresh with each line.

Take no account of stops.

Take no account of Capitals or odd words.

y^e is one letter.

Appendix E

Narrative of Bernardino De Escoban, Knight of the Cross of the Holy See and Grandee of Spain

When my kinsman who was known as the "Spanish Cardinal" heard of my arrival in Rome in obedience to his secret summons, he sent one to me who took me to see him at the Vatican. I went at once and found that though the carriage of his great office had somewhat aged my kinsman it had not changed the sweet bearing which he had ever had towards me. He entered at once on the matter regarding which he had summoned me, leaving to later those matters of home and family which were close to us both, and prefacing his speech with an assurance—unnecessary I enforced on him—that he would not have urged me to so great a voyage, and at a time when the concerns of home and of His Catholic Majesty so needed me in my own place, had there not been strictest need of my presence at Rome. This he then explained, ever anticipating my ignorance, so lucidly and with sweet observance of my needs, that I could not wonder at his great advancement.

Entering at once on the enterprise of the King as to the restoration of England to the fold of the True Church he made clear to me that the one great wish of His Holinesse was to aid in all ways the achievement of the same. To such end he was willing to devote a vast treasure, the which he had accumulated for the purpose through many years. "But" said my kinsman, and with so much smiling as might become his grave office "the King hath here at the Court of Rome one to represent him, who, though doubtless a zealous and faithful servant of his Royal Master, hath not those qualities of discretion and discernment, of the subjugation of self and the discipline of his own ideas, which go to make up the perfection of the Ambassador. He hath already many times and in many ways, to many persons and in many Countries, said of His Holinesse such things as, even if true—and they are not so—were, in the high discretion of his office as Ambassador, better unspoken. This, moreover, in an Embassy wherein he wishes to acquire much which the mundane world holds to be of great worth. The Count de Olivares hath spoken freely and without reserve of the Holy Father's reticence in handing over vast sums of money to His Catholic Majesty as due to parsimony, to avarice, to meanness of spirit, and to other low qualities which, though common enough in men, are soil to the name of God's Vicegerent on Earth! Nay" he went on, seeing that my horror was such as to verge on doubt, "trust me in this, for of the verity of these things I am assured. Rome hath many eyes, and the hearing of her ears is widecast. The Pope and his Cardinals are well served throughout the world. Little indeed happens in Christendom—aye and beyond it— which is not echoed in secret in the Vatican. I know that not only has Count de Olivares spoken of his beliefs regarding the Holy Father to his mundane friends, but he has not hesitated in his formal despatches to say the same to his Royal Master. It hath grieved His Holinesse much that any could so misunderstand him, and it hath grieved him more that His Catholic Majesty should receive such calumnies without demur. Wherefore he would take some other means than the hand of the King of Spain to accomplish his own secret ends. He knoweth well the high purpose of His Catholic Majesty, your Royal Master, in the restoration of England to the True Faith; but yet his mind is much disturbed by his recent pronouncements regarding the Bishoprics. The See of Rome is the Arch Episcopate of the Earth, and to its Bishop belongs by God's very ordinance the ruling of all the bishoprics of the Church. "Upon this Rock shall I build my Church." Now His Holinesse hath already promised a million crowns towards the great emprise of the Armada; and he hath promised it so that it be handed over to the King when his emprise, which is after all for the enlargement of his own kingdom, hath begun to bear fruit. But Count de Olivares is not content with this promise—the promise remember of God's Vicegerent—and he is ever clamorous, not only for the immediate payment of this promised sum, but for other sums. His new request is for another million crowns. And even in the very presence of His Holinesse, he so bears himself as if the non-compliance with his demand were a wrong to him and to his Master. From all which His Holinesse, consulting in privacy with me who am also his friend—such is the greatness with which he honoureth me—hath determined that, whereas he will of course keep to the last letter his promise of help, and will even exceed largely the same, he will dispose in other ways of the great treasure which he had already set aside for this English affair. When he honoured me by asking my advice as to whom should be entrusted with this high endeavour, and had shown that of necessity it should be some Spaniard so that hereafter it might not be said that the emprise of the Armada had not his full sanction and support, I ventured to suggest that in you first of all men this high trust should be reposed. For yourself, I said that I had known you from childhood, and had found you without a flaw; and that you came from a race that had gone clothed in honour since the time of the Moors."

Much other of like kind, my children, did my kinsman tell me that he had said to His Holinesse; which so satisfied him that he had commanded him to send for me so that he could have the assurance of his own seeing what manner of man I was. My kinsman then went on to tell me how he had told His Holinesse of what I had already taken in hand regarding the Great Armada. How I had promised the King a galleon fully equipped and manned with seamen and soldiers from our old Castile; and how His Majesty was so pleased, since my offer had been the first he had received, that he had sworn that my vessel should carry the flag of the squadron of the galleons of Castile. He told him also that the galleon was to be called the *San Cristobal* from my patron saint; and also that so her figurehead should bear the image of the Christ into English waters the first of all things that came from my Province. Which idea so wrought upon the mind of His Holinesse that he said: "Good man! Good Spaniard! Good Christian! I shall provide the figurehead for the *San Cristobal* myself. When Don de Escoban comes here I shall arrange it with him."

When my kinsman had so informed me as to many things he left me a while, saying that he would ask the Pope to arrange for an audience with me. Shortly he returned with haste, saying that the Holy Father wished me to come to him at once. I went in exaltation mingled with fear; and all my unworthiness of such high honour rose before me. But when I came to His Holinesse and knelt before him he blessed me and raised me up himself. And when he bade me, I raised my eyes and looked at him in the face. Whereat he turned to the Spanish Cardinal and said: "You have spoken under the mark, my brother. Here is a man indeed in whom I can trust to the full."

And so, my children, he made me sit by him, and for a long time—it was more than two hours by the clock—he talked with me about his wish. And, oh my children, I would that you and others could hear the wise words of that great and good man. He was so worldly-wise, in addition to his Saintly wisdom, that nothing seemed to lack in his reasoning; nothing was too small to be outside his understanding and considerations of the motives and arts of men. He told me with exceeding frankness of his views of the situation. All the while, my kinsman smiled and nodded approval now and again; and it filled me with pride that one of my own blood should stand so close to the counsels of His Holinesse. He told me that though war was a sad necessity, which he as himself an earthly monarch was compelled to understand and accept, yet he preferred infinitely the ways of peace; and moreover believed in them. In his own wise words, "the logic of the cannon, though more loud, speaks not so forcibly as the logic of the living day between sunrise and sunset." When later he added to this conviction that, "the chink of the money-bag speaks more loudly than either," I ventured an impulsive word of protest. Whereupon he stopped and looking at me sharply asked if I knew how to bribe. To which I replied that as yet I had given none, nor taken none. Then smilingly he laid his hand in friendlinesse on my shoulder and said: "My friend, Saint Escoban, these be two things, not one; and though to take a bribe is to be unforgiven, yet to give one at high command is but a duty, like the soldier's duty to kill which is not murder, which it would be without such behest." Then raising his hand to silence my protest he said: "I know what you would say: 'Woe to that man by whom the scandal cometh,' but such argument, my friend, is my province; and its responsibility is mine. Ere you proceed on your mission you shall have indemnity for the carriage of all my commands. You go into an enemy's country; a country which is the professed and malignant enemy of Holy Church, and where faith and honour are not. God's work is to be done in many ways. It is sufficient that He has allowed instruments that are unworthy and unholy; and as unworthy and unholy we must use them to His ends. You, Don de Escoban, shall have no pain in such matters, and no shame. My commands shall cover you!" Then, when I had bowed my recognition of his will, he resumed his instructions. He said that in England in high places were many men who were open to sell their knowledge or their power, and that when once they had accepted payment it were needful for their own credit and even for their safety, that they should further the end which they had undertaken. "These English," he said, "are pagans; and it was said of this our Holy City in pagan times '*Omnia Romae venalia sunt!*'" Whereupon there was borne upon me a recollection of years before when I was in the suite of the Ambassador at Paris, how a boy in the British Embassy who was shewing me a cipher of enclosed writing which he had just perfected had written in it with uncouth lettering as an illustration "*Omnia Britaniae venalia sunt.*" And further did remember how we had enlarged and perfected the cipher when we resided together at Tours. His Holinesse told me that in great seasons it were needful to scatter favours with a lavish hand, and that no season was or could be so great as that which foreran the restoring to the fold a great and active nation who was already beginning to rule the seas. "To which end," he said, "I am placing with you a vastness of treasure such as no nation hath ever seen. The gifts of the Faithful have begun it and enlarged it; and the fruits of many victories have enhanced it. Regarding it, there is only one promise which I will exact from you, and that I shall exact in the most solemn way of which the Church has knowledge; that this vast treasure be applied to onely that purpose to which it is ordained—the advancement of the True Faith. It will add also, of course, to the honour and glory of the Kingdom of Spain, so that for all time the world may know that the comfort of the Roman See is on the emprise of the Great Armada! In proof of which should, for the sins of men, the great emprise fail, you or those who may succeed you in the Trust are, if I myself be not then living, to hand the Treasure to the custody of whatever monarch may then sit upon the throne of Spain for his good guardianship, in trust with me."

So he proceeded to detail; and gave full instructions as to the amount of the treasure. How it was to be placed in my hands, and when; and all details of its using when the Armada should have made landing on English shores. And how I should use it myself, in case I were not told to hand it over to some other. If I were to yield up the treasure, the mandate should be enforced by letter, together with the showing of a ring, which he took from the purse where he kept the Fisherman's ring wherewith he signs all briefs, and allowed me to examine it so that I might recognize it if shown to me hereafter. All of which things of using are not now of importance to you, my children, for the time of their usefulness has passed by; but only to show that the treasure is to be guarded, and finally given to the custody of the King of Spain.

Then His Holiness spoke to me of my own vessel. He promised me that a suitable figurehead, one wrought for his own galley by the great Benvenuto Cellini, and blessed by Himself, should be duly sent on to me. He promised also that the Quittance to me and mine, which he had named should be completed and lodged in the secret archives of the Papacy. Then once more he blessed me, and on parting gave me a relic of San Cristobal, whose possession, together with the honour done me, made me feel as I left the Vatican as though I walked upon air.

On my return to Spain I visited the ship yard at San Lucar, where already the building of the *San Cristobal* was in progress. I arranged in private with the master builder that there should be constructed in the centre of the galleon a secret chamber, well encased round with teak wood from the Indies, and with enforcement of steel plates; and with a lock to the iron door, such as Pedro the Venetian hath already constructed for the treasure chest of the King. By my suggestion, and his wisdom in the doing of the matter, the secret chamber was so arranged in disposition, and so masked in with garniture of seeming unimportance, that none, unless of the informed, might tell its presence, or indeed of its very existence. It was placed as though in a well of teak wood and steel, hemmed in on all sides; without entrance whatever from the lower parts, and only approachable from the top which lay under my own cabin, down deep in the centre of the galleon. Men in single and detachments, were brought from other ship yards for the doing of this work, and all so disposed in Port that none might have greater knowledge than of that item which he completed at the time. Save only those few of the guilds whose faith had long been made manifest by their rectitude of life and their discretion of silence.

Into this secret receptacle (to continue this narrative out of its due sequence) when the final outfitting of the Invincible Armada came to pass, was placed, under my own supervision, in the night time and in secret, all the vast treasure which had before then been sent to me secretly by agents of His Holinesse. Full tally and reckoning made I with my own hand, nominating the coined money by its value in crowns and doubloons, and the gold and silver in bullion by their weight. I made a list in separate also of the endless array of precious stones, both those enriched in carvings and inriching the jewells of gold and silver wrought by the cunning of the great artizans. I made list also of the gems unplanted, which were of innumerable number and of various bigness. These latter I specified by kind and number, singling out some of rare size and quality for description. The whole table of the list I signed and sent by his messengers to the Pope, specifying thereon that I had them in trust for His Holinesse to dispose of them as he might direct; or to yield over to whomsoever he might depute to receive them whenever and wherever they might be in the guardianship of me or mine, the order of His Holinesse being verified by the exhibition by the new trustee of the Eagle Ring.

Before the *San Cristobal* had left San Lucar, there arrived from Rome, in a package of great bulk—brought by a ship accredited by the Pope, so that corsairs other than Turks and pagans might respect the flag, and so abstain from plunder—the figurehead of the galleon which His Holinesse had promised to supply. With it came a sealed missive cautioning me that I should open the package in privacy, and deal with its contents only by means of those in whom I had full trust, since it was even in its substance most precious. In addition to which it had been specially wrought by Benvenuto Cellini, the Master goldsmith whose work was contended for by the Kings of the earth. It was the wish of His Holinesse himself that on the conversion of England being completed, either through peace or war, this figurehead of the *San Cristobal* should be set over the High Altar of the Cathedral at Westminster, where it would serve for all time of an emblem of the love of the Pope for the wellbeing of the souls of his English children.

I opened the case with only present a chosen few; and truly we were wonderstruck with the beauty and richness of the jewell, for it was none other, which was discloased to us. The great figure of San Cristobal was silver gilded to look like gold, and of such thickness that the hollow within rang sweetly at a touch as though a bell sounded there. But the Figure of the child Christ which he bore upon his shoulder was of none other than solid gold. When we who were present saw it, we sank to our knees in gratitude for so great a tribute of Holinesse, and also the beauty of the tribute to the Divine Excellence. Truly the kindness of the Pope and the zeal of his artist were without bound; for with the figurehead came a jewell made in the form of a brooch carven in gold which represented it *in petto*. It was known to all the Squadron that the Pope himself had sent the figurehead of the *San Cristobal*; and as our vessel moved along the line of galleons and ships, and hulks, and pataches, and galleys of the Armada, the heads of all were uncovered and the knees of all were bent. We had not any christening of the galleon, for the blessing of the Holy Father was already on the figurehead of the ship and encompassed it round about.

None knew on board the *San Cristobal* of the existence of the treasure, save only the Captain of the galleons and ships, and hulks, and pataches, and galleys of the Squadron of Castile, to both of whom I entrusted the secret of the treasure (though not the giver nor the nature of the Trust nor the amount thereof), lest ill should befall me, and in ignorance the whole through some disaster be lost. And let me here say to their honour that my confidence was kept faithfully to the last; though it may be that had they known the magnitude of the treasure it might have been otherwise, men being but as flax before the fire of cupidity.

For myself after I embarked, I went on the journey with mixed feelings; for my body unaccustomed to the sea warred mightily with my soul that had full trust in the enterprise. The many days of storm and trial after we had left Lisbon, until we had found a refuge in Corunna did seem as though the comings of eternity had been made final. For the turmoil of the winds and the waves was indeed excessive, and even those most skilled in the ways and the wonders of the deep asseverated that never had been known weather so unpropitious to the going forth of ships. Truly this time, though less than three weeks in all, did seem of a durance inconceivable to one on land.

Whilst we lay in the harbour of Corunna, which was for more than four weary weeks, we effected some necessary repairs. The *San Cristobal* had been taking water at the prow, and we should find the cause and remedy it. Possibly it was that the bow was left unfinished at San Lucar for the better fixing of the figurehead, and that some small flaw thus begun met enlargement from the straining of the timbers in the prolonged storm. To the end of this repairing the work was given to some of the ship-men on board, Swedes and other Northerns, the same being expert calkers on account of their much experience of their repair of ships injured in their troublous seas. Among them was one whom I mistrusted much, as did all on board, so that he should not have been retained save only that he was a nimble and fearless mariner who be the seas never so great would take his place in the furlment of sails or in other perilous labour of the sea. He was a Russian Finn and like all these heathen people had strange powers of evill, or was by all accredited with the same. For be it known that these Finns can, by some subtile and diabolic means, suck or otherwise derive the strength from timbers; so that many a tall ship has through this agency gone down to the deep unknown. This Finn, Olgaref by name, was a notable calker and with some others was slung over the bow to calk the gaping seams. I made it to myself a necessity to be present, for I regarded ever the cupidity of man together with the inestimable value of the Pope's gift. Right sure was I that no Spaniard or no Christian would lay a sacrilegious hand on the Sacred Figure of Our Lord or of the good Saint who bore Him; and hitherto the esteem of all had been so great that none would dare so much. But with a pagan such considerations avail not, and I feared lest even his suspicions might be aroused. Well indeed were my fears justified. For as I leaned over the prow, I saw him touch the metal of the Christ and of the Saint as though some of the same diabolic instinct which had taught him to deal infamously with the timbers of ships had guided him to the discernment of the metals also. Then as I looked, he, all unknowing of my observation, tapped softly with his calking-mallet on both the metals which in turn gave out sounds which no one could mistake. He seemed satisfied with his quest, and resumed his work upon the oakum with renewed zeal. Thenceforth during our stay in Corunna I so arranged matters that ever both day and night there was a sentinel on the prow of the *San Cristobal*. When the day came when, praise be to God, 8,000 soldiers and sailors confessed to the friars of the fleet on an island in the harbour in which the Archbishop of Santiago had arranged altars—for we had no Bishop on the Armada—I feared lest Olgaref should make, through some inadvertence of those left behind, some attempt upon the precious gift. He was too wary, however, and behaved with such discretion that for the time my suspicion was disarmed.

On the 22nd. July, after a Council of War in the Royal Galleon in which the chief Admirals of the Fleet took part, our squadron, which had been waiting outside the harbour of Corunna with the squadron of Andalusia, the Guipuzcoan Squadron and the squadron of Ojeda, set sail on our great emprise.

Truly it did seem as though the powers of the seas and the winds was leagued against us; for after but three days of fair weather we met with calms and fogs and a very hurricane which was as none other of the same ever known in the month of Leo. The waves mounted to the very heavens, and some of them broke over the ships of the fleet doing thereby a vast of damage which could not be repaired whilst at sea. In this storm the whole of the stern gallery of our galleon was carried away, and it was only by the protection of the Most High that the breach so made was not the means of ultimately whelming us in the sea. With the coming of the day we found that forty of the ships of the Armada were missing. On this day it was that that great and bold mariner the Admiral Don Pedro de Valdes by his great daring and the hazard of his life saved my own life, when I had been swept overboard by a mighty sea. In gratitude for which I sent him that which I held most dear of my possessions, the jewell of the San Cristobal given me by the Pope.

Thenceforth for a whole week were we hourly harassed by the enemy, who, keeping aloof from us, yet managed by their superior artillery to inflict upon us incalculable damage; so that our carpenters and divers had to work endlessly to stop the shot holes above water and below it with tow and leaden plates.

On the last day of July two disasters befell, in both of which our galleon afterwards had a part. The first, was to the ship *San Salvador* of Admiral Miguel de Aquendo's squadron, through the diabolic device of a German gunmaster, who in revenge for punishment inflicted on him by Captain Preig, threw, after firing his gun, his lighted linstock into a barrel of powder, to the effect of blowing up the two afterdecks and the poop castle, and killing over two hundred men. As on this ship was Juan de Huerta the Paymaster General with a great part of the treasure of the King, it was necessary that she should if possible be saved from the enemy who were rushing in upon her. The Duke, therefore firing a signal gun to the fleet to follow, stood by her to the dismay of the English, thus baulked of so rich a prey. In the strategy of getting the wounded ship back to her place in the formation came the second disaster; for the foremast of the flagship of Don Pedro de Valdes *Nuestra Senora del Rosario* gave way at the hatches, falling on the mainsail boom. The rising sea forbade the giving her a hawser; the Duke ordered Captain Ojeda to stand by her with our pataches together with Don Pedro's own vice flagship the *San Francisco* and our own *San Cristobal*. A galleon also was to try to fix a hawser for towing; but the night shut down on us, and the wiser counsel of the Admiral-in-Chief advised by Diego Flores forbade so many ships to remain absent from the going on of the Armada lest they too should be cut off. So we said farewell to that gallant mariner Don Pedro de Valdes.

That same evening the wind began to blow and the sea to rise so that the injured ship of Admiral Oquendo was in danger of sinking; wherefore the High Admiral, on such word being brought to him, gave orders that we should keep close to her and take in our care the mariners and soldiers on board her and also the King's treasure chest; for it was said that His Catholic Majesty had on the Armada half a million crowns in bullion and coined money. It was dark as pitch when we saw the signal made when the flagship shortened sail—two lanterns at the poop and one halfway up the rigging, put out for the guidance of the fleet. Fearsome their lights looked shining over the dark heaving waters which now and again so broke with the oncoming waves that the tracks of light seemed in places to rise and fall about as though they could never be reunited. But our Mariners answered to the call, and the boats soon rocked by our sides and with a flash of our blades in the lamplight—for the battle lanterns were lit to aid them—one by one they were swept into the dark. It was long before they came back, for the wild sea made their venture impossible. But before noon of the next day they again made essay; and in several voyages brought back many men and great store of heavy boxes, which latter were forthwith lodged in the powder room which was guarded by night and day. This made greater anxiety for Senor de las Alas, in that his seamen and mariners, and worse still the foreigners, knew that there was such a store of wealth aboard.

Thenceforth we bore our part in the running fight which ensued between our Armada and the Squadrons of Drake and the Lord Admiral Howard; and also that of John Hawkins which assailed us with such insistence that we fain thought the Devil himself must have some hand in his work. At last came a time when by God's grace the flagship of the enemy was almost within our grasp, for she lay amongst us disabled. But many oar-boats of her consorts flocked to her, and towed her to safety in the calm which forbade us to follow. In this action a dire disaster had almost befallen us, and Christendom too, for a shot struck us athwart the bow and so loosened the girding of our precious figurehead that almost it had fallen into the sea. San Cristobal watched over his own, however; and presently we had with ropes haled it aboard and held it firmly with cables so that it was immediately safe. It was covered up with tow and sacking and so hidden under pretence of safety that none might discover the secret of its intrinsic preciosity. Ere this was completed we were again called to action, as for our fleetness we were required to chase with the *San Juan* of Portugal, the flagship of the enemy which was flying from our attack. For the English ships, though not so large, were swift as our own and more easy of handling; and by their prerogative of nimble steerage could so thwart our purposes that ere we could recover on following their tacking, they were well away with full-bellied sail. By this, however, we were saved much pain of concern, for when off Calais roads the Armada lay at anchor we, coming amongst the latermost, were placed on the skirts of the fleet. Thus when the English on the night of Sunday August 7th. sent their fire ships floating with wind and tide down on the Armada, so that in panic most of the great vessels had to slip their anchors or even to cut their cables, we could weigh with due deliberance and set sail northerly according to our orders from the Duke.

When by Newcastle we saw the English ships drop off in their pursuit we knew thereby that their finding was at an end and their magazines empty. Whereupon, setting our course ever northwards, so that rounding Scotland and Ireland we might seek Spain once more, we began our task of counting our scars, and thence to the work of the leech. Truly we were in pitiable plight, for the long continued storm and strain had opened our seams and we took water abominably. In that we were of the most swift of the vessels of the fleet, our galleon and the *Trinidad* of our own squadron outsailed the rest, and bearing away to the eastward, though not too much so, and thence north, found ourselves on the 11th day of August, off the coast of Aberdeyne. The sea had now fallen so far that though the waves were more than we had reckoned upon at the first yet they were but mild in comparison with what had been. Here in a sandy bay close under Buquhan Ness we cast anchor and began to overhaul.

BOTH OUR SHIPS HAD BEEN very seriously damaged, and repairs were indeed necessary which required careening, had such been possible. But it could not be in a latitude where, even in the summer, the seas rose so fast and broke so wildly. Our consort the *Trinidad*, though in sad plight, was not so bad as we were; and it was greatly to be feared that if occasion was not to be had for making good the ravages of the storm and the enemy she might meet with disaster. But such amending might not be at this time. The weather was threatening; and moreover the enemy would soon be following hard behind us. From one of our foreign seamen, a Scotchman who in secret visited Aberdeyne, we learned that Queen Elizabeth was sending out a swift patache to scour the whole northern coast for any traces of the Armada. Though we were two galleons, we yet feared such a meeting; for our stores were exhausted and our powder had run low. Of ball we had none, for such fighting as these dogged Englishmen are prone to. Moreover it is the way of these islanders to so hold together that when one is touched all others run to aid; whereby were but one gun of ours fired, even off that desolate coast, in but a little while would be an army on the shore and a squadron of ships upon the sea. It began therefore sorely to exercise my conscience as to how I should best protect the treasure entrusted to me. Were it to fall into the hands of our enemies it were the worst that could happen; and matters had already so disastrously arranged themselves that it was to be feared we should not hold ourselves in safety. Therefore, taking much counsel with Heaven, whose treasure indeed it was that I was guarding, I began to look about for some secret place of storage, to the which I might resort in case danger should threaten before we could get safely away from the shore. The Artificers said that two days, or perhaps three, would be required to complete our restorations; and on the first of these I took a small boat, and with two trusty mariners of my own surroundings I set out to explore the land close to us, which was of a veritable desolation. The shallow bay, in whose mouth we were anchored in a sufficiency of water at all tides, was lined with great sandhills from end to end save at the extremities, where rocks of exceeding durability manifested themselves even at high tide, but which shewed with ferocity at low water. We essayed at first the northern side, but presently abandoned the quest, for though there were many deep indentures, wherein the sea ran at times with exceeding violence, the simple contours of the rocks and of the land above gave little promise of a secret place of storage.

But the south side was different. There had been in times long past much upheaval of various kinds, and now were many little bays, all iron-bound and full of danger, lying between outflanking rocks of a steepness unsurpassable. Seaweed was on many great rocks rising from the sea whereon multitudinous wild fowl sat screaming; between them rose numberless points often invisible, save when the surges fell from them in their course, and amongst which the tide set with a wonderful current, most perilous. Here, after we had many times escaped overturning, being borne by the side of sunken rocks, I at last made discovery of such a place as we required. Elsewhere I have recorded for your guidance its bearings and all such details as may be needful for the fullfillment of your duty. The cave was a great one on the south side of the bay, with many windings and blind offsets; and as best met my wishes in accordance with my task, the entrance was not easy to be discovered, being small and of a rare quality for concealment. Here I made preparation for the landing of the treasure, in so far as that I took note of all things and made perfect my designs. I had left the mariners in the boat, enjoining them to remain in her in case of need, so that none of them, much though I trusted them, knew of the discovered cave. When we had returned to the galleon night had fallen.

Forthwith, after secret consultation with our admiral, I visited the captain of the *Trinidad* and obtained his permission to use on that same night one of his boats with a crew for some special private service. For I had thought that it were better that none of our own crew, who might have had suspicion of what wealth we carried, should have a part in our undertaking. This my own kinsman Admiral de las Alas had advised. When night came, he had so disposed matters on the *San Cristobal* that whilst our debarkation was being made, not even the sentries on deck or in the passage ways could see aught—they being sent below. The Captain himself onely remained on deck.

We made several voyages between the ship and the shore, piling after each our weighty packets on the pebble beach. None were left to guard them, there being no one to molest. Last of all we took the great figurehead of silver and gold, which Benvenuto had wrought and which the Pope had blessed, and placed it on the shore beside the rest. Then the boat went back to the *Trinidad*. Climbing on the rock overhead, I saw a lantern flashed on her deck, as signal to assure me that the boat had returned.

Presently a boat of our own vessel drew near, as had been arranged, manned by three trusty men of my own; and in silence we brought the treasure into the cave. In the doing so we were mightily alarmed by a shot from a harquebuss from one of the ships in the bay. Eagerly we climbed the rocks and looked around as well as we could in the darkness. But all was still; what so had been, was completed. In the darkness, and whilst the tide was low, we placed the treasure in a far branch of the cave, placing most of it in the shallow water. The sides of the rock were sheer in this far chamber, save onely at the end where was a great shelf of rock. On this we placed the image of San Cristobal, not thinking it well that the Sacred Figure should lie prone. In this far cave the waters rose still and silent, for the force of the waves was broken by the rocks without. It was risen so high in places as to cause us disquietude as we made our way out. My chosen mariners made, before we left the shore, solemn oath on the Holy Relic of San Cristobal which the Pope had given to me that they would never reveal aught of the doings of the night.

Before dawn, which cometh early in these latitudes, we were back on board ship; and sought our various quarters silently that none who knew of our absence might guess whence we came.

Morning brought only more trouble to me. I was told that in the night the harquebussier on sentry had seen a man swim from the ship and had fired at him. He could not tell in the darkness if his aim had been true. I said nothing of my suspicion; but later on discovered that the Russian Finn, Olgaref, had disappeared. I knew then that this man, having suspicions, had watched us; and that if he was still alive he perhaps knew of the entrance of the cave.

All day I took much counsel with myself as to how I should act; and at the last my mind was made up. I had a sacred duty in protecting the treasure. I should seek Olgaref if he had reached the shore and should if need be kill him; and by this and other means, secure the secret of the entrance of the cave. Thus, you will see, oh! my children, the heavy nature of the Pope's Trust, and what stern duty it may entail on all of us who guard it.

Secretly during the day I made preparation for my enterprise. I placed on board the small boat which we had used, some barrels of gunpowder, wherein I had very much difficulty for our store of armament had run low indeed and only the Admiral's knowledge of the greatness of my Trust and the measure of my need inclined him to part with even so much. I rowed myself ashore in the afternoon, and harquebuss in hand made search of all the many promontories and their secret recesses for the Finn. For some hours I searched, examining every cranny in the rock; but no sign could I find of Olgaref. At last I gave up my search and came to the cave to complete the work which I had determined upon. Lighting my lantern I waded into the shallow water which lay in the entrance and stretched inland under the great overhanging rock flanked by two great masses of stone that towered up on either hand. Patiently I waded on, for the tide was low, through the curvings of the cave; the black stone on one hand and the red on the other giving back the flare of the lantern. Turning to the right I waded on, knowing that I would see before me the golden figure of San Cristobal. But suddenly I came to an end and for a moment stood appalled. The Figure no longer stood erect as placed on the wide shelf of rock, but lay prone resting on something which raised one end of it. Lifting high the lantern, I saw that this mass was none other than the dead body of Olgaref.

The wretched man had after all escaped from the galleon and in secret followed us to the cave. He had climbed upon the shelf and in an endeavour to steal the precious figure had pulled it over on himself; and the weight of the gold which formed the Christ had in falling killed him. He had evidently not known of the other treasure, and had followed only this of which he had knowledge. As I was about to shut the entrance to the cave until such time as I could come with safety to open it, I did not disturb the body, but left it underneath the Holy Image which he had dared to touch with sacrilegious hand.

At the Judgment Day, should the treasure not be recovered, he will find it hard to rise from that encumbrance that his evil deed had brought upon him.

With sad heart I came away; and then, for that I had to guard the Pope's treasure, I fixed the barrels of gunpowder in place to best wreak the effect I wished. After piling them with rocks as mighty as I could lift, I laid a slow match which I lighted; then I stood afar off to wait and watch.

Presently the end came. With a sound as of many cannon, though muffled in its coming, the charge was fired, and with a great puff of white smoke which rose high in air together with stones and earth and the upheaval of a great mass of rock which seemed to shake the far off place on which I rested, the whole front of the cave blew up. Then the white cloud sank lower and floated away over the grass; and for a few minutes only a dark thin vapour hung over the spot. When this had gone too I came close and saw that the great stone pinnacles had been overthrown, and that so many great rocks had fallen around that the entrance to the cave was no more, there being no sign of it. Even the channel of water which led up to it was so overwhelmed with great stones that no trace of it remained.

Then I breathed more freely, for the Pope's treasure was for the present safe, and enclosed in the great cave in the bowels of the earth, where I or mine though with much labour could find it again, in good season.

In the dark I came back to the *San Cristobal* where my kinsman the admiral told me that already rumours were afloat that I had gone to hide some treasure. Whereupon we conferred together, and late that night, but making such noise that many of the soldiers and mariners could hear what was being done and give news in secret of our movements, we made pretense of making a great shipment into the *Trinidad* so that the suspicions of all were thereupon allayed.

In the morning the Armada—all that was left of it—hove in sight; and joining it we began a dreary voyage, amid storms and tempests and trials and the loss of many of our great ships on the inhospitable coast of Ireland, which lasted many days till we found ourselves back again in Spain.

Thence, in due season, anxious to see that the Pope's treasure had not been discovered, I made my way in secret again to Aberdeyne where there overtook me, from the rigours of this northern climate and from many hardships undergone, the sickness whereof I am weary.

Where and how the place of hiding will be found I have told in the secret writing deposited in the place prepared for it, the chart being exact. I have written all these matters, because it is well that you my sonne, and ye all my children who may have to look forward so much and so long to the fullfillment of the Trust, may know how to look back as well.

These letters and papers, should I fail to return from that wild headland, shall be placed in your hands by one whose kindness I have reason to trust, and who has sworn to deliver them safely on your application. Vale.

BERNARDINO DE ESCOBAN

A Note About the Author

Bram Stoker (1847–1912) was an Irish novelist. Born in Dublin, Stoker suffered from an unknown illness as a young boy before entering school at the age of seven. He would later remark that the time he spent bedridden enabled him to cultivate his imagination, contributing to his later success as a writer. He attended Trinity College, Dublin from 1864, graduating with a BA before returning to obtain an MA in 1875. After university, he worked as a theatre critic, writing a positive review of acclaimed Victorian actor Henry Irving's production of *Hamlet* that would spark a lifelong friendship and working relationship between them. In 1878, Stoker married Florence Balcombe before moving to London, where he would work for the next 27 years as business manager of Irving's influential Lyceum Theatre. Between his work in London and travels abroad with Irving, Stoker befriended such artists as Oscar Wilde, Walt Whitman, Hall Caine, James Abbott McNeill Whistler, and Sir Arthur Conan Doyle. In 1895, having published several works of fiction and nonfiction, Stoker began writing his masterpiece *Dracula* (1897) while vacationing at the Kilmarnock Arms Hotel in Cruden Bay, Scotland. Stoker continued to write fiction for the rest of his life, achieving moderate success as a novelist. Known more for his association with London theatre during his life, his reputation as an artist has grown since his death, aided in part by film and television adaptations of *Dracula*, the enduring popularity of the horror genre, and abundant interest in his work from readers and scholars around the world.

A Note from the Publisher

Spanning many genres, from non-fiction essays to literature classics to children's books and lyric poetry, Mint Edition books showcase the master works of our time in a modern new package. The text is freshly typeset, is clean and easy to read, and features a new note about the author in each volume. Many books also include exclusive new introductory material. Every book boasts a striking new cover, which makes it as appropriate for collecting as it is for gift giving. Mint Edition books are only printed when a reader orders them, so natural resources are not wasted. We're proud that our books are never manufactured in exce
quantity they need to be read and enjoyed.

Discover more of your favorite classics with Bookfinity™.

- Track your reading with custom book lists.
- Get great book recommendations for your personalized Reader Type.
- Add reviews for your favorite books.
- AND MUCH MORE!

Visit **bookfinity.com** and take the fun Reader Type quiz to get started.

Enjoy our classic and modern companion pairings!

Printed in the USA
CPSIA information can be obtained
at www.ICGtesting.com
JSHW022205140824
68134JS00018B/878

9 781513 271514